# Tempted by the Storm

## by

## Maxine Mansfield

Tempted By The Storm

Contact Information: info@thewildrosepress.com

Cover Art by *Diana Carlile*

The Wild Rose Press, Inc.
PO Box 708
Adams Basin, NY 14410-0708

Visit us at www.thewilderroses.com

Publishing History
First Scarlet Rose Edition, November 2012
Print ISBN 978-1-61217-716-8
Digital ISBN 978-1-61217-717-5

Published in the United States of America

**There was only one word that could describe the creature standing before him.** *Wonderful.*

"Did you say something?" the woman whispered.

He shook his head. "Nothing, I just can't believe my luck. You really are real and here with me."

She smiled, but her smile didn't extend to her eyes.

Before another heartbeat passed or another breath taken, he stood at her side. With tenderness, he gazed into her gentle, masked face and took both of her hands in his. He was humbled as her fingers trembled even more than his own did. "We don't have to do this if you'd rather not."

She smiled wider, and her eyes gleamed with mischief. "I suppose we might as well. After all, we're already here, and you're at least halfway undressed."

Sliding his hands up her arms and around her shoulders to her back, Sarco felt for and found the clasps holding her gown together. With the flick of a wrist, they gave way, and with a swish, the silky fabric fell to her hips exposing lush, rose-tipped breasts. Just the right size to hold in both hands, to fondle, to caress, to taste.

"Hmm, it seems you're halfway undressed yourself."

## Dedication

To the incomparable Miss Cherry Adair, thank you for telling me to sit my ass in the chair and write the damn book. I did.

And thank you David Kuropkat for your hours of brainstorming and the use of your wonderful Leeky Shortz.
Thanks to my critique group, especially Lizbeth Selvig, Morgan Q O'Rielly, Tam Linsey, Jennifer Bernard and DeNise Woods. Your input and shoulders to cry on are as always, beyond price.

And last but certainly not least, thanks to my wonderful editors and cover artist Lori and Diana... you guys make me look really good.

Touched by the Magic,
Tempted by the Storm,
Taken by the Passion…
A New Love is Born.

*"It's ice and fire*
*that forms a maiden's desire.*
*It's searing heat*
*where metal and gemstone first meet.*
*It's with love in mind*
*that a treasure becomes divine.*
*It's a champion you must defeat*
*for a heart you wish to seek.*
*It's your choice to make*
*for the wife you will take."*

## Chapter One

Lark sighed.

If ever a man was born to be laid upon silken sheets and devoured like an ice cream sundae, the handsome, dark-haired high-elf across the room was that man. He leaned nonchalantly against a pillar and my, oh my, how she'd like to practice a little good, old-fashioned debauchery with him.

What was she thinking? Even though this was the pleasure city of Carnalval and not only was lusting after strange men acceptable, but expected and condoned, that didn't mean she could simply stroll over and take what her heart desired.

Still, she gazed at him with longing and let her mind wander where it would. Perhaps, if given the chance, she'd even top that man-sundae with hot fudge and whipped cream, sprinkle it with nuts and cherries, and slowly lick off the entire concoction. The thought made her smile and her tongue tingle with anticipation.

Even with his face partially concealed by a mask, he was gorgeous. Absolutely, mind-bogglingly, breathtakingly, gorgeous. In all her twenty-one years, Lark had never seen anything or anyone to compare with the sight. She sighed once more as her mind filled to overflowing with the possibilities.

What would it be like to have those long, robe-covered legs nestled between her own? How would it feel to lace her hands through that thick, black mane of hair? To tease, stroke, and draw him down beside her? When would be the perfect moment to kiss those lips, delve into their recesses, and taste heaven? Where in Albrath was there a place private enough to have him buried deep within her and adequately secluded so they'd be free to shout their pleasure to the rooftops?

For once in her boring, predictable life, Larksong Hammerstrike would very much like to be desired and taken by a man such as this one.

She adjusted her feathered mask, drew a deep breath, and took a step toward him when she recognized another woman making a beeline straight for the man of her dreams.

Lark stepped back into the shadows. There had never been a time in her life she could compete with her sister, Aryanna, and she certainly wasn't going to start trying now.

Why had she come to this silly ball in the first place? Why had she come to Carnalval for that matter? Lark took another deep breath and squared her shoulders. She would not feel sorry for herself tonight. She had long ago recognized her place in this world and, if she were completely honest with herself, was comfortable in it.

She understood and accepted her duty and, though there were those who didn't appreciate her abilities,

Lark knew she was good at what she did. Darkly handsome men were meant for women of stature and beauty, like her sister, not those relegated to companion status, such as herself.

Despite her resolve, tears threatened and Lark fought a losing battle to stave them off. Perhaps she should make it an early evening and go back to the castle. A good wallow in self-pity and a warm cup of cocoa would be perfect. The day had been long and exhausting. She wouldn't have even been at this asinine ball in the first place if Ary hadn't insisted upon it.

Lark turned from the vision of the handsome, masked man across the room smiling down at her sister and headed toward the door. Perhaps it was for the best if she left the debauching to those more suited to it.

\*\*\*\*

He tried to concentrate on what the female before him had to say, but couldn't. Sarco Sunwalker was having too much trouble trying not to chase after the beautiful barbarian female walking toward the door. He'd noticed her the moment he'd stepped into the room and had been about to go speak with her, when he'd been waylaid. For a heartbeat, he'd been sure the feather-masked beauty had meant to come to him and then, she simply hadn't.

Sarco shook his head. Carnalval on its best day was a strange place, and this season had certainly proved to be no exception to that rule. Why had he even come? Intimately cavorting with strangers had never been on the top of his to-do list.

The damn gnome, that's why. He shuddered. There would be time to dwell on Leeky Shortz and his motives later. Right now, he needed to catch the fleeing beauty.

Knowing he was being rude but unable to stop himself, Sarco bowed quickly before the woman in front of him and headed toward the door. He caught a quick glimpse of the barbarian beauty slipping into the darkness.

With only one thought in mind, he followed. If he must be at Carnalval, he meant to make the best of this one night, his last evening of no responsibility. Tomorrow, he'd head back to the Academy of Magical Arts and to his duty, but for this one last night, his life was still his own.

He found her standing silently in the shadows of the late summer evening, her face tilted to the pale light of the three moons of Albrath and her eyes closed. In her mask and glittery white gown, she reminded him of a fabled goddess he'd once read of. He was almost afraid to speak, fearful she would be but a figment of his imagination and disappear before his eyes. Sarco gathered his courage.

"Warm, don't you think?"

The woman startled at the sound of his voice. The air whooshed from Sarco's lungs. She was even more beautiful up close than she'd been from a distance. Hair the color of warm amber cascaded down pale shoulders. Eyes of molten silver gazed back at him through the white feathers of her mask. Lips full and pink—the kind begging to be kissed—curved upward in a slight smile. There was only one word that could describe the creature standing before him. Wonderful.

"Yes, it is a little warm, I suppose." Her voice was warm honey.

Much like an untrained schoolboy, for the first time

in his twenty-six years, high-elf wizard Sarco Sunwalker stumbled for something to say. "Umm, may I have this dance?"

He longed to touch her. The low-cut gown she wore clung to—but still did too good of a job hiding—her full breasts and lush, womanly curves. He yearned to caress her naked skin and discover the different textures of every inch. Her sigh broke into his erotic thoughts.

"There's no music," she whispered.

"There's music all around, my dear Wonderful, if you but close your eyes and listen."

He watched, enthralled, as long, dark lashes caressed white feathers. Her eyes closed and a smile graced her gentle features.

"Can you hear the music now?" he whispered. "Do you not notice the melodies sung by the birds of the night, the tempo of the wind, the added harmony of tiny insect wings in flight, mixed with the percussion of our very own heartbeats?"

He leaned in close and inhaled the fragrance of wildflowers mixed with lust. His cock hardened. "Can you not feel the music, Wonderful? Allow it to seduce you, give into the moment. Taste it, embrace it, dare to embrace me."

She opened her eyes and nodded.

Sarco held out a hand, "Shall we then?"

Sweeping her into his arms and close against his chest, he twirled her to the rhythm of nature's night song.

\*\*\*\*

If she could have, Lark would have pinched herself to make sure she wasn't dreaming. He had called her

5

*Wonderful*, and in a voice so rich and deep, it rumbled all the way to her toes. No man had ever left her so breathless.

Her skin tingled and tiny shivers skittered along her spine. Being held in the arms of the most mystifying man in all of Albrath and dancing, actually waltzing beneath the stars, were what dreams were made of. Not reality.

Not wanting to break the spell, she chanced a glance at his face anyway. Although his simple, black half-mask concealed his identity, nothing could hide those eyes. They reminded her of the hungry eyes of a large cat—rich brown, streaked with gold, mesmerizing. Where had she seen eyes like his before? An inkling of a memory stirred, but Lark pushed it away.

Now was not the time for dwelling. Now was the time to misbehave. This was Carnalval. This was allowed.

Crisply pointed ears told her of his high-elf heritage. And his lips…Lark trembled with the desire to lift up on tiptoes the mere inch it would take to savor their fullness, to chance a nip, to slide her tongue deep inside and relish a taste. The sly smile he gifted her with told Lark this man knew exactly what she'd been thinking, and heat warmed her cheeks.

His arms tightened about her, and for the first time in her life, Lark knew what it meant to be under a spell. Looking away wasn't a possibility as, ever so slowly, his head dipped. He was going to kiss her, and even though she told herself to relax and breathe, her treacherous heart pounded erratically.

He tasted of exotic spice and stardust, of sweet

passion and the promise of sizzling desire. His tongue teased and tempted. His hands roamed, his body molded to hers. She was lost and knew it. Whatever this man wanted, he could have. He needn't ask, simply take.

What was wrong with her? It wasn't as if she were some virginal schoolgirl. Her barbarian father's castle was well staffed with a team of professionals to teach all the specifics of carnal knowledge. Lark had not only passed, but excelled in her sex education classes and graduated with honors.

Why, then, did this man make her knees feel they could not hold her weight? Why did her heart pound near to bursting with just a kiss?

"Shall we find somewhere more private to continue our…dance, Wonderful?"

The whisper against Lark's skin sent shivers racing straight down her spine, tightening her nipples along the way before scattering throughout her belly. "Do you mind if we go to your room? Laycee, my gnome— umm—governess, would never forgive me if I brought a man back to mine."

He chuckled against the skin of her neck and Lark quivered.

"I understand that statement, Wonderful. I too have a pesky gnome in my life."

Lark couldn't stop the soft moan that escaped as she struggled to maintain her composure while his lips continued their exquisite exploration. "Does your gnome have rules for every situation he demands you follow, like Laycee Titwilder does to me?"

The sound of the man's laughter and his softly spoken words of, "Oh yes, his name should be 'Rules' instead of Leeky," warmed Lark's heart and settled the butterflies fluttering in her tummy.

He unwrapped himself from around her and tucked her arm in his. Together they strolled the lantern-lit lane.

The man turned slightly toward her and grinned. "Leeky Shortz really does have a rule for everything. For this trip to Carnalval alone, he had three in particular."

He held up three fingers. "One," he lowered his ring finger, "stay at the biggest castle you can find. That way if you get too intoxicated you can still find your way back to your room or find someone to at least point you in the right direction." His middle finger joined the others. "Two, divide your money into three equal parts; one part in your tunic, one in your breeks, and one in your boots. That way, if you end up losing everything except your boots, you might be naked, but you still aren't broke. And last but not least," he shook the remaining finger, "never venture down a dark alley alone, because that's just dumb."

Lark laughed. "Your Leeky should meet my Laycee. They sound much alike."

The man grinned, and Lark's heart hammered in her chest. He leaned in close and nuzzled her neck. "Let's not waste time talking gnomes, Wonderful. All I want to discuss is how long it's going to take before I have you naked and squirming beneath me."

She looked him straight in the eye. "Me, too."

****

Sarco knew himself to be undeserving of the gift waiting before him and yet, at the same time, he couldn't force himself to walk away. In a matter of no more than a season—and certainly by the appearance of the once-a-century, triple-full-phasing of Albrath's three moons—he was duty-bound to take a wife. And not just any wife, but a barbarian-human princess of a wife.

So why was he here now, doing something so completely foreign to his character? One-night stands and lusty encounters for the sake of sexual release alone had never been his style.

And yet, here he stood in the middle of his rented room, facing a lovely stranger and set upon a path of total intimacy with her. There was something about this woman, something he couldn't resist.

Something beyond her obvious beauty drew Sarco to her. Something he didn't understand and wasn't sure he wanted to. Something almost spiritual had called to his soul the moment he glimpsed her standing across the expanse of the ballroom, and yet he dare not even ask her name. The freedom of Carnalval came with few restrictions, but anonymity was the most important one.

The trembling of his hand as he undid the closures holding his tunic together and slipped it awkwardly over his head told him more about himself than he wanted to know. When had he last made love to a woman for the purpose of pure, simple pleasure? He couldn't remember. Had he really allowed his life to become so burdened with day-to-day responsibilities that he'd forgotten how to live?

Perhaps Leeky Shortz had been right when he told him, "Boy, life is much too short ta not enjoy every single breath. Live life like ya're arse is on fire. That's my motto."

Sarco chuckled.

"Did you say something?" the woman whispered.

He shook his head. "Nothing, I just can't believe my luck. You really are real and here with me."

She smiled, but her smile didn't extend to her eyes.

Before another heartbeat passed or another breath taken, he stood at her side. With tenderness, he gazed into her gentle, masked face and took both of her hands in his. He was humbled as her fingers trembled even more than his own did. "We don't have to do this if you'd rather not."

She smiled wider, and her eyes gleamed with mischief. "I suppose we might as well. After all, we're already here, and you're at least halfway undressed."

Sliding his hands up her arms and around her shoulders to her back, Sarco felt for and found the clasps holding her gown together. With the flick of a wrist, they gave way, and with a swish, the silky fabric fell to her hips exposing lush, rose-tipped breasts. Just the right size to hold in both hands, to fondle, to caress, to taste.

"Hmm, it seems you're halfway undressed yourself."

With a fingertip, Sarco grazed one pert nipple and was rewarded with the soft sound of a gasp. Replacing the finger with his lips, he sucked, then grinned to himself as the woman before him forgot to breathe and shivered. Easing the gown slowly over her hips and down her legs until it floated quietly to the floor, Sarco stepped back an inch to gaze. "Exquisite."

Although she still wore a mask, Sarco didn't miss the look of doubt as she opened her silver, passion-filled eyes.

Slowly, he caressed her cheek, running a finger

down her neck, between her breasts, across her belly and resting it lightly at the top of her smooth mound before reversing and retracing his way back up.

"It isn't necessary to say pretty words and tell me things like I'm exquisite," she whispered. "I've always known I'm not. Being ordinary is fine with me, really it is. Let's simply enjoy what we have to offer each other for this one night. This is Carnalval. It's the only chance we'll ever have."

Confusion muddled his thoughts. Was it possible this woman really didn't know how very beautiful she was? Sarco placed his hands on her shoulders and turned her until she faced a tall mirror standing behind her. He took her hands into his, and one at a time, positioned them firmly on the sides of the mirror's dark-wood frame. He held them there. Sliding a foot between her feet, he pushed with his knee and slightly parted her legs.

His voice was more a growl than a whisper when he dipped his head and nuzzled the skin below her ear. "Watch yourself, Wonderful, and see the woman I see."

## Chapter Two

If ever a man was more sexy, more hot, more tantalizing than the one standing behind her, touching her, caressing her this very moment, Lark couldn't imagine such a man. Vibrations rolled over and through her as he raised his arms above his head and clapped. Thunder shook the walls, and a chilly breeze filled the room and cooled her heated skin. The whoosh of air snuffed out the candles scattered throughout the small space, plunging them into darkness save for the streaks of moonlight filtering through the windows.

Lark couldn't take her eyes from the mirror even if she'd wanted to. The man's hands glowed with light and pulsed with energy. *A wizard. He must be a wizard to do such magic.*

Gently, he caressed her cheek and ran a finger over her partially open lips. "You, my lady, are the very definition of exquisite. Your skin's as soft as the first flower buds of spring, Wonderful, and your lips taste of rich, sweet nectar. Your scent entices me. You smell of wild flowers and raw need."

Lark gasped as his long, lean body came into full contact with her back and ass. His cock was hard against her, throbbing, pulsating, ready.

His glowing fingers slid first to her throat then to her shoulders, and his lips followed their path. "Your body is beyond even exquisite, Wonderful. It was made to hold a man close and surround him with your warmth."

Lark shivered with excitement as his fingertips caressed and playfully slid up and down her arms.

"Shoulders wide enough to help carry the day-to-day burdens of life, yet hands small enough to reach out and seek comfort when you need it. Arms long enough to wrap around a man's body, and legs strong enough to hold him close. Oh yes, Wonderful, you are definitely exquisite."

No one had ever spoken to her this way. Lark shivered and her breath came in quick gasps as his glowing hands wrapped around her waist and tugged her in closer, tighter.

For long moments, they stood just like that. He holding her, and she absorbing feelings she'd long denied. It wasn't until her breathing calmed that he continued.

His fingers trailed lower, down across her belly, and between her parted legs.

Liquid heat filled her as his fingers delved into her pussy. She burned. Every nerve ending screamed, every heartbeat pounded, and every breath warred with the next to be her last. Lark needed this man as she'd never needed another, and she needed him now.

"Please," she whispered.

His thumb slid over the sensitive nub of her clit while his fingers played and teased at her opening. "Watch me, Wonderful," he chuckled. "Watch me pleasure you. See how beautiful you are when you soar."

Lark hadn't realized she'd even blinked, but she opened her eyes wide now and marveled as long, glowing fingers slid in and out of her pussy. A throbbing so intense it threatened to buckle her knees overcame her. For a second, she let go of the mirror's edge and grabbed for his arm to steady herself. He gave a simple twist of his wrist, and in the flash of light that followed, Lark's feet left the floor until she floated inches above it.

"Put your hands back on the mirror's frame." He commanded, but there was no censure in his voice, only passion.

She did as he asked.

His hands circled her hips, lifting and angling her toward him. With a swift, confident plunge, he slid his cock into her awaiting pussy.

Lark sucked in a deep breath as his thick shaft stretched her. He was big and hard, virile and hot. As hot as the sun that would surely rise much too soon in the morning, as hot as the inferno of the fires in the Valley of Torment must be. Lark giggled. Thoughts of sins and where she'd end up when she committed them were not welcome right now. This was Carnalval. This was allowed, encouraged even.

"I do believe you're the first woman ever to have laughed when I've entered her. If you didn't look so smugly satisfied with yourself, I think I'd be insulted."

She gazed at his reflection in the mirror, then looked at herself and even she could see the transformation. No longer was the woman before her plain and ordinary. Her body glowed with life and energy. Her eyes gleamed with pleasure and passion. Her insides throbbed with need and excitement. She was beautiful, vibrant, and oh God Draka, she was sexy.

Lark tucked her feet back behind his knees, locked them in place, and smiled at his gorgeous face in the mirror. "I am quite satisfied with myself. You said you wanted to watch me soar? Well then, magical man, continue with this spell you've cast and come fly with me."

There was little time left for words. Bodies melded into one another as muscles bunched and strained. Breaths came in quick, hurried spurts. Fingers caressed then held tight as he plunged harder and faster, and she answered, stroke for stroke, with a force of her own.

His hands were everywhere at the same time. On her neck, then breasts, her belly, then clit. Over and over with a sure, steady, lover's touch. His front pressed against her back, and Lark could feel the rippling of his muscles as she gloried in the barely restrained power of this man. His cock slid in and out, with strong, sure thrusts, slick and slippery, faster, then slower.

The cadence of his heartbeat matched hers, and a throbbing of delight formed deep in the pit of Lark's belly and radiated outward. The pleasure grew, expanding until her toes curled, her throat tickled, her insides contracted, and each individual hair on the top of her head zinged with an electrical charge.

When it happened, Lark wondered at the shout she wasn't sure came from her lips or his, as they both exploded together with mind-numbing ecstasy. Wave after sweet wave of rolling, effervescent spasms shook their bodies until, at last, with a satisfied sigh, he lifted her off his cock and carried her to his bed.

He gathered her close, spooning them together. "I know there's not much forbidden during Carnalval, except inquiring your name, and I wouldn't think of it. But I do ask one more thing. For the remainder of this one night, stay with me, Wonderful. Let's make love until the sun beckons. For tomorrow, I must return to my responsibilities."

Lark turned in his arms and placed one of his hands against her heart. "I pray the night wins its battle with day and the sun doesn't rise. In your arms is the most amazing place I've ever been," she sighed. "But we both know that won't happen. The sun will come up as it always does, and I too have responsibilities. But yes, for this night, I agree. Let's make love, again and again."

He slid his hands over her body. Lark moaned and trembled as his fingers and lips explored once more. He touched her in reverence, and she gloried in it.

The world inside the room became everything, and nothing beyond the walls existed. They were simply a man and a woman enjoying a passion they both knew must fade with the coming of the dawn.

Lark sighed. It would have to be enough.

****

Hours passed as the wind carried the melody of night birds mixed with the fragrance of late-summer flowers along the well-worn paths of the pleasure city of Carnalval. The skies were alight with the twinkling of fireflies, so thick they competed with the stars for attention. The three moons of Albrath, one new, one quarter, and one full, each cast shimmering rays of light, illuminating the dark corners of the room and adding to the magic.

Sarco lay on his side with one arm behind his head and the other draped across the luscious breasts of the lady sleeping peacefully beside him. It had been more than a turn of the hourglass since his third time making love with this beautiful woman. His mind craved more even while his body knew it wasn't possible. Never before, not in any woman's arms, had making love felt so right. He sighed and closed his eyes. How could fate be so cruel?

One peek. Surely one quick peek under her mask wouldn't be so horrible an indiscretion? He had to know. Perhaps he had no choice but walk away tomorrow and never again hold her, never again make love to her, but, by God Draka, he could take the memory of her sweet face with him.

Gingerly, so as to not waken her, Sarco lifted the white-feathered mask away and gazed at the sleeping beauty before him. A sprinkling of pale freckles crisscrossed her nose and dotted her cheeks. Her dark, sable lashes lay peacefully against her skin. Her full, slightly puckered lips moved gently in slumber, and Sarco longed to partake of their taste once more. He memorized every feature. The small roundness of her ears, the slope of her forehead, the tilt of her chin. Finally, with a soul deep sigh, he let the mask slip back in place.

He should have never looked. There were reasons for the rules. Sarco had always been about the rules. Had always followed them. Why had he gone against them this time? For the rest of his life, he'd be tormented by the memory of this silver-eyed beauty who could never truly be his.

He couldn't resist her allure, however, and neither could his cock. Once more, he woke her with a kiss.

\*\*\*\*

Lark smiled at the man sleeping peacefully beside her. What had it been? Three, no four, possibly five times he'd expertly pleasured her beyond her wildest dreams during the much-too-short night?

Streaks of early morning light filtered through the window and chased away shadows as Lark gazed to her heart's content at the beautiful male specimen beside her. She should rise and dress, slip quietly from the room without a word, and be on her way. She didn't move. She couldn't quite bring herself to let it end.

What would it hurt to lift the edge of his mask and gaze upon his face? She would never see him again. No one would ever know. Tentatively, Lark stretched out her hand, but then quickly drew her fingers back.

No, this was Carnalval. To break this city of pleasure's cardinal rule of maintaining anonymity and get caught at it would mean being banned from here forever. She weighed her choices—spend the rest of her life wondering or, so unlike her nature, take a chance? Lark smiled.

Her fingers trembled as, ever so slowly to avoid awakening him, she lifted his mask. One glimpse to last a lifetime, that's all she would take, then she'd slip the mask back in place. Fate couldn't be so cruel as to expect her to go on year after year, always wondering, never knowing.

A ray of sunlight illuminated the chiseled planes of his features and Lark's heart stopped. She gasped and skittered away from the sight so quickly her feet tangled in the sheet and, with a thud, she landed in a heap upon the floor.

There was stirring and the definite sound of the man turning over, and Lark held her breath and silently prayed, "*Please don't wake. Lord God Draka, if you care for me in the least, don't let him wake.*" The movement stopped, he settled, and the room once more became quiet except for the deafening roar of her pounding heart.

Oh God Draka, what had she done?

As quickly and silently as she could, Lark rose, gathered her clothing, and dressed. She was almost out the door when she remembered the mask. She had to put it back. There was no way he could be allowed to know she'd seen his face.

Stealthily, she crossed the room and with quivering fingers, put back what she should never have removed.

It was all she could do to keep from caressing his cheek one last time as tears clouded her vision and a lump too big to swallow formed in her throat. Of all the men in Albrath, why did this one have to be who he was? Of all the males in the world, why did he have to be the owner of the one face forever forbidden to her?

She'd been right after all. He was a wizard. Not just any wizard, however, but High-Elf Wizard Sarco-Keltoris Titus Sunwalker himself. A man born and bred to be the next lord and leader of the elfin kingdom of Landis. He was also the newly appointed Master Wizard Instructor at the Academy of Magical Arts. A man known throughout all of Albrath for his single-minded dedication to family, duty, honor, and responsibility.

The man her parents spoke of incessantly, sometimes kindly, sometimes not. And, most heartwrenchingly of all, he was the man her sister, Princess Aryanna Zahanna Clemencia Hammerstrike, intended to marry.

Chapter Three

If ever a man had been in the wrong place at the wrong time, Sarco Sunwalker was certainly that man.

Lark closed her eyes, rested her head against the back of the seat as the coach rocked along the country road. Outside, the wind howled and the rain pounded the stones beneath the wheels. The horrid weather matched her mood. What had begun as a sunny morning had quickly developed into a full-blown storm before Lark even left the courtyard of the castle she and Sarco Sunwalker had spent the night in. The dash back to her own castle room had left her not only drenched, but melancholy.

*Sarco, why did it have to be you?* Lark groaned as lightning flashed and thunder roared so loudly it shook the coach.

"Stop doing that!"

Lark opened her eyes and glared at her sister. "It isn't me. It's just a summer storm, Ary."

Princess Aryanna rolled her eyes. "Of course it's you. All manner of foul weather blows when you're upset about something, and you know it. How long must we suffer before you tell us what really happened last night?"

Tears stung Lark's eyes. "Nothing happened. Nothing's wrong. I simply don't feel well."

The female gnome sitting across from Lark

snorted, "That's what ya've been telling us all morning since ya got back ta our rooms, late, I might add, and it's still poppycock. I've raised ya since the first day ya were put ta yare wet nurse's tit, and ya can't fool me, little missy. Ya forgot ta cast yare protection from disease and pregnancy spell like I told ya ta do, didn't ya? Probably hooked up for the night with some smooth-talking devil of a dark-elf and now ya're worried about the consequences. Well, serves ya right if ya did. And don't come crying ta Laycee Titwilder, expecting me ta get ya out of this mess. No ma'am, not gonna happen."

The gnome governess made a production of adjusting her ill-fitting blond wig while glaring at Lark.

A single tear escaped and slid down Lark's cheek. She swiped it away and scrunched her eyes tightly closed, determined she'd not let her sister or governess see her cry.

"I wouldn't have been late if I hadn't been following your stupid take-no-money-with-you-because-the-men-should-pay rule. I had to walk back to our castle instead of renting a coach. And I didn't forget my PDUP spell. I even said it twice, just as you asked. I didn't spend the night with a dark-elf, and I'm not causing this storm. I simply had too much ale last night and don't feel well. Now, leave me to my misery, please."

Just like Laycee Titwilder, Aryanna wasn't having it. "So, where did you spend the night then, and with whom?"

Lark cringed, not wanting to lie but seeing no way around it. "In the lobby of some castle. I passed out. End of story. I wasn't the one who wanted to come to

Carnalval in the first place, remember? I would've been perfectly content to go elsewhere, anywhere, even home."

Aryanna gasped. "So now you're blaming me. You know perfectly well this trip to Carnalval was to be my last few days of freedom. And how did I spend my final night before I must go and do my duty? Did I have a secret tryst with some handsome elf, barbarian, human, or even troll? No, I didn't. I got turned down flat and spent the entire night with Laycee and her...her blow-up doll, Tug, worrying about you and waiting for you to get home."

Lark squirmed in her seat, knowing her sister was just getting started.

"And...and you may not be responsible for every single storm, but I would bet anything you're the cause of this one. You can't tell me you aren't. Even though we don't speak of it often, we both know what you are.

"I remember being snowed in more weeks than I want to think about because you were upset about something. And you haven't forgotten the time you got angry with the twins for yanking your hair, have you? Father was so worried it was going to flood and ruin all the crops because it rained so hard that season. Try and deny it all you like, but that doesn't change the facts, my dear spiritmaster of a sister!"

Aryanna's voice droned on and on, but Lark turned away and blocked it out. She pressed her face against the small window and watched the landscape roll by. Field after field of wildflowers in every color of the rainbow calmed her spirit.

Gentle hills sloped here and there as the cobblestone roadway meandered northward toward the horizon, toward the ring of portal stones, toward home.

How many times in her life had she heard those same words? *You're different, Lark. You don't fit in, Lark. People are afraid of you, Lark.*

She closed her eyes and concentrated on breathing, gulping the warm air of the confined coach as deeply as she could. Ary was right. She must calm herself before the storm washed away the road, leaving them stranded in the middle of nowhere.

Yes, she was different from other people, always had been. If she wasn't careful, she could see into others' minds without their being aware of it, and sometimes even change their thoughts to her way of thinking. More often than not, though, it backfired and people became stubbornly adamant in their own opinions, and no amount of reason could change their views. Experience had taught her to be careful when playing around in other people's heads.

And then there was the weather. The skies almost always matched her mood, and certainly on more occasions than she'd like to take credit for. There were times her father blamed her for the long winter nights and heavy snowfalls, though they lived in the far, far north where huge drifts of the powdery white stuff were perfectly normal.

Grandmother Ava had once told her being different—being a spiritmaster—was a gift. On days like today, though, Lark wasn't so sure about that. What Grandmother Ava called *spirit magic* could be as much a curse as a gift.

Lark chuckled and the rain slowed to a drizzle. A streak of sunlight shone through the thick, black clouds.

Grandmother Ava was the one constant light in

Lark's life. Her true age was a mystery, but rumor had it she was close to a century old, if not older. Bent over and as frail as a raven's bone, no one would guess the strength hidden beneath the folds of long, silk robes, or the gentleness of her arms as they held and rocked her grandchildren, let alone the wisdom and knowledge tucked away in the recesses of her still lightning-quick mind. Grandmother Ava was security, she was home, she was love.

It was on Grandmother's knee as a small child where Lark had come to terms with the fact she'd never be like everyone else. For hours on end, she'd listened avidly to the stories of her maternal ancestry. Stories of the spiritmasters—a human, nomadic group of people who were strong in the ways of mind-over-mind and mind-over-matter. Spirit magic was old magic, almost as old as the dragons themselves who had gifted only a handful of humans with the power.

Not well-respected and, more often than not, feared and hunted because of their ability to control the minds of others, the spiritmasters had become all but extinct, and scattered to the winds of Albrath. Those who were left lived in seclusion, fearful of being discovered.

Lark had been taught at a young age to hide her particular talent, or shame, as her parents referred to it. And not just hide her abilities, but never practice them, and even deny their existence. If she tried harder to repress them, she hoped, perhaps her curse would fade away in time.

The rain slowed to a drizzle, and the sun broke through the clouds. A rainbow of pastels streaked across the sky. Lark glanced over at Aryanna and smiled. "I don't suppose you'd be willing to give me credit for the good weather along with the bad, would you, Ary?"

Her sister grinned and playfully poked Lark in the ribs. "Well then, I'm putting in an order for rainbows and sunshine the rest of the way to the portal and home. It hurts me to see you unhappy, Lark."

Lark nodded. "I'll do my best. I promise."

Ary leaned back against the seat of the coach and closed her eyes to nap.

Lark studied her sister. How could anyone be so beautiful and so thoughtful? Not that she wasn't a prissy, prima donna princess all the way to the tips of her manicured toes, but Ary had a spirit that naturally made people smile and wish to do her bidding. She was regal yet fair, conceited yet accepting, spoiled yet giving. She would make Sarco Sunwalker a fine wife.

Pain laced with guilt stabbed Lark's heart and thunder crashed overhead. She forced the vision of Sarco as he had looked last night, with passion smoldering in his eyes, from her mind.

Ary opened her eyes, leaned over, and patted her hand. "I wish you would tell me what's wrong," she sighed. "Though I know you won't. At least all will be well when we get home. You just wait and see. It'll be different this time."

Lark cringed and the clouds opened up in a deluge.

Home. She was barely tolerated at the dinner table let alone in the castle on a daily basis. It had gotten to the point over the years that weeks could go by without Lark seeing either of her parents. She didn't mind. Being in the presence of King Alfred and Queen Allanna usually meant she'd once again displeased them in some manner.

Lightning flashed across the sky and thunder rolled over the carriage as it swayed in the fierce wind, while Lark relived the only time she had purposely sought her mother out.

It was on her sixteenth birthday and curiosity finally got the better of her. She found Queen Allanna alone in her private solar.

"Mother, may I have an audience, please?"

The queen turned toward her and, at first, didn't seem to recognize her. "Lark? Oh, it is you. Don't stand there slouching, girl. Get on with it. What is it?"

Lark curtsied. "May I ask a question?"

The queen twisted so as not to look directly at her but nodded.

"Why did you name me Larksong? I mean, not that I don't think it's a perfectly lovely name. It's just that it isn't like the others. I mean, it doesn't start with an A like Aryanna, Adan, Ally, and Audrey. And…and there isn't even a middle…" Lark's voice trailed away until the last of her words were no more than a sigh.

Queen Allanna walked to the window and stared off into the distance. "You were never like the rest of the children. Not even the day you were born. You were so difficult. Eighteen hours I labored with you, and for what? I expected more, I expected a son. Another son would have been prudent. After all, I had already given your father three daughters. There certainly was no need for a fourth.

"It would've made the king happy if you'd been a male. But you weren't. And then you opened your eyes and I knew God Draka had punished me for wanting another son so badly. You were marked. Those cold, soulless, gray eyes. Eyes of the cursed spiritmasters."

26

The queen twisted toward Lark and pointed a perfectly manicured nail toward her. Lark felt the sting of it to the core of her soul.

"I could no more name you as I did the others than I could throw myself from this window. Can't you understand? It would've tainted our name, it would've been sacrilege. Even someone like yourself must realize that.

"The entire time I labored with you, an irritating bird screeched outside this very window. Your cry sounded much the same as that incessant noise, so since I had no choice but to name you something, I named you Larksong in its honor. Appropriate, don't you think?"

That had been the last time Lark had sought out her mother for any reason.

And now, after traveling this last season as Aryanna's companion, she was headed back to a home where she wasn't wanted.

At least Grandmother Ava would be there to greet her, and her brother Adan and her twin sisters Ally and Audrey. Did it really matter if her parents found her an embarrassment, a disappointment, a disgrace?

What would they think if they knew she'd bedded her sister's future husband? Casual sex for pleasure certainly wasn't considered taboo. It was completely normal. Sex with your sister's intended was another matter entirely. Once a man or woman was spoken for, they were off-limits, especially to other family members.

What would Ary think if she knew? She probably wouldn't be offering comfort or patting her hand. The thought of her sister's face contorting with pain and betrayal was more than Lark could take. She'd rather hurl herself from the highest peak of the Alarian Mountain Range than cause a moment's suffering for Ary.

Lark wondered how she was ever going to live the rest of her life knowing the man she'd already begun to fall in love with belonged to someone else. And not just anyone else, but her very own sister.

Glancing at Ary's kind, trusting face, the dam of tears Lark had been valiantly holding back all morning burst wide open.

Aryanna wrapped her arms around Lark's shoulders, hugging her close as she whispered, "Oh, Lark, sweetie, someone really has broken your heart, hasn't he? Tell me who it is, and I'll have Adan hunt him down and pummel him. You go on and cry all you want, honey. It's all right. If it floods, we'll just turn this old coach into a boat and row our way home."

Lark cried harder.

## Chapter Four

If ever a man should pack his bags and run as quickly as he could this very moment, Sarco Sunwalker was that man, and he didn't even know it. The fate awaiting him, if he stayed where he now was, made Lark shudder. She believed with all her heart, when her sister's coach rolled through the entry to the Academy of Magical Arts next week, Sarco wouldn't have a clue what was about to hit him.

Not that his eventual marriage to beautiful Princess Aryanna could be considered a horrible existence. For Lark genuinely believed any man would be lucky to call Ary his wife. It was the fact he would be getting the king and queen as in-laws in the bargain that made Lark ill. If these last days at home had taught her anything, it was the farther from her parents she, or anyone else, could get, the better.

Her parents, King Alfred Zavier Caden and his wife Queen Allanna Zanlynn Calista Hammerstrike, were a sight to behold. Songs attesting to the perfection of their union had been composed and sung by minstrels from one end of Albrath to the other for as long as Lark could remember.

The dark and brooding King Alfred, a hulking barbarian warrior, was a handsome man used to getting his way in all things. That is, as long as his way coincided with the wishes of the queen. She was the true ruler, and everyone knew it.

The beauty of Queen Allanna, a petite human, was renowned throughout the land. Her golden tendrils and deep-sea-blue eyes were the subject of poet, minstrel, and artist alike. But then, the poets, minstrels, and artists were not privy to the coldness of the queen's heart.

Everyone in the kingdom looked upon King Alfred and Queen Allanna as the perfect couple, ruling over their perfect kingdom, with their perfect life and their perfect children. All their children, that is, except for Lark. She'd always been a disappointment, a freak of nature, a mistake. Unlike her siblings, Lark didn't fit into the vision her parents had of the perfect family.

Lark grimaced. Getting away from her parents tonight wasn't going to be an option. The entire family was in attendance for Princess Aryanna's farewell dinner, with King Alfred holding court at one end of an enormous oaken table while Queen Allanna sat in all her regal splendor at the other end.

Lark sat to the left of her father, sandwiched between Ally and Audrey, the twins. Her brother, Adan, was on their father's right, with Grandmother Ava beside him and Ary beside Mother.

The conversation all evening had revolved around Sarco *this* and Princess Aryanna *that*, the fulfillment of a prophecy, the wedding of the century, and the joining of two dynasties. It was nauseating.

Lark tried to block out the voices and concentrate only on the food she kept shoving around her plate, but the sound of Ary's voice and what she was saying snapped her back to attention.

"Lark's going to accompany me to the Academy.

As a matter of fact, I insist she does. Who knows, she might find her very own wizard to marry while there. Wouldn't that just be the sweetest thing? We could have a double wedding."

Her sister's smile was open and genuine, and guilt about her jealousy toward Ary filled Lark. After all, it wasn't Ary's fault she was destined to marry the only man Lark wanted for herself.

The screech of humorless laughter coming from the far end of the table stopped all conversation in the room. Lark's mother glared at Ary, as if Lark wasn't even in the room. "Lark, marry a wizard? There'll be no marriage between your youngest sibling and a wizard or anyone else for that matter. I can guarantee you that.

"Why, it would be almost criminal. Could you imagine the talk if she actually produced offspring? I won't hear of it. This royal household has a standard to uphold. Just because we endure Lark, doesn't mean we have the right to pawn her off on some poor, unsuspecting soul. Perhaps she should stay home where an eye can be kept on her."

The room became silent as a tomb. Heat wicked up Lark's neck, her face burned, and a lump formed in her throat. She couldn't swallow.

Grandmother Ava stood, tossed her napkin upon the tabletop, and faced the queen. "There are days I'm embarrassed to admit you are even my daughter, Allanna."

Tears pricked Lark's lashes as her grandmother's kind old eyes filled to overflowing. "She is your daughter, too, and Lark *will* go with her sister to the Academy. Do you hear me?"

Grandmother Ava pointed a bony finger toward

Lark's mother. "I have put up with much over the years to keep peace with you, but this, I'll not abide. For the very last time, there is nothing wrong with what Lark is. She will go, or else!"

Queen Allanna glared at her mother but didn't utter another word.

Lark was grateful her grandmother defended her, but at the same time, she wanted to find a place to crawl inside and hide. Being the center of her mother's attention was never a pleasant experience.

King Alfred wasn't any better when he interjected a moment later. "Don't worry yourself about it, Allanna dear. Your mother is right. Let the girl go. What can it hurt?" He waved his fork in Lark's direction. "And don't forget, the crops aren't quite ready to harvest. No sense running the chance she'll get upset again and ruin them."

He wiped his mouth with his napkin. "I don't see what you're so concerned about anyway. No man, wizard or not, will give Lark a second glance with our lovely Aryanna in the vicinity. Nothing to worry about, I say."

The king turned his smile on Lark, and the lump in her throat tripled to boulder size. "And as for you. You're a daughter of my loins too and, though plain and undoubtedly different, when the time does come, I'll find some man willing to bind himself to you. I don't even care if it costs me a fortune to convince him to do so. And if by chance there are children from the union and they're, umm, different like you, I'll simply instruct the lad to build above flood level."

Lark rose from the table and fled the room as clouds opened outside, thunder crashed, and rain poured.

****

Sarco waited patiently near the front of the receiving line and took what he hoped would be calming breaths. He tugged at the stiff collar of his scarlet-colored wizard's robe.

This was the moment he'd been dreading since the day the first part of the prophecy had been fulfilled.

The procession of snow-white carriages drawn by sleek, matching horses moved through the gates of the Academy with all the pomp appropriate to the arrival of a princess. A flash of lightning streaked across what, moments before, had been a cloudless blue sky, and thunder roared overhead. Fat drops of rain pelted the long line of awaiting dignitaries.

Sarco smiled to himself. At least the weather knew sunshine wouldn't be appropriate today.

The first carriage stopped directly in front of the long red carpet and a doorman came forward to open the coach door. Sarco held his breath.

A vision of female perfection stepped out. She was lovely, there was no denying it. Long, cascading curls of spun gold flowed across petite shoulders and swung gracefully against a tiny waist. Her form-fitting gown accentuated her high, full breasts and was the exact shade of her deep violet eyes. Full, pink lips smiled easily and Sarco caught himself smiling back in response to her open friendliness.

Princess Aryanna was beautiful, graceful, and everything any man should ever hope for. Why, then, did Sarco feel only a passing appreciation for her beauty? The memory of silver eyes and soft sighs haunted him.

As if the mere thought could conjure the woman he would never forget, Sarco felt her presence as clearly as if she'd touched him. He glanced up quickly and watched as Wonderful stepped from the carriage. Her gaze locked with his, searching for him, expecting him, knowing he would be here. It was her, really her, and she looked…guilty.

God Draka, she knew who he was.

Anger warred with confusion. Had she known all along? Had she known that night at Carnalval? Had it just been a game of take-the-princess's-future-husband-to-bed? Who was Wonderful to the princess? A friend? A relative? More than likely, she was naught but a servant.

He heard…no, he *felt* her voice in his mind as clearly as if she stood right beside him, whispering in his ear, "*Please don't let on we know each other. Act like we've never met. It's not what you think. Give me a chance to explain. I beg of you.*"

He wasn't sure if he'd imagined her voice inside his head because he didn't wish to believe her capable of deception or if she really had such a remarkable ability. Right now, though, there was no time to dwell upon it. The procession had begun.

The princess moved down the reception line, and Sarco waited tensely as she was presented to Headmistress Seychelle. He had to give Princess Aryanna credit for poise. She didn't even blink as she took in the strange pair standing before her.

Headmistress Seychelle was an entity unto herself. Coldly beautiful and well-known as a powerful enchantress, she certainly looked the part. Dressed in black leather that kissed and caressed sleek curves, she was a sight to behold. Tall, even for a high-elf, her skin was so pale it almost appeared translucent, and crisp, pointed ears peeked from a mass of black curls. In her hand, she held the end of a silver chain. The other end of that chain was linked to Ray.

Sarco sighed. Why had the woman insisted on bringing her mangy-looking human pet with her today of all days? Couldn't she have left him behind just this once?

Ray choose that moment to punctuate Sarco's point. He grinned up at Princess Aryanna and said the only three words Sarco, or anyone else for that matter, had ever heard him utter.

"Ray loves cock!"

Princess Aryanna jumped so quickly she almost tripped over the hem of her gown. She would've if Wonderful and the female gnome tagging along behind hadn't caught her.

Headmistress Seychelle shook her finger toward the skinny, almost hairless, little man. "Not right now, Ray. We're busy. Mistress will give you cock later, sweetums. Now, be a good boy and sit still."

"Ray loves cock. Ray loves cock. Ray loves cock."

Headmistress Seychelle sighed and jerked lightly on the leash. "Behave this moment, or I'll call for Briar." Immediately, Ray sat at his mistress's feet and whimpered. "That's a good boy."

Sarco glanced toward his silver-eyed beauty to see her reaction to Ray. Wonderful's eyes shone with laughter, so much so, Sarco couldn't help but smile himself. The dark clouds overhead parted and streaks of sunshine lit her head and shoulders. He couldn't take his eyes from her. She looked ethereal, radiant, and beyond lovely.

The clearing of a throat brought Sarco back to attention. The princess now stood directly in front of him and the assistant administrator, Mr. Ohmni, who was making introductions.

"Princess Aryanna Zahanna Clemencia Hammerstrike, might I present Sir Sarco-Keltoris Titus Sunwalker, heir to the Lordship of Landis and Master Wizard Instructor Extraordinaire."

Sarco bowed as the princess curtsied.

She held out a hand, and Sarco graciously took it into his own and imparted a light kiss upon her wrist. "It's a pleasure to finally meet you, Princess Aryanna."

His words were meant for the princess, but his gaze strayed to the woman standing silent behind her.

Princess Aryanna cleared her throat. "It's my pleasure to finally meet you, sir. Please call me Ary. All my friends do."

She turned toward her two female companions. "May I present my youngest sister, Princess Larksong, and our governess, Miss Laycee Titwilder?"

Sarco caught himself smiling even though he wasn't sure he shouldn't still be angry. Guilt did away with the last vestiges of irritation. After all, he'd broken the rules of Carnalval himself when he gazed upon her face while she slept. No matter her reason, could he fault her for knowing who he was?

Larksong. How pretty. It fit her. Now he had a name to go with the face that haunted his every waking moment and the dreams that tortured his soul nightly. He and Wonderful stared at each other for a few moments before Sarco realized he hadn't responded to the princess's introductions. Heat flooded his face.

"Umm, it's a pleasure to meet you." He nodded at the governess and at Larksong, where his gaze lingered.

He knew she hadn't uttered a word out loud, because he couldn't force his gaze from hers, but Sarco felt—heard—her voice ring clearly in his mind.

"*It's Lark. Just Lark. And it's nice to officially meet you, too.*"

\*\*\*\*

Lark tossed and turned but sleep eluded her. With a sigh, she settled for staring out the floor-to-ceiling windows of her room. The three moons of Albrath, all in different phases, shone brightly in a star-filled sky.

What was wrong with her? She should be sound asleep. She was exhausted after unpacking not only her own but all of Ary's trunks. It certainly wasn't because the room or the bed was uncomfortable. This was not a student dormitory. This was a suite, and Lark had a room all to herself.

Nervous energy made her restless. Tomorrow, the agreed-upon semester before the actual engagement would begin. Tomorrow, both she and Ary would start classes. And tomorrow, she would be forced to face Sarco.

Sarco. What was she going to do about Sarco? Tears clouded her eyes as Grandmother Ava's words came back to haunt her. "Be truthful and honest in all things, child, for only in a truthful heart does real magic abide."

Well, she hadn't been the least bit truthful with her sister concerning Sarco, and now she found herself in a serious dilemma. Ary was insisting Lark take the Elemental Wizard class—taught by Sarco—in her place.

Their conversation earlier in the evening played over in Lark's mind.

"So, what do you think of my future husband, Lark?"

Lark couldn't remember if it had been the tone of Ary's voice or her flippant attitude concerning Sarco that first angered her and then made her feel the need to defend him. "I think you're a lucky woman. He's tall, he's handsome, well educated, and has a nice smile. And did you notice his hands? They're huge and so strong looking."

Heat crept up Lark's neck and warmed her cheeks as she remembered the feel and texture of those hands touching her, stroking her.

Ary simply shrugged her shoulders. "I've seen better. His brother Cyrrick is certainly more handsome, in my opinion."

For the first time in her life, Lark wanted to violently shake her big sister.

"Cyrrick? You think Cyrrick is better looking than Sarco? He isn't nearly as tall. They might look remarkably alike, but Cyrrick's hair isn't as black as Sarco's and his eyes don't have those lovely streaks of gold. You just like Cyrrick better because he's a diplomat and you understand diplomacy. Sarco is a wizard, for God Draka's sake. How on Albrath can you not be attracted to the core of your very bones by that fact alone, if nothing else?"

Ary smiled at her, that sly smile she always got when she knew she was going to get her way. Lark should have seen it coming, but when Ary spoke, her words were the last ones Lark expected to hear.

"Then you take the wizard class in my place if

wizards impress you so much. I have no use for that form of magic. Especially first thing in the morning, five days a week. Instead, I do believe I shall add another class on magical plants and herbs, or possibly music. Do make my apologies to Sarco, won't you?"

Aryanna walked over and placed a small, worn leather book in Lark's hand. "Oh, and give this to him from me. I found it in Father's study and, knowing Sarco to be a scholar, thought perhaps he might enjoy it as a pre-engagement gift. I can't even tell you what it's about. Ancient languages bore me."

Lark's jaw dropped open, and she snapped it shut as her fingers clenched the small tome. "You can't be serious? The whole purpose in coming to the Academy was to show the future leader of Landis your interest in his lifestyle and work. Everyone in his family is a wizard, remember? I can't be a substitute for you, Ary."

The princess just continued smiling. "Cyrrick isn't a wizard, and he's certainly an important part of his family. If I'm not good enough for the snooty wizard just as I am, then I simply won't marry him. As far as I'm concerned, it's settled. You'll take Sarco's boring old wizard class in my place, and I'll take other subjects that interest me. That way we both get what we want."

Aryanna then turned on her heel and walked from the room.

That had been hours ago.

Lark had no doubt Ary slept peacefully, without a care in the world, confident Lark would handle this matter as she did most things. It wasn't fair, and it wasn't right. What was she going to do? It wasn't as if Sarco wasn't going to notice the switch. And her parents…if this courtship and engagement didn't go smoothly, there was no doubt she would be blamed. But one thing was evident. If she didn't get to sleep soon, she wouldn't be fit to face Sarco, or anyone for that matter, in the morning.

Sarco. She sighed and the vision of his handsome face filled her mind. Where was he right now? Was he slumbering, warm and cozy in his bed? Was he sleeping alone this night?

Lark's throat tightened at the thought of Sarco with another woman, any other woman, even Ary— especially Ary—and she clamped a hand over her mouth to prevent the cry that would have escaped. He wasn't meant for her and never would be. He belonged to Aryanna.

Her mind wouldn't listen to reason, though, and she desperately longed for him anyway, for a touch, a taste, a moment. The physical need for him grew strong, and she fought it as long as she could. Knowing she must find a way to resist going to him or bringing him to her, Lark looked toward the wooden chest at the side of her bed.

Opening the chest's top drawer, she withdrew one of her favorite toys. It was a small, smooth, golden orb. She clicked on the switch, and the soft hum of the vibrations brought a tiny smile of promised relief to her lips. *Soothe my raging fire so I can sleep* was her only thought as she touched the pulsating orb lightly to her clit and held it in place.

Closing her eyes, Lark sought the object of her desires. *Sarco, where are you?*

In her mind, she saw the Academy's outer courtyard and followed the cobblestone paths as they meandered throughout the grounds. Feeling drawn to a particular window, Lark's heart leapt at the sight of a dark head resting upon a pillow. It was Sarco. Her ability had found him.

Applying a little more pressure against her clit with the golden vibrating orb, she delved wantonly into his mind.

*"Sarco, make love with me. I need you, please."*

His essence came off the bed with hers, and out the window they flew. High into the sky they soared until, with gentleness, he laid her upon a cloud. A soft breeze blew, stars twinkled, and birds of the night sang a lilting melody.

Nothing separated them, not clothes, not a hair, not even a breath, and Lark gloried in the sight and feel of Sarco's magnificent bronzed body against hers. Strong arms enveloped her. Arms honed by hours of casting spells with sheer will and concentration.

His lips found hers as they teased, tasted, and tormented with ease. Hands roamed freely as his fingers stroked to attention first one taut nipple then another. His cock was heavy against her belly, and Lark longed to have its length deep within her.

*"Please, now,"* she begged into the silence of the night.

Sarco's chuckle tickled her ear, and goose bumps pimpled her flesh. *"Oh, not yet, Wonderful. Not yet."*

In her mind, his tongue took the place of the small orb. Over and over, he lavished her pussy with swift, confident strokes. But he didn't stop there. His tongue tantalized one thigh, traversed her tummy, and delved into the recesses of her belly button, then down the other thigh, before suckling her clit once more. His tongue probed deep within her, mimicking the action of his glorious cock she remembered so well.

Lark squirmed, moaned, begged for release, and at the same time, pleaded with him to never stop. He brought her numerous times to the brink, then backed away at the last possible moment.

When Lark knew she would surely die if she didn't find release soon, he took pity on her and, with a swift plunge, filled her pussy with his hard, vital cock. He rode her for long minutes, stroke after confident stroke hitting its mark. She locked her legs about his hips and held onto his arms. They were her life rafts, and she was lost at sea.

Finally, with one last plunge and a roar of satisfaction, Sarco filled her with his hot seed. Lark cried out his name as spasms of rippling pleasure coursed through her soul.

With a smile on her face and a sigh on her lips, Lark clicked off the toy and slept.

****

Sarco came awake with a start. He couldn't remember any other time a dream had seemed so real. He could smell her on his skin, feel the heat of her pussy still surrounding his cock, and taste her upon his lips.

Lark. The woman had bewitched him.

His hand went to his still partially erect member and came away with a surprise. Flipping back the cover, he stared at himself in disbelief. A hot blush crept up Sarco's neck in the darkness of the room. The last time he'd experienced this kind of lack of self-control had been when he was a young lad. Certainly not anytime in the past ten years. What was this woman doing to him?

Sarco rose and headed for the shower. He thought at first perhaps cold water would cure what ailed him. Looking at the aftermath and mess of his all-too-real dream, he chuckled. It was a little late for a cold shower to take care of this problem. This was definitely a job for hot.

## Chapter Five

If ever a man had the right to demand an explanation, Sarco Sunwalker was certainly that man. The problem was, Lark couldn't think of even one intelligent reason she was willing to give him.

Not for why she'd known who he was at Carnalval.

Not for how she'd gotten into his mind yesterday and begged him not to say a word.

Not for any of it.

After all, spiritmasters were still feared in many places. Ignorance died hard. And she certainly had no reasonable excuse for why *she* stood before him now, a full turn of the hourglass before the start of class, instead of the woman he'd been expecting to see today.

And then there was the fact that he glared at her as if she were the last person on Albrath he ever wanted to lay eyes on again. Being hauled into his office and the door slammed before anyone roaming the halls had a chance to see her had been embarrassing enough without being subjected to what could only be called an interrogation.

The soft low growl of his voice startled her, and Lark audibly gulped.

"Miss Hammerstrike—Lark—not that it isn't a pleasant surprise to see you this morning, but it was your sister I expected to come to my office and officially register for my class, not you. Care to tell me why you're here and she isn't?"

Lark opened her mouth to speak, but before she could, Sarco held up a hand.

"Before you give me some lame excuse that is just going to waste my time and make me angry, let us get one thing perfectly straight. This is a class, *my* class, and I am the instructor. Not your friend, not someone you or your sister can manipulate to suit the whims of a princess. Do you understand me?"

Lark nodded as the sound of thunder rumbled in the distance. She held out the small leather volume her sister had given her to give to him. He took it, glanced at it, and dropped it on his desk.

"A gift from my sister." Lark fidgeted. "Ary, umm, that is, Princess Aryanna sends her apology. She…umm, well, elemental magic isn't a strong point with Ary. Not that she isn't talented, because she certainly is, just not when it comes to wizard stuff." Lark twisted her hands together. "The princess felt I would get more from this class than she would, so she sent me in her place."

Sarco stared at her so long, the silence grew uncomfortable. Lark gently probed his mind, curious as to how angry he truly was.

*"I wonder if she tastes as good this morning as she did last night in my dream?"*

Lark gasped and retreated from Sarco's mind. She knew she'd yanked him into her fantasy the night before, but she hadn't realized he was aware of it. Though she'd practiced for years the skill of peeking into other people's heads without their knowledge, never before had she allowed someone else into her own, and certainly not into something as private as a sexual fantasy.

At least Sarco didn't seem to be aware it had been mind control and not really a dream.

Heat rushed up her neck and settled on her cheeks. Lark squirmed, wanting to escape his regard.

"You can't take her place, Lark. You aren't her." He took a deep breath and continued, "I don't believe it would be a good idea for the two of us to spend much time together. I'm a man of honor and duty, but even I have my limits. I think it would be best if you didn't take my class. After all, we do have a...history."

Fighting back a mist of tears, Lark probed his mind once more and saw herself as Sarco did, gloriously naked, with passion gleaming on her face. She was beautiful and happy. Nothing like the way she looked when her refection stared back at her from the mirror. The woman in Sarco's mind was...amazing.

How could she turn and simply walk away from a man who saw her like that? Even though she knew she should, she couldn't. If she gave into Sarco's demand and walked out of his class and out of his life, she would always regret it.

Yes, it had been foretold by prophets that he was destined to wed a barbarian princess and she him. But to VoT with the prophets—to the Valley of Torment with them! They were apparently so nearsighted that all they could see was Aryanna. After all, Ary wasn't the only barbarian princess around. And Ary had made it painfully clear she wasn't the least bit attracted to this man and didn't wish to marry him. Sarco was only an unpleasant duty to her.

Even if, in the end, Ary and Sarco were forced to marry, would it truly be so wrong to grasp what little happiness she could while there was still time? And as for the prophets, they truly did belong in the Valley of Torment if they couldn't understand that happiness here and now should be more important than ancient history.

She chewed her botton lip. Was it fair to Sarco, though, to disrupt his life this way? Was it fair to Aryanna to steal what happiness she could at her sister's expense? Probably not.

Lark warred with herself. Yes, life would be simpler for Sarco, for Aryanna, and for everyone else involved if she left this very moment and never looked back. But her feet refused to cooperate.

Even if she had him in her life for just a short period of time, couldn't that be enough? Wouldn't it be worth it? It had to be. It would have to last her a lifetime.

Guilt tore at her gut as tears once more stung Lark's eyes. She fought them back, unwilling to give into what she considered a weakness. All of her life, she'd been trying to fit in, trying to make things easier for other people at the expense of her own happiness. When was it her turn?

The old adage *all is fair* came to mind, and Lark squared her shoulders as she looked Sarco Sunwalker in the eye. Not this time. Duty be damned.

"Honor is important to me also, and so is my word. I gave my sister my word, you see? I promised her I would take your class in her place, and that's what I intend to do." She crossed her fingers behind her back. "I'm sorry if my presence here makes you…uncomfortable. You are the instructor, and I *am* now one of your students. You'll simply have to deal with me as you will."

The look on Sarco's face was priceless. His mouth dropped open, and his eyes grew wide with disbelief. Lark almost smiled. She was pretty sure the heir to the Lordship of the elfin kingdom wasn't used to anyone, least of all a mere student, questioning his dictates. She had to give him credit, however. It only took Sarco a moment to mask his emotions and recover.

"Well then, Lark. It is okay to call you simply Lark, isn't it? I am normally on a first-name basis with my students. And even though we have been…intimate in the past, you will receive no special consideration."

The word *intimate* was said with such clinical coldness that for a moment Lark thought perhaps she'd been wrong about the man after all. Then despair mixed with desire flashed in Sarco's eyes and it told Lark a completely different story. He was having just as hard a time keeping his distance from her as she was from him.

"Since you insist on continuing in this situation, let me assure you, Lark. I expect you to put forth the effort it takes to learn. There are no princesses in my class, only wizards. If you can't take the heat of a fireball, I suggest you stay as far away from me as you can get."

Beams of bright sunlight filtered through the window. "*Wonderful*, Mr. Sunwalker. Trust me, I can take whatever you care to dish out. And I would expect no less from a…umm…stodgy old instructor such as yourself."

Sarco chuckled, but the sound was more predatory than it was humorous. "Stodgy? I'll show you stodgy."

The lights of his office suddenly dimmed and the bolt to his door clicked to the locked position. "Old? Tsk-tsk. It is such a bad idea to provoke me, Lark."

She gulped. "Have you forgotten so quickly that you intend to wed my sister?"

"Have you forgotten already how you melted in my arms?" Sarco chuckled.

She shook her head no.

Sarco took a deep breath. "No, Lark, I haven't forgotten, But I'm not bound to Princess Aryanna today, and I won't be bound to her tomorrow or for several cycles of the moons yet—if ever. Only time will tell. I do have to be honest with you, though. In the end I will do my duty to my people no matter where that leads. It is who I am."

"I understand." She nodded and wrapped her arms about herself. "So, where do we go from here?"

He held out his hands. "I can't help myself, I want you. I probably shouldn't but I do. I can't even promise you more than right this moment, but at the same time, I can't forget how many times you screamed your release to the rafters while we were at Carnalval. Was it once, twice? No, I believe it was four times."

He suddenly grinned. "I counted. Perhaps for the time being we can put whatever the future holds on hold and give each other a…refresher course?"

His eyes gleamed with mischief. "It truly is unfortunate this stodgy old elf can't promise you anything except pleasure. I have to admit, there is something about you I can't seem to resist.

"And, I don't see any reason why we should resist this pull between us. After all, the simultaneous full phasing of the three moons of Albrath and the need to fulfill the prophecy is still a very long ways off. Aryanna and I haven't even really spoken of it yet, let alone made promses to each other."

He moved toward her, his cat-like, golden-brown eyes beckoning. "Until then, until such time as I am forced to take another as mate, if you're willing to settle for what I do have to offer, come to me now, and I'll remind you of just what we did share."

He held out a hand.

Lark gulped. This was wrong. She shouldn't have baited him. She knew better. Making love with a total stranger was one thing, but the man standing before her, for all intents and purposes, might very well someday belong to her sister.

With her mind made up, Lark took the outstretched hand and melted into Sarco's embrace.

As his lips touched hers, Lark swallowed the last of her guilt. Ary didn't know Sarco like she did, nor did she want to. Ary had no idea that his lips could devour with just the perfect mixture of pressure and heat. And she had no clue how deep his tongue could probe, how sweet his taste could be, how close to paradise just being held in the circle of his arms really was.

Would it really be so very wrong to enjoy a few stolen moments of bliss? Would she regret it the rest of her life if she didn't? Perhaps she could protect her heart, build a wall around it. Accept the encounter for what it was, simple sexual gratification, and finally get him out of her system, rid him from her heart. And then, by the time Sarco was forced to do his duty and marry Aryanna, she'd have no regrets left. She'd simply smile at the memories and wish them both well then fade away into the shadows.

A moment later, Lark knew she'd made a mistake. As his kiss deepened and his arms encircled her even tighter, shivers of anticipation raced along her spine, and her heart pounded so hard she was afraid it would burst wide open. How could she have ever thought anything concerning Sarco Sunwalker would be simple?

His lips plundered hers, and all coherent thought fled Lark's mind. He tasted of the freshness of the first snowflakes to fall during an Alarian winter, sweet like the last drops of summer's dew upon the grass. Crisp and invigorating, refreshing yet sizzling hot.

His tongue probed deeper, drinking in her small gasps of pleasure, ridding her of all doubts, and branding his mark upon her soul.

She'd been a fool, and she wanted to cry. There was no way she could walk away from this man, ever. It hadn't been a possibility from the moment she'd first laid eyes on him. She just hadn't known it then.

His lips made their way along her neck, down her throat. "You are overdressed, Wonderful." With the flick of his wrist and a flash of light, her tunic fell away.

Lark gasped as the cool office air accosted her bare skin. She wasn't cold for long, however. Sarco ran his hand lightly over her breast and tweaked a pebbly hard nipple between his fingers, rolling it back and forth before taking it into his mouth and sucking. Heat pooled in her belly, and the liquid fire he was stoking moistened her pussy.

"God Draka, you are so beautiful." Sarco's eyes darkened with passion, and his words sounded breathy to Lark's ears. "I can't help myself when I'm anywhere near you. All I can think about is touching you, kissing you, ramming my cock deep into that sweet pussy of yours."

"Then do it, Sarco. Make love to me now, please. I need you inside of me."

A brilliant flash of light momentarily blinded her.

Where had the warm fur rug she was now lying upon come from? The roaring fire? She hadn't noticed them in the office before. And when had Sarco undressed? For he was certainly as naked as she was.

His glorious cock stood thick, long, and proud. She spread her legs in invitation and smiled.

For the space of eighteen heartbeats, he simply gazed at her brazenness. Heat crept up Lark's neck and settled in her cheeks. Never had she been so bold. Then his eyes locked with hers, and the appreciation she saw shining back had her heart skipping a beat.

"Exquisite," Sarco whispered. He positioned himself between her thighs and with one sure, fluid thrust, he entered her.

Lark closed her eyes and arched toward him. She wrapped her legs around his back and her arms around his shoulder. Time and space lost all meaning as over and over Sarco's cock filled her, teased, and tormented. Like the ebbing and surging of a tide, he rode her.

Lark's clit throbbed with every single stroke. Pressure built—intense pressure, superb pressure, *wonderful* pressure. But she wanted desperately to make this encounter last. She didn't ever want it to end, but end she knew it would. When, if ever, would she get another chance to be held in this wizard's arms, cradled in his embrace, stroked by his own brand of fire?

He must have felt her fears, perhaps even shared them. For, a moment later, he slowed his pace and gently kissed her lips. "Open your eyes, Lark. Look at me. Watch how perfect we are together."

She did as he asked and gloried in the sight and feel of their joining as Sarco once more picked up the pace. He plundered her pussy unmercifully with his cock, slamming and ramming, slick and wild. She answered him in kind, meeting each thrust with abandon.

When her orgasm burst upon her, it wasn't a slow, gentle quaking, or even the rolling ripples of pleasure she was used to. The intensity shocked her. It started at the very roots of the hair on the top of her head and built like an eruption of lava from a volcano.

Her breath caught in her chest, her heart stopped beating altogether, her nipples tingled, her arms trembled, her belly quivered, her legs turned to jelly, and her pussy spasmed as swell after swell of paroxysmic perfection left her unable to do so much as lift a finger.

If the all-male roar Sarco bellowed a moment before collapsing on top of her was any indication, he'd found his release, too.

She should care that she'd just had mind-blowing sex with her sister's intended, she really should. But all Lark could manage to do right this moment with any real consistency was breathe in, breathe out, breathe in, breathe out.

"Play time's over, Wonderful. Get up. It's time for class."

****

"You're late, knave," Aryanna pouted. "I've been waiting in this damp, humid place for over a full turning of the hourglass. I suppose I should be honored you bothered to show up at all. Especially since you stood me up at Carnalval."

The man chuckled, wrapped his arms around the princess, and kissed her soundly.

"Don't be angry with me, Ary. I couldn't make Carnalval. I was stuck in negotiations. How many times must I apologize before you'll forgive me? And I had important research to do in every library I could find between your home and mine before I could get away. I'm here now. That's all that matters. And this isn't a damp, humid place. It's an arborarium filled with beautiful plants and fragrant flowers fit for a princess like you."

He drew her down onto the soft bed of moss beneath their feet and cradled her within his arms.

"Now, did you give it to her?" he whispered.

She wanted to be angry with him, she really did. The problem was, she found it impossible to remain angry when he was kissing her neck with lips that drove her to distraction and a warm tongue that flicked in and out of her ear. Aryanna giggled.

"Cyrrick-Keltith Tomas Sunwalker, stop it. I can't think when you do that."

He made a production of giving Aryanna loud, sloppy kisses all over her face as they both fell into a fit of laughter.

Cyrrick snuggled Aryanna into the crook of his arm. "Okay, okay, business first, my sexy little princess. Then pleasure, much pleasure. Did you give her the book?"

Aryanna frowned as she nodded. "Are you sure this is the only way? If this doesn't work, Lark's never going to forgive me, let alone Sarco forgiving you."

Cyrrick sighed. "It has to work. If it doesn't, my

love, forgiveness isn't the worst thing we'll have to worry about. The wrath of the ancients is."

Aryanna sat up. "Bah, I don't believe all that ancients stuff. That war and prophecy was forever ago. We hadn't even been thought of yet, not even by our parents. What could those old stories possibly have to do with us? I think we should forget all this intrigue and elope. I don't want to do this, especially to Lark."

Cyrrick shook his head. "I wish there was another way. God Draka knows I've searched and searched for one. Trust me, Ary, if there was any other path, we'd take it. I know you don't believe in prophecies and such, but I was raised in a magical family. The stories are all too real, and there are consequences that must be considered, my love."

Tears wet Aryanna's lashes, and she blinked them away. "Make me understand, Cyrrick. Tell me again why we must deceive the two most important people in our lives."

Cyrrick closed his eyes. "Almost nine hundred years ago, Castle Kuropkat was an elfin jewel of trade and prosperity—"

"Oh my God Draka." Aryanna punched his shoulder. "Not the whole flipping boring story. I know the visiting barbarian princess seduces the elfin heir, blah blah blah, and the two kings got pissed off and started a war, blah blah blah."

Cyrrick nuzzled Aryanna's ear. "Then what don't you understand?"

Aryanna sighed into his embrace, not really wanting to listen or think about any part of the story but also realizing she had no choice. "I just want to understand our part in all of this."

Cyrrick nipped her soft bottom lip then captured her mouth in a kiss that took her breath away. "Wouldn't you rather spend what little time we have making love instead of talking? I so need to plunge my cock as deep as I can get it, straight up that sweet pussy of yours and pump until both our heads explode." He grabbed her hips and brought her hard up against him, mimicking the very action he'd just described.

Aryanna glared. "How romantic." She pushed against him. "But business first, remember?"

"It's my Uncle Arizon's fault," Cyrrick sighed. "He's the one who spoke the dreadful words. It's the second part of his prophecy we have to worry about. Uthiel Dragonheart, with Sarco's help, fulfilled the first part last year. They saved a dragon and other stuff that doesn't matter to us.

"What does matter, though, is the time is now for the second part of the prophecy to be fulfilled. The blood of the elfin heir must be joined with the barbarian-human princess, and it must take place when the three moons of Albrath are all in the full phase."

A sob caught in Aryanna's throat, and she swallowed it down. "Stupid-ass prophecies. I don't even believe in them," she proclaimed.

Cyrrick took a deep breath. "It doesn't matter if you or I believe in them, my heart. It only matters that the entire rest of Albrath, and Sarco, and the Council of Elders do."

Aryanna seethed. "Fine, let them. I still don't understand. We really could just ignore the whole damn thing and run away."

Cyrrick held her so tight, breathing became difficult.

"I wish it was that simple," he said, loosening his grip just a hair and gazing into her eyes. "We can't run from this, Aryanna. Are you willing to spend the rest of your life hated, shunned? Because we would be. We would be considered without honor. Our children, if we have any, would be outcasts. My brother would be disgraced."

"I don't care about honor. I don't care about your brother. I care about us, you…our children," she sobbed. "You're right, though. We—we can't take chances with our, our children's future."

It felt like a death toll to her dreams. "So…if our plan doesn't work, I'll…I'll…ma…marry Sarco."

Cyrrick caressed her cheek. "It's not going to come to that. I won't let it. This is going to work. Trust me. Your parents may have chosen you to marry Sarco, but if what we've put into motion continues to the conclusion we hope for, Sarco will be the one making a choice."

She shook her head. "But what if—"

"No what-ifs." Cyrrick cupped her face. "This will work. Making it possible for Sarco to choose his bride is our only hope, and the only way to accomplish that, is with the quest. You've already made sure the seeds of a romance were sown when you insisted Lark accompany you to Carnalval."

Aryanna opened her mouth to protest but didn't get a chance as Cyrrick continued excitedly, "Didn't I tell you Lark was just his type?"

She nodded.

"Now we just need to nurture those feelings. If we manage to pull this off, by the time the quest is upon us, Sarco will be hopelessly in love with Lark and he'll go against convention and choose her over you."

Cyrrick laughed and the carefree sound of it lifted Aryanna's spirit.

"Your insisting Lark attend Sarco's class was a stroke of pure genius, too, by the way. But it's still going to take all the skill we both have, a couple of miracles, and an enormous amount of luck to succeed. In the end, though, we'll all get what we want and live happily ever after. I just know we will."

Aryanna leaned over and nipped Cyrrick playfully on the chin. "Then we'd best get on with this lovemaking you've been teasing me with, knave. We have work to do."

Cyrrick didn't need further enticement. Before Aryanna realized what happened, he had her flat on her back, naked, with her legs spread wide. She grinned up at him.

"Fuck me, Cyrrick. Do it now." Her voice sounded husky even to her own ears. "Put your cock in my pussy and pound me so hard I can't think. I command it of you."

He chuckled, "Ahh, my sweet, it always pleasantly surprises me when such naughty words come out of that pretty, little mouth of yours. But when will you learn I don't take orders well?"

With a growl, he slid down the length of her body, parted her folds, and captured her clit between his teeth. He nipped, and ripples of pleasure shook Aryanna's small frame.

With a gasp, she cried, "Oh my god Draka, I love it when you bite."

Cyrrick flicked out his tongue and licked. "Well, if you liked that, let's see what you think of this."

Slowly, he inserted a finger into her ass, past the second knuckle, then latched onto her clit and sucked with ravenous delight.

Aryanna was undone. She struggled to take in deep enough breaths to remain conscious while pounding against the finger pumping her ass and grinding her clit against Cyrrick's mouth.

It was naughty. It was delightful. Shivers of excitement skittered along every nerve ending she possessed. By the time Cyrrick gave into her wishes and slid his cock deep into her welcoming warmth, it took no more than a handful of thrusts before they both shuddered with spasms of release.

## Chapter Six

If ever a man should be drawn and quartered, then slowly roasted over a fiery pit, Sarco "The Tyrant" Sunwalker was that man.

Lark groaned as she shifted in her seat later that afternoon. Muscles she hadn't been aware she even had ached and burned with a persistent throb.

First day of classes, and could a nice, welcoming lecture with perhaps a simple homework assignment be sufficient? Oh, no, not for Sarco "The Tormentor" Sunwalker.

After listening to a full hour of mind-numbing facts on ancient wizard history, the class had retired to the arena for what Sarco "The Sadist" Sunwalker described as weeding out the weak.

Lark closed her eyes and concentrated on trying to suck sufficient air into her lungs. The ache in her ribs reminded her that deep breathing wasn't a function she'd be performing again anytime soon. Nausea threatened to rid her of what little she'd been able to force down at lunch as images raced through her head of what Sarco "The Evil Spawn from the Valley of Torment" Sunwalker had gleefully labeled *Wizard Lab*.

She relived the lecture he'd given in the arena to his students.

"There are three things imperative to becoming a successful, elemental wizard—intelligence, agility, and talent. Without an abundance of all these, you might as well save yourselves—and me—a lot of time and discomfort and take up trade skills. I've been told there is a huge need for tailors, armor crafters, engineers, even cooks."

All twenty students had been riveted on Sarco "The Cruel" Sunwalker, but none more than she was. His persona demanded attention. Energy radiated from him. His voice was hypnotic, compelling, and powerful. His next words had been a warning Lark now knew she should have heeded.

"Drop your protective force fields. This is a game. A game, which, if you lose, you're out of my class."

Sarco "The Insane" Sunwalker chuckled, "I like to call this little competition *Dodge Fireball*. The point being, I'll cast and throw fireballs as fast as I can, and if I get a direct hit, don't waste my time by showing up tomorrow. I'll cast twenty of them, so keep count if you can."

Sarco stopped talking for a moment and held up a hand. "Don't fret. They'll be low-level fireballs, and although you might sustain a minor burn or two, they will not kill. If you are hit, please move out of the field of play. May the fastest, smartest, most competent of you succeed."

Lark shuddered at the memory and even that small movement sent spasms of pain shooting down her arms and legs. What proceeded after Sarco "The Mad Wizard" Sunwalker's instructions had been complete pandemonium. She couldn't stop her mind from recalling—almost moment by moment—the dreadful test.

Fire had flown through the air, and white-robed

novices scattered. The first fireball missed Lark's head by mere inches and hit the dwarf standing several yards behind her as it arced toward the ground. Lark didn't even have time to see which dwarf had been hit before she was jumping sideways to avoid the next ball of fire.

Burning cinders rained upon them, and Lark winced at the painful stings. Dodging yet again, she slipped, and her hip met the dirt of the arena floor with a thud. She scrambled to regain her feet as another blue-flamed orb exploded against the chest of the poor barbarian unlucky enough to have run in front of her. He landed squarely across her chest, momentarily knocking the air from her lungs.

Lark glared at Sarco. The man was purposely trying to hit her. She caught his eye, and he smiled and winked. Lark seethed with anger. How dare he cheat by singling her out.

She not-so-gently probed his mind and screamed into it, "*Why?*"

He surprised her by answering, "*You are a distraction I can ill afford, Lark. There can be no repeat of this morning. Give my regards to your sister.*"

Another fireball missed Lark's head by no more than a breath and her rage grew. "*I see you, too, can delve into the minds of others. I wouldn't have believed before today, however, you'd be capable of stooping so low as to use your powers against a student. And here I thought you were a man of honor, Professor Sunwalker.*"

Sarco grinned at her, but there was no humor in his smile. "*Telepathy is a new talent it seems I've acquired since I met you. There is much you don't know about me, Wonderful. And it's not only my honor, but also yours, I'm trying to protect. Now be a good girl and stand still. I can't promise you it won't sting a bit, but I can promise it'll be over in just a few moments."*

The heat of the flame Lark hadn't even seen leave Sarco's fingers singed her hair and stung her skin but missed a direct hit by no more than a heartbeat. It pissed her off.

*"Well, turnabout is fair play then, Professor Sunwalker. You won't get rid of me that easily."*

Lark concentrated on her fellow students, and the arena became like a pinball machine as Sarco threw fireballs and Lark used mind-control on her classmates to dodge them. One after another, the other students took turns receiving the hits Sarco had intended for her. Though she still had to duck and weave, and fall and get up, she avoided a direct hit. More than once she landed so hard Lark was sure she heard things that shouldn't crunch do precisely that.

Then, suddenly, it was over and only six students were left standing—one dwarf, one troll, one high-elf, one dark-elf, one gnome, and herself.

Sarco"The Arrogant" Sunwalker smiled at the students remaining in the middle of the arena. "I'll see those of you who passed my test in the morning. Class dismissed."

To Lark, he sent a message. *"I must admit, first victory has gone to you, Wonderful. Let's see what tomorrow brings."*

Without another word or a backwards glance, the man had turned and whistled a tune as he walked away.

The whole ordeal had occurred six short turns of the hourglass ago, but to Lark, the suffering would never end. She sat in Channeling, her last class of the day, and tried her best to concentrate.

Lady Dragonheart, or Briar as she had instructed the students to call her, was lecturing. Though Lark valiantly tried, she found it hard to pay attention. All she wanted in the whole of Albrath was to go to her room, soak in a hot tub for a couple of hours, and sleep for a week.

How was she ever going to keep up this pace? If every day of Elemental Wizard class was destined to be like this one, she wouldn't last another day, let alone a full semester.

After the two-hour wizard class had come Mysteries of the Mind, with a dark-elf instructor whose name she couldn't even remember or pronounce. Then there had been History of Magic, with Mrs. Wanglehopper, a dwarf female with a gray beard long enough to rival most men's. She was so old and boring, Lark had twice drifted off to sleep during her lecture.

Then had come lunch.

Lark winced. Lunch had been another nightmare all in itself. There was no doubt about it, this was going to be a very long semester.

Lark had hoped lunch would be uneventful. She'd needed a few minutes' peace.

No such luck. Because lunch was when she'd officially met Sherman Bobert Limburger the Ninth.

She sighed. What was she going to do about Sherman? A bone-weary tiredness she rarely felt seeped deep into her soul.

Again, Lark's thoughts drifted from Briar's lesson. The images from the lunchroom were vivid and still painfully embarrassing. She covered her eyes with her palms.

When the short, pudgy man had walked over to her table with a tray of food balanced in his beefy hands and asked if he could sit with her, Lark's first response had been to tell him she wanted to be alone. After the morning she'd had, she wasn't in the mood for company.

Then she noticed his appearance and realized who he was. His thick, mud-brown stubs of hair stood in spikes, and the ends of them were so singed that when he walked, gray ash sprinkled like dirty snowflakes onto the shoulders of his tunic that was now anything but white. She wanted to crawl under the table so she wouldn't have to face him, but she couldn't. Horrified, Lark stared at the poor creature standing before her.

He was the same halfling she'd used mind control on earlier in the day to avoid Sarco's final fireball.

He was pathetic looking. One bushy eyebrow was, for the most part, intact, but the other had been entirely burned away. His thick, oval glasses were bent almost in half and melted in places. They were taped together in the middle and barely covered his tear-reddened brown eyes.

Soot smudged his cheeks and tiny blisters made his already pouffy lips appear even bigger. Not tall to begin with, he stood slightly bent over, as if straightening would cause too much pain.

"Umm…did you hear me, Miss? Do you mind if I sit here? You're the only person in the room that looks remotely familiar."

Then he shook his head. "Ah, never mind, I just realized you weren't one of the losers from this morning's class so you probably wouldn't want to share a table with the likes of me anyway. I don't blame ya. I wouldn't sit with me either if I didn't have to."

The halfling turned to leave, and even though sharing her table, let alone her lunchtime, with him was the last thing Lark wanted to do, she couldn't let him just walk away.

The smell of singed flesh, burnt hair, and smoked cheese was so thick, Lark gave it her best effort to speak without breathing any more than absolutely necessary. "No, please, I'd be honored, really."

The halfling quickly sat down, extended a hand, introduced himself, and then broke into tears. Not gentle, sliding-silently-down-tender-little-cheeks tears, but loud, sobbing, soul-racking, nose-leaking, streaking-lines-down-the-soot-on-his-face, drawing-attention-from-every-corner-of-the-room tears.

His head dropped to the tabletop where his forehead hit with a loud smack. A cloud of soot, singed hair, and particles with origins of which Lark didn't want to speculate, drifted over everything, including her food. She pushed her tray away, her appetite gone.

"What's wrong, Mr. Limburger? Umm, Sherman, wasn't it? Please, stop crying. Nothing can be as bad as all that, can it?"

The halfling looked at Lark from the puddle he'd made on the table. "As bad as all that? My life is over. Is that bad enough for you? I'm a failure. I can never go home again. I was to be the first halfling from my kingdom to go to the Academy and make something of himself. And what do I do on the first day? I flunk out of Elemental Wizard class, that's what I do.

"Oh, the shame. I can never face my folks or the townspeople again. My parents took out a mortgage on their castle, more than half the town's residents donated every spare platt they had for my tuition, the church had a fundraiser, and my girl back home even offered to pawn the little engagement ring I gave her last year. All with one single, shining hope, that I, Sherman Bobert Limburger the Ninth, would come back and save us all."

Lark groaned, but Sherman didn't notice.

"You see, my father's kingdom survives by selling the cheese we make. To craft excellent cheese you must feed the cows and goats superb grain. In order to grow such magnificent grain you must have outstanding weather. An elemental wizard can ensure a plethora of sunny days and still plenty of rain to water the crops. I've been taking classes and preparing for this all my life, and now I've failed, and on the very first day to boot."

Sherman stopped, wrenched a large handkerchief from somewhere deep in his pocket, blew his nose with the force of a small gale, then proceeded with his tale. All Lark could manage to do was stare and listen.

"I still don't understand how it happened. Even being a portly type of guy, I'm normally fast and steady on my feet." He lifted one big, bare, hairy foot, plopped it right in the middle of the table, and shook his head. "With feet as impressive as these, I just don't get it. I could have sworn I was out of the way of that final fireball. Then, from out of nowhere, I tripped over something—must have been a rock—and, *bam*! I was on the ground and a ball of fire hit me right in the kisser."

Lark grimaced as guilt once more filled her.

"I went back after class and searched the arena floor for more than the turn of an hourglass and couldn't find one single stone big enough to trip over. God Draka must be punishing me and my kingdom. I know there's no way to make you understand because you're barbarian. I took a class on barbarian culture once. I know your kind are never clumsy. It isn't your way. Go ahead, ask me anything about barbarian. I'll tell you. Not that it matters now."

Sherman sobbed once more, and all Lark could do was silently cry along with him. Even though she had given up eating when the ash and singed hair had settled over her food, a large lump remained stuck in her throat. She remembered the last fireball very well, and here sat the poor, unsuspecting halfling on whom she had so thoughtlessly used her power. What was she going to do? She couldn't allow what she'd done to ruin Sherman's life.

Grandmother Ava's voice came back to her clearly, as if Lark were still a small child sitting on her lap during lessons. *"With the privilege of magic comes much responsibility, Lark. Abuse the powers you've been given and innocent people will be hurt. If you make a mistake, child, fix it."*

She stood, swiped at her eyes, and faced Sherman.

"I know Professor Sunwalker told everyone who was hit not to come to class tomorrow, but please come anyway. I'll talk to him for you, I promise. I don't know yet what I'll say, but I'll do my best to make it better. Trust me."

Lark hadn't waited for his reply but turned and fled before she gave into her urge to cry again.

After lunch, she had had to endure Spell Casting 101 and History and Theory of Magic before coming to Channeling class.

Lark uncovered her eyes and looked up at Briar. Oh, would this day never end? Almost as quickly as that thought formed, the last grains of sand in the hourglass trickled down and a bell tolled.

Slowly, Lark stood, mindful of aching joints and sore muscles. She picked up her stack of books and headed for the royal suite, grateful the trauma of her first day was finally over.

A dense fog settled over the Academy.

## Chapter Seven

If ever a man was more confused by the difference between his duty and his heart's desire than Sarco was, he'd hate to see that man.

Not knowing what else to do, he picked up the small leather volume Lark had given him earlier and flipped it open once again.

A sound distracted him, and he looked from the yellowed pages to his brother. Tossing the book toward him, he asked, "Any idea what this is? I can't seem to make heads or tails out of it."

Cyrrick flipped through it for a few moments then smiled. "Why, I do believe this may be the answer to all of your problems. If I'm not mistaken, and I'm pretty sure I'm not, it's an extremely rare volume of *Barbarian Protocols and Etiquette*. I remember hearing somewhere there are only two left in existence."

Sarco shook his head. "So why would the princess give me something so valuable? And this is going to help me how?"

Cyrrick drew up a chair and straddled it. "It can teach you the proper way to ask for the hand in marriage of a barbarian princess, for one thing. How's that going, by the way? Courting Princess Aryanna, that is?"

Sarco closed his eyes and rubbed his forehead, hoping the heat and pressure of his fingertips might actually alleviate the dull throbbing pain that had been persisting and growing since class this morning. It didn't help, so he opened them once more and faced his brother.

"There hasn't been any courting. I've only met the woman once and that was when she first arrived. She was supposed to be in my class, but the chit sent her sister instead. I don't see why I need to bother with courting her anyway. It's an arranged marriage, remember? It's not like either of us has any say-so in the matter."

Cyrrick rocked forward on the legs of his chair. "Protocol, my dear brother. Everything has to do with protocol and diplomacy. Barbarians are a proud people. Remember, the war that was responsible for this mess was because the elfin lord was insulted. That can't happen this time, brother."

Sarco glared at him.

"Great-Uncle Arizon and the entire Council of the Elders will be counting on you. At the Yulemass Ball, you must officially ask King Alfred for the hand of his daughter in marriage, and you must do it with pomp and circumstance."

Cyrrick playfully leaned across the desk and punched Sarco's arm. "Anyway, courting could be fun. Princess Aryanna might be a little snooty, but you have to admit she's not bad on the eyes."

Sarco chuckled but the sound held no humor. "Yes, the princess is beautiful. I'll give her that. Kind of spoiled for my taste, but then again, what does it matter? It's not as if I have much of a choice."

"If you could choose, brother, who would it be?" Cyrrick leaned in close and his voice became almost a whisper.

Sarco smiled at Cyrrick. "I think I'd choose not to marry at all, as it stands right this moment. But I have to admit, Princess Aryanna's sister, Lark, does intrigue me."

"Well, I think it best we keep that little tidbit between the two of us," Cyrrick grinned. He suddenly reached across the distance and tapped Sarco lightly on the hand. "Do you remember when I told you I wanted to become a diplomat instead of a wizard? You were the only person in the entire family to encourage me and to accept my decision. You told me then to follow my heart, and I did."

Sarco nodded, but he didn't understand what the change of topic had to do with this conversation. Cyrrick, though, just kept talking.

"The family is happy I made that choice now, but for a while things weren't pleasant, especially with father. I'm asking you to put your trust in me again. No matter how bad things may or may not seem, I'll stand by you and any decisions you make. Give me a chance to show you your faith wasn't misplaced."

Sarco stared at his brother as Cyrrick grabbed the book and opened it. He pointed to an underlined passage.

"Practice these words over and over until you can say them without thinking, even in your sleep." He handed the worn book back to Sarco, stood, nodded once, and strode from the room.

Sarco stared at the frayed, old parchment pages for a long time. He had the strangest feeling something important had just been conveyed and somehow he'd missed it.

\*\*\*\*

Leeky Shortz knocked once more, louder than the time before. Impatience caused him to shift his Miss Bunny 2000 from one arm to the other in order to use his ungloved hand to pound harder.

*Don't people realize a gnome has better things to do than stand outside a door half the day?*

From somewhere deep within the royal suite, Leeky heard a high-pitched, nasal twang. "Come in."

He did, then stood in shock at what he saw.

A saucy female gnome moved back and forth across the room. What she was doing to the poor blow-up doll in her hands was a more traumatic sight than any eyes should ever have to behold.

"What the fungus-infested toe jam of a green-eyed cave-troll are ya doing ta that poor thing, lass?"

The female gnome wore a poor-fitting blonde wig, he noticed, when she turned toward him and glared. "Who are ya and what are ya doing here?"

Puffing out his chest, Leeky smirked. "Ya mean ya don't know? Everyone who's anyone knows who I am. I'm Leeky Shortz, rogue gnome, friend and confidant ta rulers and princes, oh, and I'm the Academy handyman. I was told there's a job ta be done. Now what are ya doing ta that…that…thing, lass?"

"The name's Miss Laycee Titwilder ta ya, Handyman. Not 'lass.' I'm governess ta Princess Aryanna, and what does it look like I'm doing, ya daft gnome? I'm vacuuming, of course."

A long hose extended from where the blow-up doll's cock would have normally been. Laycee had a firm grip on it as she pushed it along the floor. The poor doll's balls were two long, green plastic bags, so bloated with air they looked painful and near to popping.

Leeky gulped and fought the urge to check and see if his own parts were where he'd last left them. "There's just something wrong about using a lad that way. I've heard of multi-purpose dolls, but this is going a step or two over the line, if ya ask me."

She rolled her eyes, sighed, and spoke as if he were a small child who needed slow, careful explanations. "This is a Tug McGroin. He's the latest, top-of-the-line model available. Guaranteed ta be the last all-purpose companion a girl will ever need, or money back. And trust me when I tell ya he cost a pretty platt."

She stopped talking for a moment and stroked the dark, berber-like, artificial hair on the doll's plastic chest. "He comes with a multitude of handy attachments and can do everything from making a girl's toes curl ta mixing a pitcher of margaritas. Watch this."

Laycee took hold of Tug's chin and yanked. His plastic mouth flopped open and out rolled a moist-looking, pink tongue, at least eight inches long. She tweaked the doll's nose and the tongue vibrated in a slow, circular motion, mimicking the licking of its lips.

Laycee grinned at Leeky and wiggled her eyebrows suggestively. "Didn't I tell ya he's capable of making a girl's toes curl?"

For the first time in his very long life, Leeky Shortz was speechless.

Laycee, however, didn't seem to have that problem. "Well, ya gonna just stand around and stare all day, or ya gonna get that job done?"

"Job, umm, what job?" Leeky spluttered. "Are ya in need of a good doing then? Ya want ta have sex?"

She placed her stubby hands on her hips and glared. "I was talking about the job I put the request in for. And, just for the record, I'm a lady and I don't go around having sex with strangers, especially strange gnomes." She crossed her arms and raised her nose an inch into the air.

Leeky grinned. "Ya don't do strangers? Well then, show me this job while we get ta know each other better, lass."

She pointed to a box in the corner. "Put that together and hang it over my bed."

Setting his own blow-up doll gently on a chair close to the door, the gnome-handyman walked toward the box.

"Hope ya don't mind that I brought my Miss Bunny 2000 along with me. She gets mighty lonely when I leave her at home."

Laycee rolled her eyes, but Leeky didn't stare for long. He turned his attention to the box. "A Swing of Love, huh? My, but aren't ya just full of surprises."

Leeky's grin grew of its own volition until he was sure if it got any bigger, his face would split in two. He ripped open the cardboard box, put on his chartreuse hanging-things gloves, and proceeded to put together and hang the swing.

"So, what's up with the gloves?"

Leeky smiled at her. "What the red arse-cheeks of a nakey ogre streetwalker plying her trade on a snowy day do ya think they're for? Didn't I already tell ya I'm a rogue, lass?"

He held up his long-fingered hands. "These finely tuned instruments are my fortune and a national treasure. There has never been a lock made these fingers couldn't pick, a knife they couldn't wield, or a lady they couldn't pleasure, so I must protect them. During the war, the government insured them for a million platt, and that was when I was still a mere novice. Priceless, that's what they are now."

"The war?" she cackled. "That was well over eight hundred years ago. Ya look old, but not that old. Now I'm sure you're full of more hot air than my Tug."

He grinned. "Think what ya will, lass. So, ya wanna have sex when I get this done? Try it out, make sure it's sturdy?"

Laycee sighed. "Is that all ya ever think about? Even a three-balled troll humping a dead goat thinks about more than just sex."

Leeky continued to swagger toward the box, but he glanced back over his shoulder at her and winked. "Well, I am what I am, lass. So is that a yes?"

She sputtered, and her false teeth flew from her mouth. "Well, I need time ta consider it. Get back ta work, silly gnome."

Leeky licked his eyebrows, showing Laycee that her Tug McGroin doll wasn't the only talented fellow in the room. He grinned what he hoped was his most lecherous smile. "Time, huh? I'll give ya time, I'll even give ya the bonus plan."

Her eyes popped wide with surprise, and he laughed. If she was impressed with the length of his tongue and his naughty suggestions just wait 'til she got a gander at his package.

"So…what? Ya need like five minutes ta think it over? I'll be done with this contraption by then and we can…" He placed both of his fists upon his waist and rocked his hips back and forth suggestively. "Ya know, do a little humpity bumbity."

She crossed her arms, shook her head, sighed, and continued to stare at him while he worked.

A few minutes later, Leeky hopped down, took off his chartreuse hanging-things gloves, and replaced them with his soft, fuzzy, pink, touching-a-lady gloves. "So, ya wanna have sex?"

Laycee giggled.

\*\*\*\*

As Lark entered the royal suite, a low, growl-like sound came from somewhere deep within. She rushed forward, frightened something terrible might have befallen Ary or Laycee.

The sound came again, this time not quite so loud, from directly behind Laycee's door.

Hesitating for a moment, Lark chided herself for being such a coward. Laycee might be injured, might need her. With a trembling hand, Lark turned the knob.

A noxious, gaseous green cloud hit her square in the face. Her eyes watered, her skin crawled, her toes curled, and her stomach heaved. Lark slapped a hand over her mouth and gagged.

A voice roared at her, "What the crawly vermin's nest in the beard of a one-legged dwarf dancing a jig on the top of a troll's belly do ya think ya're doing, lass? Close the door. Ya're letting out the hard-earned fruits of our labor, and I was winning."

Lark's eyes stung as she looked toward the sound of the voice. Immediately, she wished she hadn't. Some kind of bright-red leather swing contraption with shiny, metal coils was hanging lopsided from the ceiling directly over Laycee's bed. Worse, the frightening device wasn't empty.

Swinging back and forth was a male gnome with an overly large nose and thick, bushy eyebrows who Lark had never seen before. And he was, for the most part, naked.

The only things he wore were Laycee's blonde wig, which sat askew on his nearly bald head, and a pair of bright-orange gloves. His short legs hung over the edge of the swing, and thankfully, he was cradling a large mug of ale between them, shielding Lark's eyes from a sight she had no desire to see.

In his stubby hands, he held what looked to be a large bowl of steaming chili, and on his face, he had an ear-to-ear grin.

The sound of a loud *phruurapppp* tore Lark's eyes away from the little man and toward the red-faced female gnome sitting beside him in the swing.

Laycee in her birthday suit was a sight Lark would not soon forget. With her wig now gone, tufts of brown hair stuck out at odd angles from various spots on a head that had always been too big for her small gnome frame.

Breasts that at one time had probably been impressive now resembled saggy, half-filled bags of marbles. Their nipples pointed toward the floor and swung at belly button level. Her wrinkles had wrinkles and, thankfully, like Laycee's male companion, her most private area was concealed with a large mug of ale and a bowl of chili.

What was strangest of all, though, was the little governess looked truly happy. Lark couldn't remember another time she had seen Laycee smile so widely.

"I do believe I just took the lead with that one, Leeky. Lark, be a sweet girl and close the door on ya way out, will ya?"

Lark couldn't move. Two blow-up dolls, squeezed onto the swing on either side of the gnomes, stared back at her, looking just as perplexed as she was.

Dragging her gaze from the swing, Lark glanced around. It looked like a war zone. Pieces of plaster had fallen from the ceiling, various articles of clothing littered the floor, and covering every horizontal surface was an array of toys about whose functions Lark didn't even want to speculate.

"I think something's wrong with the lass, Laycee. She doesn't look well."

Lark glanced back toward the voice, trying to make sense of the scene before her.

"Oh, she'll be fine, Leeky. She's just not used ta seeing folks have a good time."

Laycee leaned in close to the male gnome and whispered, although Lark heard her plainly, "Comes from a stick-up-the-butt kinda family, if ya know what I mean."

He laughed. "You've never been in a good old-fashioned farting contest, have ya, lass? Ya haven't lived 'til ya do."

Another loud, drawn-out *phruurapppp* lifted the male gnome a good three inches off his seat before dropping him back in place. He grinned at Laycee. "Dare ya ta top that one."

Smiling at Lark, he added, "Close the door, lass, grab a mug and a bowl of that fine pig's feet chili Miss Laycee here made, and I'll have Miss Bunny and Tug move over ta make room for ya. We'll have a grand time, ya'll see."

Lark turned and fled.

\*\*\*\*

"*You awake?*"

Lark stirred, not sure if the voice in her mind was a dream or real. Then it came again, louder this time.

"*Lark?*"

Tears that embarrassed her for the weakness they revealed welled in her eyes. Why did it have to be this man who had the power to twist her heart into a pretzel with just the sound of her name on his lips?

"*I'm awake, Professor Sunwalker. What do you want now, a middle of the night rematch? Didn't you get to inflict enough pain earlier? And why didn't you tell me you were telepathic?*"

She could almost feel his sigh against her skin.

"*I don't understand what's happening to me. I've never been telepathic before, and it's only your mind I seem to be able to connect with. It sure didn't work with my brother when I tried to get inside his head earlier tonight.*" He was silent for a moment, then added, "*About today…umm…I just wanted to say, I'm sorry. I had no right to take my frustrations out on you. None of this is your fault. Truce?*"

Even in her mind, Lark couldn't keep the catch out of her voice. "*If you'll stop trying to get rid of me, we can have a truce.*"

She felt his smile against her own lips.

"*G'night, Wonderful.*"

"*Night,*" she smiled into the darkness.

Lying in her room, she stared through the windows at the thick patch of fog swirling outside. Why would Sarco suddenly develop the power to probe her mind, and just her mind, no one else's? The niggling memory of a lesson surfaced and just as quickly was gone. There was something she should remember, but it just wasn't there.

Grandmother Ava would know. Why hadn't she thought of her before? She would ask Grandmother next time she saw her. Grandmother Ava always had the answer.

Oh, and she had forgotten to ask Sarco about Sherman, the halfling. For a split second, Lark almost sought a link with Sarco again, then changed her mind. She yawned, and her ribs reminded her that such an action was still a bad idea. Turning in bed, Lark winced as joints and muscles protested.

Tomorrow she would worry about Sarco and why he had this newfound power, and tomorrow she would worry about Sherman Bobert Limburger the Ninth and the fate of his kingdom, but for tonight she was just plain too tired.

## Chapter Eight

If ever a man had earned each and every one of the deep furrows currently lining the middle of his forehead, Sarco Sunwalker was certainly that man. Lark silently watched him from the doorway of his office.

Yes, after what Sarco had put her through yesterday, a furrowed brow was the least of the things he deserved. Why, then, did it take every ounce of effort she could muster to keep from rushing to his side and smoothing those vertical lines with her fingertips...and her lips?

There wasn't time to think about how his skin would feel, or the heat pulsing throughout every inch of her body right now, though. In a matter of minutes, the doors of the wizard's classroom would open, and there was still important business to discuss before then.

Lightly, Lark rapped on Sarco's open office door. "Sarco, may I speak with you a moment, please?"

Long, strong-looking fingers closed the brown leather volume he'd been concentrating so intently on, and his handsome face lifted toward her. "Come in, Wonderful. What do you need?"

Lark crossed the floor and took a seat opposite his desk. For a moment, guilt for having to bother him seeped into her soul. He looked tired this morning. It was obvious to anyone with eyes, Sarco Sunwalker hadn't slept much the night before. His black hair was tousled, his eyes bloodshot, and even his high-elf pointed ears were drooping. His royal-blue robe was wrinkled, as if he'd tossed and turned in it, and weariness emanated from him.

She had no choice, though. This couldn't wait.

"I need to speak with you concerning Sherman Bobert Limburger the Ninth, the halfling I used to block your final fireball yesterday. I'd like you to give him another chance."

Sarco didn't look up as he shook his head. "It doesn't matter how it happened. He was hit. He's out. If I change the rules for him, I'd have to change them for everyone."

Lark pursed her lips and arranged her arguments in her mind before she spoke.

"I realize without rules there would be anarchy, but this is a special circumstance. His entire family and kingdom are counting on him, and if it wasn't for my interference, he wouldn't have been hit at all, and you and I both know it."

She hesitated a moment, locked gazes with Sarco, then continued, "I'm willing to let him take my place, if need be. You're welcome to tell the other students anything you like. You can even tell them I cheated. I don't care. That way, you don't have to bend your rules, and you'll get what you wanted yesterday—me, out of your class and out of your life."

Sarco didn't break his gaze as he stood, walked around his desk, and took her by the arms.

"Is this halfling really that important to you, Lark? Even if he hadn't been hit, I didn't sense the talent in him it takes to become a great wizard."

She squared her shoulders. "It's important to me

that I'm not the reason he fails. Sherman may or may not succeed, but you'll never know unless you give him a fair chance. Will you?"

Sarco's hands caressed her, and a shiver she hadn't anticipated scampered down her spine. His warm gaze held her in its embrace.

"Even though it's without a doubt wrong, I don't want you out of my class or my life, Lark. I'd rather be tortured knowing you can never be mine, than be devoid of the sight of you."

Heat that had everything to do with Sarco's words and the nearness of his body shot through her and landed like lightning in the pit of her belly.

"If allowing Sherman back in class means that much to you," Sarco continued, "I'll find a way to make it happen. However, there is something I want…no, wish…*beg* of you, in exchange."

Lark held her breath, hoping.

His head dipped, and he nibbled her ear. She clung to his arms, needing the anchor they formed to steady her. The heat she'd known earlier exploded once more deep within, and with abandon, she leaned into his embrace.

"Anything," her voice trembled. "I'd do anything you ask."

He shuddered against her.

"Ahh, Wonderful, how you tempt a man beyond reason," he said, kissing her neck and then backing away to look into her eyes.

"This, then, is my request. Let the halfling take your place as my student, and you become my apprentice, my lover. Spend what time with me we have until I'm forced to wed."

The reminder that this man was meant for her sister and not for her brought tears to Lark's eyes. She fought them back, a job made all the harder with his next words.

"I can't believe I'm asking this of you," he sighed deeply. "It's wrong. I know it's wrong, but, Lark, you're like the air I breathe. I need you."

Lark couldn't prevent a tear from slipping past her defenses and sliding down her cheek. "What of Aryanna?"

He shook his head. "I don't wish to hurt your sister, and I know my duty. I'll do what I must when the time comes. But for now, share with me what little time we have left. I can see in your eyes you want me as much as I want you. What we can have these next few weeks will be enough. I know it will. It has to be."

The tears Lark refused to let fall clung precariously to her lashes. "Though I know it's wrong, it seems there is nothing my heart can deny you."

With a flick of his wrist, Sarco closed the door to his office. The paperwork scattered on his desk skittered to the floor, and the lights dimmed. His lips captured hers in a searing kiss of ravishing need, and Lark melted into his embrace. Tongues darted in and out, mimicking the act of love, teasing, tempting, and tasting each other.

One moment, Lark stood before Sarco, kissing and caressing him, and with the next heartbeat, she lay flat on her back on the top of his desk. The white novice-robe she'd been wearing was nowhere in sight.

He parted her naked thighs and the lecherous grin he bestowed upon her had her trembling in anticipation. "I haven't broken my fast this morning, Wonderful.

May I feast?"

He didn't wait for her answer as he dipped his head between her thighs, and his fingers tenderly parted the lips of her pussy. Lark gasped and arched her back as hot breath touched and tantalized tingling membranes. Closer his kisses came to the tiny swollen nub, only to dart away at the last possible moment.

A moan escaped her lips as she shifted and lifted toward him, trying unsuccessfully to draw his head to where she so desperately needed it to be. He chuckled against her bare skin, and the sensation sent goose bumps racing down her legs, curling her toes.

"Please," she pleaded.

Sarco kissed the inside of Lark's knee while a single finger stroked lightly across the nub of her swollen clit. He slid the finger downward and darted in and out of her pussy. His eyes blazed with passion.

"Lesson number one, my sweet apprentice. A wise wizard knows how to master the art of patience, for timing is everything."

Sarco's lips captured her clit, and his teeth nipped the tender bud playfully. Lark lost all sense of time and space as reality faded away and pure pleasure took its place. He sucked and licked the tiny pearl-like globe of flesh, bringing Lark to the very pinnacle of a shattering orgasm, then backing off. Over and over he repeated the process. She begged, but her pleas fell on deaf ears as he feathered kisses up and down her lower body before returning once more to the engorged clit throbbing for his touch.

Lark writhed beneath him, unable to remain still, trying to escape the torture of a joy too great while, at the same time, seeking to get closer, wanting more, needing more, craving all Sarco had to give.

"Lesson number two, my delicious little apprentice. A wise wizard knows the prize comes to those who persevere."

The deep, passion-filled rumble of Sarco's voice flowed through Lark's every nerve ending, igniting sparks of anticipation along the way, and skittering them across her tender torso.

Sarco latched onto Lark's clit with renewed vigor. He sucked without pause as spasm after spasm of mind-shattering pleasure quaked every fiber of her being.

Lark held onto his shoulders like they were a lifeline keeping her from drowning in the turbulent sea of enraptured release.

"Lesson number three, my beautiful apprentice. A wise wizard knows to take proper care of his wand, for within the wand lies the capacity for great magic."

Lark gloried in the feel of skin against skin as Sarco, with a single, confident plunge, entered her.

The width, weight, and length of him infused her with a heat of such magnitude, her body pulsed with it. She wrapped her legs tightly around him, rising to meet each thrust with an abandon born of pure need. Stroke after stroke, she gloried in the feel of him sliding in and out of her pussy as her muscles contracted, seeking to hold him tight.

Intense pressure rocked her core once more and spread down and outward, pounding in her blood with a life force of its own. Lark gloried in Sarco's powerful, unrestrained thrusts, until with a final plunge, he stiffened in her arms and shouted her name.

The magnificent spasms of his cock and hot flow of his essence sparked ripples of such pleasure the world about her splintered into a million fragments of light and Lark's own climax gave way to a feeling of completeness she had never before experienced.

"Lesson number four, my Wonderful. A wise wizard knows that when his lady is well satisfied, so shall he be."

Outside, the sun shone brightly from a cloudless blue sky for the first time in days.

****

"Well, did she give it to him?"

Cyrrick Sunwalker grinned at the petite blond beauty scowling before him, her cute little nose stuck in the air, hands fisted on her hips, and a bejeweled foot tapping the floor impatiently.

"You know, until you open your mouth, my love, no one would ever guess you're half barbarian."

She socked him in the shoulder before he could move out of her range. He grasped her around the waist, tumbling her with him as he fell, laughing, onto the bed in the middle of his room.

"And such a fierce little barbarian you are, my lady."

Aryanna glared at him. "I'll show you fierce."

She struggled until she managed to get on top of him. Cyrrick laughed as she straddled him, pinning him beneath her.

"How's this for fierce?" she purred close to his ear while slowly rocking back and forth along his expanding cock.

In a single movement, he flipped her over and burrowed his hardness against the welcoming softness between her thighs. "God, Ary, what you do to me."

Panting hard, as if he'd run a mile, Cyrrick quickly

divested them both of the garments separating him from the flesh he craved to touch.

With the wag back and forth of a single finger, Aryanna stopped him. "No…no…no, you don't. There'll be no fooling around until you've answered my question, knave."

He sighed and rolled over, bringing her with him and snuggling her under his arm with her head resting on his chest, close to his heart. "Of course, she gave it to him. You know Lark. She is nothing if not dependable and, before you ask, yes, I made sure to tell him to memorize the passage with the word changes we made, exactly the way we discussed it. Now can we make love, Ary? I have a powerful need to be inside you."

He watched as she chewed her bottom lip.

Cyrrick caressed Aryanna's cheek. "Don't worry so much, my lady, it'll work. It has to. Trust me in this."

"I hate deceiving them, Cyrrick. You should've seen Lark last evening. She looked horrible, and I heard her crying long into the night. What if Sarco doesn't say the words just as we wrote them? What if he refuses to take the challenge and do the quest? Oh my God Draka, what if he fails? What am I going to do if Lark finds out I manipulated her and threw her and Sarco together?

Cyrrick took a deep breath and blew it out. But he knew Aryanna wasn't finished ranting yet, so he remained silent.

"I can tell she's already more than halfway in love with the man and feeling guilty because she thinks she's being disloyal to me. If this doesn't work and they don't end up together, she's going to hate me forever and I won't blame her. This could backfire on us so easily. Then what would we do?"

Cyrrick wrapped Aryanna tightly in his arms and cradled her once more close to his heart.

"It'll work. I know my brother. Sarco is honorable. He'll take the challenge, he'll do the quest, and he will not fail. There's no other way, Ary. This must work. Without you at my side, life would have no purpose. Lark hasn't realized you can probe minds yet, has she?"

Cyrrick felt the shaking of her head before she spoke. "No, she doesn't realize. She never has. Just like the rest of my family, she thinks I'm all lace and ribbons, jewels and gems, the proverbial pampered princess. Sometimes I wonder what she'd think if I opened up and allowed her to see who I really am. I'm almost as powerful as she when it comes to mind control."

Aryanna laughed. "Even as a child I could manipulate both my parents and they never suspected a thing. My brother and all my sisters did whatever I wanted whenever I wanted and never once questioned why. It's the only spiritmaster trait I inherited."

Cyrrick patted her bottom. "I'm glad of that. I'd hate to see the weather change as often as your mood does."

Aryanna glared up at him, but that was her only response to his statement. "I could never use my powers on Grandmother Ava. I can get inside her mind but not control it. She's much too powerful for that." Aryanna poked Cyrrick squarely in the chest. "You, my love, seem to be the only person in all of Albrath whose mind I can't get into at all. How do you manage to block me out?"

Cyrrick chuckled. "Self-preservation, princess. If you could read my mind, my thoughts would either make you blush or get me smacked."

Aryanna leaned closer and the look of pure mischief glowing in her eyes made Cyrrick's heart pound. "I don't need to be able to read those thoughts to know what you're thinking, knave."

Aryanna laughed and the tinkling of it, like the sound of fine crystal, didn't do a thing to alleviate the persistent problem he struggled with whenever he was in her presence.

Blood pounded through his veins, and his cock throbbed. Her small hand's not-so-gentle cupping and squeezing almost made him embarrass himself by finishing before they even got a chance to start.

"I'll take pity on you this one time, knave," she giggled, then leaned close to his ear and whispered, "I'm in control, though, and I'll have my way."

Cyrrick moaned as she quickly slid up the length of his cock and took him into her hot pussy. "God Draka, Ary, ride the damn thing. Don't just sit there torturing me."

She laughed again. "Quiet, knave, and let a princess work."

He clenched his jaw as she teasingly slid her way back up, only to suddenly plunge down—all the way down. His breath whooshed out, and he forgot to take the next one.

"You like that? Want more, want faster, want deeper?"

Cyrrick hissed, "You're killing me, Ary. Have pity."

Her eyes gleamed with mischief. "If you insist."

A moment later, his balls were begging his cock for a quick reprieve as she clamped her muscles tightly about him and quickened her pace. She rode each stroke harder, faster, and deeper than the one before.

"Like this?" she smiled.

Cyrrick didn't even have the presence of mind to nod. All he could do was hold tight to Aryanna's waist, grin like a fool, and enjoy the ride.

## Chapter Nine

If ever a man carried the heavy burden of responsibility resting on his broad shoulders with more finesse than Sarco Sunwalker, Lark would like to see that man. Sarco truly was a prince among men. Was it fair any mortal should have to live with the fact that not only did the future of his entire race and the peace of his lands lay completely and totally in his hands, but also that he must set aside his own desires and hopes for happiness for the good of countrymen he didn't even know?

Lark sighed as she followed Sarco from student to student, carrying his clipboard, taking notes, being his apprentice. With each passing day, she'd grown more convinced that never in the history of Albrath had there been a man more loving, more handsome, more intelligent, more patient—in fact, simply *more*—than this man.

It wasn't so much what Sarco said or did that distinguished him from other men. It was what he didn't say or do. He didn't need to resort to being loud or using force to gain respect or get his point across. His mere presence commanded unspoken respect and loyalty. Students flocked to him as a natural leader and hung on every word he uttered. He was magnificent—as a lover, as a friend, as a mentor—and, for a little while yet, he was hers.

The last few weeks had flown by like the grains of sand in a broken hourglass. The semester was more than a quarter of the way over, and she dreaded its coming end. The end would herald the Yulemass celebration, and the Yulemass celebration would herald the arrival of the rest of her family and the horrid Sarco-asking-for-Ary's-hand-in-marriage ceremony.

Lark and Sarco didn't speak of it. Ever. When they lay in each other's arms, they both pretended the need to fulfill the prophecy didn't exist. But the knowledge was there, always between them, always in the back of their mind, and Lark knew it. There was no escape from it or from the guilt.

Ary. What was she going to do about Ary? What kind of a person was Lark to sleep with the man she knew was intended to be her own sister's husband? Where was God Draka when a girl needed him, and why hadn't he struck her down for the evil creature she obviously was? But, no, not even the threat of a curse of warts or a plague of rashes could make her stop and reconsider her wicked ways.

And Ary herself certainly wasn't helping matters. Her comments of, "I'm glad it's you and not me who has to spend time with that boring wizard," and "Sarco who? Oh, yeah, him," didn't lend well to self-restraint. If Ary didn't care enough about the man to even want to be in his presence, then why should Lark feel guilty for stealing what few precious moments of happiness she could get?

Lark heaved a sigh. Not even in her own mind could she justify her actions. Would that stop her, though? She knew it wouldn't. Right or wrong, her heart was now in the sole possession of Sarco

Sunwalker. All she could do was love the man with all she was for as long as she could and pray for a miracle.

The distinct sound of someone sniffling drew Lark out of her introspection, and she glanced down the line of students. At first, she didn't notice anything different in any of the faces she had come to know so well.

The high-elf, Rysen, still had his nose an inch higher than everyone else's and a look of complete boredom on his face, as he did every day. Barlomas, the dwarf, had his normal scowl and the remnants of his breakfast poking out from his long red beard. Even the dark-elf vixen, Deedra, looked as she always did, with her indigo-blue skin shimmering, her long snow-white hair flowing down her back, and her breasts impressive enough few noticed the blood red of her eyes or the cruel turn of her mouth.

Nothing was amiss with this crew.

Then the sound came again. Lark whipped her head back down the line at the same moment Deedra shifted her stance slightly. Now Lark could see who was crying. It was Sherman.

What on Albrath could be wrong now? The first few days after Sherman rejoined the class had been trying, but after that, he'd settled in nicely and, in all fairness, was thriving.

Lark wanted to go directly to the little halfling and ask what the matter was but knew she couldn't.

The beginning of every week was the same. Sarco greeted and lectured as he walked the line of students, and Lark followed behind him, taking notes. The students looked forward to this. It gave them an idea as to what the rest of the week would hold, and it let them know where they stood in their studies.

No, she couldn't disrupt the class. Only three more students to talk with, and then she and Sarco would be standing in front of Sherman who, as usual, was last in line. That would have to be soon enough.

"Mr. Rysen." Sarco's voice rumbled low and deep. "I realize you feel practice is somewhat beneath you, but not only were your fireballs mediocre at best last week, but your spells were too. You can do better."

He held up his hand as the high-elf opened his mouth to speak. "*Show* me, Mr. Rysen, don't *tell* me. That is all."

Rysen nodded.

Sarco moved down the line.

"Barlomas, how are you this fine morning?"

The dwarf grimaced. "How do you think I am, sir? My arse still smarts where I landed on it the other day after you hit me with that damn fireball. I still say it wasn't a low-level one either. Singed my beard near off, it did. Fairly roasted to ashes a fine piece of Alarian mountain goat I was saving for me lunch."

Sarco chuckled and the sound of it sent shivers of delight racing down Lark's spine.

"You're probably right, it may well have been a medium-level spell. I'll check more closely next time before I chuck one at you. I'm sorry about your arse, and, umm, your lunch."

Lark watched intently as Sarco approached Deedra, the dark-elf. True to form, the first place his gaze landed wasn't her face. Lark's instinct was to kick him in the shins to get his attention back on task. She settled for clearing her throat.

The almost translucent high-elf skin of Sarco's face pinkened as he raised his gaze to eye level with Deedra.

"Umm…Miss Deedra, umm, you did a fine job last week. You have very good, umm, form. Yes, form. Keep up the good work, and you will do fine on the final breast—I mean, *test*."

Lark closed her eyes, took a deep breath, and shook her head. Men! What was it about an extra-large set of mammary glands that turned them all into drooling idiots? Looking at her own less than adequate cleavage, Lark sighed. She couldn't blame Sarco for looking at the beautiful dark-elf. After all, he was every inch a man and Deedra was exquisitely lovely to look upon.

Lark had to admit, if she were male, she'd probably lust after the dark, blue-skinned beauty herself, so how could she fault Sarco?

Somehow that thought didn't make her feel any better as she prodded him in the ribs to get him moving. She might have to accept the fact that Sarco Sunwalker was undoubtedly all male, but she didn't have to let him know it.

Finally, they arrived at Sherman. It took only a glance to tell something was wrong. Behind the taped-together rims of his big, round glasses, Sherman's eyes were bloodshot and watery. His face was blotchy, and his one bushy eyebrow drooped. His lips quivered, and every couple of seconds, he sniffed and wiped his nose on his sleeve.

Lark's heart went out to him, and she almost stretched to hug him before she remembered they were in class and it wouldn't be appropriate. The sound of Sarco's voice saved her from embarrassing the halfling.

"Sherman, what's wrong?"

It was like a dam burst as loud sobs rang through the room. The halfling covered his face with his hands, sank to the floor on his knees, and cried as if his heart was breaking.

"Class dismissed," Sarco shouted above Sherman's wails.

Lark marveled at Sarco's tenderness as he bent, scooped the halfling up, carried him into the office, and deposited him gently into a chair.

Kneeling before the distraught man, Sarco offered him a towel. "Want to talk about it?"

Sherman took the piece of cloth and loudly blew his nose. "She does…does…doesn't love me anymore," he sobbed.

Sarco shook his head. "Who doesn't love you anymore, Sherman?"

"Miss…Miss…Miss Sedona Cheddar, that's who." Sherman's howls became so loud, the walls vibrated.

Sarco patted the halfling on the back. "Come now, it can't be as bad as all that."

"As bad as all that, you ask? I tell you, I'm ruined. My life is over. There's no reason to go on. All is lost." Sherman sniffed, swiped at his eyes and nose, then continued, "We had plans, she and I. Sedona is her parents' only child and heir to their fortune. We had dreams and aspirations of a two-cheese dynasty. Now all is ruined. My love, my life, and my beautiful dreams are all gone. How…how…how could she possibly leave me, Sherman Bobbert Limburger the Ninth, for that useless Karl Xavier Gouda? He doesn't love her. He just wants her family's money."

The halfling was once more overcome with grief, and his sobs tore at Lark's heart. "Now, now, it'll get better, you'll see." She patted the Sherman's shoulder.

After a few moments, the halfling composed

himself. "We were once friends, Karl and I. As children we used to play together. But not one day in his rotten life did Karl ever do the right thing. I was the only person to befriend the backstabbing girlfriend stealer. Now, Karl has my beautiful Sedona and I have nothing."

Sherman moaned while clutching a soggy, tear-stained piece of paper. Lark patted harder.

"See this letter?" Sherman hefted the paper and shook it. "Ruined, I tell you. Thrown over for a Gouda, of all things." The halfling sighed. "Now, I—Sherman Bobert Limburger the Ninth—am destined to go down in history as the man who stank at love."

\*\*\*\*

As far as ideas went, this probably wasn't one of Sarco's best. Lark purposely dragged her feet in an attempt to delay arriving at her rooms. Why had she even told Sarco where they might find Leeky Shortz at this time of day? And what on Albrath would make the man think that Leeky the gnome could help Sherman?

The sound of Sarco's voice made her jump. "If we go any slower, Lark, we might as well be walking backwards. What's wrong with you?"

She scowled, but continued ambling toward the rooms she shared with her sister and Laycee. The door was only steps away. "Me? Nothing is wrong with me. I was just about to ask you the same thing. Why would you ask Leeky Shortz to help with anything, let alone with Sherman? Leeky is a very disturbed little man—gnome—whatever. You have no idea the things I've seen."

"You just don't understand him, Wonderful, "Sarco sighed. "I admit, he's a little rough around the edges, especially when it comes to women, but he has life experience that is invaluable. I'm sure if anyone can do it, Leeky is the man—gnome—whatever, to help Sherman regain his self-confidence. It's worth a try. What do we have to lose?"

Lark cringed as she hesitated with her hand on the doorknob, not wanting to open it. "That's precisely what I'm worried about. I've seen Mr. Shortz at work. Poor Sherman doesn't stand a chance."

Sarco took Lark gently by the hand and smiled. "Trust me in this, please."

Lark shrugged. After all, how much worse could it get? As she swung open the door, the word *worse* took on a whole new meaning.

"What the tainted tonsils of a two-toed troll trollop are ya thinking, lass? Close the door before stuff seeps out inta the hallway. Now that would be a mess ta clean, wouldn't it?"

Whipped cream—piles of it—were everywhere. Lark wanted to close her eyes, but morbid curiosity prevented her. Leeky Shortz sat on the tiled floor with some kind of a game laid out between his outstretched legs. The game board looked to be fashioned from a pair of very big panties, of all things. He held a set of dice in his brown-gloved hand.

The gnome was dressed in a cowboy hat, a pair of chaps, and spurs. The only other accessory to his outfit was a red candied cherry sticking precariously out of his belly button. Whipped cream circled his nipples, and what she hoped was chocolate sauce made a ring around his mouth.

"I found the nuts and sprinkles, love."

Lark turned toward the sound of Laycee's voice

coming from the other room and groaned. If Leeky looked like this, what of her gnome governess?

It only took a moment to find out. Miss Laycee Titwilder strode into the room, wearing a black-and-white cow costume complete with plastic udders and little pink cow ears perched on top of her blond wig. She had a ring of whipped cream around her mouth that suspiciously matched the one circling Leeky's nipples, and she carried two bowls in her hands.

The look on her face when she saw they were no longer alone was almost worth the trauma of seeing the two of them.

"Oh, my, I didn't realize we have company. Why didn't ya tell me, Leeky? Aren't ya supposed ta still be in class, Lark? It's the middle of the morning. Oh, and I see ya brought along that nice Sir Sarco fellow. Let me just clean this mess up a bit."

She took the bowls and plopped them into the lap of the blow-up doll in the corner. The colorful sprinkles and nuts clashed with the dominatrix outfit poor Miss Bunny had been dressed in today. She looked almost as surprised as Lark felt right now.

Lark gasped as she realized what Laycee meant to do. "No, it's all right, really. Sarco just wanted to ask Leeky a question. I can see we're intruding though, so we'll come back later." She yanked at Sarco.

Laycee laughed, "Nonsense, ya aren't intruding a bit. Are they, Leeky? I'll just have Tug help me clean this mess, and we can have tea and chat."

Lark winced as Laycee grabbed Tug. The only thing that made this whole situation tolerable was the look on Sarco's face as the female gnome lifted the skirt of the frilly little maid costume she had Tug dressed in, and used the hose where his cock should have been to suck up the whipped cream that was all over the floor, while quickly chanting a spell. Then, she sprayed the white stuff down the drain hole she'd just magicaly created.

"Multi-purpose doll," Leeky shouted above the noise of the hose. "Ain't technology wonderful? So, what did ya want ta see me about, Sarco?"

Lark looked at Sarco out of the corner of her eye and almost felt sorry for the man. Almost. She jabbed him in the ribs.

He jumped and glared at her.

"Why didn't you tell me about this?" he hissed.

Lark grinned. "I tried to, remember? You wouldn't listen."

Sarco sighed and his hand shook as he ran it through his hair. "Well, next time kick me or something, okay?"

Lark nodded. She watched him look at the expectantly waiting Leeky, then straighten his shoulders, and clear his throat.

"Umm…yes, I wanted to ask a favor of you, Leeky."

His voice trailed off as his gaze followed Laycee in her cow costume, its long tail wagging behind her and Tug, the maid, under one arm while she held onto the doll's cock hose with the other. Whipped cream spurted out the end of the long, flesh-colored hose. It really was quite hysterical, Lark decided, but there was another matter more pressing at the moment to be dealt with.

Lark jabbed Sarco once more and spitefully enjoyed watching him shiver and take a deep breath before finally looking directly at Leeky. *Perhaps next time, Sarco will listen to me.*

"One of my students just got thrown over by his girlfriend back home and is distraught. I was wondering if you'd be willing to take him under your wing and help him get back some of his self-confidence? I'd really appreciate it. Although you don't need to show him, umm, everything you know."

Leeky Shortz cackled, "Why, I'd be more than happy ta help ya student. It's been a mighty long time since I had someone ta impart my vast knowledge ta. Might be entertaining. Ya send the lad ta see me tomorrow. Now have a seat and play a round with us. It's my turn."

Leeky rolled the dice and got double sixes. "Woot!" he yelled as he grinned at Laycee. "Ya know what that means."

Laycee sat Tug down and walked over to the panty play board, placed her hands on her hips, and scowled at Leeky.

"Again? Ya landed on the Ride 'Em Cowboy square again? That's not fair. All I ever get is *Use plenty of whipped cream*, or *Give your partner a massage without using your hands*, or *Time for toys*. Why don't I ever get Ride 'Em Cowboy? Are ya using loaded dice again, Leeky Shortz?"

The male gnome looked positively innocent as he placed a hand over his heart, smearing the whipped cream circling his nipples. "Laycee, ya wound me, lass. When it comes ta games of love, would I ever cheat ya?"

"I suppose not," she sighed. "Ya sure seem ta be having extraordinarily good luck today, though." She got down on all fours, facing away from Leeky.

Reaching behind her, she flipped open the button-up closure where the cow tail had been, exposing her saggy, pasty-white bottom. "Okay, Ride 'Em Cowboy…again."

Leeky smacked his hands together and giggled with glee.

This time when Lark tugged on Sarco's arm, he followed her out the door immediately.

## Chapter Ten

If ever a man needed to be kicked in the shins for the smug, self-satisfied smile gracing his face this morning, it was Sarco Sunwalker. Only two weeks remained before both of their families were due to descend upon the Academy and the scheduled Yulemass celebrations, and what was he doing?

Not preparing for their relatives' arrival.

Not trying to avoid marrying Aryanna.

Not even concentrating on his class.

No, Sarco Sunwalker was spending his time helping Leeky turn poor Sherman into even more of a freak then he'd been before.

It wasn't just Sarco and Leeky either. They had recruited help in the form of Sarco's poor, unsuspecting friend, Sir Uthiel Dragonheart, who had arrived only two days earlier to visit his wife Briar for the holidays.

Men! What was it about a man that turned his brain to mush and brought out the naughty little boy when faced with what he perceived to be a challenge? As each new attempt at setting the halfling up with various women over the last few weeks had failed, Sarco and Leeky had become more and more desperate. They were determined, with the added help of Uthiel, to turn Sherman into a debonair ladies' man. Lark sighed.

"What the blistered bunions on the feet of a Mountain of Geiger billy goat were ya thinking with that 'do, lad? Ya need more hair cream," Leeky grumbled.

Lark simply shook her head as she stood quietly in Sarco's office, watching the proceedings.

"I don't know, Leeky," Sarco interjected. "Any more and he's going to look like his head is as plastic as Tug's."

The gnome scoffed as he slipped off his light-purple, eyebrow-plucking gloves and replaced them with his bright-chartreuse, hair-combing ones.

Uthiel poked Sarco in the ribs. "I see our little friend still has his glove fetish."

The ruggedly handsome human pointed in the direction of the gnome, and Lark let the corners of her mouth tilt up in a small smile.

Leeky, however, didn't seem to be finding it amusing. He scowled. "It's not a fetish. I'm just particular what touches me where. A rogue can never be ta careful. These hands are irreplaceable, ya know."

The gnome surveyed the halfling. "It's better ta look plastic than it is ta have the whole mess sticking up every which way. If'n he's gonna be attracting the opposite sex, his hair has ta be tidy. Girls like that sorta thing. Being able ta lick your eyebrows doesn't hurt either."

Lark choked, and the ensuing coughing fit had her eyes watering. The men didn't even notice, though, as Leeky switched the topic of conversation back to Sherman.

"We've put him in new duds. We've trimmed his toenails, fixed his glasses, even shaved the hair off the tops of his feet. It's the little touches that matter the most."

Sherman shuffled from foot to foot. "I don't know, Mr. Shortz. I really appreciate you trying to help me out and all, but I've never been much of a looker. I once flunked a grooming class."

"Nonsense," Leeky declared. "All ya need is confidence, lad. Repeat after me. I am a sexy man."

The halfling giggled nervously. "I am a sexy man."

"All women secretly want me."

Uthiel laughed out loud while Sarco simply rolled his eyes. Lark snickered.

"All women secretly want me," Sherman mumbled almost inaudibly.

Leeky raised himself to his full three-and-a-half-foot height. "Ya've gotta believe in ya self or nobody else is gonna believe in ya. Now say it with meaning this time, lad. I am a sexy man, all women secretly want me. I am the Shermanator."

The halfling's eyes lit. "Oh, I like that, Mr. Shortz. I am the Shermanator. Kinda catchy. Rolls right off the tongue. Don't you think? Oh, yes, the ladies won't be able to resist a man who calls himself the Shermanator. I am a sexy man. All women secretly want me. I *am* the Shermanator.

Lark threw up her hands and walked away.

****

"No, I won't do it. You simply must find another way."

Cyrrick kissed Aryanna's forehead as he held her in his arms and sighed. "I wish there was some other way to handle it, Ary. If you have any suggestions, I'm all ears."

"Ear comments coming from a high-elf aren't funny." Her voice broke with emotion. "I can't do it,

Cyrrick. I can't hurt her that way. Who would've thought the stupid fine print on a thousand-year-old-quest would be so important? If something is that vital, it should be in big bold letters, not tiny little words you can hardly even see."

He tucked Aryanna under his arm, close to his heart and smiled sadly into the dimness of the room. "Unfortunately, my love, the fine print is always important. We must deal with this problem. Lark can't be allowed to help Sarco in any way with the quest. The wording is very specific, and, trust me when I say I went over it thoroughly. The only way I can see to prevent her interference is to find a way to keep them separated after the ceremony. If she helps him, even with her mind control, he can't choose her. The council will know. I've already set into motion the only thing I'm sure will put a damper on his amour for a little while anyway. The rest, my sweet princess, sadly, is up to you."

She shivered against his side, and he held her tighter.

"You don't know what she's like when she's hurt, Cyrrick. Things…happen. Lark has had so much pain in her life, it isn't fair. She's so in love with Sarco, and it's because of our manipulation. Now we have to tear apart what we set in motion? Why can't we just sit them both down and explain it? They'll listen. They'll understand. I know they will."

The weight of so many people's future happiness was like a heavy stone on Cyrrick's chest.

"I wish we could, Ary, I truly do. Are you willing to take the chance Lark will be able to resist helping Sarco, even if she perceives him to be in danger? You yourself didn't expect the mental bond that formed between them to be so strong. What did you call it again?"

"Spirit Union, that's what it's called. It's so rare, it's almost never heard of anymore. So why this time?" she groaned. "Why them? It's even stronger than marriage vows. Only death can break it, and then only temporarily, I've been told. Lark hasn't realized what she's experiencing yet. Let's hope she doesn't figure it out until this is all over with. I wouldn't want to be stuck outdoors if and when she comes to that particular realization after we rip her entire world apart."

Cyrrick hugged Aryanna close. "So you'll do it? Years from now we'll sit around and laugh about this, you'll see."

The wetness of her tears touched his skin.

"I doubt I'll ever find anything about this situation funny, no matter how much time has passed. I suppose I don't have a choice, though, do I? If I don't, I may very well end up married to your brother, whose mind and heart will forever be bound to my sister. I don't have to like it, though, and I don't have to be happy about it, and you, my dear diplomat, are just going to have to put up with me that way, for a long time."

Cyrrick kissed the lips of the woman who possessed his soul. "It's my sincere wish to put up with you for the remainder of my days, my love."

****

It had been a long day, and Lark was glad it was almost over. After her last class, she had come back to Sarco's office to go over tomorrow's schedule and, of course, to see the man himself. Just watching his long, strong fingers writing out the next morning's class plan was a pleasure. Her body warmed at the memory of those same fingers upon her skin, and her senses tingled with desire.

For a moment guilt tugged at her conscience. This wasn't right. He wasn't really hers. He would never be.

Lark shook her head. Ary didn't even want him, and she so desperately did. Was it really so very wrong to take what she could while she could?

Every inch of Sarco Sunwalker was perfection and then some. From the tips of his jet-black hair, to his crisply pointed ears, to his sensual, full lips, his strong chin, his broad chest, and his oh-so-talented hands, he was everything her heart had ever desired. And that wasn't even taking in consideration what lay just south of his perfectly indented belly button. God Draka help her, she wanted him with a passion that knew no bounds.

"I hope I'm who you're thinking about, Wonderful. You're positively glowing."

Heat crept up her neck, and still Lark lifted her gaze to meet his without hesitation. "I was just remembering the way your hands feel on my body and wishing they were there right now."

Sarco held out a hand. "Come to me, then."

She shouldn't. Even if Ary didn't want him, this was wrong. One of Grandmother Ava's sayings came to mind. *If you have to do something in secret, child, then it's probably not what you should be doing.*

Lark stubbornly ignored the voice in her head and teasingly lifted the hem of her tunic over her head and tossed it carelessly on the floor. She tamped down the last vestiges of her guilt as she slowly sauntered forward until she stood directly before him. She would be strong tomorrow, she silently promised. She would end the relationship then. Really, she would. But not today. She wasn't strong enough today.

Holding out a hand for help, she giggled as she climbed up, straddled his thighs, and settled herself firmly on his lap.

With a wink and a pucker, Lark touched her lips to his. He was hot, familiar, safe, secure, and oh, so sexy. It was like coming home to a welcoming fire on a chilly day and finding a brightly wrapped present just waiting to be opened. Sarco was home, her haven, her holiday, and everything else all rolled up into one.

"I need you now, Wonderful. I can't wait another moment to be inside you." He tugged his robe up past his hips and freed his cock. Lifting her along the hard planes of his body, he slid her down until she could feel the head of his large, hard cock probing the opening of her pussy.

Lark sighed as he entered her and slid his cock in so deep, it touched her womb. She wrapped her arms around his neck, arched her back, and rode.

The door banged open with a resounding thud that shook the entire room.

Sarco jumped so quickly Lark landed on the floor in front of him in a heap. "Mother! Father!" He quickly slipped his robe back down over his still-rock-hard cock. "I wasn't expecting you until next week at the earliest."

Sarco stepped over and in front of Lark, somewhat blocking her from his parents' view.

Lark lifted the hem of Sarco's wizard robe and peeked between his legs at the two people in the doorway. She wanted nothing more than to find a hole to crawl into so she could hide.

A high, trilling voice sang out, "Sarco, my dear. We thought you knew we'd be arriving today. We spoke with your brother just yesterday. Tsk, tsk, never leave details to others that you should attend to yourself, I suppose."

Lark's mouth gaped open, and she snapped it shut. Her mind raced. How to best explain who she was and what she was doing here, sitting naked on the floor in the middle of Sarco's office? She almost laughed. At least things couldn't look worse than they were already.

"And you, dear, you must be Princess Aryanna." Sarco's mother spoke again as she bent and gave a small wave.

Lark gulped as heat flooded her face.

"Why, of course you are." The woman grinned. "How silly of me. Who else would you be? I've been so excited about meeting you and about the upcoming wedding. I have ideas and details galore to go over with you. It's good to see you children getting on so splendidly."

Lark grabbed for and fumbled with her tunic.

Lady Sunwalker stood back up and poked her husband. Lark cringed as she watched the man, who looked much like an older version of Sarco, shake his head and look at his wife. The woman was positively gushing.

"Oh look, Ty. Just look at those hips, will you? Aren't they simply perfect for carrying babies? And those breasts, though not huge, they're impressive. I bet she could feed twins without any difficulty at all."

Sarco's mother clasped both of her hands to her chest and beamed, "I've wanted grandchildren for ever so long. I'd almost given up. You, my dear daughter-in-law-to-be, have renewed my faith."

"Mother, stop."

Lark wanted to cry, and the desperation in Sarco's voice didn't help alleviate her feelings of doom. With one last quick tug, she finally forced her tunic into place.

Sarco bent and helped her up from the floor.

Lark stood, still partially behind him, glad for the barrier his body provided.

"What are we going to do?" she whispered.

Sarco shook his head. "I don't know. Leave it to me. I'll handle it."

Lark nodded, squared her shoulders, and, out of sight of his parents' eyes, took Sarco's hand in hers.

The tall elfin woman looked much like her son. They shared the same crisply pointed ears, raven-black hair, and gold-streaked eyes. She continued smiling as if nothing were amiss, although she lost some of her bubbly excitement when thunder shook the building.

"Oh, my, what is with the weather these days?" Lady Sunwalker said. "We haven't been here but a quarter turn of an hourglass and the sky was clear and the sun shining brightly when we arrived. Yet look at it now. The clouds have rolled in, and the wind has whipped up something fierce. I do believe it just may rain."

Lark cringed.

"Now, Son, properly introduce us to your bride-to-be."

Lark held her breath and glanced sideways at Sarco's face, drawing what comfort and strength she could from his warm hand still tucked into hers. "She's not Princess Aryanna, Mother. She's...she's my apprentice."

Lark's heart stopped. She was sure it had. If it hadn't, she would be feeling something, anything, not this cold numbness seeping into every crevice of her soul. She let go of Sarco's hand, and hers fell to her side.

"I don't understand, Son. She isn't the princess? She's...a...a companion or servant of some kind?"

Sarco's father cleared his throat. "Now, now, Jillian, don't be getting yourself in a tizzy. You know what it does to your blood pressure. Can't you see what's going on here? The boy was simply...working, yes, working with his assistant-type person. Nothing wrong with that. Better he gets it out of his system before the wedding. Wouldn't you say?"

Sarco's father winked at them, and a heavy weight of guilt settled deep into the pit of Lark's stomach.

Sarco's mother sighed. "But she has such nice hips, Tylindius. I do so want grandchildren. Oh, well. Do you do laundry, my dear? I have this irritating spot on my favorite royal purple robe, and I did so wish to wear it to the engagement ceremony next week. Would you be a dear and see if you can get it out for me? I'll have one of my girls send it over when they unpack my things."

Sarco glanced at Lark, but his eyes were distant and cold. "An apprentice isn't a servant, Mother. She won't be doing your laundry."

Lady Jillian Sunwalker placed her hands on her hips and glared at her son. "Well, does your apprentice at least have a name, or do we simply call her your apprentice?"

Sarco opened his mouth. "She's...umm..."

Lark stared at Sarco willing him to say something, anything, but he didn't utter another word. She looked from Lady Jillian to Lord Tylindius Sunwalker. They smiled back benignly.

Pushing Sarco aside, she stepped forward and extended a hand. "I'm Lark, and I am indeed your son's apprentice. It is a great honor to meet you both. As for your robe and its pesky spot, please do send it to me, Lady Sunwalker, and I'll be glad to see what I can do. If you would excuse me, please, I'll leave you and your son to get reacquainted."

Then, without a second glance at Sarco or his parents, Lark stepped out the door into the howling wind. With her spine ramrod straight and her chin held high, she headed toward the rooms she shared with the real and future Mrs. Sarco Sunwalker.

Lightning flashed across an angry sky as the clouds darkened. Fat drops of cold rain pelted the ground and stirred the dust beneath her feet.

Lark seethed.

## Chapter Eleven

If ever a man should've been shot, then drawn and quartered, and roasted over a spit before a single tear could've been shed for him, Sarco Sunwalker was that man. Why, then, could Lark not staunch the persistent, irritating flow of the small droplets trickling down her cheeks?

His *apprentice*? She was nothing more to him than simply his apprentice? And, when asked, he hadn't even been able to remember her name?

She rationalized it for the hundredth time since laying her head upon her pillow. How would she have handled the introduction if the tables had been turned?

Lark understood how difficult it must've been for him. After all, Sarco couldn't have said, "Mom, Dad, I'd like you to meet Lark. She's Princess Aryanna's younger sister. We've been fucking each other's brains out for the past couple phases of the moons, even though I'm supposed to propose to and marry Aryanna soon. Not that I've given much thought to the spoiled little princess anyway, mind you."

It didn't matter. Saying only that she was his apprentice, then not even remembering her name—*that* wasn't the right way to handle the situation either.

Men! Damn all their souls to VoT.

Lark fluffed her pillow, then punched it for good measure, wishing with all her heart it was the traitorous

Sarco Sunwalker's jaw. She sniffed twice, blew her nose into a wad of soggy tissue for the umpteenth time, and scrunched her eyes tightly shut.

A warm feeling radiated from the core of her mind outward, and Lark braced herself for what she knew was coming. Then he was there in her head, as if simply thinking about him had conjured him to her.

"*Wonderful, you still awake?*"

Lark stiffened. "*It's* My Apprentice *to you, Professor Sunwalker and, no, I'm asleep. Go away. I'm in the middle of dreaming about a man who actually knows my name and isn't afraid to say it.*"

She felt his sigh just as strongly against her skin as if he were lying right beside her.

"*I deserve that. I'm sorry, Lark. Please forgive me. I panicked. I didn't know what to do. I mean, what else could I have said? They caught me off guard. None of this is your fault. The last thing I want is you hurt. I was trying to protect you.*"

Lark shook with anger. She could feel it coursing through her body and wasn't anywhere near ready to listen to reason. "*Oh, so forgetting my name was a form of protecting me? Admit it, if not to me, then at least to yourself. You were ashamed. A younger sister isn't good enough for your highly esteemed family.*"

Fragments of light exploded behind her eyes in every shade of red as Sarco's frustration projected outward. "*Is that what you really think? Let me tell you one thing, Miss Princess Larksong Hammerstrike, then I'll leave you alone. I've spent the entire evening racking my brain for a way to make this whole mess right. You're not good enough for my family? I'm the one who's unworthy. I'm the one who has been seducing you even though I know I'm expected to marry your sister. Don't you think I know what a low-life, dishonorable piece of gutter scum that makes me? And still I can't help myself. I love you, you're in my head, my heart, my very soul."*

He shuddered, and Lark caught herself reaching out for him, though all her fingers met was empty air. *"Oh, Sarco. I love you, too. And it's not really you I'm angry with at all. It's me. It could've just as easily been Ary who walked through that door as your parents. Can you imagine how hurt, how upset, she would have been? What kind of woman has sex with her own sister's intended without a thought of the damamge she's doing? I'm not very proud of myself right now. And what are your parents going to think of me, of us, when they find out who I really am?"*

His heartbeat doubled, and she felt it pounding in her own chest. *"Don't worry about my parents. They've never been the kind to judge. But what are we going to do, Lark? Time is running out, and I can't marry your sister while loving you as I do, and I can't not marry her if I can find no way around the prophecy."*

Lark swallowed twice, afraid that even though she was communicating with thought and not speech, her despair would show. She didn't want that. She was the one who'd started this. Sarco hadn't really wanted her in his class or in his bed to begin with. He'd tried to warn her. She'd known this would end badly, and she'd insinuated herself into his life anyway. So she was the one who now needed to be strong. *"Perhaps it would best for everyone involved if we simply didn't see each other again?"*

His gasp rolled through her, leaving her chilled.

*"No. I can't give up on us yet. I need you too much. We still have time. We still have options. Give me another chance to fix this, please."*

She wanted to cry, and at the same time, she wanted to believe. *"Do you really think there may be a way to fix this mess?*

She felt his nod. *"There has to be. We'll start working on it first thing in the morning. But for tonight, tell me you forgive me, Wonderful, for how badly I acted today. I can't sleep unless you do."*

She smiled into the darkness of the room and with her mind stroked his cheek. *"There is no reason for forgiveness. We were both caught off guard."*

He mentally smiled against the skin of her neck and nuzzled. *"'Night then, Wonderful. I'll see you in the morning."*

Her blankets became his arms as she nestled into his embrace and let slumber dry her tears.

*"G'night,"* she whispered.

Lark's last words were like a kiss upon his lips and Sarco smiled sadly into the darkness. He closed his eyes and tried to relax enough to sleep. Morning was but a few short turns of the hourglass away, and with it would come the time for decisions. What was he going to do?

Lark was a complication to his life for which he would eternally be grateful but that didn't make what he was contemplating any easier. His choices were simple yet, ultimately, excruciatingly difficult. Disappoint one woman and himself, or devastate all of his family, the council and, last but certainly not least, his people?

There was no way he could think to retain both his

love and his honor. He wished, not for the first time in his life, he had Cyrrick's skill at diplomacy. Explaining his reservations to those who mattered would be so much simpler if he did. And Cyrrick. What would he think of being thrown into the forefront of the fray?

Sarco sighed and rubbed the dull ache at his temples. Since the moment of his birth, he'd been groomed, trained, and decreed as the next Lord of the High-Elves. It defined him, had always been who he was and what he would become.

Years of tutoring on every subject from sitting in judgment of wrongs to kissing babies and shaking hands, from swords and fireballs, to prophecies and legends. They'd all been for one purpose. He was Sarco-Keltoris Titus Sunwalker. *The heir*. How could he simply turn his back on his people and walk away? Yet that was exactly what he was contemplating. Wasn't it? The thought made his heart heavy.

Could he do it, though? Could he stand and face the Council of the Elders and Princess Aryanna's parents, then turn to his own family and abdicate his right to be Lord of the Realm to his brother? Would Cyrrick then be duty bound to fulfill the prophecy by marrying Aryanna?

Honor and duty had been drummed deeply into his soul from the moment he took his first breath, and now he was considering his own wants and needs before those of his people, before those of even his brother. This didn't feel honorable, this didn't feel right. But what else could he do? Spend the remainder of his life in a cold, loveless marriage to the sister of the one woman on Albrath he did love?

Sarco shuddered to his core. Ultimately, he was

who he was and could not be another. Tomorrow was a new day with new possibilities, and the ceremony was still almost a week away. There was still time.

Tomorrow he would make it a point to find the time to visit Uncle Arizon and ask him if there was anything in the prophecies and legends that might help them find a way around the rules. Tomorrow he would spend every possible moment he could with Lark so when and if their time together had to end, she'd know his love was real and she was the one and only woman who would ever truly own his heart. For tonight, though, he lifted his eyes toward the heavens and prayed.

****

The door to Sarco's office banged open so hard it shook the walls. "What the pierced, puckered nipples of a big-nosed, pot-bellied, red-eyed, ugly ogre woman were ya thinking, lad?"

Lark gasped. Next to Leeky stood Sherman Bobert Limburger the Ninth with his robe singed and tattered. His glasses were askew, and his face was beet red and blistered. The stubs of his still smoldering hair stuck straight up, both eyebrows were now gone, and the corner of his mouth twitched spasmodically every few seconds.

"What happened?" The sound of Sarco's and Uthiel's combined voices reverberated off the walls.

Sherman continued twitching silently with a blank expression on his face while Leeky explained. "The Shermanator here had a small error in judgment, that's all. Just need ta get him cleaned and fixed up a bit, then I'll take him back out. Don't worry about a thing. I've got it completely under control, and I'm pretty sure

Briar will forget about it before ya know it."

Lark jumped at Uthiel's roar.

"Briar? What has this to do with my wife?"

The gnome shuffled from one foot to another. "Now, now, Uthiel, ya know how she is. It was a simple misunderstanding really. I told the Shermanator here ta walk up ta the prettiest woman in the lunchroom, give her a solid smack on the arse, and grab a good cheek full. Ya and I both know women secretly like that kind of stuff. How was I ta know Sherman would think Briar was the prettiest? Not that she isn't, mind ya. Pretty as a picture, I always say."

Sir Uthiel's entire head turned red and Lark feared that at any moment now, the poor man would simply explode.

Then he did.

"You mean to tell me this…this halfling-wizard-wannabe grabbed my wife's arse?" Uthiel unsheathed his sword and advanced on a trembling Sherman.

Leeky jumped in front of the traumatized halfling and spread his arms wide. "Just a minute there, big fellow. If ya be wanting ta carve up someone I guess ya best start with me. Sherman didn't know she was your wife and, trust me, he got the worst end of it. The lunchroom's gonna need repairs, too."

Uthiel sighed, lowered his sword, and shook his head. "What happened, what is it going to cost me, and do I really want to know any of this?"

Lark tried unsuccessfully to follow the conversation. "I don't get it. What did Lady Dragonheart—I mean, Briar—do?"

Leeky grinned sheepishly. "Oh, that's right. Ya weren't here last year, were ya, lass? Ya don't know about our girl. Briar has a tendency ta set things on fire when she's surprised or upset. She channels, ya know, and with her protective force field up, sometimes the results are, shall we say, catastrophic.

"Uthiel himself spent more time without eyebrows last year than he did with them. And Ray, the headmistress's pet human...why, ya can't get him ta go anywhere near her. Singed every hair on his body clear off and near ta ruined his favorite toy, she did. Sweet child, though, really, she is. Still, I think it's best if the Shermanator and I stay clear of her for a while, just ta be safe."

Lark frowned. She and Sarco hadn't had even a moment alone to talk this morning, and now, with the addition of Leeky and Sherman along with the now everpresent Sir Uthiel Dragonheart, it looked as if they wouldn't be getting the chance anytime soon.

Sarco wasn't smiling either.

Leeky sighed. "I had such high hopes for the lad." He patted the halfling on the back. "Sherman. The next woman ya lay eyes on, I want ya ta walk right up ta her, grab a good-sized handful of arse, and tell her something ta make her laugh. Women like a man with a sense of humor. Just make sure it isn't Briar this time."

No sooner were the words out of Leeky's mouth than the office door opened once again and in sauntered Headmistress Seychelle with her human, Raynorel, in tow.

Everyone except Sherman froze. They tried to signal the halfling before he made a horrible mistake, but there was no helping it. As Headmistress Seychelle walked past Sherman, he sank both hands up to his knuckles into the black, silver-studded, leather material stretched tight against her rounded derriere and squeezed for all he was worth.

"I once took a class on joke telling so I know how to do this. Did you hear the one about the halfling with the small pecker? No? That's because there isn't one." Sherman doubled over in laughter.

Lark shook her head and covered her eyes with one hand, not wanting to watch Sherman destroy himself. She couldn't block out his voice, though.

"Do you have halfling in you? Want one?"

Lark couldn't help herself, she peeked.

Sherman grinned up at the tall, darkly beautiful high-elf, with her mass of midnight-black curls and blood-red lips, obvious adoration plastered across his face.

Headmistress Seychelle glared at Sherman. "Out of tens of thousands of sperm, yours was the fastest swimmer your father could produce? Really? How sad. Do you have a death wish, little man?"

Sherman's lips trembled, but Lark was proud of his courage as he leaned in close and sniffed the air at Seychelle's pussy level before opening his mouth once more. "You smell scrumptious. Reminds me of a fine, aged limburger."

Lark groaned and braced herself for Sherman's untimely demise.

Instead, Headmistress Seychelle surprised her. The sound of the woman's tinkling laughter brought the first smile of the day to Lark's lips, and she watched in fascination as the headmistress stretched out a long, red manicured nail and stroked the halfling's cheek.

"My, what do we have here? Adventurous, cheeky little fellow, aren't you? I may have underestimated you." Seychelle bent and ran her fingers from the tip of his nose, down his robe, and stopped just short of his groin. "You'll follow me back to my office when I'm done here. I have things to…show you. Do you understand me, little man?"

Sherman was grinning from ear to ear and bobbing his head up and down.

Lark didn't know what to say. Apparently, neither did Sarco, Uthiel, or Leeky as they stared at Sherman in awe.

It took Seychelle clearing her throat to get their attention. "Sarco, I came to inform you a reception dinner for your parents has been planned for this evening. It will be last minute, I'm afraid. I wasn't expecting them until next week. We'll manage, however.

"Dinner will be served right as the last rays of the day's sun fade so don't be late. Oh, and it's formal."

She turned toward Uthiel. "You may come along if you wish, Mr. Dragonheart. We could spend some time getting reacquainted after dinner if you like. Leave your wife behind, however. You know how she upsets poor Ray."

Ray chose that moment to add his own two cents' worth. "Ray loves cock."

Lark almost laughed as Uthiel twitched.

Turning back toward the door, Seychelle crooked her finger, motioned for Sherman to follow, and exited the room.

The halfling straightened his glasses, grinned at his friends, and pantomimed plucking two six-shooters from an invisible holster and firing them in the air. "I am a sexy man. All women love me. I am the

Shermanator." He swaggered out the door.

Sarco was the first to regain enough composure to speak. "How long do you think we should wait before we go rescue the poor little guy?"

Uthiel shook his head. "I'm not sure we should or even could rescue him. Once Seychelle gets a victim, umm, I mean a man in her office, she isn't likely to let anyone just walk in and take him away before she's done playing with him. Personally, I can't think of a better person to teach our young Mr. Limburger the Ninth the ropes, so to speak."

Lark shook her head in disbelief.

Leeky, though, didn't seem to realize anything was amiss. As a matter of fact, if anything, he looked like a proud new papa. "*Rescue* him? What the purple pustules on the bare, hairy arse of a red-headed dwarf are ya thinking, lads? Did we just witness the same scene? Headmistress Seychelle taking on a new conquest, let alone our little Sherman, is as rare an event as bath day at a troll's house. It's been years since she's taken a personal interest in anyone, other than our Briar last year, but she doesn't count 'cause she's a girl, and well, that was a mistake. What I wouldn't give ta be in our little Sherman's shoes right now."

Lark cringed, but Leeky didn't seem to notice.

The gnome wiped away a solitary tear and grinned at his companions. "I've taught Sherman Bobert Limburger the Ninth everything I possibly can, and today he's made me proud. I say it's time to celebrate. Let's grab the other two lasses, take the rest of the day off, and go on a picnic. I know the perfect spot."

Lark and Sarco locked gazes. Finally, a chance to be alone and talk.

\*\*\*\*

It took just a little more than half a turn of the hourglass to get everyone assembled, then Sarco, Lark, Uthiel, Briar, Leeky, and Laycee set off to the portal.

Lark lingered at the back of the group, hoping to get a few private words with Sarco. It didn't happen. Everyone was talking excitedly at the same time, and being heard over the likes of Laycee and Leeky was an impossibility.

"What the pulverized bunion on the big toe of a Barbarian backstabber were ya thinking, lass? Can't ya leave that…that…Tug thing at home once in a while? We don't need ta take him everywhere we go. Ya're slowing down the progress and lagging behind."

Laycee glared at Leeky and the female doll he had tucked firmly beneath his arm. "Oh, but we need Miss Bunny, I suppose? Why didn't ya leave *her*? At least Tug is useful. He has an umbrella attachment ta keep the sun off of us during our picnic so we don't burn. And his arse has a built in refrigeration device ta keep the drinks cool. What's Miss Bunny gonna do for us, mix the drinks? Oh, wait. She can't. She's plastic and her hands don't do anything, do they? If I'm not mistaken, it's just her orifices that are somewhat useful."

Sarco stepped between the gnomes. "I think everyone is a little on edge, worrying about the upcoming events. How about if we forget school, classes, and responsibilities today and just have a little fun? I know I could sure use some relaxation."

Although they grumbled about it, both Laycee and Leeky agreed, and the group continued toward the portal. They rounded a corner, and the sounds and sights coming from an open door stopped them all in their tracks. They were standing directly in front of Headmistress Seychelle's office.

Lark gasped and couldn't help but gape into the room, at its décor, its occupants, and the activity inside.

It was like no office she had ever seen before. The floor was covered completely with snow-white fur. The walls reminded her of a medieval castle made of cold, dark, damp stone with strange, torturous-looking devices hanging here and there. The ceiling gave the illusion of a night-time sky, complete with stars and full moon. Clouds moved across the horizon and a gentle breeze blew outward into the hallway.

Lark could only see two objects in the entire room. One was a huge, black, shiny throne, fitted with straps and shackles. The other appeared to be some kind of upright, stainless-steel rack, and attached to the rack in the most bizarre costume Lark had ever laid eyes on, was Sherman Bobert Limburger the Ninth.

The halfling was strapped spread-eagled onto the contraption, and beads of sweat pebbled his forehead. His mouth was covered with a thin piece of leather, and a shiny steel ball had been stuffed into it. Around his neck, he wore a silver- studded, spiked, black leather collar. Attached to the ring in the middle of it was a set of chains. The chains led to Sherman's hairy, now-pierced nipples.

The sound of Sarco's gulp and his, "That must've hurt," distracted Lark for only a moment. She closed her eyes, not wanting to see anymore, but morbid curiosity forced her to open her lids.

Sherman was also wearing a black leather thong below his poochy, hairy belly. Lark cringed. The bare cheeks of his pimply little ass were on display for the world to see. She felt sorry for him. "Isn't there something we can do? We can't leave him in there like that. We have to help him."

Headmistress Seychelle came into view and Lark shuddered. Black leather kissed and caressed her skin as her stiletto boots sank into the fur-covered floor. In her hand, she held a black, vicious-looking, silver-tipped whip, and the crack of it made not only Lark but also Laycee and Briar jump.

All three women held their breath.

Ray flounced to the base of the rack and dropped an orange, knobby, dildo-looking piece of rubber at Sherman's feet.

"Ray loves cock!" he yelled.

Sherman shook his head quickly back and forth. He looked toward his friends in the hall with desperation and just a touch of fear in his eyes.

The headmistress caressed his cheek with one long red nail before running it along his chin, down his neck, his chest, and circling the depths of his belly button before reversing her path.

The halfling grinned and a giggle escaped his gag.

The whip cracked once more and Sherman's eyes crossed. The shiny metal ball flew from his mouth and hit the wall across the room with a thud. His knees buckled inward and his toes curled.

The sound of Uthiel's voice startled Lark. "My God Draka, did she just flick him in the nuts with that thing?"

Sherman looked pleadingly toward the group with tears in his eyes. He slowly and very distinctly mouthed the words, "Help me."

Leeky cackled, "Naw, she didn't actually hit him *there*. She just got close enough to get his undivided attention."

The door slammed shut and the sound of bolts tumbling in place reverberated off the walls.

"Well, then, what the tainted tonsils of a four-fingered, one-legged, lopsided high-elf harlot would ya make of that, lads? Our little Sherman taken under the gentle wing of the most distinguished dominatrix of our time. One thing about it. Sherman Bobert Limburger the Ninth will come out of that room a real man."

Lark looked at Sarco, Leeky, and Uthiel as if seeing them for first time. They were all bobbing their heads, grinning from ear to ear, and patting each other on the back as if they had done something truly amazing.

"You can't mean to leave him in there with her, can you?"

Sarco and Uthiel chuckled as Leeky answered.

"Leave him. VoT, lass, we would've been willing ta pay Headmistress Seychelle for the service she's rendering Sherman for free. Don't be fretting so. The headmistress hasn't killed anyone...yet. At least that can be proved."

Leeky winked.

## Chapter Twelve

If ever a man warranted a relaxing afternoon at the beach, Sarco Sunwalker was that man. Lark lay on her side, watching his gloriously naked profile as he slept peacefully on the warm sand beneath the shade of a palm tree. For at least the hundredth time today, guilt for the predicament she'd helped put him in filled her.

Fewer than seven rotations of the sun and her family would be here. Only fourteen rotations of the sun and the ceremony to ask for Aryanna's hand in marriage would come to pass, and Sarco would be lost to her forever.

Lark stared at the glowing orb high in the sky and wondered how something so warm and inviting could herald the end of any chance for happiness she would ever have. But it did.

Time trickled away from her. What was she going to do?

She knew it would be impossible to convince her parents to choose her instead of her sister. They barely tolerated the fact she breathed. She couldn't ask Sarco to give up his place in the world for her, as they'd discussed. They had both come to the inevitable conclusion that before long, he wouldn't be able to live with himself if he did. She couldn't change the more than eight-hundred-year-old prophecy or what it meant to the people of Albrath. She certainly couldn't stand in the way of her own sister's future happiness, but she also couldn't stop loving Sarco Sunwalker any more than she could stop the grains of sand from sifting through the hourglass.

So, what could she do?

Lark closed her eyes and concentrated on what she did have control over, and that was her own self-will. She could step aside with grace even before the ceremony and walk away. She could leave Sarco and Aryanna in peace. She could hold her head high and smile, at least while others were watching. And lastly, she could politely disappear into the far reaches of Albrath.

But then, where would she go? She had no platt of her own, no marketable skills, and no connections.

A tear slipped from between her lashes, and Lark swiped it away. Remaining at the Academy after the ceremony was not an option. She could and would give up the only man she was capable of ever loving for the good of all, but there was no way she could stay and watch him become a husband to her sister.

There were no choices left.

Lark shuddered as a chill eneveloped her that even the sun couldn't chase away. Although it was the one place she'd hoped never to see again, she'd have to return home.

She felt the warmth of Sarco's breath upon her skin before she heard his voice.

"What's wrong, Wonderful? Why are you crying?"

Lark opened her eyes, and the loving concern reflecting back at her from Sarco's own dark-brown depths almost melted her reserve. How could she leave this man? She took a deep breath, and did the only thing she could think to do.

She lied.

"Nothing's wrong. As a matter of fact, nothing has ever been so right. The picnic was great, I was famished, and the food delicious. This beach is beautiful." Lark grasped and scooped a handful of fine, white sand and let it trickle through her fingers.

"I've never been to the Tambian Sea, so this is a treat for me." She flung out her arms and smiled. "And this secluded cove you found for us is amazing. Oh, and the feel of the warm sun and the gentle breeze is heaven. The best part, though, is having you all to myself, if only for a few hours. My tears are happy ones, Sarco, really they are. Thank you for bringing me here."

He smiled and Lark's heart twisted painfully.

"I like it when you're happy, Wonderful. How about if you roll over here and show your man just how happy you are?" Sarco wiggled his eyebrows and grinned lecherously. Lark laughed.

His skin was like molten steel beneath her fingertips. She gloried in the sharp intake of his breath as, ever so slowly, she allowed a single finger to wander its way from the tip of one of his pebble-hard nipples, downward, sweeping across each rib to swirl in and out of the indentation in his sculptured abdomen, before finally coming to rest on the very tip of his expanding cock.

His barely restrained control, and the sound of his harsh breath coming hard and deep, brought a smile to Lark's face.

"Like that?" She purred as she ran her fingers up and down the length of his shaft.

His response was almost a growl as he lifted toward her touch. "Oh, I like."

Lark giggled. "Then you'll really enjoy this."

She rose and covered him with her body, sliding down until her chin was almost even with the tip of his cock as she nestled it snugly between her breasts. She rocked her body up and down, slowly, methodically, with precision and forethought. With every upstroke, her breasts caressed and cradled his cock, and on the stroke downward, she flicked out her tongue and tasted the tip. Just enough to tease, to torment, and to tantalize. He quivered, and she gloried in her power.

Lark laid her face against the warm skin of his taut belly and breathed in the essence of the man. Tears stung her eyes, and a lump formed in her throat as she fought to memorize the cadence of his heartbeat, the textures of his skin, the plains and valleys of muscle and sinew, all the things that made Sarco Sunwalker uniquely himself. How could she give this man up? How could she not?

She sat, straddled him, and gazed into the chocolate warmth of his eyes, trying with all her heart to convey the feelings her tongue refused to speak. She couldn't say those words to him anymore. It wasn't her rightful place. How unfair would it be to continue declaring a love that was doomed before it had a chance to blossom? No, she couldn't say what her heart was screaming for her to proclaim, but with time running out, this might possibly be the last chance she would ever have to show this man how much she loved him. To tell him goodbye.

With painstakingly slow precision, Lark rose, guided Sarco's rock-hard cock to her pussy, and eased down the length of it, completely sheathing his life force deep within her body. She threw back her head and closed her eyes as tiny swirls of red-hot heat skittered throughout her core and exploded in a tempo matching the rhythm of their joining.

Lark opened her eyes and smiled at the beautiful man beneath her. Locking gazes and fingers, she slowly slid up and down the velvet shaft. He tried to speed the cadence, but she simply shook her head and he acquiesced.

With each glide up his magnificent cock, Lark arched her back and gloried in the erratic beat of blood coursing through his veins and the quivering hot flesh within her. And with each plunge back down, she took the time to look, really look at the man beneath her and relegate to memory another detail.

The fine crinkle lines around his eyes, the width of his brow, the crisp points of his high-elf ears, and the flare of his nostrils, the rich fullness of his lips, even the strength in the line of his jaw. Every nuance was a precious piece of the whole that made up the man Sarco Sunwalker.

Lark lifted her face toward the heavens as clouds rolled in and partially obscured the sun. A fine mist of rain moistened her cheeks like tears. The wind ebbed in cadence with the sea, and Lark realized the weather today was just as confused and uncertain as she. Strangely, it comforted her. She embraced it.

The sound of waves crashing close by became the beat of her heart as the sea breeze swirling around them became her breath. The lilting songs of birds carried upon the winds were a melody to her soul.

The warmth of the sun mixed with the coolness of

the misty rain upon their skin and fused her to Sarco, joining them as one. Nothing else existed in this, their world—in this, their moment in time.

She closed her eyes and rode him while holding tightly onto the safe anchor of his fingers intertwined with hers. She lost herself in the wonder of the miracle she knew Sarco Sunwalker to be. With every movement and gesture, her body whispered, *I love you, Sarco,* though not one word escaped her lips.

The pressure built, at first no more than a deep throbbing in her pussy that, before long, couldn't be ignored. Lark tried to stave off her orgasm, not wanting this time with him to end, not ready for this part of her life to be over.

When the first wave of electrifying spasms shook her, she cried out. A second later, the feel of hot seed flowing and hard flesh convulsing deep within told her Sarco had achieved his pinnacle of pleasure also. The world was perfect, and she was where she belonged.

Without warning, tears fell. Hot and salty, they coursed silently down her cheeks. With a sob wrenched deep from her soul, Lark forced herself to open her eyes and look at Sarco, the man she loved with every fiber of her being. How could the greatest joy and pleasure she had ever experienced and the greatest sorrow and pain she would ever have to live with be one and the same?

"What's wrong, Wonderful? Please tell me."

The look of concern on Sarco's face brought out the protectiveness in her. She didn't want him to know pain, especially her own. She wouldn't lie to him again, but she knew she didn't have to tell him the whole truth either. "That was the most amazing lovemaking I've ever experienced. It was perfect. You were perfect.

Promise me, Sarco, no matter how old we grow or how far away we may be from one another, you'll never forget this day."

Sarco smiled and was about to respond when a completely different sound caught both of their attentions.

"What the blue-painted farts of a backwards-walking troll were ya thinking, lass? Ya should've known better than ta put that untrustworthy scoundrel, Tug, anywhere near my sweet little Miss Bunny. Now look what's happened. He's trying ta run off with her."

Sarco and Lark scampered to their feet, grabbed their clothing, and looked toward the sound of Leeky's winded voice and the waves crashing onto the beach.

A high-pitched screech rent the air. "Sweet little Miss Bunny? It's that harlot's fault in the first place, I tell ya! I've seen the way she looks at my poor innocent Tug when ya're not watching. Just wait 'til I get my hands on ya evil Miss Bunny, and I'll show ya what a blue-painted fart really looks like."

About ten feet offshore, something pink bobbed up and down in the water with a bright green and red stripped umbrella sticking out of it. Sarco and Lark shaded their eyes from the glare of the sun and looked harder. There was Tug, stretched out on his back with an umbrella sticking up where any remotely normal male—who wasn't plastic—would've had a cock, and Miss Bunny appeared to be straddling him. The pair were completely naked, and Lark could swear they were smiling even bigger than usual.

The sight on the beach was more disturbing than the one in the water. There stood the two naked-as-the-day-they-were-born, sunburned gnomes with sand-covered asses and angry faces, yelling and pointing at each other and the blow-up dolls.

Sarco cleared his throat. "I suppose we should go help them recover their, umm, dolls before they get themselves drowned or kill each other."

Lark nodded and giggled. "It would be the honorable thing to do."

They looked at each other and could contain their mirth no longer. Together they fell to the sand in a tangle of arm and legs as they burst into a fit of laughter.

Sarco encircled Lark within his arms. "I have another idea, Wonderful. Instead of helping gnomes fish dolls out of the ocean, let's take a quick trip to my home. It's still early afternoon. We can take the portal and easily be back before Seychelle's dinner party tonight. Landis is an amazing place, and I really need to speak with Uncle Arizon before the Yulemass is upon us and it's too late. If anyone knows of a way to get around the dictates of the prophecy, it would be the man who spoke the words in the first place."

****

Landis was so much more than she could've imagined. Lark marveled at the view all around and below them. They were standing just outside the portal, high up on the side of a mountain, and the unimpeded panorama was breathtaking.

A cascading, blue waterfall split the mountain in half, thundering into a sparkling, rushing river running through a lush, green valley. The air smelled of jasmine and was filled with the lilting songs of birds. The lights of homes and businesses dotted the mountainside, and from her high perch, Lark could see movement within many of them.

An intricate roadway of swinging bridges linked everything together, and a cobblestone path led ever downward toward a grand-looking castle with high towers, many balconies, and cultured gardens.

"Oh, Sarco, what a beautiful, magical place your homeland is."

The feel of Sarco's arms tightening about her and the smile he sent her way had Lark's heart soaring. "I'm glad you like my home, Wonderful. It's my fondest wish that someday it'll be your home also."

The warmth of his hand in hers as he led her down the path brought a sense of oneness. No matter what his uncle might say this day, no matter what the future may hold, her heart would now and forever belong to Sarco Sunwalker. No prophecy could ever change that.

They stopped just inside a courtyard, and Sarco led Lark to a small enclosed garden, complete with a tall, bubbling fountain in the very center. Roses of every color of the rainbow bloomed in well-kept beds and the air was filled with their fragrance. A feeling of contentment settled over Lark.

"Would you mind waiting for me here, Wonderful? Next time, I'll introduce you to Uncle Arizon, I promise. For today, though, I think I should speak to him privately. I shouldn't be long."

Lark smiled and nodded as she took a seat on a nearby bench. "Take all the time you need. I could stay here forever."

\*\*\*\*

"Why does it have to be me? Why does it have to be now? Why does it have to be Aryanna who I marry? Tell me again, make me understand, Uncle." Sarco ran his fingers through his hair in frustration. Even after a full turning of the hourglass, he still didn't know any more than when he'd first arrived.

He paced back and forth before his great-uncle, the High-Elf Arizon Windstrider, who stood silently staring off into space as if he were no longer aware of his nephew's presence.

Just when Sarco's irritation level attained its peak, Arizon spoke. "I didn't realize the ramifications of the prophecy at first. I had no idea the impact it would have. It stopped a war, you know? Right then and there, they laid down their weapons—elves, barbarian, and humans alike. Those words came directly from God Draka's mouth himself, even though it was I who uttered them. Words are powerful things, nephew. Once spoken, they can never be taken back."

Arizon hung his head, as grains of sand silently filtered through the hourglass.

Finally, the old man looked up and stared at Sarco with an unfaltering gaze. "Why does it have to be you, you ask? That's simple enough to answer but probably not what you'll wish to hear. It can only be you, Sarco. The prophecy clearly states the firstborn heir of the elves must marry a princess of barbarian-human descent. Even if you wanted to abdicate your Lordship for this woman you've been ranting on about for the last turn of the hourglass, your brother could not take your place. He can never be firstborn. That is, of course, unless your life comes to an untimely end. Only upon your death can your bother step into your rightful role."

Sarco sighed, and even the very beating of his heart became painful.

Arizon Windstrider slowly made his way to a bench and sat. His long white beard hung nearly to the ground and the consequences of living almost nine hundred years showed on his weathered face. "Why does it have to be now, you wonder? Because the time is upon us and the stars are aligned. The three moons of Albrath will soon all be in full phase for the first time in centuries. Who knows when that will happen again?"

Sarco ran his fingers through his hair. "But, but…"

High-Elf Wizard Arizon Windstrider held up a hand. "What has been set in motion will stay in motion until it connects with an unmovable object. That is a universal law, not mine, and so is unchangeable by man or magic. The fable of Castle Kuropkat was solved, and with your help, I might add. That single incident set into motion the need for the second part of the prophecy to be fulfilled by the rotation of the next triple full-moon phase."

"But why does it *have* to be Aryanna I marry? She isn't the only barbarian-human princess," Sarco bellowed.

It was as if Arizon hadn't even heard him.

"Peace came to Albrath with the first part of the prophecy being satisfied, and continued peace depends on the second part being seen to its conclusion in a timely manner."

Arizon closed his eyes and was silent for long moments. Sarco was afraid the old man had fallen asleep until, with a deep gasping breath, the wizard continued. "Why does it have to be Princess Aryanna you marry? For no other reason than she is who her parents have chosen. It's their right by Barbarian law to choose and you must not go against their wishes. Keep in mind what is truly important here, Sarco, and that is the fulfillment of the prophecy and maintaining peace throughout the land. Your people are counting on you. Don't worry so about the wife part. Take it from me, I've lived a very long time, and after awhile, one woman is much like any another."

Sarco shuddered.

Arizon looked thoughtful a moment. "You've never known war, nephew, and I hope you never do. It's an ugly, cruel thing. Women wailing for their lost husbands. Children weeping for their dead fathers. The last mournful cries of a dying dragon. Blood and pain, atrocities beyond your imagination. It's always amazed me what man is capable of doing to man. When God Draka came to me in that long-ago dream and gave me the prophecy to speak, he also gave me a warning. The races must be joined. If the prophecy is not fulfilled, a war such as no man's eyes have ever seen will come to pass. The streets will run red with the blood of men and dragon alike 'til the sins of their ancestors are washed away from the land."

Sarco hung his head.

"From the time you were old enough to hear and comprehend our ways, you've been told this day might come. You've always known you're the heir and upon your shoulders the fulfillment of the prophecy might come to rest. Don't allow doubts of yourself or frivolous feelings for a female to stand in the way of what you know must be done. It's your duty, Sarco, your burden to bear, and the continued well-being of your people depends upon it. Have I made myself clear enough this time, nephew? Have you any more questions? Did I succeed in helping you understand?"

Sarco nodded. "I have no further questions, Uncle. I'll do what I must. My duty is clear. You've more than succeeded in your explanation. I now completely understand."

He hung his head in defeat.

\*\*\*\*

"Mmm...you smell more tempting than warm ambrosia, Ary, my sweet, and I'm ready for a snack before this boring dinner party. How about if we slip away somewhere for a quick little nibble while we have the time?"

A satin-clad slipper stomped on his foot, and Cyrrick jumped backwards. "What was that for?"

Princess Aryanna's snapping violet eyes glared holes right through him and he wished he hadn't asked.

"*What was that for?* What was that for!" she hissed. "Am I really that easy to forget? Where were you all morning while I was left waiting alone in your room? After all, it was you who set up the rendezvous with me, remember? Then, today you simply forget I exist? Or were all those sweet words and promises you were whispering in my ear yesterday a figment of my overactive imagination?"

Cyrrick looked around Headmistress Seychelle's office-now-banquet-room to make sure they weren't causing a scene. Luckily, they were the first guests to arrive and the only other people milling about were those still doing setup. He gave a sigh of relief. The last thing any of them needed at this point was to be embroiled in a scandal. The culmination of all their preparations was too close for stupid mistakes now.

He ran his fingers through his hair and took a deep, calming breath. "I take it you didn't get my message then? I left you a note, Ary. I personally watched your gnome governess tuck it into one of the pockets of that silly doll's pants. You know, the one she's always carrying around with her? And she swore she would give it to you the moment she saw you today."

Aryanna looked like a petulant little child playing dress-up, and Cyrrick had to restrain the smile he almost let show, knowing the sight of it would simply make her angrier.

"But I haven't seen Laycee today, or even Lark for that matter. The whole world has deserted me."

Instead of grinning, Cyrrick took her gently by the arm and led her into the shadows of the room, away from curious eyes. He wrapped his arms loosely around her middle, with her back snuggly warm against his chest. Resting his chin on the top of her head, he finally gave in to his urge to smile.

She was beyond beautiful tonight. Her long, sun-kissed curls hung about her shoulders like a shawl spun of the finest gold. They accented perfectly her rose-tinted cheeks and cotton-candy-pink kissable lips. Her form-fitting gown of deep-red velvet clung to every luscious curve like a caress. For a moment, Cyrrick had trouble remembering what they had been discussing.

"Ahh, Ary, how I do love your flare for the dramatic. No one has deserted you, my love. I'm not sure where Laycee and Lark disappeared to, but as for myself, I was roped into showing my parents around the Academy and couldn't slip away. Sarco was supposed to do that duty himself, but he seems to have disappeared on us as well. And since wherever Sarco is, you'll probably find Lark, we should be happy instead of grumpy about the situation. Don't you think?"

Cyrrick felt Aryanna's sigh as if it were his own.

"I suppose you're right. It's just the closer it gets to the ceremony, the more nervous I'm getting. So much is riding on the outcome. I could end up married to your brother instead of you and having my baby sister despise me for the rest of my life if things don't go as planned."

Aryanna paused and shuddered. A mournful sob racked her delicate frame. Cyrrick hugged her closer.

"She cried half the night, you know. Lark, that is. I have no idea what happened yesterday, but it must have been very traumatic and it somehow involved Sarco and your parents because I heard her whisper their names over and over between sobs. This has to end soon, Cyrrick. I simply can't take it much longer."

Aryanna turned in Cyrrick's arms and laid her cheek against his chest as she wrapped her arms around his waist.

"I didn't get a wink of sleep last night, either, and I'm sure I have dark smudges under my eyes and look simply dreadful. Lark blames me for this mess, even if subconsciously, I know she does. And she's in her right to do so. It's my fault we're all in this situation. If I hadn't gone and allowed myself to fall in love with you, life would've been so much simpler. But I did, and I wouldn't change that for anything in the world now."

Aryanna shuddered again, and Cyrrick did his best to envelope her in his warmth.

"Do you know what she did last night? She made it rain in my room. Just in my room, directly over my bed, and nowhere else. I don't think Lark was even aware of it. The harder she cried, the more it rained. I had to sleep in the hallway on a settee all crunched up into a tight little ball. It was horribly uncomfortable, and I kept waiting for lightning to strike me dead. I'd probably deserve it if it had."

Her tears fell faster and faster. He held her tightly and let her continue to vent.

"And your parents, my future in-laws, what are they going to think about me if they ever find out our role in all this? I'm sure they're wonderful people, Cyrrick. I'd hate to see disapproval or disappointment on their faces every time they look my way…for what?…the next hundred years or so? Oh, wait. High-elves live much longer than humans or barbarians. Make that only-God-Draka-knows-how-long, and probably even well into the afterlife."

Cyrrick rocked her slowly back and worth as if she were a small child. All the while trying to organize his thoughts before he spoke. "Let's try and take this one day at a time, shall we, Ary? Tonight, let's just get through dinner then tomorrow we'll worry about Lark, Sarco, my parents, and the next hundred years or so. Don't even think of Lord Tylindius and Lady Jillian Sunwalker as your in-laws right now. Tonight they're just two ordinary people you're socializing with at a dinner party."

"You, my pretty princess, are an expert at socializing." He leaned over and kissed the top of her head. "You know how to win people over with your charm and that beautiful smile of yours. Those qualities are bonus reasons you'll make the perfect diplomat's wife. When this is all said and done, everyone will realize just how perfect and giving you truly are."

Cyrrick tweaked her nose playfully and planted a quick kiss on the tip of it. "My parents will love you,

Ary. Not quite as much as I do, but they'll love you. Trust me, you'll see. This will all be resolved soon, and, in the end, everything will work out as it's meant to be. I believe that with all my heart. I have to. Anything less is unacceptable."

She nodded against his chest, but he could feel her reservations and fears as strongly as if they were tangible. He wanted desperately to alleviate those fears, to drive them away, to see her carefree smile once more. Her next words reminded him that her fears were his also and had a very real basis.

"Right now it feels like nothing will ever be resolved, and I have no choice but to think of Lord Tylindius and Lady Jillian as my future in-laws, Cyrrick. It may not yet be decided which Sunwalker son I'm going to end up married to when this disaster is all said and done, but there's no doubt whatsoever who my in-laws are going to be."

Ary's voice broke, and her tears fell once more.

Cyrrick did what was in his power to do. He lifted her face to his own and kissed her soundly—not caring who in Albrath might see.

## Chapter Thirteen

If ever a man was born to be a lord, Sarco Sunwalker was that man. He was resplendent tonight in his royal-purple robes and winning smile. Only his eyes held a hint of telltale sadness when he glanced her way. Lark wished with all her heart she could kiss away his worries. She knew that wasn't possible, though. It wasn't her place or right.

And Aryanna, standing regally at his side. How could one woman be so beautiful? Lark was proud of her sister, even if she did envy her the man who would soon be her husband. If anyone deserved to be happy, Aryanna did. She'd always had a kind heart, even when she hid it under her princess façade.

And what a façade that was. From the top of her golden curls all the way to the tips of her jewel-encased shoes, she was completely without flaw. She and Sarco were the perfect pair.

If only Sarco's Uncle Arizon could've offered them even a grain of hope. He hadn't, and the gloom that enveloped both of them on the trip back from Landis was almost more then she could bear. They'd talked and made decisions. They'd accepted their fate, but that didn't prevent the tears from threatening to fall.

Lark felt ill.

Trying her best to look at anything other than Sarco and Aryanna, she glanced around the room. Lark almost didn't recognize the office. Mistress Seychelle had certainly outdone herself tonight.

The white fur covering the floor was the only thing that remained the same. Gone was the large throne with its straps and the rack poor Sherman had been leashed to mere hours before. In their places were long, elegant tables set with shimmering china and sparkling crystal.

Even the walls were different. No longer did they resemble a dungeon. Now they gleamed as white as the fur floor and were ensconced with glittering, golden lights flickering like fireflies.

Above Lark's head, stars shone in a cloudless night sky. A gentle, flower-fragrant breeze warmed her skin.

She scooted farther into the corner and braced her back against the wall, not wanting to bring attention to herself. She knew she was drab and colorless compared to the other guests at the party, and especially compared to her sister.

Wearing the same plain white gown she'd worn the night of the Carnalval ball hadn't really been planned. They'd gotten back so late from Landis, she'd simply grabbed the first thing available in her closet.

Now, however, Lark was grateful she blended into the background. Tylindius and Jillian Sunwalker looked totally besotted with their new daughter-in-law-to-be. Lark didn't wish to remind any of them she existed.

"Champagne, Miss Hammerstrike?"

The sound of the familiar voice brought a smile to Lark's face. The sight of the halfling standing before her with a gold-rimmed fluted goblet in his stubby hand had Lark's mouth dropping open and her eyes widening. She quickly schooled her countenance. Sherman Bobert Limburger the Ninth truly was a changed man. He positively glowed.

What was it about putting a man, any man, even a halfling, into formal attire that totally changed how they were perceived? The midnight-black tux with tails fit Sherman as if it had been tailored with him and only him in mind. The crisp white shirt beneath it gave testimony to the fact that he was in better shape than Lark had first thought.

Though his mud-brown hair still stood in random, unruly, singed tufts for the most part, it had been slicked into somewhat of an orderly fashion, and his chubby cheeks sparkled with health and happiness. The only disturbing thing about him was the spiked collar he still wore about his thick neck, like a cherished trophy. And his hairy feet were conspicuously bare.

"Miss Hammerstrike? Lark?"

Rudely appalled at the realization she had been staring, heat crept up her cheeks. Holding out her hand, she accepted the goblet the halfling offered. "Thank you, Sherman. It's good to see a friendly face, and, umm, you appear to be just fine. So, everything went…well with the headmistress, I take it?"

Lark had never seen eyes the color of powdered cocoa turn to melted chocolate so quickly, but she did now as Sherman's normally dull brown irises lit and became pools of warm, liquid excitement.

"Oh, I'd say it went much better than well, Miss Hammerstrike. It was the best class I've ever taken in my entire life. *My Mistress…*" Sherman leaned in closer toward Lark and whispered, "That's what Headmistress Seychelle insists I call her. Anyway, My Mistress is a most amazing woman. She showed and taught me things I've never seen or done before. Why, what that woman can do with a—"

Sherman hesitated and his cheeks pinkened. "Well, it doesn't matter what she can do. What matters is she is extremely talented. It was an experience of a lifetime."

Lark didn't have a clue how to respond. "That's nice, Sherman."

The very person they'd just been discussing chose that moment to make her debut in typical Headmistress Seychelle flare. With trumpets blaring and her signature, form-fitting black leather swishing, the headmistress didn't take a backseat to anyone. She was amazing, and Lark stared, her mouth agape. From the top of the headmistress's raven mane of curls to the tips of her stiletto boots, she was magnificent.

Even the strange little man hopping along on the end of a thin gold leash attached daintily to the headmistress's wrist couldn't distract from the beauty of his owner.

Until he opened his mouth. "Ray loves cock," he screeched.

Lark shook her head, and embarrassment for the beautiful woman filled her as all eyes turned toward Ray. Headmistress Seychelle, however, didn't seem the least perturbed by the outburst. She leaned toward Ray and patted him lovingly on the head.

"Not right now, pet. Mistress is busy. If you're a good boy, mistress will give you cock later."

Seychelle continued to move through the crowd.

Ray wasn't having any of it. He threw himself to the floor and flailed his arms and legs about. "Ray loves cock. Ray loves cock. *Ray. Loves. Cock.*"

Lark sought Sarco with her gaze and was surprised at the humor she saw gleaming back at her. The man was completely enjoying the spectacle. His parents weren't, though. Their high-elf complexions had gone even paler than normal, and they gasped like fish attempting to breathe out of water.

Aryanna had turned a scarlet red to match her dress and frantically fanned a faint-looking Lady Sunwalker while talking over Ray's yelling, apparently, in hopes of drowning out his tantrum. It wasn't working.

"Ray loves cock. Ray loves cock. Ray lovesss—"

The door burst open and in strolled Uthiel Dragonheart with his wife Briar on his arm. All eyes turned, even Ray's. With a yelp, the strange little man leapt from the floor, broke the thin gold chain in his haste, and fled from the room without a backward glance.

Headmistress Seychelle now looked perturbed. She motioned for a servant to follow Ray before turning back to her guests.

Overhead, bells tinkled to silence everyone so the headmistress could address the crowd. "My dear guests, it is a pleasure to have with us this evening true royals of the realm. Join me in welcoming the great Lord of the Elves and ruler of Landis, Tylindius Sunwalker, and his lovely wife, Lady Jillian."

Applause reverberated off the walls.

"Please take your seats and enjoy the feast," the headmistress graciously nodded.

Lark chose the end seat of the table farthest from the guests of honor, not wanting to bring attention to herself and really not wishing to cause herself unnecessary pain by watching Sarco and Aryanna together. She smiled as Sir Uthiel and his Lady Briar chose seats close by, glad that at least she would have someone she knew to chat with.

She turned toward the beautiful half-elf who taught her Channeling class, her curiosity overcoming her natural propensity for proper etiquette. "I've heard just sketchy bits and pieces, Lady Dragonheart, but I'm dying to know why Ray is terrified of you? If you don't mind me asking?"

With her slightly pointed ears, waist-length auburn hair and laughing, forest-green eyes, the young woman glowed as a pink blush crept up her cheeks. At the sound of Uthiel's chuckle, she stuck her tongue out at him. "Please, call me Briar. About Ray, well, it was simply a horrible accident."

Uthiel coughed and it sounded like he was choking. Lark laughed when she realized Briar kicked him under the table.

"It was an accident, and you well know it, Uthiel Dragonheart!" Briar scowled at her husband, who simply shook his head and winked at Lark. Briar ignored him and continued her story. "It happened when I was taking my finals last year. I didn't mean to cause an explosion or blow anything up. I wasn't aware I was even channeling at first." Briar paused for a moment. "That probably sounds silly since I am the channeling instructor, but, at first, I had no idea that drawing energy through yourself and projecting it outward was channeling. It had always been just a normal part of who I am. I thought everyone did it. Anyway, umm, Ray got in the way of a channeling mishap and ended up with no hair anywhere on his body and, umm, he was kinda singed around the edges.

"From what I've been told, it took a few days to locate Ray, and the headmistress was at her wit's end by the time they did find him. I don't think he or Headmistress Seychelle has forgiven me for my teensy mistake. She never says anything out of the way or cruel, of course. She simply keeps her distance and makes sure Ray is nowhere near if I'm around. So now I try to stay away from them both, if I can manage it. I don't wish to make anyone uncomfortable—even Ray—if at all possible. It's for the best, I do believe."

Briar smiled, and nodded, adding, "Yes, that pretty much sums it up. By the way, I'm told he wasn't always the way you see him now, you know. Ray, that is."

Lark was stunned. "Really? What happened to him?"

"It was before I came to the Academy, so I never knew Ray when he was normal. Headmistress Seychelle herself told us Ray was once her assistant. And not just any assistant but a brilliant one. Then she loaned him out to High Mystic Purrell to help with an editing job, and what you see today is what she got back. I hope you never have the displeasure of meeting High Mystic Purrell, Lark. He's…scary."

Briar shuddered as she stared off into space. Uthiel gave her shoulder a quick squeeze, and she must have shrugged off the unpleasant memory, She caught Lark's eye again and chuckled. "Ray, though, is harmless. When he yells what he yells, all he actually wants to do is play fetch with his horrid dildo. I feel kinda sorry for the poor little guy."

A flurry of movement around the table distracted Lark as servants bearing food arrived. She folded her arms across her lap to give them better access to her place setting. A sense of contentment settled into her being. With Briar and Uthiel for company, it appeared dinner wasn't going to be such a horrid event after all.

The first course—a creamy white soup with chunks of savory vegetables—was delivered.

Lark was about to ask another question of Briar when the door suddenly flew open and Lark glanced up.

Her fragile feeling of contentment evaporated in an instant.

Even though she had known her family was scheduled to arrive sometime within the next week, the sight of her mother's haughty, cold eyes and the sound of her venom-laced voice were startling and unexpected—and Lark could have done without them for the rest of her life.

"Seychelle, dear old friend, I certainly hope we haven't arrived too late for what looks to me suspiciously like an engagement party."

Her mother sauntered across the room, her hips swaying, her golden curls bobbing to and fro, and a look of pure malice adorning her picture-perfect complexion. Lark gulped and dropped her gaze, wishing she could as easily block out the sound of the woman as she could the sight. She couldn't, though; Queen Allanna had never in her life known when to keep quiet.

"It seems our staff must have misplaced our invitations—if they were even sent," the queen sniffed. "If that is indeed what transpired, trust me, the staff will be decisively dealt with. Unless, of course, that isn't the case at all…? Which means it's simply a matter of you playing favorites, since the groom's parents are high-elves like yourself."

Her voice rose an octave. "You wouldn't do that,

now, would you, old friend?"

Silverware clattered as it dropped from stunned fingers of people seated at the tables around the now completely silent room.

*Oh Lord Draka*, Lark moaned. *Everyone is horrified, and I don't blame them.* Although she was on the opposite side of the room, she felt the vibrations of Headmistress Seychelle's chair being suddenly pushed back, then teetering before it toppled to the floor with a resounding crash.

Lark held her breath.

Seychelle, in her haste to jump to attention, got a heel caught in the hem of her leather garment and stumbled forward, but the headmistress recovered nicely. Lark sighed with relief. She caught herself inwardly cheering as Seychelle managed to make her near-disaster seem part of the fluid movement of announcing her newest guests.

"Queen Allanna, and King Alfred Hammerstrike! Oh, my goodness, what a wonderful surprise. This is truly an honor. I'd never plan an engagement party without the bride's parents. You should know that. This is simply a welcome dinner for the Sunwalkers, and now for your family also, of course." Headmistress Seychelle spread her arms wide. "Look, everyone, Princess Aryanna's parents have arrived…and earlier than expected. What a treat."

With a huff and her nose held high, Queen Allanna Zanlynn Calista Hammerstrike, with the king in tow, whisked past Lark on her way to the table of honor without a passing glance for her youngest daughter. *Bless the Lord Draka for small favors.*

But the lump that had been forming in the pit of

Lark's stomach since the moment she left Landis now doubled in size when the remainder of her family didn't follow suit, but actually stopped at her chair. One by one, they greeted and hugged her—first her brother, Adan, then the twins, Ally and Audrey.

At least her siblings were starting to move on after saying hello, and for a moment, Lark thought she'd get away with remaining in her little corner of the room.

Then she saw Grandmother Ava and knew it was a hopeless cause.

"Lark, you look pale, child. You haven't been eating well and you've been studying too hard as usual, haven't you?" The old woman held up a weathered hand as Lark opened her mouth to respond. "Don't even think of denying it. A grandmother knows these things. Come along now and sit with the family."

Somewhere off in the distance, thunder rumbled.

Knowing it wasn't a request but an order, Lark didn't balk. And considering it came from her grandmother, she quickly gave her apologies to Uthiel and Briar, then followed as bidden.

She had no sooner taken her seat and her first bite of food from the plate placed in front of her, when her mother let her know that even if she hadn't formally acknowledged her, she was acutely aware of her presence.

"Must you always gulp your food like a commoner, Lark? It's one thing to do it at home, but I can hear you chewing all the way down here. And do sit up straight. At least try to act like the princess you were born to be. I swear, you are a constant embarrassment."

Lark tried to swallow her bite of partially chewed Alarian Mountain Beefalo, but even water wouldn't make it go down.

*How can someone so beautiful on the outside be so ugly where it really counts?* From the tips of her golden curls done up in a stylish fashion, to her petite figure in a stunning gown of crystalline white, the queen was perfection to gaze upon. It had always been amazing to Lark what evil a pretty shell could hide.

Lark's face burned with increasing heat. Her eyes watered with unshed tears, and her chest constricted to the point where breathing became painful. She couldn't bring herself to look at her mother, and she certainly couldn't look at Sarco, who sat nearby with Aryanna. The last thing she wanted to see in his eyes was the pity she was sure was there.

A new voice made her wish for a hole to open up and swallow her. "Personally, I like to see a girl with a good appetite. These days, most eat like birds. Much too thin, if you ask me."

Lady Jillian Sunwalker's attempt to defend her was even worse than her own mother's hatefulness. Hatefulness she could deal with, hatefulness she was used to.

Pity was another story.

But Lady Sunwalker wasn't done yet. "A nice pair of hips can be an asset, especially for carrying grandchildren. You might wish to keep that in mind."

Finally swallowing the now-tasteless morsel, Lark held her head high, raised her gaze, and scanned the table. One by one, the guests looked away. Even her own siblings were embarrassed for her.

Except for Grandmother Ava, who glared at her own daughter and wasn't looking in Lark's direction.

Jillian and Sarco Sunwalker, though, they were

both looking straight at her. And they had identical expressions in their eyes. It wasn't pity—it was acceptance! Lark could have kissed them both.

Her father's deep baritone voice broke the silence. "Allanna, my dear, let the child eat in peace. This is a celebration, after all."

Lark's mother glared at her husband, and her words slithered off her tongue. "Don't be such a barbarian, Alfred. You've always had a soft spot for the one *flaw* in our otherwise perfect family. Manners and etiquette may mean nothing to you, but as for myself, I'm much more gently bred and demand nothing less than perfection from our children. Someone has to uphold the standards of our station."

King Alfred Zavier Caden Hammerstrike patted his wife's hand before picking up his fork. "I suppose you know best, dear."

Tears burned the corners of Lark's eyes.

She caught Sarco's eye, and he smiled that mischievous smile she so loved. A familiar warmth seeped into her mind.

"*I don't like your mother, Wonderful. How much do you want to bet she has that same sour expression on her face when your father gets up the nerve to actually ask her for sex? I'd wager she even critiques the poor fellow's performance in bed. 'To the right...no, your other right, barbarian! Faster, faster— no, slower. Oh, just get off of me and forget it.'*"

Lark covered her mouth with both hands, trying her best to suppress a laugh. Her face burned even hotter, knowing none of the other people at the table were privy to what Sarco had just thought. They probably thought she was not only a glutton and a mistake, but an idiot to boot.

"*Stop it. You're going to get me in so much trouble.*"

His slow, lazy smile made her heart thump wildly.

A moment later, the sound of her mother's voice once more made her heart want to stop. "And I can assure you, Lady Sunwalker, there'll be no grandchildren from that one. I'll see to that. Every family has their burdens to bear, and Lark is ours. As a matter of fact, if she continues to eat the way she does, I won't need to worry about it. No man would want her."

Queen Allanna Hammerstrike turned her poisonous gaze upon Lark once more. "Our trunks still need to be unpacked. We brought few servants with us this trip so I expect you to help. You appear full enough to me. Be about your duty to your family."

Sarco rose, anger flashing in his eyes. Lark stopped him with a thought.

"*No. What she wants is to hurt me. I won't give her the satisfaction that she has. She's my mother. Let me handle it, please.*"

With all the grace and dignity of a princess, Lark calmly rose. She would take no more this day. "It seems I've lost my appetite after all, and I'd be more than glad to oversee our servants, Mother."

She glanced around the table, making eye contact with each person and smiling warmly. "Please excuse me."

She then curtsied, straightened her shoulders, lifted her head high, and walked away. After few steps, Lark paused and looked back at her mother.

"Oh, by the way, Mother, I really like your hair. I especially love the intricate curls and combs. It must've taken your maid hours," she said, then glanced skyward. "A hat would've probably been more advantageous, though. It looks like it may rain."

An ominous gray cloud formed directly over Queen Allanna's head. "You wouldn't dare," she hissed.

Lark smiled. "Wouldn't I?"

Fat raindrops began slowly falling then picked up speed as they pelted the top of the queen's head and rolled down her face, then finally splashed onto the table.

The queen sputtered, "You, you will p-pay for your insolence. Mark my words!"

Headmistress Seychelle lifted her glass in a toast. "Now that's a prime example of why this school is called the Academy of Magical Arts. Shall we resume our dinner?"

Lark curtsied to the headmistress and walked out of the room with a quiet pride, her head held high.

## Chapter Fourteen

If ever a man was carrying around a bigger burden this morning than Sarco Sunwalker, Lark would like to see that man. Even from this height, she could easily spot the worry lines etched deeply in Sarco's face, and she could tell he hadn't slept any more than she.

Lark grimaced, turned from the window of the high tower, and flopped onto the small cot in the middle of the sparsely furnished room.

For what had to be the thousandth time in the past few days, she asked herself *why*? Why had she allowed herself to fall in love with a man she could never have?

As if that wasn't bad enough, what good had it done to hide herself away in this tower built specifically to block mental magic? For days on end, she'd exiled herself so as to not interfere with Sarco's interactions with both their families and Aryanna.

Yet every time she heard a knock, Lark still wanted so desperately to rush and throw the door wide open in the hope Sarco had come calling. By mutual agreement, though, he hadn't come and she knew he wouldn't. But that hadn't dimmed her desire for him one single iota.

Lark sighed as her mind drifted over the last few rotations of the sun. The mind-numbing days had crawled by slowly, but the nights had been unending torment. Long, uninterrupted hours of bittersweet memories had incessantly filtered into her dreams.

As the grains of sand slowly sifted through the hourglass, the feel of Sarco's arms, his passionate kisses, his unspoken promises, and the memory of joy beyond her wildest dreams played in Lark's mind like an unending stage tragedy.

The cost of that forbidden pleasure had been higher than she'd ever thought possible. The pain in her heart ached to the point where she eventually prayed for dreamless sleep, a short repose, even a single hour of peace. And if the look she'd glimpsed this morning on Sarco's face was any indication, he wasn't faring much better.

She knew well the toll this situation was taking on the man she loved. Each day he looked more haggard, more troubled, more desperate for a miracle they both knew wouldn't come.

Sarco was nothing if not honorable, yet here she was, wanting more than anything to welcome him back into her arms, her bed, her heart—and with enthusiasm, no matter the cost.

In reality, she should have the grace and fortitude to push him away from herself and toward Aryanna. Someone had to be strong. Lark knew it wasn't her, because all she found herself doing now was pleading with God Draka for the opportunity of one more moment with Sarco. One more chance to touch his face, to see his smile, to feel his kiss, to show him her love. One more night to be held in his arms.

She hugged herself tightly, trying without success to ward off the feeling of flying apart. An entire lifetime with Sarco would not be enough to sate her hunger for him.

How would she ever survive this?

He had become a part of her being, her very soul. After the ceremony tonight, he would be promised to Aryanna and life as she knew it would end. Her body would continue on, but she would never recover.

Lark scrunched her eyes tightly closed, trying her best to prevent the seemingly ever-present tears from escaping yet again.

Tonight, Sarco-Keltoris Titus Sunwalker, High-Elf Wizard, heir to the Lordship of the elfin kingdom of Landis, would stand before her father, King Alfred Zavier Caden Hammerstrike, and ask for the hand of her sister, in marriage.

Her sister. Not her.

There would be ceremony and chivalry, diplomacy and etiquette, magic and legend. The ballroom would overflowing with every single soul at the Academy in residence. Except her.

There would be dancing and feasting, singing and laughter galore. It would be the party of the millennium. Even the renowned twelve who sat on the Council of the Elders would be in attendance. All because of an ill-fated, eight-hundred-year-old prophecy.

Her breath caught painfully in her chest. How could fate be so unkind as to bestow on her the one and only man she would ever love then snatch him away without mercy? And there was no one she could even talk to about her pain.

When Grandmother Ava had come to visit, even though she was the only person who'd ever acted like a real parent to her, Lark had tried her best to smile and block her real thoughts from the kind old woman.

Grandmother was the moderator of the Council of

the Elders. To let Grandmother into the far reaches of her mind would've been the same as betraying Sarco.

There had been other visitors as the last couple of weeks before the ceremony had slowly drifted by. Like Aryanna, whose presence and gay chatter only served to make Lark feel guiltier if that was possible. Then had come Laycee, with her ever-present escort Leeky Shortz in tow. Even the antics of the gnomes couldn't bring a smile to her face. Her twin sisters, Ally and Audrey, with their identical smiles and mindless prattle, had come, and so had Briar and Uthiel, with words of kindness and news of the upcoming festivities.

Sherman Bobert Limburger the Ninth had even showed up to help pass the time. But no one could ease the pain in Lark's heart.

At least Sherman had been able to take care of one little problem for her. Ally and Audrey had been pestering her to show them around the Academy. When Sherman enthusiastically agreed to take on that duty, Lark could have kissed him. Though she loved the twins, the last thing she wanted was to have to entertain them.

She'd even lured Sherman off to the side and told him about the tiny scar on Ally's wrist from the bite she herself had inflicted as a child, so he'd be able to tell one sister from the other. The look on the twins' faces when Sherman told them apart right from their very first meeting had been the only thing to bring a smile to Lark's face the entire past week.

Walking back to the window, Lark breathed in large gulps of air as pain hit her anew. Just a few short hours from now, Sarco would be lost to her forever.

Even though the tower walls had been built

specifically to withstand and block the majority of mental magic, lightning flashed in the distance and thunder rolled. Clouds grayed and converged as they opened a cold deluge on the crowd below. The wind whipped viciously as the inhabitants of the Academy courtyard scattered and ran for cover.

Only one man stood his ground. Sarco Sunwalker stared upward through the drenching rain with such a look of sadness on his face it hurt Lark's heart to watch him.

"*I know how you feel, Wonderful. I miss you.*" The tremor of his whisper filled her mind to overflowing and, in the small tower room high above the courtyard, Lark wept.

****

"Think you could've cut it any closer? I swear, you're going to give me a heart attack, Cyrrick. Sarco just took the podium and is about to speak. I don't know how I let you talk me into this. It isn't going to work. I just know it isn't. Something will go wrong. It always does."

The look he gave her calmed her jangled nerves as nothing else could have. It was a gaze filled with confidence, love, trust, and just a touch of that exasperating elf arrogance she found so appealing.

"Ary, my love, don't be irritating today of all days, please. I have everything under control. Nothing is going to go wrong. We've planned this perfectly. I'm a diplomat, for God Draka's sake. This is what I do. It'll work, you'll see."

Princess Aryanna glared in his direction before turning her attention back to Sarco standing regally in his royal-purple robes and getting ready to address the

Council of the Elders and her father. "Something doesn't feel right about all of this, Cyrrick. Tell me again what exactly I'm supposed to do and what is going to happen after your brother says the words we changed."

Cyrrick sighed, but she didn't dare chance another glance in his direction.

"It's simple, love. Sarco will recite from the book. You will scream. Your father will be insulted and demand retribution. I, the diplomat, will step forward and offer the genius alternative of the quest to regain Sarco's honor. Your parents will have no choice but to accept this suggestion as it is a traditional barbarian custom."

"Oh, I can scream, all right. As a matter of fact, I want to scream now," she whispered, but the only indication Cyrrick gave of having heard her was the shake of his head as he kept talking.

"Sarco will go on and complete the quest to appease your family and restore his honor. He'll earn the right to choose his bride. He, of course, will choose your sister, Lark, and not you. Your parents won't be happy, I'm sure, but there won't be anything they can do about it."

She stomped on his foot. "How can you act so nonchalant? This is the rest of our lives you're talking about."

Cyrrick cupped her face with his hands and gazed into her eyes. "My heart's pounding like it's about to explode right out of my chest, if that makes you feel any better." He tweaked her noise. "Just remember, when the time comes, you must act sufficiently saddened by Sarco's choice. Your parents can never know they've been tricked. If this works, my love, we'll all get to live happily ever after."

She hoped so.

Sarco opened the small leather volume. A hush fell over the banquet room.

Panic rose in the back of her throat, and it was hard to breathe. "Tell me one more time this is going to work. I mean, it has to. I can't have caused my sister so much pain for it not to work, can I? You should see her. It's all I can do to not fall to my knees and beg her forgiveness every time I'm in her presence. They must end up together. *We* must end up together. Please, Cyrrick, tell me. I swear, I'll believe it."

Cyrrick smiled and her heart did a flip. "Do you trust me, Ary?"

She nodded.

"It'll work. As God Draka is my witness, it'll work."

****

Sarco waited patiently in the center of the brightly decorated hall for the ceremony to begin. The small leather volume lay open and ready in his hands. The page he'd memorized for so long blurred as his eyes burned. His mind sought Lark, needing the comfort and strength only her spirit could bring to him. He tried for a fleeting moment to connect with her thoughts before giving up, knowing she wasn't here and wouldn't be. She was in her tower. He wished, for what must have been the hundredth time since walking to the podium, for her presence. He felt so very alone.

He had dreaded this night and what he must do his entire life. There was no getting out of it, however. Duty bound him. He stiffened his spine and tugged on the collar of his robe as he took in his surroundings. He had to admit, Headmistress Seychelle had out done herself.

There was more gold displayed on the four thrones where his parents and the barbarian king and queen sat than in the coffers of most kingdoms. And the members of the Council of the Elders each sat suspended above the proceedings on cloud-like pillows.

Sarco smiled at Lark's grandmother and his Uncle Arizon, who were in their matching scarlet-red robes while the rest of the council was all arrayed in royal blue. It always boggled his mind that his uncle was alive and well after all these years.

Even though it had only been a couple of weeks since he'd seen Arizon Windstrider, and that visit hadn't turned out as he would've liked, to once more be in the presence of so great a wizard was still an honor.

From somewhere above, music played.

The room filled quickly, and the crowd spilled out onto the floor. Sarco shuffled his feet and shifted the book back and forth between his hands. He took deep breaths, hoping for a whiff of fresh air. What he got instead made his stomach rumble.

Food. His stomach reminded him he hadn't yet eaten. He'd been too nervous. He stared at the banquet tables, where a feast the likes of which he'd never seen sat ready. Alarian oxen roasted over an open pit, and trays of Geiger Mountain pheasants dripped with juice. Fruit, fresh and ripe from every corner of Albrath, spilled over the edges of platters, while vegetables of every texture and color filled large serving bowls. Breads and grains overflowed dozens of baskets, and desserts he didn't even recognize tempted his palete.

His mouth watered and his stomach growled.

He tried his best to concentrate on something else, anything else, and caught sight of a friendly face— Briar Dragonheart, his best friend's wife. She was beautiful tonight, and beside her proudly stood Uthiel. To Sarco's eye, the pair looked like a god with his goddess on his arm. They were the definition of regal, and he was grateful for their presence.

Sarco smiled once more as he noticed even Leeky had dressed for the evening. He wore his treasured golden gloves. The ones he only took out for the most special of occasions. And Laycee matched him perfectly in a gold tunic. He almost choked at the sight of their dolls. Tug and Miss Bunny both were sporting gold thongs.

Sherman, though. He surprised Sarco the most. The halfling had his hair slicked back and was dressed in a tux. He was even wearing shoes this evening. On his arms, he escorted Lark's twin sisters.

Sarco had never paid much attention to the middle sisters. He looked at them now. They really were quite lovely. Their chestnut hair hung to their tiny waists and wisps of it curled coquettishly around their heart-shaped faces. Their eyes shone with identical sea-blue clarity.

The women clung to the halfling's arms, and even though they towered over him, somehow, Sherman himself stood taller when he was with them. Both smiled adoringly whenever the halfling spoke and appeared totally enthralled with the Shermanator.

The music suddenly stopped and silence descended over the room. Lights dimmed as a spotlight illuminated Sarco's face. The time had come.

He closed his eyes for the span of a single grain of sand dropping through the hourglass, said a quick prayer to Draka, and took a deep breath. He opened his eyes once more and faced to his right. "Council of the Elders, I greet thee. King Alfred and Queen Allanna Hammerstrike, I am honored to be in your presence. Princess Aryanna, I am your humble servant."

Sarco then faced to his left. "Mother, Father, it is an honor to have you here this special night. Headmistress Seychelle, thank you for arranging this ceremony and for your gracious hospitality."

Sarco then addressed the room. "My friends, welcome."

He opened the leather volume, cleared his throat and, even though he knew his heart could never be in the words he was about to speak, he made sure his voice rang loud and true. "King Alfred, quandra dophtra, Aryanna, halla wondra mi hota ana I requsta recotmore fota toda dema tota don marna."

A deathly quiet hung over the room, and a sense of wrongness filled Sarco with dread. He had never known the meaning of true silence before this moment. Without straining his ears, he could have easily heard a breath being taken in the very back if anyone had dared to breathe. No one did.

Without warning, the lights came up and Princess Aryanna screamed. Before another heartbeat passed, the cold steel of Adan Hammerstrike's sword pressed the tender skin of his throat. Queen Allanna's face was as purple as Sarco's robe, and she bellowed for her son to separate Sarco's head from his body.

The quick sting surprised him as the blade began to slice. Sarco flinched as the warm, stickiness of his own blood made a slow trail across his throat.

From somewhere above, Uthiel and Leeky jumped in the middle of the fray, both prying the hulking barbarian off of him.

Lord Tylindius shouted for order while King Alfred yelled for war.

Sarco watched helplessly, not understanding, as his mother wept. He tried to go to her, wanting to offer comfort, but he didn't get the chance. A female dwarf council member fainted and fell off her cloud. She landed on top of Tug who looked, in a bizarrely disturbing way, to be fucking her.

Sarco shook his head. If the situation hadn't been so dire, it would have been humorous. What happened? What had gone so wrong? What had he done?

Out of the corner of his eye, Sarco watched as Cyrrick stepped up and tried in vain to regain some semblance of order. He cringed as his brother was almost trampled by a rush of barbarian guards.

Before Sarco could get anywhere near Cyrrick, table after table toppled like dominos. Food of all shapes and sizes went flying.

As if in slow motion, a bowl of steamed carrots flew through the air and landed squarely in the middle of Headmistress Seychelle's lap. She jumped out of the path of flying food, slipped, landed on her ass, and slid right through a pile of buttery mashed potatoes.

Hands grabbed at the back of his robe, and Sarco twisted, trying to free himself.

Sherman shouted, "This way, sir."

Sarco shook his head. "I will not run."

Uthiel grabbed his shoulder. "It is better to remove yourself for now. If you don't, I'm afraid there will be bloodshed on both sides. Go, and let this calm. I will come for you."

Though he didn't want to, he followed the halfling through the crowd and out the door. Uthiel was right. He had no idea what he'd done wrong, but the one thing Sarco did know, his continued presence was making the situation worse.

Taking in deep gulps of air, he rushed from the hall. He had to decide what to do. He had to think. He had to find out what went wrong. He had to talk to Lark.

He took the steps of her tower two at a time, pausing halfway to catch his breath and ease the pain in his chest. His gasps had far less to do with exertion than with the events of the past few minutes. Tonight's ceremony was definitely over and almost before it had begun.

How had everything gone so horribly wrong? One moment he'd been standing before King Alfred and the council, his voice ringing out, and the next moment there'd been total bedlam.

Finally, he reached the top of the stairs. He had to see her. He had to explain before she heard it from anyone else. Sarco pounded on the heavy wooden door with a soul-deep sorrow. How could he have made such a mess of everything?

The door opened and there she stood, eyes swollen from what looked like hours of crying, her hair mussed, her nose red. The most beautiful sight he had ever beheld.

"*Lark*," his mind screamed.

She held out her arms as she answered, "*What's happened, Sarco? What's wrong? Oh my God Draka, you're bleeding."*

She touched her fingertips gingerly to the spot on his neck still slowly oozing blood.

"Don't worry about that. It's nothing. Just a scratch."

"Let me look at your wound at least."

He shook his head. "There isn't time, Lark. Please, just listen to me."

Lark grasped Sarco's arm. He knew she only meant to help steady him, but he knew he wasn't even worthy of that much.

"It's over, Lark. I'm not sure how I did it, and it certainly wasn't on purpose, I swear, but I've somehow ruined everything. There isn't even a hope left of fulfilling the prophecy. And even worse, it means I'll be responsible for a war between our families. Only time will tell the level of destruction I have brought upon our heads."

He heard Lark's gasp, but couldn't bring himself to look at her, not wanting to see the same disappointment in her eyes he had so recently seen in the shocked gazes of her family.

Her soft hands comforted him, however. She placed them on his face and tipped it toward hers. When he finally had no choice but meet her gaze, the love and acceptance radiating in Lark's eyes calmed and humbled him as nothing else in the last few hours could have.

"It can't be as bad as all that. You're an honorable man, Sarco Sunwalker. Now tell me what happened, and we'll figure this out together."

He drew the worn leather volume she'd given him almost a season ago from a pocket deep in his robe and tossed it on a nearby table. "That happened, I think."

Lark shook her head, not understanding, as Sarco paced. His face took on the appearance of a man who'd been delivered a great, shocking blow, and words tumbled faster and faster from his lips.

"I swear, I memorized that passage exactly the way it's written on the page. Maybe I got the dialect wrong or mispronounced something, I don't know. Or perhaps the book itself has a mistake in it. There must be an error of some kind. I didn't do this on purpose, I swear. I didn't know what I should do, so I came here. I had to see you, to be the one to tell you. I didn't want you to hear this from anyone else."

Even though she realized it was shock fueling his rambling speech, frustration got the better of her as she stood and grasped his arm. "Stop. I don't care about any of that. Tell me what's happened?"

His look of total despair had her heart contracting painfully in her chest.

Sarco sat. "I have no idea. I said what I was supposed to say and then all VoT broke loose. Your sister screamed, your parents wanted me killed, and your brother, Adan, tried his level best to accommodate them. Someone, your father, I think, was yelling for war. My mother was crying, Cyrrick was almost trampled to death, and I still have no idea why any of it happened."

It was Lark's turn to pace. "I'll admit, this sounds bad. We can fix it, though, I'm sure we can. I don't know how yet, but we can. There must be a way. What exactly did you say to my father, Sarco? Word for word?"

Sarco picked up the book and flipped it open to a

worn page. He took a deep breath, sighed heavily, and repeated the passage.

He glanced at Lark. "It means, *King Alfred, your daughter, Aryanna, has won my heart and I request her hand this day in marriage.*"

Lark grabbed the volume from Sarco and stared at the page. "This can't be right. It's been altered." Her voice trembled when she spoke. "What you really said to my father is...*King Alfred, your daughter Aryanna, is a most hideous pig and I demand recompense if her hand this day I must take in marriage.*"

Sarco jumped so quickly the chair toppled over with a thud. "I said *what*? I'd never insult your sister. And...and...and the very last thing I'd suggest would be some kind of...of...payment to marry her. This can't be. How could this have happened? Who would've changed the words, and why?"

Lark shook her head. "I don't know. I wish I did."

She couldn't bring herself to look Sarco in the eye as she fought to find the words to gently explain just how dire the situation now was. She settled for staring at her feet and wringing her hands. "How well do you know our customs, Sarco?"

She chanced a quick glance at the man she loved when no answer was forthcoming. His head was bowed and his skin was turning an ugly hue of green.

Finally, he looked at her with resignation in his eyes. "I know there is no greater wrong you can do a barbarian than to insult one, especially to insult a member of his or her family. Wars have been declared for much less. Lives have been demanded as payment. I expect no less from your father, and I'll do whatever I have to do to prevent the bloodshed of my people."

Lark knelt in front of Sarco and took his cold hands into hers. "We'll find out together who did this. Somehow, we'll make it right. I don't know how yet, but we will, I promise. I won't let this happen, Sarco. I can't."

She stood and entwined her arms about his neck as Sarco's arms encircled her waist and hauled her against him. Their lips met in desperation and need, both seeking a reassurance they knew would be fleeting. It didn't matter. The desire to mesh into and draw from each other's strength was stronger than the panic of the moment. The kiss deepened. Their tongues probed and caressed. Time stood still and the world held only two.

The door banged open with the resounding boom of a cannon, followed by the unquestionable thud of many feet stomping up the stairs.

"What the protruding prostate of an overzealous troll were ya thinking, lad? Hurry, hide! Ya can't be found here, of all places."

Lark and Sarco jumped apart as if burned and turned toward the open door.

Another voice froze them to the spot.

"Didn't I tell you we'd find him here? I knew she was behind this debacle and would be harboring him. Where there is deceit and disloyalty, there has always been Lark."

She didn't want to look. She knew what she'd see. She could already hear it in the venom of her mother's voice. There was no choice, however. Lark stepped in front of the man she loved, held her head high, lifted her eyes, and faced the room, ready to do battle.

## Chapter Fifteen

If ever a man was less deserving of the predicament he found himself in, Lark knew in her heart, Sarco Sunwalker was that man. Why then, would he not, in his stubbornness, stay safely behind her, but instead push her aside as if she were no more than a pesky fly?

The small room quickly overflowed with people, and it took all of Lark's self-control to keep from summoning forth the storm howling outside her window. At least the tower would be cleared of its unwelcome guests.

She refrained though. Such action would be futile. Some things simply couldn't be put off and dealing with this situation was one of them. Instead, she stood her ground and braced herself for what was to come. She didn't have to wait long as a rush of voices drowned out the thunder crashing overhead.

"An insult to our family has been leveled. As by barbarian right and law, I demand his life be forfeited. Nothing less will be accepted or war will be declared."

Lark glared at the smug face of her mother. She wanted to strike the woman who had always made it known barbarian customs were crude and below her station. Yet now she dared try and use those same customs to hurt the man Lark loved?

Grandmother Ava sputtered, "Don't be ridiculous,

Allanna. Killing the boy won't solve anything and neither will war. The prophecy must be fulfilled, or there will truly be a war to deal with. If you but give him a chance, I'm sure he has a perfectly reasonable explanation, and this matter can be settled."

Lark could have kissed her grandmother for those words.

"Now, Mother Ava, I know you mean well, but if my queen says it's the boy's head, then that's the way it must be. Prophecy or no prophecy, war or no."

Lark huffed. She would've let her father know in no uncertain terms what her feelings on barbarian customs were but just as she opened her mouth to speak, Sarco firmly clamped a hand over it and wouldn't budge, no matter how much she struggled against him.

Fortunately, the resonance of the words spoken next by Lord Tylindius Sunwalker served to calm her as no other could.

"There must be some solution other than death or war to settle this to everyone's satisfaction. I'm sure if we sit like rational men, we'll figure this out and come to a perfectly peaceful conclusion. After all, these are modern days. We need to act civilized. I know my son to be a man of honor. He would never intentionally insult you, your family, or especially your daughter."

Lark still couldn't speak with Sarco's hand held firmly in place over her mouth, but she could nod her head in agreement with his father's words, and she did. The next sound, however, sent chills scampering down her spine from the force of Wizard Arizon Windstrider's authority.

"There will be no murder or wars declared this day.

Perhaps you should reread your history books and actually learn from them this time. I, myself, lived those long ago days. I spoke the prophecy that has brought us all together now. We'll give the lad a chance to say his piece, or it'll be my wrath you'll feel."

Lark shuddered before the imposing sight and sound of Arizon, the High-Elf Wizard and leader of the Council of the Elders. Sarco's hand slipped from her mouth and fell away. She chanced a glance back at his face. He was as much in awe of his uncle as she.

"Do not dare think you can threaten me, you decrepit old elf. I'm Queen Allanna Zanlynn Calista Hammerstrike, and I'm within my rights to demand satisfaction. It's my daughter whose name has been maligned, my family who's been wronged. I didn't become queen yesterday. I know the law, I know custom. I'll have satisfaction."

Lark saw flecks of light before her eyes and realized she'd been holding her breath. She let it whoosh out in a rush and took in quick deep gulps of air. Her fingers tingled, and the hair on the back of her neck crawled of its own accord. For not the first time today, she was eternally grateful she'd declined the evening meal. If she hadn't, Sarco would probably be wearing it right about now, along with all his other troubles.

Sarco held the small leather volume in his hands. "If you'd but please give me a moment to explain. I'm sure we can settle this peacefully. I have no idea how it happened, but the words I was to speak became altered. No insult was intended."

Lark looked pleadingly toward the crowd, especially her mother. "Please, you must believe him.

Sarco would never do this. I've been his…apprentice for the entire semester and I've come to know him well. He really is a good, honest, honorable man. Listen to him, believe him, I beg of you."

The cold, calculating smile that graced her mother's face warned Lark louder than any words ever could have. It had been a mistake to try and defend Sarco, and especially against the queen herself. Her mother's next words brought that lesson home in spades.

"*Apprentice*, is that what they call platt-diggers these days, Lark? It's obvious that's what you've become. You, even more than this…this…this," a perfectly manicured red nail shot out toward Sarco, "*elf* person, are an insult to our family. It's plain even to a blind man you're after the ladyship status you think this pointy-eared freak of nature can give you. It's so like you to covet that which rightly belongs to your sister. That has been your history, after all, hasn't it? On my life, I swear, you'll never see the day you become his lady."

Lark gasped, and tears filled her eyes. Her mother only smiled, however, as thunder filled the room. "I won't let you get away with it. Make the thunder crash 'til we've lost our hearing, the lightning strike 'til the buildings burn to the ground, and the rain fall 'til the valley floods and we all float away. You still won't save him, Lark. You've wronged your sister who was more than willing to marry below her station for the sake of that ridiculous prophecy. And now, you dare defend the criminal."

The tears burned Lark's eyes, but she refused to let them fall as her mother continued her tirade.

"If the words were indeed altered in that stupid book, it was you who altered them. You've always been a manipulative creature. From the moment you opened those gray, soulless eyes I knew what you were. I should've had the fortitude to end it then and there. I should've dropped you from the tower the day you were born. The dogs could've devoured what was left and saved our family from the wickedness you've become."

Lark didn't flinch. She was numb to it. How many times in her life had she heard basically this same diatribe from the one person who should've loved her?

Lark, the evil spiritmaster, who should've been burned at the stake before being allowed to take a breath. Lark, the creature of dark magic whose soul, by virtue of the color of her eyes, was corrupt and beyond redemption. Lark, the monster, who'd been left alive by grace and pity alone. Lark, whose only purpose in life was to serve her family and who'd failed miserably. Lark, the mistake. Lark, the freak.

She lifted her face to the crowd, not certain what she should say, just knowing she needed to say something.

"Enough!" Sarco's voice rang with a force that rattled the windows.

Lark stared up at him, willing him to not make things worse for himself by trying to defend her. It was no use. She could feel his mind so filled with rage it was closed to her pleas.

He stepped between Lark and her mother, his face red, his hands fisted. "You can say and think whatever you wish about me, Queen Allanna. After all, I made the mistake, and I'll pay for it. But hear me well. I won't tolerate one more insult to Lark. She has been nothing but kind. She is innocent in all this, and I'll defend her honor."

The queen laughed, but it held no humor. "Lark, innocent? There hasn't been anything innocent about the girl from the day she was born."

Sarco opened his hand, and a ball of blue flames formed. "What did I say about one more insult?"

The queen roared. "You dare threaten me, Elf? I'm a queen. I'll have you flayed alive, your filthy blood poured out upon the ground, and your bones fed to the crows."

A sudden movement off to the side of the room caught Lark's attention.

"You call yourself a queen? You…you…you, are no queen. You…harridan." Lady Jillian, with rage in her eyes, fought to get her hands on Lark's mother, and the sight of Lord Tylindius trying to hold back his delicate, regal wife almost brought a smile to Lark's face. It would've been humorous if the circumstances hadn't been so grave. But all Lark could feel was hopelessness as the situation continued to spiral out of control.

"*Harridan*? You dare call me a harridan, you…you…you anorexic, pointy-eared hussy."

Lark prayed for the floor below their feet to open and swallow them so she and Sarco could escape.

"For the love of Draka, get control of your wife, man." Her father's words added fuel to the out of control situation. "Can't you see my sweet queen is upset enough by your son's treachery without your wife making matters worse?"

"Sweet? My son's treachery?" Lord Tylindius's

face turned a strange shade of ruddy purple.

The elfin lord was almost across the room with both hands fisted, fire in his eyes, and murder obviously on his mind when Cyrrick burst into the room with Aryanna close on his heels. He was out of breath, his tunic askew, and a set of footprints crisscrossing his forehead.

He intercepted his father and placed himself between the two men. "If you would but allow me the chance to speak, I believe this situation can be settled to everyone's satisfaction. And peacefully, I might add."

All eyes riveted on Cyrrick as he dropped his arms, straightened his tunic, and walked nonchalantly to the middle of the room.

Queen Allanna opened her mouth to speak, but Cyrrick held up a hand and, surprisingly, not a sound came forth.

"Hear me out before any of you say another word, please. If by the time I've finished you aren't satisfied with my suggestion, then by all means settle it amongst yourselves. Kill each other if you must. There's a simple solution to this entire insult-and-honor thing. One that I'm sure will satisfy all parties involved. Let us regroup in the council chambers below where we've more room and discuss this like the royals and leaders we are."

Cyrrick turned and, without a backward glance, led the way back down the steps.

****

Sarco stood silently as he watched Cyrrick, standing tall and looking every inch the diplomat he was, on the very same platform he himself had made his life-changing mistake no more than a single turning of the hourglass ago. Cyrrick slowly perused the council chamber, making sure he made direct eye contact with kings, queens, lords, ladies, and all twelve members of the Council of the Elders before ever glancing back toward him. Sarco forced a smile on his face and nodded to his brother.

Slowly, and dramatically, Cyrrick unrolled the parchment scroll he held in his hands and cleared his throat. "Colleagues, friends, contemporaries, what I wish to suggest is simple and to the point. I propose my brother, Sarco Sunwalker, perform the ancient barbarian quest, the Maiden's Desire. That's what barbarians throughout the centuries have done when they wished to garner favor, seek forgiveness of the royal house, or claim a princess for wife. I see no reason why it wouldn't suffice in this situation."

*The Maiden's Desire quest? Has Cyrrick lost his mind? I'm not a warrior. I am a wizard. It takes more brawn than brain to complete such a quest.* Sarco swallowed past the lump forming in his throat. *But what if...?*

Cyrrick held up a hand, and the room quieted. "Unfortunately, an insult has been leveled. It wasn't intentional, but it must be dealt with all the same. By completing this quest, Sarco will prove his willingness to do whatever it takes to be forgiven his transgression, prevent war between our peoples, win his bride, fulfill the prophecy, and regain his honor."

Sarco took a deep breath. *If only.*

The room broke into pandemonium as voices became louder. "It can't be done," several people bellowed, followed by voice after voice of dissension.

Someone from the far right side of the room asked,

"Is it even legal? He's not barbarian. He's high-elf."

"It's a damn hard quest, even for a barbarian," another voice rang loud and clear from somewhere in the middle of the room. "No elf can do it, and certainly not before the deadline of the three full moons."

A contentious voice argued from the left, "An elf can do anything a barbarian can, and in less time, too!"

Barbarians and elves faced each other.

Sarco shook his head. If his brother didn't get control of the room soon, another fight would ensue.

The same voice who had spoken earlier from the right yelled, "Bah, elves are too soft and afraid of getting their lily-white hands dirty to do a quest, let alone the Maiden's Desire. It's barely been completed three times in all of history, and only then by barbarian champions."

Sarco grabbed Cyrrick's arm. "Do something, say something, before this gets out of control again."

Cyrrrick raised his hand once more and a hush fell over the room. He tapped the worn parchment of the scroll, "There's no law stating one must be born barbarian to attempt the quest. The Maiden's Desire is almost as old as time itself and the outcome as binding as any promise."

Sarco gulped. How many promises had he alone broken this day? The last one being that one way or another, he'd find a way to keep himself and Lark together. And the people of the elfin kingdom of Landis, he'd certainly let all of them down.

Cyrrick's voice rose an octave, and Sarco forced himself to pay attention to the information he had no doubt would be imperative to not just his but also the future survival of elves everywhere.

"The quest was first spoken, attempted, and completed before this world was through forming. That's how long our distinguished barbarian brethren have inhabited and ruled over major parts of Albrath. What more appropriate ending to the fulfillment of the great prophecy than by completion of this ancient quest? Would that not truly join our peoples for all time as nothing else could?"

Sweat dampened his hair and trickled down his neck as the eyes of a hundred angry barbarians bored into Sarco's back. From shoulder blades to waist, his skin prickled, but he couldn't dwell on it right now. He needed to concentrate on what Cyrrick was saying. He needed something, anything, to hold onto, to give him hope.

"As most of you know, by right of birth, I myself am an elfin prince, but first and foremost, I'm a diplomat of the people, all of the people. It is the diplomat today who implores this esteemed group of leaders to listen to the words and the spirit of the quest. Hear them not with your ears but with your hearts."

Sarco held his breath.

Cyrrick closed his eyes, lifted his head, took another deep breath, and brought the scroll up against his chest close to his heart. The lights dimmed, the sounds of the raging storm outside faded away, and not a single breath was heard as he spoke.

*"It's ice and fire that forms a maiden's desire.*

*It's searing heat where metal and gemstone first meet.*

*It's with love in mind that a treasure becomes divine.*

*It's a champion you must defeat for a heart you*

*wish to seek.*

*It's your choice to make for the wife you will take. "*

Cyrrick had looked directly at Sarco when he read the last line, and it took a moment for the impact of his words to really sink in. Could it be true? Sarco shook his head twice, afraid to believe. "It sounds more like a riddle than a quest."

"Perceptive of you, brother," Cyrrick whispered. "For it most certainly is a riddle of sorts. One that I have the utmost confidence you'll be able to solve. And best of all, the rules of the quest state you may take companions to help you in any way you see fit. The only detail you must keep in mind is that at no time may any help in any form come from the princess you *wish* to choose, or else you forfeit the right to ask for her hand in marriage."

Sarco whispered back, "Are you telling me that if I complete this quest, I not only regain my honor and am forgiven my transgression, but I also earn the right to *choose* my wife from amongst the daughters of the barbarian royal house? *Any* of the daughters?"

Cyrrick winked. "That's precisely what I'm telling you."

A moment later, Sarco realized they hadn't whispered quietly enough as a screech rent the air.

"I'll not have it. Do you hear me? My husband, the king, and I are the only two who have the right to choose and we choose our daughter, Aryanna. She's firstborn; it's her right to become Lady of Landis someday. Her name has been maligned, and I will have satisfaction. This…this…this elf will not be given the opportunity to do some stupid quest and weasel his way back into our gentle, good graces. He'll not be allowed to pick a wife from amongst our daughters. They are not prize cattle to be auctioned off to the highest bidder. It's unheard of. I'll not stand for it, I tell you."

Queen Allanna looked almost pleadingly toward Wizard Arizon. "The prophecy. There must be some rule in our favor, right?"

The old wizard looked thoughtful then slowly shook his head. "All the prophecy states is the firstborn heir of the high-elves must join in marriage to a princess of barbarian-human descent and forever merge all three peoples into one race. It doesn't say he can't do a quest and earn the right to choose which princess. We just presumed he would go along with your choice of Princess Aryanna. I mean, why wouldn't he? Sarco knows his duty. After all, it was her hand he was trying to ask for when he bungled the job so badly."

Sarco smiled as the first rays of hope he'd felt in days settled into him.

Queen Allanna screeched. "That's not the point. Him choosing can't even be acceptable as a consideration. Don't you think this situation has been traumatic enough? We were already forced to agree to a marriage between an…an…an *elf* and one of our precious daughters, and now you're allowing the pointy-eared misfit the right to choose? The only thing worse would be a match between one of our princesses and a…a…" She scanned the crowd. "A halfling! It's unheard of."

Queen Allanna swooned, and the king caught her.

King Alfred fanned his wife as he addressed the council. "Can't you see what's going on here? What this is doing to my dear wife? I smell treachery. I don't mind the boy going on the quest to regain his honor and prevent war, but do you actually expect me to allow him to walk back in here and choose a mate from amongst my daughters like nothing happened? Prophecy or no, I have a problem with that."

The wizened old elf shook his head. "As it stands this moment, I don't see what choice you have but to accept the terms of the quest. Unless war is exactly what you wish for…?"

Sarco mentally sought Lark. *"Wonderful, we finally have a chance."*

Her excitment flooded his mind. *"Yes, my—"*

Sherman Bobert Limburger the Ninth stepped forward and cleared his throat. "Point of order, if you please." Heads turned toward the sound.

"If it pleases this body, I mean group, I mean council…umm…"

King Alfred stopped fanning his wife for a moment and shook his fist at the little man. "If you have something to say, spit it out. If not, step back. We're discussing important business here."

Sherman once more cleared his throat and tugged at his collar. "It's just, sir, madams, council members, umm, if the only sticking point here as to whether Sarco gets to do this quest to be forgiven or not rests solely on who he can or can't choose to marry, then there is something everyone seems to be overlooking."

He tugged at his collar again.

King Alfred motioned him forward and dread filled Sarco. He had no idea what the halfling was about to say, but with Sherman's history, the chances of it being in Sarco's favor weren't good.

Sherman made his way through the crowd and walked right up to the barbarian king. "I took a class once on the human race so, well, I'm somewhat of a trivia buff when it comes to their laws and customs. Section nine, page two hundred thirty-four, paragraph five, of the sixth volume of *Rules of Being Human,* plainly states, 'In the matter of marriage in royal families, daughters of the same house must marry in the order of their birth. Your daughters are not full-blooded barbarian, but are equally human. So, you see, sir, it doesn't matter who you and your wife chose for Sarco to marry, or who he would've chosen if he does complete the quest. By human law, it's Princess Aryanna he must marry."

Sarco closed his eyes, and Lark gasped within his mind. He opened them once more. Like watching a tragic event unfold, he couldn't look away from the carnage.

Clouds obscured the moon and heavy shadows formed in the hall. A sudden booming clap of thunder startled the halfling and his voice faltered briefly. "I, I don't mean to babble, sir, r-really I don't. It's just that the prophecy clearly states the marriage between the high-elf heir and the barbarian-human princess must be consummated while the three moons of Albrath are all in their full phase. That will happen in less than a fortnight.

"So you see, sir, when Sarco does go on this quest, it can only be with the hope he'll succeed and be awarded forgiveness, regain his honor, and marry Princess Aryanna, for she is the oldest and must marry first."

Rain suddenly pelted the roof of the hall so hard, Sherman was forced to yell. "You've nothing to worry about. I mean, what's he going to do? It's not like he can find husbands for your other daughters and do a quest at the same time?"

His heart thudded with defeat so powerfully that Sarco was certain it was going to burst. He didn't care. If he couldn't have Lark, what good would his life be? How could he ever have been willing to go through with the stupid proposal ceremony in the first place while hoping for a miracle? What a fool he'd been. And now, both he and Lark would pay for his stupidity for the rest of their lives.

****

Tears stung Lark's eyes as the realization she'd never have Sarco for her own sunk into her soul. She felt Aryanna's gasp and thoughts almost as if they were her own.

*"Section what of what? How could this have happened? Married by who was born first? We did all this for nothing? Oh Lord Draka, what've we done?"*

Lark's head hurt with the force of Aryanna's thoughts, and she projected her own pain back to the sister she couldn't even look at right now. *"It was you? You changed the words? How could you do that to me, to Sarco? Why would you?"*

Two words floated back from Aryanna's mind to Lark's. The anguish and helplessness of those words settled deep in Lark's heart like a heavy stone. *"I'm sorry."*

A silence like death hung over the hall as a piercing cold seeped in and surrounded the inhabitants. Each individual breath in the room hung suspended in icy crystals of air. In unison, every soul turned toward the floor-to-ceiling windows gracing the west wall and stared in horror and awe at the sight outside.

For the first time in the history of Albrath, the heavens above the Academy froze. Clouds took on the appearance of ice mounds and slowed their movement midflight.

Then, it snowed, one flake at a time. Slowly at first, with the momentum picking up quickly. Finally, the skies burst wide open and large flakes of perfectly formed snow bombarded the ground where snow had never, ever, fallen before.

## Chapter Sixteen

If ever a man needed a friend more than Sarco Sunwalker did this very moment, Lark would like to see that man.

Sarco's shoulders drooped. His head hung low. The promise of pain to come was etched deeply on his face, and he looked defeated.

Lark wondered if he was as numb as she. Numbness was preferable to the anguish she knew to be swirling just below the surface. The anguish waited patiently for both her and Sarco to let down their guard and allow it in to destroy what was left of their hearts.

She forced herself to stay put and not rush headlong to Sarco's side and into his arms. She wanted to hold him and be held. Anything to keep the gut-wrenching pain at bay for a few more turns of the hourglass. She couldn't, though. It wasn't her place or her right.

A voice boomed from the council members and put all other thoughts on hold. "Enough discussion. It's late, and I'm an old man sorely in need of his bed. Let us be done with this."

The great wizard Arizon pointed in the direction of the barbarian king, and Lark held her breath in anticipation of his words. "King Alfred, will you or will you not accept Prince Sarco's apology for his unfortunate mistake if he completes the quest?"

The king looked to his wife. Queen Allanna scowled toward the high-elf prince but, after a moment, nodded.

The king stood. "Aye, the barbarian throne will accept his apology if he successfully completes the quest."

The wizard then trained his eye on Sarco. "And you, great-nephew, heir of Landis, wizard in your own right, will you accept the terms of the quest?"

Sarco lifted his head and straightened his shoulders. "I accept," he said, his spine ramrod straight.

Lark let out the breath she hadn't realized she'd been holding.

The old elf wizard clapped his hands above his head and every candle in the hall burned with a flame so white it bathed even the deepest crevices of the room in a warm light. Every face was illuminated. "Then choose your companions, Sarco Sunwalker, and choose them wisely. May God Draka watch over and bless your journey."

Sarco raised a hand and pointed. "Sir Uthiel Dragonheart, the greatest paladin I've ever known and my dearest friend, will you lend me your sword and quest with me?"

Lark smiled as the tall, handsome man stepped forward with the look of a proud warrior on his face. "My sword and my loyalty are yours. Of course, I'll quest with you, Sarco. Did you really think you could've gone without me?"

Uthiel stepped forward, grasped forearms with Sarco, and took his place at the wizard's side.

"Leeky Shortz, the greatest rogue Albrath has ever known, guide to kings and warriors alike. Dear friend, will you quest with me?"

Lark rolled her eyes and then grinned as the gnome stepped proudly forward.

"What the oozing, purulent zits on the underbelly of a two-platt chubby ogre harlot are ya thinking, lad? Did ya even need ta ask? Aye, I'll quest with ya." Leeky removed his golden go-to-a-special-meeting gloves and replaced them with what Lark guessed were his indigo-blue questing ones. He tucked the ever-present Miss Bunny firmly under his arm and joined the other two men.

Sarco once more spoke. "Sherman Bobert Limburger the Ninth, though I can't say with complete honestly you're my best student, you do try the hardest and you certainly have the biggest heart and mouth. Will you quest with me?"

Lark's heart pounded as Sherman rushed forward to Sarco's side.

"Oh, Sarco, sir, this is the greatest moment of my life. You won't be sorry you picked me. Just you wait and see. I'll make you proud. I can't wait to write my parents and tell them about this. They'll never believe it. I took a class once on questing but never dreamed I'd ever actually go on one and especially with the great wizard Sarco Sunwalker, and Sir Uthiel and Leeky. I don't know what to say." His sobs prevented him from continuing.The man who owned her heart spun toward the section where the majority of the royal barbarian family was seated and surprised Lark with his next request.

"Prince Adan Zeth Conner Hammerstrike, your reputation for being just and your sense of fairness are well known throughout the land. When this quest is over, I don't wish there to be any question as to whether all the rules were followed to the letter of the law. Will you quest with me?"

Lark knew if she wanted to, she could trespass into her brother's mind and manipulate his answer. She shuddered at the thought. They were no longer children and this wasn't a game. This was all too real, too important. She wouldn't consider it even for a moment. Instead, she waited like everyone else.

The tall, blond barbarian warrior stood. "Earlier this evening I would've gladly killed you, Sarco Sunwalker. It wasn't for lack of trying that I did not. But I do believe in fairness and giving a man, even an elf-man, a second chance."

The huge barbarian stepped forward. "Perhaps you didn't intend insult to my family, I'm not sure. What I do know, however, is, if you're willing to do the Maiden's Desire quest, then you must be serious about seeking forgiveness, for it's not a simple task. As long as you realize that I am not your friend and will scrutinize your every move each step of the way, I'll be glad to go."

Sarco nodded. "I'm counting on it."

Adan joined the group.

Sarco faced to his left and the look on his face as he gazed with pride at Cyrrick swelled Lark's heart. "All my life you've stood by my side, brother. I've watched you put your own wants and needs aside when you thought mine were more important. They weren't then and they aren't now. Because of you, I am who I am. Watching you fight and work and struggle without ever once giving up while going after your dream of becoming a diplomat taught me more about honor and duty than anything else could've. Cyrrick Sunwalker, my brother, my friend, will you quest with me?"

Her breath caught in her throat as Lark waited. Cyrrick wrapped his arms about Sarco's shoulders and they stood in a silent embrace.

Finally, Cyrrick let his arms drop back to his side. "I'd be honored to quest with you, Sarco. I do worry, however, as to how much help I can be. I'm not a paladin like Uthiel or a warrior like Adan. I have no skills with a sword in which to watch your back. I'm not a rogue like Leeky or a competent wizard like you or even a passable one like Sherman. I'm but a man who gets by with words. What good will words do you where you're going? It wouldn't hurt my feelings if you choose someone more…useful than myself. Perhaps another of your students?"

Sarco smiled at Cyrrick, but even if no one else did, Lark noticed the hint of sadness to it. "You've never understood or appreciated your own worth, brother. It is you I need. No other will do."

Cyrrick acquiesced. "It's settled then, let us quest."

The sound of wizard Arizon's voice snapped everyone back to attention. "Are we done then? I'm tired."

Sarco nodded. "We're almost done, Uncle. Your head will know its pillow soon, I promise." He faced his companions. "We quest at daybreak. Meet me in the courtyard and be ready to ride. We've a long journey ahead of us."

He faced the council and the royals. Lark's heart pounded, waiting for his words. "I know my duty, and when the light of morning comes, I'll gladly do it. The remainder of this night, however, is mine, and I have much to attend to. If I'm going to be gone from the Academy for any length of time, I must confer with and prepare my apprentice to handle my affairs. I bid you a goodnight."

Sarco's gaze locked with hers. The determination she saw in his eyes should've warned her of his intentions but when Sarco walked through the crowd and stopped directly before her, shock coursed through her veins. No more than a breath separated them, and her pulse hummed with excitement. With something akin to a fear to hope, she boldly returned his steady stare. He didn't utter a single word. He didn't have to. But the heat of his thoughts had Lark's heart soaring before its next beat.

"*I have need of you, Wonderful.*"

She smiled almost shyly at the weary-looking man. "*I have need of you also, Wizard.*"

Sarco gave a quick wink Lark knew was meant for her eyes only before speaking loudly for the benefit of the crowd. "Come along, Apprentice, and don't dawdle. I'm a busy man and we've much work to do before morning. I've no doubt it'll take most of the night."

\*\*\*\*

The door to the high tower room no sooner slammed shut than Sarco was upon her. He couldn't wait another moment. Lark's sudden gasp in the silence of the room only served to fuel his lust. Quickly, he stripped her of her tunic and himself of his own clothing, discarding them at his feet.

"Now, Lark. I must have you now. It's been too long. I can't wait another moment."

She didn't comment, and he was glad for it. There was no need. They both knew what they wanted, needed. Instead, she wrapped her arms about his neck and her legs about his waist. He pushed her up against the wall and entered her, fast and hard. The coolness of the stone against the palms of his hands and the heat of the woman he loved against his front was a delicious, erotic treat.

He pounded furiously, his cock growing thicker and harder as each stroke went deeper than the last. It stretched the inner walls of her pussy to accommodate its size, and Sarco gloried in the rippling sparks of pleasure her sheath created.

His teeth nipped the tender skin of her neck as his hands tightly held her hips. She moaned. He captured her lips, and his tongue delved deep into the recesses of her mouth, warring with her tongue, possessing her, loving her. The hair on his chest rasped her pert nipples, and Sarco shuddered and smiled at the glorious sensation.

Sweat glistened his skin as the sound of his own breathing roared in his ears. She clenched around him and cried out his name as pressure built, and streaks of fiery bliss shot straight down his balls and up through his ass. Like the eruption of a volcano, his seed burst forth and he exploded with ecstasy.

Still joined, he carried her to her bed, and collapsed upon it.

Sarco sighed as his cock slipped free of her pussy. "I didn't mean to take you so crudely. I couldn't help myself. You deserve much better."

Lark smiled into the darkness as she leisurely ran her hand up and down the taut muscles of his back. "Don't fret, my love. It was perfect. It always is."

"I'm glad you think so, because I have a powerful

need for you again, now."

Lark grasped his once-again-thickening cock. "So I see." She giggled. "Then what are you waiting for?"

He didn't hurry this time. Slowly, he took her mouth in a kiss that curled her toes. His hot tongue delved and played, stroked and explored until Lark was left gasping for air and quivering with anticipation. Only then did he move on to her neck.

Shivers of excitement skittered along her spine and landed deep in her belly. Her pussy throbbed. She sighed as she tugged on his shoulders. "Now. Fuck me, now."

He chuckled, and the feel of it against her skin had her tugging on him harder. "Patience," he said. "I hunger for the taste of you, and tonight, I feast."

And feast he did. Her mouth, her neck, her shoulder blades, and even the cleft between her breasts. Lark squirmed beneath him, unable to remain still as his hot raspy tongue burned a path of pleasure all the way to the center of her pussy. Then, he leaned back up, captured a nipple in his mouth, and sucked, hard. Lark's spine bowed of its own volition as rippling sparks of electrifying heat shot all the way to her toes. Her pussy ached.

Again, she begged. "Now, Sarco, please."

"Shh." His mouth moved lower. Down across her ribcage, nipping and kissing as he went. When his tongue darted into her belly button, Lark almost came up off the bed. The throbbing of her pussy was so intense, she slid a finger between her folds and stroked hard to ease her need.

Sarco captured her hand and pulled it away while shaking his head. "Oh, no you don't, my love. There'll be many nights to come when you'll have the opportunity to pleasure yourself. Tonight's my turn." He locked gazes with her, and the despair in his eyes made Lake want to weep. "I have no idea how long I'll be gone, Lark, or how this will all end. I have only this night to worship you, to love you, to make sure you never forget that it is you and you alone who owns my heart and always will. Allow me this night to show you with my body in ways my words can not."

How could she deny this man anything? How could she ever give him up? Lark smiled into the eyes of the man she would die loving. "I am yours. Do with me as you wish."

Time lost all meaning as Sarco once more bent to his purpose, nuzzled his head between her thighs, and captured her clit with his hot tongue. Her hands gripped his hair, and her panting breaths were the only sound she heard.

He nipped, and shockwaves of delight rolled over her. He sucked her swollen nub over and over again, and jolts of fiery excitement rocked her insides. Her heart pounded so hard that her pussy's pulse matched its beat.

She was just on the precipice of release when he suddenly pulled away. She locked her fingers in his hair, trying desperately to hold him in place.

Sarco chuckled as he untangled her fingers and flipped her over. "Not yet, Wonderful."

She groaned, "But I need—"

He didn't chuckle this time. Sarco gave a full belly laugh as he positioned Lark on her hands and knees with her ass facing him. He slid his cock up the cleft of her pussy and slammed it home. "Now, my love, you can come with me now."

*Oh my God Draka!* The sheath of Lark's pussy contracted and spasmed around him. Her breath caught in her throat, and her heart forgot to beat. Faster and harder, he fucked her. His balls slapped her ass while his cock embraced her very soul. They were one, and nothing in this world or the next could ever change that fact.

On and on, they fucked. Both trying to delay the inevitable and yet knowing that too soon this night would end and, with it, their hopes and dreams. But, too soon, tremors of perfect pleasure she could no longer hold back overtook her and engulfed her in their wake.

Lark cried out Sarco's name a moment before his own orgasm overtook him, and he shuddered as he fell to the bed, taking her with him. He held her close to his heart with a desperation that left it hard for her to breathe. She didn't care, though. She'd crawl inside him and go with him in the morning if she could.

Then he slept. He was exhausted. As well he should've been after the love they'd just so ardently made. Sarco had been nothing less than a man possessed.

Tomorrow, she'd feel the aftermath of this night in every bone, muscle, and fiber of her body. She counted on it.

Lark lay on her side, watching the man who owned her heart slumber. A look of peace finally graced his handsome face. Her fingers toyed absently with an errant strand of his midnight-black hair. She was not yet willing to relinquish the joy of simply touching him, being near him once more.

She threaded her fingers through the silky strands

all the way to his warm scalp. She focused on scratching and massaging his head in hopes of staving off her own sleep. Her other hand gently stroked the soft skin of his cock, savoring the memory of the pleasure it had given her such a short time ago.

There would be time for sleep tomorrow. Lark knew she'd even welcome it then. It might help ease the pain of losing him, if even for a few short turns of the hourglass. For tonight, though, he was hers, and she was determined sleep would not rob her of one grain of sand's worth of the time she had left with Sarco Sunwalker.

His gold-flecked eyes fluttered open, and Lark's heart did a flip-flop in her chest as he smiled at her.

"I didn't mean to wake you. You need your rest."

His arms encircling her and drawing her close filled Lark with such a feeling of contentment, she snuggled in closer and yawned widely.

A chuckle rumbled through him, and the vibrations tickled her ear. "Oh, no you don't, Wonderful. You don't get to entice me awake so thoroughly with your touch, then simply fall asleep."

Lark drew back a little and smiled up into his face as she tried valiantly to stave off the tears suddenly threatening. She'd relegated to memory every line and nuance, every crease of his pointed ears and even the dark stubble adorning his chin. So this was it, then? Their very last opportunity to be together this way, to share in a love that had been ill-fated from the day it had begun.

She wasn't going to cry. She wasn't!

Tonight she would show Sarco all the love she'd stored in her heart to last a lifetime. There was nothing more important than these last few turnings of the hourglass. They were more precious than all the platt in Albrath, and even each single grain of sand falling was to be cherished and not taken for granted.

She ran a single fingernail lazily up and down his chest and gloried in his shiver before finally gripping his cock.

"I'm getting chilled here, woman. Stop your torture and come warm me, Wonderful."

Though she wanted to cry with the pain of her impending loss, Lark forced herself to chuckle. "Why, Professor Sunwalker, you don't feel the least bit chilled to me. That's definitely not shrinkage beneath my fingertips. As a matter of fact, it's growing rather nicely. Remember how to use it?"

With a playful growl, he came up off the bed and grabbed her around the waist. With a single twist of his body, he had her beneath him.

"My lady, I do so love it when you squirm."

The purr of his voice against her skin sent ripples of pleasure skittering down her spine, and now it was her turn to shiver.

"Ah, so you're chilled too, I see," he laughed. "Let us warm each other, Wonderful."

The wet heat of his tongue on her skin was like being bathed in spring sunshine as he sampled first her lips, then the tender flesh of her neck before working his way to the taut buds of her nipples. A throbbing deep in her core radiated outward. It matched the cadence of her heartbeat.

When his head dipped lower and teased the inside of her thighs, she quivered with anticipation. For long minutes, his tongue made lazy paths back and forth from the inside of her knee, up her thigh, to the outside lips of her throbbing pussy.

Just when she was sure she'd die from need, he captured her clit with determination and flicked the tiny, sensitive nub with the very tip of his tongue. Her entire body grew as tight as a percussion instrument as he, the talented drummer, played a steady staccato upon her body and honed her desire with precision.

Over and over his tongue lavished and his teeth nipped as, with relish, he sucked, probed, tapped, and teased. She squirmed beneath him, striving to get closer still, striving to fuse them into one being.

*If only. If only.*

Lark was at the pinnacle of release when Sarco suddenly stopped.

She stared at him through lust laden eyes. "What's wrong?"

His boyish grin was more enticing than should be allowed.

"Oh, nothing is wrong, Wonderful. I just want to prolong the joy of you writhing beneath me." He nipped the tender skin of her inner thigh, and Lark jumped in response.

She shuddered. "Enough, Wizard. Give me what I crave. Now."

The feel of his warm breath touched tender parts once more as his hot tongue flicked out, capturing her clit.

This time there was no pause. This time there was no mercy. This time there was only pleasure. Soaring, body-spasming pleasure so intense that when the explosion of ecstasy finally came, it left her with the feeling of floating somewhere high above her own body.

Nothing had ever felt as right as this moment. There were no words she could speak to express the love coursing through her every fiber for this man, words simply weren't strong enough. She settled for snuggling into Sarco's embrace as he slid up her body, knowing instinctively that sometimes, contented silence spoke louder than the most elegant of speeches.

Lark smiled into the darkness as Sarco sighed. Though she may not need words right now, it was apparent he needed to talk.

"I'm not always good with saying the right things, Lark. That's my brother's talent, not mine. But there is something I need you to know. I never meant for you to be hurt, and I truly regret that you have been. You've changed my life in ways you can never imagine. I hope you realize that."

Sarco flipped onto his back beside Lark and turned her face gently toward him. "Because of you, I look forward to waking each morning. Because of you, I know there's nothing I cannot do. Because you're in my world, my life is no longer empty. I don't yet know how I'm going to make this right, or even if there is any way I can. I just know I must try. I can't face the thought of a life without you."

Lark gazed deeply into Sarco's shining eyes and whispered, "We'll make it right together, somehow."

Sarco smiled, but it held a touch of melancholy. "With the coming of the dawn, we'll face those problems, and you're right. Even though we'll be separated by distance, we'll do it. For these last few precious hours, however, let's put the problems from our minds. I have a powerful need to feel you sheathed about me, Wonderful."

Lark giggled like a schoolgirl as the vision of gnomes, whipped cream, and a certain naughty board game popped into her mind. "You mean like Ride 'Em Cowboy?"

Sarco groaned and chuckled. "Oh Lord Draka, please don't remind me of that sight. I do not want to embarrass myself right now, Wonderful. The thought of gnome sex isn't conducive to the *stiff* frame of mind I mean to maintain, if you understand my meaning."

Lark leaned over his body, winked, and playfully feathered kisses across his face, neck, and chest. "I suppose you're right, although I did so want to play Ride 'Em Cowboy with you."

Slowly, she straddled him and gloried in the feel of the big, powerful muscle beneath her fingertips as she cradled his cock with both hands. How could something be so baby-soft and at the same time so very hard? It pulsed and jumped beneath her touch with a life force that more than matched hers. It was magnificent.

"This little ole thing? This is what you wish me to ride?" Lark couldn't stop the grin that split her face.

"I'll show you *little*," he growled as he lifted Lark, positioned her above his waiting cock, and plunged deeply into her pussy. With a hand on each hip, he slid her up and down the length of his shaft.

"Ohhhhh," she moaned. "That's nice. That's really, so very...very nice."

The pace quickened. She rode him even faster as sparks of tingling excitement scampered through every nerve ending Sarco's cock touched. Her ass slapped against his thighs, and their eyes locked in concentration. His nostrils flared as she ran her hands down her own body. She tweaked her nipples and rubbed her clit. Their bodies sang the same tune, and their sweat mingled as his fingers dug into her hips, holding her tighter as if he meant never to let her go.

At a frenzied pace, they fucked, looking into each other's eyes, both seeing the lust burning hotter than the desperation of the moment and glorying in it. Together they strove for completion.

Lark knew Sarco was close to release. The telltale spasms jolted her with every plunge of his cock. They excited her as nothing else could've. With a vigor born of need, she rode him even harder, even faster.

Close, so very close.

Her eyes closed, her heart pounded, her breath came in quick bursts. Just as the first ripples of hot liquid burst forth to fill her, Lark's muscles clenched and contracted. Sparks exploded behind her eyelids, and her body shuddered with a pleasure so sweet and complete, she sobbed with the joy of it.

"Sarco," she shouted.

Outside, the snow had long ago stopped falling and a warm, gentle breeze melted away the last remnants. Stars shone brightly and the three moons of Albrath bathed the surrounding landscape in soft light.

Inside the tower room, high above the Academy courtyard, Lark nestled contently into the haven of Sarco's arms. Love so strong it radiated from the man lying beside her, infusing Lark with its warmth. Their limbs intertwined, their breathing slowed, their minds eased.

Tomorrow would bring what tomorrow would bring. For tonight, though, no blankets were needed.

## Chapter Seventeen

If ever a man was more alone in the world than Sarco Sunwalker appeared to be this morning, Lark would hate to see that man.

She watched her lover, content for the moment to simply be nearby while he sat silently on the edge of her bed staring out the window. Streaks of faint light appeared in the eastern sky.

Gone this morning was the wizard's robe she was so used to seeing him wear, and in its place was traveling apparel she had never seen him don. A sturdy, white linen shirt clung to his broad chest, a pair of well-worn black breeks hugged his hips, and fine leather boots graced his feet. He was magnificent.

When, during the night, had he slipped from her chamber to exchange his clothing, and had he even slept? If the worry lines embellishing his handsome face this morning were any indication, he hadn't rested much.

Lark wondered if she should tell him about the thoughts she'd intercepted from Aryanna last evening. She knew in her heart she couldn't bring herself to do it right now. The man had more than enough to deal with, without her adding to his worries.

Besides, what, really, did she have to tell him, after all? She'd heard nothing substantial, just a few random thoughts, and she wasn't even sure they'd been whole thoughts. They were more like strong emotions—grief, shock, and guilt. Oh, yes, definitely guilt.

Lark knew she'd have a hard time forgiving Aryanna if her sister was somehow involved in putting Sarco in danger. Not wanting to marry a man was one thing, but almost getting him killed was entirely another. And what or who had she meant by *we*? Ary had most assuredly included someone else in her thoughts.

Was it Aryanna who'd changed the words in the leather book? After all, it was Ary who had insisted Lark give the text to Sarco as a gift.

Doubts filled Lark's mind. She thought she knew her sister well. She wasn't sure now. What she did know, however, was as soon as Sarco was safely away, she was going to find out how Ary was involved.

For now, she wouldn't tell Sarco her suspicions. As a matter of fact, unless she could prove her sister's involvement, she might never tell him. It could only serve to hurt him no matter who he ended up married to.

But Lark was going to have a chat with her big sister just as soon as Sarco was gone. Oh, yes, they were definitely going to talk.

So lost in her own thoughts was she, the sound of Sarco's voice startled her and she jumped.

"Sit with me, Wonderful. There's something I must ask of you before I go." His sadness enveloped her, and she felt his pain. The turmoil of his thoughts mixed and swirled together within her mind.

She sat at his side, taking his hand into hers, and looked deeply into his eyes. "Anything. You may ask anything of me. There is nothing I can or would deny you. You should know that by now."

He faced her. "I keep thinking there's something we must be missing. Some way around all these stupid rules and regulations of who marries whom and when."

He cupped her chin gently in the palm of his hand. "I have a project for you, Wonderful. While I'm gone, see if you can discover anything helpful. For every rule, there's usually a loophole, somewhere, somehow. Research it, Lark. See what you can find. When I return, I'll do my duty. I must. It's who I am, and the peace and future of our peoples depend upon it. But my soul will know no peace, and my life will be endless, empty days without you at my side."

Lark nodded. "I'll spend every waking moment until you return searching for a way for us to be together, I promise."

Sarco cleared his throat, stood, and paced before the window. "I have one more thing to ask. Something of vital importance."

A shiver of dread seeped into the recess of her mind and worked its way down her spine. She had no idea how she knew she wasn't going to like what Sarco said next. She just knew she wouldn't.

"We have no choice. We must say the blocking spell, Lark."

Panic clouded her vision. How could he ask this of her? Not only was she to lose his physical presence, but their mental bond as well? She couldn't do it. It was more than she could bear. A familiar warmth seeped into her mind and cradled her, as sobs she could no longer hold back shook her frame.

*"Don't cry, Wonderful. It won't be forever, but it must be done. The rules of the quest adamantly state I*

*cannot receive help in any form from the one I wish to choose for a wife, or I may not choose her. I wish with all my heart, by some miracle of fate, to be able to stand before your father and choose you when this is done. I love you, Lark. You must know that to be true. I also know if you in any way were to perceive I was in danger, you wouldn't be able to stop yourself. You'd help."*

She lifted her chin a notch and gazed at him pleadingly as words tumbled forth from her lips. "Is there no other way?"

Slowly he shook his head and let his mind speak the words his lips could not. "*Not that I know of, Wonderful.*"

Lark nodded. "Then let us be done with this quickly before I lose my nerve."

Sarco placed five candles in the center of the floor. With a flick of his wrist, a bright blue flame appeared in the palm of his hand. A warm light infused the room as the flame leapt from his fingertips and lit the candles. The room pulsed with magic. The air vibrated with it.

"I love you, Larksong Hammerstrike. Never doubt that," he whispered.

Lark sighed, "I love you, too, Sarco Sunwalker, with all that I am."

She closed her eyes and held tight to Sarco's hand. Their minds meshed, their hearts became one, and together they spoke the words of the ancient spell they both knew they'd no choice but to cast.

*"Across time and distance between your mind and mine,*

*For now, sever the bond only magic can unbind.*

*For a season, an hour, a grain of sand,*

213

*Let our thoughts now be solitary*
*Until together we once more stand."*

The warm feel of Sarco's arms as he caught her up in a tight embrace was more torture than comfort. She trembled with despair. Gone. He was gone from her mind.

She had never known the true meaning of loneliness before this moment. Even as he bent his head toward her, kissed her lips gently, and caressed her cheek, she couldn't shake the feeling of abandonment.

Then, without another word or a backwards glance, he made his way to the door and walked out. The closing of the door brought home the full impact of what had just transpired, and isolation came crashing in upon her.

Solitude enveloped Lark like the darkest of nights.

****

Aryanna fidgeted with the edge of the blanket, seemingly unaware of the wet splotches her tears made on the fabric. "Don't go. Please, don't go. I need you here."

Cyrrick couldn't take his eyes from the tearstains as he sighed and tucked her tightly against his length, as close to his heart as he could get her.

"It's not my wish to leave you, love, but I must go. Sarco wouldn't be doing this damnable quest in the first place if it hadn't been for my arrogance and interference. I don't understand what went so wrong, Ary. There wasn't supposed to be violence. I thought I had the situation under control. I swear on my life, I never for a single moment thought things would get so far out of hand. For God Draka's sake, I nearly got my brother killed. I've ruined everything—our lives,

214

Sarco's and Lark's lives, and possibly the lives of our people. How can I even look my brother in the face this morning without him seeing my guilt? I doubt I can."

Warm, fresh tears ran down his side as she lifted her head, sniffed loudly and hiccupped. "It's that…that…that halfling's fault. He's ruined everything. Now we'll never be able to marry."

He kissed the top of her head and stroked her shoulder gently. "Don't blame Sherman, my love. If you must blame anyone, blame me. I'm the one who didn't take your human half into consideration. I'm the one who didn't do his research thoroughly. No, Sherman Bobert Limburger the Ninth didn't ruin anything. I did. Perhaps he may have even done us a huge favor."

Red-rimmed, deep violet eyes starred at Cyrrick, and his heart contracted painfully at the glimmer of hope he saw flicker there. "What do you mean, a favor? Do you think there still may be a chance?"

He took a deep breath and carefully thought out his words. "I have to be honest with you, Ary. Things are pretty grim, and I'm not sure if there is anything we can do about it. But as long as there is breath in our bodies, there's a chance we may find some way around the human rule of who marries first. At least now, there's a little time to research it. If it hadn't been for Sherman, we wouldn't have found out about the rule until after the quest was done. By then it would've really been too late. That's what you can do while I'm gone. Find an exception to that rule, Ary. There must be one, it's just a matter of locating it. I bet you can even get Lark and the twins to help, if you ask…nicely."

The mention of Lark's name brought with it a new

flood of tears. "Oh my God Draka, I forgot to tell you about Lark. She knows, Cyrrick. She heard my thoughts and she knows. She hates me. I just know she does. I could feel so much anger and hurt radiating from her. And she's probably told Sarco by now, so I bet he hates me, too."

Cyrrick yanked the blanket over her body and tucked it under her chin, trying his best to infuse warmth into her and alleviate the shivers cascading through his own skin. "What thoughts did she intercept, Ary?"

Aryanna sat up, wrapped the blanket tightly around her bare shoulders and looked nervously toward Cyrrick. "I can't be positive. You know how thoughts are. Sometimes they're just a jumbled mess all strewn together. I know I was angry with Sherman, and I know I was frustrated because all we'd so carefully planned was falling apart."

Aryanna hesitated for a moment then continued, "I remember feeling guilty because we'd hurt Lark and Sarco, but I have no idea which of those thoughts I completely formed or she actually intercepted. I do know she heard at least parts of them."

He tugged her back into his embrace, not wanting her to see the concern in his own eyes. "Don't worry so. I doubt Lark even realizes what she heard, and if she does and if she's spoken to Sarco about it, we'll deal with it. Your sister loves you, Ary. That will never change, and if any two people in all of Albrath can possibly understand our motives, they'd be Lark and Sarco."

Aryanna tried to jerk away, but he prevented her from doing any more than lifting her face toward him.

He took full advantage of the opportunity as he covered her mouth with his. When he finally had her panting against him, he released his hold and chuckled. Even to his own ears, the sound of his humor fell pathetically short.

"Let me worry about what Sarco does or doesn't know, my lady. Don't give it one more thought. You just concentrate on your sister and on finding a way for us to marry when I return, okay? Now, let your man up from this bed and give me the clothes you hid last night, or I'm going to be late. You've had many turns of the hourglass to have your sweet, wicked way with me."

Cyrrick grinned and planted a kiss on the tip of her nose. "I love you, Ary." He leaned over and swatted her soundly on her smooth, naked ass and gloried in the way she bristled against him. "Be a good lass and fetch my boots while you're at it, woman. I can't be letting a perfectly good quest get underway without me, now, can I?"

"*Be a good lass*? I'll show you how I can be a good lass."

He knew he deserved the swift and sudden punch from her tiny fist as it impacted the middle of his belly. To have the last glimpse of the woman he loved be of her gazing at him and grinning like a mad woman, with fire and mischief blazing in her eyes instead of tears, was a joyous sight indeed.

\*\*\*\*

Sarco paced beside his steed and shook his head. He glanced toward Uthiel, Cyrrick, and Adan, shrugged his shoulders, and sighed. Where were Sherman and Leeky? The first rays of the morning sun were already ablaze, and dawn was well upon them. They'd been assembled in the courtyard for at least half a turn of the hourglass, and still there was no sight of the halfling or the gnome. Anger and frustration coursed through him. Five more minutes, that's all he was going to give them. If they weren't here by then, quest or no quest, he was leaving without them.

The out-of-place sound of giggling caught his attention, and he turned toward the source. He shook his head in disbelief.

Sherman Bobert Limburger the Ninth led his horse at a snail's pace with both of Lark's twin sisters fast on his heels, nearly dancing in circles about him.

Each twin's hair looked like it could use a good brushing, and all three of the little group grinned like lunatics from ear to ear. The trio appeared to be suspiciously well satisfied with themselves, and it was obvious they'd dressed in a hurry. Sherman's shirttail was half tucked into his pants, and if Sarco wasn't mistaken, his boots were on the wrong feet.

The princesses, Allyssa and Audrey, were no better. One's gown was conspicuously laced wrong and hung at odd angles while the other had mistakenly put her dress on inside out. Though he still couldn't tell one from the other, it was the first time Sarco had seen them not look completely identical. Just what had the girls and the halfling been up to all night? It was on the tip of his tongue to ask when Adan beat him to it.

"Ally, Audrey, don't tell me you've been cavorting with this…this halfling?" the barbarian bellowed loud enough to wake the dead. "I can see it in your faces. You want him, both of you. Mother will stroke if she finds out. And have you no shame? One man between the two of you? On second thought, don't worry about

Mother, you'd best be worrying about me. As your brother, I won't permit it. Do you hear me? Other cultures might get away with acting like heathens, but it isn't the *barbarian* way."

Sarco almost felt sorry for Adan, almost. He might have if the blade nick on the side of his throat the hulking warrior had inflicted yesterday hadn't stung at that moment, reminding him Adan didn't need or deserve his sympathy. And then there was the idea of Lark's mother stroking. That thought was so appealing, he couldn't have prevented his lips from smiling even if his life had depended upon it.

He grinned like a fool as Ally and Audrey both answered their brother, "Whatever do you mean, Adan? We simply came to see Sherman off. You've never understood us, and you don't even try."

Adan held up a hand, and Sarco forced himself to conceal his pleasure at the other man's obvious discomfort.

"Oh, no, you don't. That's not going to work on me. You can't tell me there isn't more going on here than what you're both 'fessing to. My God Draka, look at how you're dressed."

The twins folded their arms across their chests and stared at their brother with identical innocent expressions, but it was Ally who spoke. "We did dress in somewhat of a hurry this morning, I suppose, and may not be our normal tidy selves. After all, we didn't want to take the chance we'd miss wishing Sherman *Godspeed* and a safe journey. It would've been unforgivable on our parts if we had. He's been so generous while acting as our personal guide this past fortnight. And there may be a tiny grain of truth to your concern that we find Sherman appealing, but then, that's perfectly normal."

A chuckle escaped Sarco's lips, and though he knew the glare Adan leveled on him was meant to have the opposite effect, it only made him laugh harder.

"You should see how girls look at him, Adan," Audrey wailed. "All the women secretly want him. He's a very sexy man and famous to boot. And I bet you didn't know he's as much a prince as you are, and he's even a lord, like Sarco will be one day? His kingdom is just very far away and small. That's why not many people have heard of it or his status."

Sarco almost fell off his horse. His gut ached from the attempt to hold in the laughter dying to spill forth. Just when he thought Adan's face couldn't get any redder or the story couldn't get any wilder, Ally chimed in.

"And...and, what if we do both like him? What's wrong with that? We've always done everything together. Would you expect anything different from us now? You'd like him if you'd give him a chance, Adan. Sherman is known far and wide throughout the land, not only as a prince among men, but also as a great wizard and a very good cheesemaker. He's also a scholar. He's taken classes on every subject imaginable. He told us so."

Both girls giggled, "He's the Shermanator!"

That did it. Sarco gave up trying to hold it back and bent double with laughter.

Adan roared, "A prince? A great wizard? A learned scholar? The Shermanator? Sometimes it amazes me you two can manage to breathe and walk at the same time. Get back inside the Academy before anyone else sees you, and don't say another word about the Shermanator to anyone. I don't have time to deal with this now. We'll discuss it further and settle it once and for all when I return."

The barbarian prince then glared at the halfling. "It's a good thing you're going with us. I'd have to kill you right now instead of later, if you weren't."

Sarco shook his head as Sherman stopped staring at the girls and grinning like a fool. He watched his student gulp, pinken, and look toward him, seeking sanctuary. "Forgive me for being late, sir. I was, umm, unavoidably delayed."

Uthiel's coughing and Adan almost jumping off his horse was more than enough to make up for having to wait for the halfling in the first place.

"It's quite all right...Lord Sherman. A great prince, famous wizard, and experienced cheesemaking scholar like yourself is worth waiting all day for, if need be."

Sherman's pink cheeks turned a fiery red.

Sarco squinted his eyes and peered out into the shadows. Now, where was the damn gnome?

He didn't have long to wonder as a familiar gravelly voice split the air. "What the shaved bare arse of a rock-climbing, purple-painted Alarian billy goat are ya thinking, lass? I told ya, let go of me leg. I'm late."

Sarco wasn't exactly sure what he'd expected to see when he looked in the direction of the voice, but he knew it couldn't possibly be the sight he beheld. Leeky limped toward them with his blow-up-doll under one arm, the lead to his horse in his other hand, and Miss Laycee Titwilder bumping along behind with both her hands gripped tightly about his right ankle, clinging on for dear life.

Sarco stared, wondering if the day could possibly get any stranger.

"I won't have it, I tell ya," Laycee squealed. "Ya won't be taking that plastic two-bit hussy with ya and leaving me behind."

Leeky stopped, set Miss Bunny astride the horse, bent and extracted his ankle from Laycee's grip and gently helped her to her feet. "Ah, lass, ya know I wish I could take ya with me, but I can't. Miss Bunny here is a tool. That's it. Simply a tool is what she is. Ya're more than welcome ta ask Sarco how handy a blow-up doll can be on a quest. Why, during the trip we made last year, my Miss Kitty doll gave her very life to save us." Leeky swiped at his eyes. "We even had a fine funeral for her."

The gnome turned toward the waiting group. "Didn't we, Sarco?"

Sarco shuddered at the memory of last year's journey. The trip to find and save Uthiel had become the stuff of legend and nightmares. The search had ended once Sarco, Leeky, Briar, and her father had traveled halfway across the world to eventually find him. When all had been said and done, Uthiel had been saved, the fable of Castle Kuropkat solved, and Uthiel made leader of the Paladins of Albrath and protector of the dragons. He and Briar now presided over Castle Kuropkat and all its adjoining lands.

What had Sarco gotten for his trouble, though, other than rescuing his friend? The task of fulfilling the second part of a prophecy he now spent most nights trying to forget? If need be, he'd do it all over again, of course, because Uthiel was worth it. But that didn't stop the nightmare images of angry seas, a burning ship, a huge dragon, Briar's scary, uncontrolled magic, and a punctured blow-up doll as a flotation device from invading his sleep.

Leeky waited for an answer, however, so Sarco opened his mouth to speak and found the lump in his throat too big for words to get past. He settled for nodding.

"See, didn't I tell ya? I have ta take Miss Bunny. Ya never know what might pop up."

Laycee punched Leeky in the shoulder, but Sarco could tell it didn't hold much force. "It's what might pop up that worries me, ya blasted gnome."

Leeky blushed. "Aww, Laycee, ya've nothing ta worry about, lass. Ya know my heart belongs only ta ya. Matter of fact, I got something for ya as a kinda going-away present, just ta prove it."

The gnome dug deep into one of the many pockets gracing the military-style, camo pants he wore and plucked out a shiny, golden key. He held it out to Laycee. "This here's ta my rooms in the underbelly of the Academy, and I want ya ta take it. While I'm gone, go there and make it as homey as ya like. That's where we'll live when I get back. Umm, ya might have ta move off ta the side a few pairs of…uh, panties here and there. It's a harmless hobby of mine. I've collected a pair or two over the years. Unused, of course."

Sarco smiled as the female gnome grabbed the key from the notorious, rogue panty thief and pressed it to her heart. "Does this mean ya wish ta marry me then, Mr. Leeky Shortz?"

Leeky's eyes grew big and he coughed. "Marriage? Well, someday long, long in the future, perhaps, lass, but for now, I was thinking more along the lines of just having my way with ya whenever I want without any of the responsibility."

Laycee grinned, stretched up on tiptoes and planted a kiss on Leeky's cheek. "Ya sure do know how ta sweet talk a girl, Leeky Shortz. There's no doubt about that."

Leeky grinned and wiggled his eyebrows. "Ya think that's sweet. Wait till ya see what else I got ya." He dug once more into his pants-of-many-pockets and retrieved something long, thick, smooth, and green. He handed it to Laycee.

The female gnome turned it back and forth in her hands and, for a moment, looked perplexed. "It's a…a…a cucumber."

Leeky threw up his hands. "What the saggy, baggy, hanging tits on an overused, older-than-dirt troll harlot did ya think it would be, lass? Of course, it's a cucumber. It's ya favorite vegetable, isn't it? I was planning ta take it along for my own lunch, but it's so big and stiff, I couldn't help but think of ya. I wouldn't want ya ta be overly lonely while I'm away. We both well know how useless Tug is in *certain* departments lately, with his gear issues and all."

He patted her on the head. "I'm a sensitive gnome, ya know? I'm a modern guy, and I keep in touch with my feminine side and all that stuff. And just think about it. After a few days when ya've gotten ya use out of it, and it gets a tad mushy around the edges, ya can always slice it up and toss it in a salad. Can't beat getting double duty out of a gift, now, can ya?"

Laycee threw her arms about Leeky's neck. "Ya're one of a kind, Leeky Shortz. Ya certainly are."

Leeky untangled himself from Laycee and mounted his horse. "What the multi-colored puke down the front of a one-legged, drunken, black-eyed ogre are we waiting on, lads? There's a quest ta be done. Let's ride."

Sarco glared, anxious to be on his way. But Leeky didn't seem to notice or be in any hurry. He simply continued to sit astride his steed, his blow-up doll across his lap, while his girlfriend gazed up at him adoringly and stroked a cucumber—*that* was a disturbing sight.

He shuddered and turned toward Sherman, which was an even bigger mistake. There sat the halfling with both twins still dancing around his horse and extolling the fame of the Shermanator, but now in song…and horribly off key. Sarco cringed and closed his eyes for a moment to wash clean the slate of his mind.

When next he opened them, he glanced at Adan. The huge barbarian looked ready to commit murder and didn't appear to care who it might be.

Searching for normal, Sarco's eyes found Cyrrick. For a fleeting moment, his brother looked right at him then turned away. The strangest feeling came over him. What was it he'd glimpsed in Cyrrick's eyes? Remorse, sorrow, even a touch of guilt? He couldn't tell. He made a mental note to speak privately with him as soon as the opportunity presented itself.

Finally, glancing toward Uthiel, Sarco smiled. Normal at last.

That bubble burst a moment later when Uthiel spoke, "I suggest we get going real soon, Sarco. I had to drug Briar with her own brew of sleeping tea in order to keep her from tagging along. You know her, she's going to be spitting mad when she wakes and finds us long gone. I'm almost afraid for the Academy. The woman wouldn't take no for an answer, though, and she wouldn't let me sleep a wink 'til I tricked her into drinking that cup of tea."

Uthiel grimaced. "I added a few drops of rose hips to disguise the taste. Then told her it was a rare aphrodisiac tea I'd brought as a special Yulemass gift for the both of us and had been waiting for just the right moment to present her with it. You should've seen her face, Sarco. She was so excited. And the sexy little kittenish way she climbed into my lap as she drank it." He sighed. "I'm such a dead man when we return."

Sarco gulped, and Uthiel continued to explain. "But what else could I have done? She wouldn't listen to reason, and she kept insisting we needed a healer with us. And not just any healer but her in particular. I love her with all my heart, and she means well, but you know how stubborn she can be, Sarco, and the kinds of things that tend to happen when she's anywhere near. Oh, yeah, my friend, we'd better be riding fast and hard. We'd best be many, many miles down the road before Lady Briarlarn Dragonheart next wakes."

A small tic twitched Sarco's right cheek as he mentally rolled his eyes. Yelling, "Lets ride," he took off at a gallop—as much to get away from his crazy companions as to get started.

It was going to be a long quest and to begin it he needed to find…a flower formed from nothing but ice?

## Chapter Eighteen

If ever a man looked more lord-like sitting astride his steed than Sarco Sunwalker did this very moment, Lark would like to see that man.

The sight of *her* man's raven-black hair fluttering in the breeze, his white shirt clinging to his broad, muscular shoulders, and his black breeks caressing the smooth leather of his saddle caused more than a few erratic heartbeats.

The only thing Lark could think about as she watched him gallop away atop his snow-white stallion was an ardent wish for just one more quick round of Ride 'Em Cowboy. Oh, to be that lucky pony for just a short time. The thought brought a secretive smile to her lips as a giggle burst forth from the depths of her soul.

Even though her heart ached with loneliness as she watched the men ride through the courtyard and out the gates of the Academy, Lark forced herself to think only pleasant thoughts and to will the sun to continue shining upon them. She may not be able to help the man she loved with his quest, but she could ensure Sarco's leaving took place without gloom.

Fifteen minutes more, that's all she needed. A quarter turn of the hourglass and it wouldn't matter what the weather outside was like. A short ride north and Sarco would be through the portal, well on his way, and beyond the boundaries of any havoc her power might wreak on his group.

A mere quarter turn of the hourglass, then she'd search out Ary, get some much-needed answers, and not care if the clouds obscured the sun.

Lark sat on the edge of the bed and let the warmth of the sun's morning rays seep into and calm her impatient soul. She watched each grain of sand as it sifted through the hourglass. Fourteen minutes and counting.

****

"Where is she, Laycee?" Lark stood in the middle of the rooms she once shared with her sister. With her hands on her hips, tapping her foot and glaring at her insolent-looking governess, she tried her best to appear intimidating but could tell it wasn't having the effect she'd hoped for.

"Don't be trying ta give me the evil-eye, missy. That don't work. I've known ya since ya still pooped yourself. Do I look like ya sister's keeper ta ya? How am I ta know where she is? She's a woman full grown, and where she spends her nights is her business. I'll be glad ta tell her ya were here asking after her, though, next time I do see her."

Laycee turned and walked away. She had Tug under one arm and a cucumber in her other hand. For a moment, Lark thought to ask why the female gnome would be carrying vegetables around this time of the morning then decided it was probably best if she didn't know. What was important was finding the traitorous Miss Aryanna Hammerstrike.

She softened her voice and tried a new tactic. Demanding had never gone over well with Laycee. Perhaps begging might bring better results. "Laycee, please. Pretty please with whipped cream and cherries on top. I really need to talk to her. It's extremely important. If you have any idea where she is, tell me."

Laycee set her cucumber on a nearby table and Tug in a chair. She removed her wig, plopped it on the doll's head and scratched her own before turning back toward Lark.

"Ya know I don't like tattle-telling and rumor spreading. Just this once though, I suppose it can't hurt. I haven't seen it with my own eyes, mind ya, but I've heard she's been sneaking up the west tower and having a tryst with some young buck. If ya find her, don't be telling her I told ya where ta look. Gotta stay neutral where ya girls are concerned, ya know? If not, I can't effectively do my job. Don't want ta be accused of playing favorites. Now, get on out of here before the twins get back, and for the love of Draka, don't be asking me what those two are up ta. My heart can only stand so much."

Lark made her way up the long winding staircase of the west tower. She'd never been here. There'd never been a reason. At the top, a doorway came into view. The door stood slightly ajar as if someone had exited in a hurry. Peeking in first, then lightly shoving the door open, Lark stepped inside.

She stood in awe. There lay Ary on her back, in the middle of a large bed, with a blanket tucked tightly about her chin. Tears had pooled in the shallow indentations beneath her eyes and overflowed her cheeks making wet tracks on her otherwise flawless face. Her golden curls surrounded her head like a halo, her mouth puckered prettily and her chin occasionally quivered. Even now, even though it was obvious she'd cried herself to sleep for some reason, Princess Aryanna Hammerstrike was beautiful.

It took every ounce of will Lark possessed to not go to her sister, hug her close to her heart, and rock her until all her tears were no more than a memory. She stopped herself, however. She had to be strong, she had to find out, she had to know.

Tearing her eyes from her sister for a moment, Lark took the opportunity to look about. The room was fairly standard, much like her own in the tower on the other side of the Academy. The bed in the middle of the room took up most of the space. A simple table with a couple of chairs sat in one corner, a desk and chair in the other. A glimpse of something royal purple draped across the seat of one of the chairs caught Lark's eye, and quietly she tiptoed over to investigate. Gingerly, she lifted the garment and held it up for inspection.

It was a robe. Not just any robe, but a robe of the royal house of Sunwalker. For a heartbeat her breath caught painfully in her chest. Sarco had left her room sometime during the night.

She shook her head. She knew Sarco better than that, and she knew without a doubt if she went directly to his room, this moment, she'd find his robe there.

No, this was *not* the robe of the man she loved. Whose then? Her thoughts raced. It could only belong to one other.

Cyrrick. This must be Cyrrick's room. And it must be Cyrrick's robe, which could only mean Ary was sleeping in Cyrrick's bed. *Cyrrick* was the *we* in Ary's thoughts?

It became as clear to Lark as the sight of her sister still sleeping in the bed before her. Sarco's brother had betrayed him. Sarco's brother and her sister had done this together. Why? What on Albrath did Cyrrick and Aryanna have to gain by destroying Sarco's life? There was only one way to find out. Lark walked over and not so gently pinched her sister.

"Ouch!" Aryanna sat straight up in the bed and glared. "Why'd you do that? I thought something bit me."

Lark glared right back at her. "If I could produce a swarm of locusts to accommodate you...*Princess*, I would."

Outside clouds gathered.

Aryanna stood, wrapped the blanket tightly around her naked body, and though she tried to hide it, a glint of guilt and sadness flashed in her eyes.

"So I guess I was right after all, you did intercept some of my thoughts last evening. I suppose you must be angry and confused right about now?"

Lark's left cheek twitched. "Angry? You suppose I must be angry? And confused? That's an understatement if I ever heard one. Just which thoughts do you think I intercepted, Ary? I want to hear you tell me what I heard out loud."

Outside the sky rumbled and darkened as if evening approached instead of midmorning.

Aryanna retrieved clothing discarded on the stone floor. "So, exactly which thoughts would you like to hear first, Lark? The thoughts about how my life is over and nothing really matters anymore? Or perhaps the ones where I've made a mess of everyone else's life and deserve the worst punishment that could possibly be thought up? I'm afraid you need to be a little more specific." She dropped the blanket to the floor and proceeded to dress.

Lark paced back and forth as the sky became as night and lightning flashed in the distance. Finally, she stopped directly in front of her sister, and looked her straight on. "I have to know, I need to hear you say it. Were you or Cyrrick in any way responsible for altering the words in the Barbarian Etiquette book, and the fiasco that almost got Sarco killed yesterday?"

Aryanna sat. "It's not that simple to explain."

Thunder crashed so nearby, the tower shook from the force.

Lark stood over her sister and said only one word. "Try."

She didn't want to feel sorry for her. She wanted to hold tight to her anger and use it as a shield, but when Aryanna rose and paced until finally stopping before the window, Lark's reserve slipped a notch. Her sister looked like a fish out of water, gulping air into her lungs as if there wasn't enough of the invisible stuff to be had. For a moment, the skies outside almost calmed.

"S-sit down, and…and I'll ex-ex-plain."

Lark's rebellion bubbled forth. All her life she'd been taking orders. She was tired of it. "I'd rather sip this particular cup of poison standing, if you don't mind, thank you."

Aryanna's face crumbled, and the pleading sound of her voice touched a warm spot deep in Lark's heart even though she fought it. "Please, Lark. Please sit down and give me a chance to explain."

Lark sat reluctantly on the edge of the bed.

Outside, rain pelted the cobblestones of the courtyard below, the sound reverberating off the walls of the small tower room.

Aryanna moved closer to Lark, drew up a chair, and sat. Clearing her throat, she looked Lark in the eye. "Yesterday wasn't supposed to happen the way it did, and I'm so sorry," her voice trembled. "No one was supposed to get hurt. That wasn't the way it was planned. I'm not even sure where to begin."

Lark folded her arms. "How about the beginning?"

Aryanna nodded. "Fair enough." She got a faraway look in her eye. "Do you remember the first time Cyrrick came to our castle? He was so handsome. I remember being surprised when I learned he was acting as an ambassador for his family and had come to talk about the fulfillment of the prophecy.

"It became my chore to keep Cyrrick entertained and out of our parents' hair while they pondered their decision, so we spent innumerable hours together going over boring history books in the library. We talked about every subject you could possibly imagine, from first crushes and broken hearts, to favorite foods and authors, to the dreams and goals we had for our lives. Oh, Lark, the hours we spent out in the garden…I can still smell the fragrance of roses in moonlight every time I think about it.

"We didn't plan it, Lark. It just happened. We fell in love. We even denied it for a long time, but we couldn't keep up the pretense. Our feelings for each other were simply too strong. We discussed going to Mother and Father and asking them for their permission to allow us to wed."

Lark glared. "So why didn't you?"

Aryanna lifted her chin. "We tried. Mother and Father wouldn't hear of it. They demanded I marry Sarco. I didn't know what else to do but try and find a way around it. The thought of a lifetime married to the brother of the man I love is torture. And to know I will forever lose the splendor of being held in his arms is pure torment. Even though I knew I was no longer free to pursue another, I couldn't seem to help myself. I pursued Cyrrick with a passion. I even seduced him…many times."

A cold realization seeped into Lark's heart as Aryanna fidgeted on the chair. How so very alike the two sisters really were. Wasn't that exactly what she herself had done with Sarco?

The rain froze and turned to flecks of ice as Aryanna continued, "I talked him into helping me search for a way around the rules of the prophecy, and he found the quest. He really is an amazingly intelligent man, Lark." The hail grew to the size of small pebbles as the sound of Aryanna's voice morphed into a steady hammering in Lark's already pounding head. "I threw you and Sarco together. I needed to make sure you and he would be exposed to each other at Carnalval. I had a feeling you'd be perfect for each other. I have to admit, though, I was concerned when you cried all the way home from festival that perhaps you two hadn't hit it off after all.

"Then I saw the sparks fly between the both of you when we were introduced the day we arrived here. Sarco didn't even look at me. He only had eyes for you. So I tricked you into taking his Elemental Wizard class in my place. I knew the two of you wouldn't be able to keep your hands off each other, and I was right, wasn't I?"

Lark nodded and stared off into space, unseeingly, as the wind howled outside.

"To answer your question, Lark, yes, we did change a couple of the words Sarco was to memorize in that silly book. We couldn't think of any other way to get him to insult our family, and it was imperative he do so. It was the only way to trick him into having no choice but to do the quest. We both wanted Sarco to be allowed to chose whom he married. Then, we sat back and allowed nature to take its course."

The sounds of the wind whipping, hail falling, and thunder crashing barely registered in Lark's mind. She was beyond angry now. Ary was smiling and sounded practically cheerful about the ordeal, as if she and Cyrrick had done Lark and Sarco a favor and should be thanked for their efforts. Lark's fingers itched to feel the skin of Ary's throat beneath them.

"You've both exceeded our wildest expectations in the attraction department, you really have," her sister continued, her expression and gestures animated. "But we never, ever meant for anyone to get hurt, Lark. If you don't believe anything I tell you, you must believe that. And you have to admit, if it hadn't been for that stupid human rule the halfling had to go and tell everyone about, our plan would've worked. Sarco could've completed the quest, chosen you, and fulfilled his destiny with the woman he does love. Cyrrick and I would've been free to be together at last."

Ice the size of small stones pummeled the ground and structures below. The onslaught sounded like firecrackers popping.

"Please don't look at me as if you wish my blood spilled upon the floor, Lark. If you really do, you're welcome to it. Trust me, you can't possibly think worse of me than I do of myself. I know what a mess I've made, and I take full responsibility for my actions. My only hope is that someday you'll be able to find it in your heart to forgive me." Aryanna covered her face with her hands and wept.

Lark stood. Rage competed with guilt. She fought to form a coherent thought as she stared at her sister's bent head. "Why didn't you come to me? Why did you feel the need to trick me into falling in love with Sarco? I'm your sister, Ary. I would've understood. I would've gladly helped. You should've trusted me. There isn't anything I wouldn't have done for you."

She fisted her hands to her sides. "Do you have any idea how much guilt I've been carrying around all these weeks? And Sarco, God Draka, this has almost killed him, and still may. You ask me to forgive you? I ask you, why didn't you trust me, Ary?"

Aryanna slowly lifted her head. Tear tracks marred her once-perfect face. "It was never you I didn't trust, Lark. It was always me."

Pain, too intense to be held in, flowed up and outward, as Lark's ears rang with the beating of her heart and the pounding of her head. She knew this was as much her fault as it was Ary's, probably even more so.

Yes, she and Sarco had been thrown together, but Lark knew in her heart she'd wanted him, and in the end, it hadn't mattered to her that he'd been meant for her sister. She had taken what she wanted, just as Ary had. If truth be told, they'd all four played equal parts in this debacle.

Lonely, empty years without either the man she loved or the sister she'd always adored stretched endlessly before Lark, and despair chilled her from the inside out. Shivers she couldn't control shook her entire frame.

Outside, lightning struck so close, a tree beside the tower split in two, and the crashing of it jerked Lark from her trance. Chunks of ice now pelted the ground, and the wind whipped so viciously it whisked away a statue of a previous headmistress, tossing it across the front of the window before depositing it on the other side of the bailey.

Lark couldn't take her eyes from the out-of-control tempest. She was so absorbed in her own pain and the storm outside, she didn't hear the footsteps on the stairs. The door burst open with a resounding thud, and a pair of surprisingly strong hands grasped both of Lark's arms and shook her.

"Get yourself under control, Granddaughter. You must cease this minute. If you don't, the Academy itself could be lost. Lark, can you hear me, girl?"

Lark crumpled into her grandmother's arms and sobbed, "I can't. I've only ever been able to control it to a point. I'm sorry."

Grandmother rocked her, and the wind lessened. The feel of Grandmother Ava's gentle fingers stroking her hair eased her soul. "You must try, child," Grandmother whispered. "Just as water tempers fire, flesh tempers spirit. Look deep within yourself. The power is there."

Lark lifted her head and looked into the kind face of the only parent she'd ever known. "You're right, Grandmother. I'll try." She stood and walked to the window and gasped. The sight of the destruction below was far greater than she could have imagined and it frightened her. "I did this?"

Grandmother Ava nodded. "And now you must stop it."

Lark shook her head. "Mother was right, after all, wasn't she? I am a monster."

Tears fell in earnest and obscured the view. The feeling of a hand strongly grasping her own, a body standing beside her, and a warmth invading her mind brought comfort. Thoughts floated together as Lark and Aryanna's minds meshed into one.

"*Don't ever believe that, Lark. You aren't the monster, she is. You're special, and Mother could never see past her fears to recognize that in you. It's her loss, not yours.*" Her sister's love enveloped her. "*I'll understand if you can never forgive me, really I will. I'm not sure I can ever forgive myself. I'm afraid I even bungled the explanation badly, didn't I? I was so nervous. But then how could I ever justify using my own sister? A sister I love with all my heart. I really only ever wanted happiness for both of us, and I know in my heart Sarco is the man to make you happy, just as Cyrrick is the only one for me. But please don't blame Cyrrick for any of this. It's my fault.*"

Lark turned to her sister and gazed in Ary's eyes. She wasn't sure who cried harder. For the first time, she saw a sister she'd never seen before. This Ary was just as vulnerable, scared, and insecure as she was. Gone was the prissy, proper princess she showed the rest of the world. The woman who stood before her today was simply the big sister who'd made a mistake. It was time to stop the blaming.

"*I forgive you, Ary, and it wasn't just you. We were all in the wrong. We'll work this out together, you'll see. Right now, though, I need your help, please. I can't stop the storm alone."*

Aryanna squeezed her hand. *"You've always had the power to stop it. It's within you, but I'm honored you asked my help. I think I know just the thing. It always worked when you were a squirming, squalling baby."*

Lark peeked at her sister and smiled. She closed her eyes as Ary's voice rang with the strains of a lullaby. The words sounded vaguely familiar. They flittered through her mind.

Outside, the winds calmed, the hail ceased, the dark clouds gave way, and order once more reigned.

*"Ary, how could I have not realized all these years that you, too, see into other people's minds and connect with their thoughts?"*

She felt her sister's sigh as strongly as if she'd heard it. *"Because I'm the quintessential princess, Lark. That's all most people ever care to see."*

Lark placed an arm around her sister's shoulder, and Aryanna draped one of hers about Lark's waist.

*"I'm sorry, Ary."*

*"Me too, Lark."*

\*\*\*\*

Sarco was cold. No, cold wasn't nearly a strong enough word for what he was feeling right now. It was nose-hairs-sticking-together, cheek-burning, breath-crystallizing-in-his-lungs, finger-numbing, toe-tingling, freezing-arse *cold*, and they hadn't even begun the long trek up the mountain yet.

He drew the edges of his woolen cloak tighter about himself and glanced upward toward the Alarian mountain range. White clouds obscured the peaks while a gray sky hid the sun. He shivered, as a gust of frigid wind found its way once more up and under the edge of his garment. If it was this cold down here, what would it be like way up there, in the small valley with the flower they sought?

The very recollection of warmth eluded him, and he wondered fleetingly if he'd ever know warmth again.

Warmth had only been a quarter turn of the hourglass ago. That's how long it had taken the six of them to ride out of the Academy courtyard, up the road, and through the portal. Warmth was no more than a distant memory here, a thing of the past.

The barbarian city of Alaria stretched out before them, coldly beautiful in its wintry, frozen silence. Ice hung like crystal daggers from leafless branches, while structures dotting the barren landscape glistened.

Soaring towers rose in the middle of a sprawling city. They stood proud and tall, yet, to his eyes, the castle adjacent to them appeared bleak and isolated. So this was Lark's home, where she'd grown up? Loneliness filled him. His mind sought a connection while his heart reminded him just how futile wishing could be.

Sarco sighed, looked toward the heavens, and gaped. The sky here was like a living entity unto itself as it pulsed and moved with energy. Ribbons of light danced across the horizon. Shades of reds and greens blended and swirled together with golds and purples, so close he could almost grasp and touch them. The sight struck awe in his heart.

Why had they been forced to come to this particular place? This farthest, most-northern point of land in all of Albrath? This vast homeland of the barbarian people?

He shivered as he turned in a circle and stared out at a pristine blanket of white. There was only one reason why anyone traveled this far north in the dead of winter. Where else would a barbarian quest begin but in Alaria?

## Chapter Nineteen

If ever a man was more missed than Sarco Sunwalker, Lark would like to meet that man. Even though her small tower room was filled close to overflowing with guests, she might as well have been completely alone. Her heart ached, and she wondered—for at least the hundredth time since she'd watched him ride through the gates and off into the distance this morning—how he was faring. Better than she, Lark hoped.

The discussion with Aryanna earlier had left her not only physically but emotionally exhausted. Not to mention the energy it had taken to finally stop the storm. Lark wanted nothing more than to lay her head upon her pillow, cry herself to sleep, and drift off into dreamless oblivion for a few short turns of the hourglass.

That wasn't possible yet, though. There would be plenty of time for tears and sleep later. Right now, this meeting needed to get underway.

Lark glanced around the room, not sure where to begin. Five faces stared silently at her. Well, six, if she counted Tug. Aryanna, the twins Ally and Audrey, Laycee, and Briar sat waiting.

Lark took two deep breaths to try and calm the nervous rumbling of her tummy and cleared her throat. "First, let me say thank you in case I forget to do so before we've finished here this evening. Second, I need to assure all of you if at any time you wish not to be a part of this, Aryanna and I will understand and in no way hold it against you. This is our problem to deal with, and though we'd love all the help we can get, we don't wish to cause anyone a moment's trouble."

Lark fidgeted with her hands as she glanced toward her Channeling instructor. Nerves momentarily caused her to pause and gather her thoughts before continuing. "Briar, you've become much more than a teacher to me. You've become a trusted friend and advisor, but you're the only one here who is neither directly related, nor in the employ of this family. There is always the possibility being a conspirator with us could cause you difficulties in your position. We'll most certainly understand if you don't wish to be involved."

The tinkling sound of Briar's laughter helped settle Lark's nerves. "I'm honored you and Aryanna trust me enough to ask for my help. I'm not concerned about my position. It's secure. And believe me, right now, I need something to keep me occupied so I don't go chasing after my sneaky husband and do more than burn his eyebrows off. Do you know what he did to me? He tricked me into drinking my own sleeping potion so I couldn't go with them. Just wait 'til he gets home. Oh, yes, I need to be kept busy. Count me in. I'll do anything I can to help."

Lark laughed. "Thank you, Briar. And I wouldn't want to be Uthiel when he gets back, though I wouldn't mind watching the fireworks."

The room broke out in a round of giggles as Lark turned her attention back to them. "All right then, I'm going to tell you what Aryanna and I have decided and what we plan on doing about it. When I'm done, if you're all still willing to help, it'll be greatly appreciated."

Heat crept up Lark's cheeks. The thought of divulging a secret she'd kept close to her heart for so long left her feeling vulnerable. Still, she took a deep breath and plunged onward. "Ary and I have decided to go against the dictates of our parents."

A hush fell over the room.

"Ary is in love with Cyrrick and doesn't want to marry Sarco. I'm in love with Sarco and wish to spend every moment of the rest of my life with him. So you can see our dilemma. We need help finding a way around the humans' who-marries-who-and-when rule."

Soft gasps and almost inaudible whispers filled the air. Laycee responded first, just loud enough to be heard by everyone in the room. "Have ya both lost ya minds? Has the entire world gone crazy? Ya can search 'til VoT freezes over for all the ways ya want around any rule and it still won't matter a hill o' beans. There's no way around ya parents' dictates, and they've declared it's Ary who'll marry Sarco. Love, bah! What has love ta do with duty? As ya governess, it's my responsibility ta tell ya ta cease this silliness immediately, be good girls, and do what ya parents say. End of story."

Laycee's eyes twinkled as she stood, fisted her hands, and placed them firmly on her hips. "Now, as ya probably-soon-ta-be-out-of-work friend, what can I do ta help?"

"You can count us in," Ally cheered.

Audrey chimed in. "We've never agreed with all the letting-the-king-and-queen-do-the-choosing-for-you thing anyway. Being a princess shouldn't mean giving up all rights to happiness."

Lark held up her hand, and a hush fell over the room. "It's settled, then. First thing tomorrow morning, we'll meet in the library. We'll read every single word of every page in every history book ever written on the human race. Somewhere, in one of those books must be the answer we're searching for. There is nothing more we can think to do."

"What about asking Grandmother Ava?" Ally interjected. "She knows more about humans than anyone else I've ever known."

Lark shook her head. "We can't involve Grandmother. She's the moderator of the Council of the Elders. She can't be expected to go against tradition, and I don't want to get her into trouble. We'll have to do this one on our own, I'm afraid."

Audrey looked at Ally, then back toward Lark. "So, I guess I'm the one who's gonna ask the question everyone is wondering about but is afraid to ask. What happens if we do read every page of every book on humans and still don't find a way around the rule?"

Lark's breath caught in her chest.

Aryanna stood and answered for her. "If we don't find a way around the rule, then I'll do what is expected of me and do my duty to my people. I'll have no choice. Above all else, the prophecy must be fulfilled." Her voice broke. "We've discussed it, and neither Lark nor myself can fathom being responsible for a war or the loss of a life. I pray it doesn't come to that."

Aryanna shuddered then continued. "I want to thank everyone for coming. Before today, I thought I was alone in this. I was wrong. I've learned so much this day. I've learned to trust, I've learned to listen, and I've learned to accept. But most importantly of all, I've learned I don't have to do this alone. You are my sisters, some of my blood and all of my heart. Together, we'll succeed."

Lark crossed the distance between them and enclosed Aryanna in a warm embrace. Ally and Audrey joined in as arms wrapped about arms. A heartbeat later, Laycee and Briar made their way across the room. Hands were clasped together in solidarity and promises forged.

The meeting was adjourned.

\*\*\*\*

"What the green slimy snot running down the fat lip of a red-eyed ogre with a nasty head cold are ya thinking, lad? Take those oversized paws of ya off my doll and step away from Miss Bunny, or ya'll be feeling the depth of my blade in ya backside."

Sarco quickly jumped between his little friend and the barbarian. He held one hand on the top of Leeky's head while his other rested on Adan's broad chest. He might be able to keep them physically apart, but he couldn't prevent the barbarian from escalating the argument.

"What's wrong with you, gnome? The doll stays here with the horses. I'm more than willing to help outfit us in proper gear to climb mountains, but I'll not be seen traveling with a blow-up doll, of all things. Being in the company of a halfling, an elf, a human, and a gnome is bad enough. I draw the line at dollies. I have my pride. I'm the prince of this kingdom. These are my people and they look up to me. It isn't seemly, and I won't do it."

Though Leeky barely came to the level of Adan's knee, it was all Sarco could do to keep his small friend from getting past him and attacking the giant barbarian.

"Miss Bunny won't be staying here all alone in the cold. Go ahead, Sarco, ya tell him. There's no more valuable piece of equipment ya can take with ya on any journey than a good blow-up doll. She goes."

Adan's face turned a deep red. "She stays."

Leeky slipped between Sarco's feet and kicked at the barbarian. "She goes, I tell ya."

Sarco picked Leeky up and struggled to hand the squirming gnome unceremoniously to Uthiel. Then he once more faced Adan. "I appreciate all the help you're giving us, especially with these thick, warm coats, leggings, gloves, and snowshoes, but I've been through some mighty tough situations with Leeky, and I trust his judgment."

He smiled at the gnome who was still trying to squirm his way out of Uthiel's grip. "More than once his ingenuity has saved my life. If he wishes to cart his doll, along with all his gear, up that mountain, then that's his business, not yours. As for going along and being seen with us, that's up to you."

Uthiel set Leeky down. Adan scowled but didn't say another word as he strapped on his backpack and took his place at the front of the line to guide the group up the mountain.

Leeky picked up Miss Bunny, draped a coat about her shoulders, and strapped her onto his back with the rest of his gear. Her feet bounced along the ice, her arms flailed back and forth, and her blond curls bobbed above the back of Leeky's head. The movement made it appear as if she were shivering right along with the rest of them.

Sarco grimaced at the disturbing sight and looked to his brother. "What exactly did you find out about the quest, Cyrrick, other than the fact it begins here? Oh, and in case I forgot to tell you, thanks for spending your last hours at the Academy doing research for me."

Cyrrick didn't look at Sarco, or anyone else, as he drew a small notebook from a pocket. His voice was flat and almost lifeless as he addressed the group. "The quest was originally called *To Appease a King.* Catchy title, huh? From what I've read, this first part consists of gathering a single flower. Sounds easy, I must admit, until you take into consideration what flower they're talking about.

"The definition of A Maiden's Desire, straight from the reference books, states, 'Found only in one spot in all of Albrath: a small, secluded valley high in the Alarian Mountains.' The description given of the flower is quite poetic really. 'A flower as strong as its elements, as delicate as a breath. The touch of a finger can bring its untimely death.'

"The section I read on the Maiden's Desire states they bloom but once a year and that is the week after Yulemass. They can only be picked successfully while in bloom. This, my friends, is the week after Yulemass, so it looks like we've lucked out." Cyrrick flipped his notebook closed.

Once again, the strange feeling Sarco had been getting all day when he looked his brother's way seeped into his soul. Something was wrong and he needed to find out what. It was on the tip of his tongue to ask Cyrrick for a few moments of private discussion when Sherman distracted him.

The halfling held up his hand as high as he could get it and hopped up and down.

Sarco grinned. "This isn't class, Sherman. If you have something to say, just say it."

The halfling blushed. "So will you be using elemental magic then to gather the flower, Mr. Sunwalker, sir? I'd sure like to see that. I took a class once on flowers."

Sarco sighed. "I have a better than average understanding of the use of the element fire, but I get the feeling it may take all four elements—soil, air, water, and fire—to accomplish this quest. Only Uncle Arizon still practices all four. It takes an amazing amount of energy and concentration to do truly elemental magic. Father is a fire wizard like myself, and Mother is water. Over the years she has shown me a few tricks, and I did practice some air and soil one semester, but I'm really not proficient with anything other than fire. I hope I'm up to the task, but only time will tell. It's been years since I dabbled in anything other than fire."

Uthiel patted Sarco on the back. "If anyone can do it, I know you can."

Not another word was spoken as the group headed out single file up the narrow mountain trail with Adan in the lead. Sarco rubbed his forehead. He tried his best to convince the pounding in his head that hadn't ceased all day to finally stop and go away. He failed utterly. He missed home. He missed Lark.

The sky darkened and became laden with heavy, unfallen snow. The air turned crisp and grew thinner the higher they climbed. A chill wind blew so sharply it whipped through the thick coats and the group shivered.

Time slowed and lost all meaning. All that mattered was following the footsteps of the man directly in front and adding your own footprints to his. Onward and upward they trudged.

****

They were about halfway up to the mountain plateau surrounding the valley they sought when Cyrrick first noticed Leeky looking back over his shoulder at him.

"What the mangy patches on the underbelly of a green-eyed billy goat is wrong with ya, lad? I realize I don't know ya half as well as I do ya brother, but even I can tell something isn't sitting right with ya."

Cyrrick scowled at the gnome. He'd decided to be last in line for a reason. He didn't want to be bothered with anyone right now, especially not a nosey gnome with a doll strapped on his back. All he wanted was to be left alone so he could best decide how to tell Sarco what a traitorous, no-good piece of dragon dung he had become.

Knowing he had no choice but answer Leeky or be subjected to further questioning, he chose his words carefully. "Nothing's wrong. I'm just not much of a cold-weather person. I prefer sand and sunshine to mountains and ice."

Leeky didn't even look back over his shoulder when next he spoke. "And here I was thinking your conscience was probably bothering ya a bit because ya've been monkey-twiddling the woman ya brother's suppose ta marry. Guess I was mistaken."

Cyrrick stumbled over his own feet and almost choked. "You know?"

Leeky cackled. "Not much goes on at the Academy

I don't know about, lad. I may well be a janitor by day, but I'm a rogue all the time. I get around, ya know. And unless ya're kinkier than me, which I seriously doubt, I wouldn't call what ya were doing last night as research for ya brother. Which meansya've known about the quest all along."

Leeky chuckled, "So, Mr. I'm-Good-With-Words, what ya going ta do about getting ya brother out of this mess? Ya did do that too, didn't ya, get him inta this mess of a quest in the first place, I mean?"

Cyrrick hung his head. "It's not that simple, Leeky. I admit, I was trying to find a way for Aryanna and myself to be together. I love her and she loves me. But I also love my brother and I want him to be happy. I thought if he could just do this stupid quest he'd be able to choose which princess he wished to marry. He loves Lark, you know he does, and he would've chosen her."

Cyrrick shrugged his shoulder. "It's my fault, all of it. I didn't do my homework thoroughly. I didn't find out about the human rule until it was too late. I've put my own brother in danger for nothing, hurt three other people, and probably lost the only woman I'll ever love. I can't bring myself to even look Sarco in the eye right now, I'm so ashamed of myself. Let alone know how to ask his forgiveness. I know I'll never be able to forgive myself for what I've done."

The climb became steeper, but the gnome didn't sound the least bit winded when he asked his next question. "Are ya a man of worth or no, Cyrrick Sunwalker?"

Cyrrick nodded slowly even though he knew Leeky couldn't see it. It was habit. "I try to be. I always thought I was before this. Now, I'm not so sure, I guess."

Leeky turned toward Cyrrick and winked. "What the bleeding bunions on the bare feet of a tap-dancing, onion-farming ogre are ya talking about? Who ya are ain't determined by the mistakes ya make, lad. It's how ya go about setting them ta right that defines ya. A man's worth's measured by only three things in this world—his thoughts, his words, and his deeds. The sum of these is honor. Ya are an honorable man, Cyrrick Sunwalker. Everybody knows that. I've no doubt when the time comes, ya'll know exactly what ta do and ya'll be doing the right thing. Until then, quit lagging behind. Ya're slowing us down, waiting for ya. I want ta be getting ta that valley and inta a warm tent while I can still feel my feet. Why, my poor balls are so cold right now and they've shrunken so far up inside me looking for a warm spot, that there're near ta poking out my arse."

Cyrrick smiled for the first time all day, his heart feeling lighter. He quickened his step as he spoke to Leeky's back. "From what I've heard about gnome balls, old man, they're too little and inconsequential to worry about poking out of anywhere."

Leeky Shortz cackled, "You'd be surprised, diplomat. Why, if it weren't for my snug undies, I'd have bruised knees from all that heavy skin flapping back and forth."

Cyrrick laughed for the first time in days.

## Chapter Twenty

If ever a man appeared to be more flustered than the tall, white-haired, indigo-blue-skinned dark-elf pacing back and forth behind the counter, Lark would hate to see that man.

The librarian stopped suddenly, as if he'd just noticed them. "I certainly hope you didn't intend to use the facilities today. Just look at this mess."

He spread his arms to encompass the room, and even though she didn't really wish to, Lark glanced around. It was chaos and then some. Windows were broken, shelves overturned, books strewn, and puddles of water stood everywhere. Her face warmed with embarrassment as she made contact with the intense, purple eyes of the librarian.

"Yes, that was a rather nasty storm we had yesterday, wasn't it?" Lark's voice rose an octave higher than normal and squeaked.

The dark-elf, whose bright-red name badge read, Mr. Authorn Hawthorn, Head Librarian, appeared almost beside himself.

"Nasty? This…this…catastrophe is what you call simply a nasty storm? Oh, no, a nasty storm is when I have to wear my waders to work the next morning. This is a disaster of epic proportions. It'll take weeks to put to rights, if it can be accomplished at all. I scarcely dare to hope none of the truly valuable works of literature have been damaged beyond redemption. I simply don't understand how this could've happened." The librarian placed a hand over his heart. "It's almost more than I can take. A lifetime of work in total disarray. Wherever shall I begin?"

He shook his head and looked like he might cry. "This has been the strangest season for weather I've seen in my entire life. I wonder if it has anything to do with the three moons coming into full phase soon? One of them is already full and the second is two-thirds of the way to becoming complete, you know. Less than a phase now and they'll all be fully round, glowing orbs in the night sky. I hope it's not lunar interference causing this havoc. If it is, I fear what the next weeks may bring."

Lark plastered a smile to rival Miss Bunny's on her face, trying her best not to allow the dark-elf to see her guilt. The trip to the library had been one reminder after another of yesterday's lack of control. "I doubt there'll be another storm like that one again anytime soon, Mr. Hawthorn. I'm sure it was simply a freak of nature and has little or nothing to do with moon phases."

Mr. Authorn Hawthorn blinked rapidly, sniffed loudly, straightened his shoulders, and addressed the group of ladies yet again. "Please, call me Authorn. Mr. Hawthorn sounds so pretentious and old, don't you think? Now, is there something I can help you with? I really need to get back to cleaning this mess." He bent and retrieved a soggy book. It dripped fat drops of water on the marble tiled floor, making a disturbing plopping sound.

Lark cringed. "We need to take a quick peek in the section on human history if it isn't too much trouble,

Authorn. If we find it in disorder like the rest of the library, we'll be glad to put it to rights. It's the least we can do."

Authorn didn't even look at the women, his entire attention still focused on the waterlogged book. He pointed toward the right side of the huge room. "Human history is in the non-fiction H row over there, but due to storm damage, we're closed. I'm very sorry, ladies, you'll simply have to wait until tomorrow. No matter how much we do or don't get accomplished today, we'll reopen then."

Lark sputtered. "But—but—but, you don't understand. This is a very important matter. It's imperative we see the section on human history today. You won't even notice us, I promise. Oh, and if it makes any difference, we're princesses."

The dark-elf librarian glanced at the group of women with a look of exasperation on his deep-blue face. "Human history is just that, dear lady. It's history, and as such, can certainly wait one more day. You seem to be nice girls even if you are princesses, but if Headmistress Seychelle herself were to walk through these doors today and demand to use the facilities, I simply wouldn't be able to comply. These books are precious, some even irreplaceable, and must be handled by specially trained individuals only. Surely you understand the importance of my task? Now, off with you, I have much work to do."

Defeated for the moment, Lark turned to the waiting group of women. The pressure of Aryanna's warm hand coming to rest on her arm offered comfort, and the sound of her voice brought with it a sense of camaraderie. "Well, what are we to do now?"

Laycee plucked something shiny from deep inside a pocket. "We could go and take a quick look-see at where I'm going ta be living when Leeky gets back. He gave me the key ta his apartment and told me ta fix it up as I saw fit."

The rest of the group nodded and embraced the idea enthusiastically. Lark wasn't so sure. All she could do was shudder at the memory of sex swings, farting contests, whipped cream, Ride 'Em Cowboy, and bare-arsed gnomes on the beach. The thought of what she might find lurking in the depths of Leeky Shortz's apartment was more than a little frightening.

****

At least they had sunshine, unlike the previous days' weather during their quest. That was the only pleasant thing Sarco could think of, because the quest certainly wasn't going well.

Six fully blooming Maiden's Desire flowers, with ice-white stems, and as delicate as single snowflake leaves, had been growing fairly close together in a patch upon a wide, layer of ice. Now, only three remained.

His first three attempts to pick a flower had failed. Three times the combination of timing and magic had been incorrect. And with each failure had come the breaking away of a section of the ice. Not just any section, however, but a thick section spanning the frozen shelf hugging a huge snowbank. If Sarco didn't succeed soon, the remainder of the ice would give way and the packed snow would inevitably become an avalanche barreling down upon their heads.

Sarco paced back and forth before the last three flowers and contemplated his next move. "Anyone have a suggestion as how to proceed before I get us all killed? We've searched this valley twice and this is the only patch of Maiden's Desires we've found, and we don't have many left. I'm fresh out of ideas. I mean, what else can I try that I haven't already?

Uthiel sighed. "I really thought this part of the quest was going to be easy when you picked that first bloom. But it melted as soon as your hand touched it, even though you took Leeky's advice and wore gloves. I'm sorry my friend, I don't know what else you can try."

Sherman jumped up and down with his hand held high.

Sarco rubbed his temples. "Yes, Sherman."

"You should try summoning one again. I mean, you almost had that second flower when you beckoned it with your wand. If you hadn't had to touch it when it got to you, it would've worked. I just know it would've."

Leeky slapped his leg. "What the shriveled-up nut sac betwixed the legs of an older-than-fart-dust troll troubadour do ya think we should do? Personally, I liked it when ya tried ta thaw the ice around the third one and scoop it up in the frigid water. It still dissolved into nothingness, but the idea has potential."

Suddenly, the wind shifted, and with a loud crack a segment of ice holding two of the three remaining flowers gave way and slid into a deep crevasse.

Sarco stared into the abyss. "Well, men, there's only one flower left and just a small section of ice still holding back all that snow and keeping us from tumbling into that frozen darkness. What am I going to do?"

Sarco glanced toward his brother. "Any ideas?"

Cyrrick didn't disappoint. "You could try using us. Perhaps together we may be able to accomplish what one alone can't."

Sarco shook his head. "This is my quest. If anyone is to be put in danger, it must be me."

Cyrrick shrugged. "I realize you've always prided yourself on being able to take care of your own problems, but there must've been a good reason why the quest rules allowed you to choose companions. I doubt the purpose of our being here is solely to keep you company."

Though it took a few moments to come to terms with what his brother had said, Sarco acquiesced. "You're right, Cyrrick. I do tend to get a little self-absorbed, don't I? So, how do *we* go about plucking this damn flower and staying alive long enough to get it off this mountain?"

Cyrrick paced. "I think Leeky's right. Do you remember what Uncle Arizon told us about magic? A true elementalist must be able to control all aspects of his environment. The way I see it, we have a three-part problem, and though the solution could prove to be dangerous, I do believe it's doable."

Sarco nodded. "Go on."

"First, we must pick the flower and somehow prevent it from dissolving." Cyrrick hesitated for just a moment then continued, "Then, when the ice shelf does give way, we must somehow keep the snow behind it at bay long enough to get a head start." He sighed and shook his head. "And, finally, we must find some way to beat a mountain of snow down to Alaria or get buried alive in the avalanche. I have a suggestion for the first two problems. The third, though, I have no idea what to do."

Sarco was relieved as, for the first time in days, Cyrrick stood before him and looked him directly in the eye. No deception, no guilt, no subterfuge, just brotherly concern. "I suggest we put Sherman to use. I sat in on a couple of your classes, remember, and I know for a fact Sherman can control fire, for a short time anyway. What good's having an extra set of wizard hands along if you don't make use of them, right? While he employs elemental fire magic and melts the ice away from the base of the last flower, you draw on the wind."

Sarco started to turn away. "It won't work. I'm not an elemental air wizard, let alone a water one."

Cyrrick grabbed Sarco's arm and halted his movement. "Hear me out, brother, before you discount my idea. Using your elemental air and water magic—and you and I both know you are competent in at least the basics of both—you will then take the water Sherman's melted and quickly form it into a ball. When you have the water spinning fast enough, position it over the flower and open it up like a sphere. When it's surrounding the flower, combine the water and air together and freeze the globe solid. That should allow you to simply bend down and scoop up the flower, for it will be suspended in solid ice."

Sarco rubbed his chin and nodded. "That might work. But the surrounding ice will still break away beneath the flower and the snow will surge down upon us."

Cyrrick shook his head. "I won't allow it to. Even though I'm a diplomat by trade, I'm nonetheless a

Sunwalker. I'm not as powerful a wizard as you, but there are still some things I remember how to do. I can hold back the snow for a short time, Sarco. I can hold it long enough for the rest of you to get safely away. Mother spent many hours teaching me water magic. Snow is simply another form of water. I can do this. I need to do this for you, for Aryanna, for all of us."

Sarco gazed into the set of eyes so similar to his own and finally saw what he'd been afraid to see for so long. Signs he'd ignored so he wouldn't have to face their consequences. They were all there right before him. He could ignore them no longer.

The conversation about the small leather book came back to him in full force. His brother's words from almost a season ago burned through his mind. *If you could, Sarco, who would you choose?* And then, *Practice these words over and over and over until you can say them without thinking, even in your sleep.*

Sarco paced, needing the time it gave him to think. Not giving a thought to what anyone else around him was doing, he immersed himself in memories.

It had been Cyrrick who'd changed the words in the book? But why? Other scenes flooded his mind. Memories of Cyrrick with Aryanna fast on his heels as he ran into Lark's tower room after the disastrous ceremony. And Aryanna demanding Lark take her place in his class. Even the leather book itself had been a gift from Aryanna. The glances between the two he'd seen so many times and ignored. Why hadn't he realized it before? How could he have missed something so obvious? Cyrrick and Aryanna, they were in love, and…desperate.

Sarco wanted to kick himself. He knew why he'd

missed the signs. It was because he'd been more concerned with his own problems and station than his brother's feelings. But then, if Cyrrick and Aryanna had wanted to be together, why hadn't they simply asked for his help? He wasn't unreasonable. Was he?

Even the answer to that question made Sarco cringe. Cyrrick knew him well, and knew Sarco would have protested loudly if his honor had been brought into question. Honor had always come first, even before family. How had he allowed himself to become so shallow that his own brother didn't feel he could confide in him?

He chanced a quick glance Cyrrick's way and was stunned by the determination he saw etched on his brother's face. His brother was willing to lay down his life for him.

Now he understood the true reason why this quest must be completed, and completed successfully. It wasn't to restore his own honor and be granted forgiveness from a throne he cared nothing for. It wasn't for the sake of the prophecy. It wasn't even for the opportunity to choose whom he would marry.

From the moment the words during the betrothal ceremony had left his lips, even before he'd realized something was wrong with the words he'd spoken, Sarco had known deep in his heart he'd made a mistake.

He could not marry Princess Aryanna, no matter the outcome of this quest or the dictates of kings, councils, and rules. She'd never been his to have. She'd always been Cyrrick's and he hers.

The true reason for the quest was simple. Cyrrick had cared enough about Sarco's happiness to try and find a way for him to choose a wife of his heart and still retain his honor and do his duty. His brother was even willing to risk losing the woman he loved if the quest didn't work. It was important to Cyrrick for Sarco to finish what Cyrrick himself had set into motion. Cyrrick believed in him and his abilities to do this. If nothing else, that was ample reason.

Sarco remembered the look on his brother's face when he'd said, *You were the only one who stood by me when I decided to become a diplomat, and I'll make you proud someday.* He'd always been proud of his brother, and was more so now than ever before.

There was much they needed to discuss, but the time to talk would have to come later. Right now, Sarco needed to prevent his brother from sacrificing his life because of a sense of misplaced guilt.

He stopped pacing, turned, and looked Cyrrick in the eye. "And how would you get safely away from the avalanche, Brother, after I pick the flower? I won't chance losing you, Cyrrick, not for a quest, not for a kingdom, not for a prophecy, not for a woman, not for anything. You mean that much to me. There must be another way. Either we both get back to the women we love or neither of us do."

Cyrrick looked shocked. He looked to be about to argue the point, but never got the chance.

"What the pickled innards of a patchy, red-spotted, nearly bald, drunken ogre dancing a jig on the top of a tavern table are ya thinking, lad? I've got the perfect solution right here in front of ya and ya aren't even seeing it." Leeky pointed toward Miss Bunny and grinned. "Didn't I tell ya she's the most important piece of equipment we could bring with us?"

Sarco wasn't sure he wanted to know what the gnome meant. He ran his fingers through his hair and scratched his chin. "I guess I'm not quite grasping it, Leeky."

The gnome puffed out his chest and looked indignant. "Why, isn't it obvious? We'll use Miss Bunny here ta beat the snow down the mountain."

Sarco's left cheek twitched. "You mean as kind of a…a…sled or something?"

Leeky cackled and rubbed his hands together. "Precisely, lad. Now ya've got it"

His neck was stiff and Sarco rubbed it, trying to work out the kinks not only in the muscles but also in his mind. "I can see using the doll as a sled of sorts, really I can. What I don't get though is how all six of us are going to fit on her. Even if we figure out a way to keep Cyrrick from being buried alive when he lets the snow loose. He can't hold it back forever."

Uthiel spoke up. "Not to encourage Leeky because, well, we know what happens when he gets an idea. But we could make a chain from the ice to the doll. I'll hold onto Cyrrick and Adan can hold onto me. Leeky can straddle the doll's head and have her in position and ready to steer down the mountain. Once you and Sherman work your magic and gather the flower, each of you run, grab onto a doll shoulder and hang on.

"When you guys are ready, Adan and I can yank Cyrrick toward the doll as he continues to hold back the snow. Right before Cyrrick lets the snow loose, Adan will jump onto Miss Bunny's body and help hold Leeky in place while he steers. Cyrrick and I'll each dive for a thigh and bring up the rear, so to speak. If we time it right, it'll probably be one wild, crazy ride, but it just might work."

Sarco shook his head. "We can't chance it. It's too dangerous. Someone could get killed."

The sight of Prince Adan Hammerstrike bristling before him almost brought a smile to Sarco's face. "I'll not have a coward for a brother-in-law, Sunwalker. It sounds like a fine plan to me. All except the part about riding that damn doll down the mountain. I'll admit, that's more than a little iffy, but I'm game if everyone else is." Adan glared at Leeky and the sight almost brought a smile to Sarco's face. It the circumstances weren't so dire, it would have. "If you get us killed, gnome, I swear I'll rip your doll's head off with my own two hands and shove it up your arse. Do you hear me? But if this plan of yours works, I'll personally carry Miss Bunny on my own back for the rest of this crazy quest."

Leeky smiled and held out a hand to Adan. "It's a deal."

Sarco shook his head, amazed, as, after the handshake, Leeky dug into his pants-of-many-pockets and hauled out a pair of bright red mittens. He made a production of slowly taking off the black fur gloves he'd been wearing and firmly slipping on the fuzzy mittens in their place.

He laid Miss Bunny gently on the ground and straddled her neck with his bottom, resting just above her breasts. His stubby legs stuck straight out alongside her ears, and he enclosed both his fists into her flowing, blonde hair.

For a split second a completely bizarre image of Ride 'Em Cowboy invaded Sarco's mind and he shuddered.

Leeky looked back over his shoulder and grinned. "What the red, inflamed hemorrhoids poking out the backside of a constipated, green-eyed dragon are ya waiting for, lads? We've a quest ta be getting on with and a ride down the mountain ta be taking. My sledding gloves are in place and Miss Bunny's raring ta go."

The men looked at each other and nodded.

Sarco positioned himself before the bloom with Sherman at his side and took a deep breath. "All right, let's do this."

The heat from Sherman's fire magic melted the ice at the base of the flower, and Sarco closed his eyes as he dug deep into his memory for the spell to call forth the power of the wind to his fingertips. "From the four corners of Albrath I summon the air. Let the wind now do my bidding without a care."

The melted water spun in the small pool around the flower until the Maiden's Desire bloom itself could no longer be seen.

Again Sarco relied on his memory of magic. "From water to ice you will now be. Freeze solid this sphere I command of thee." The water stopped spinning and a ball of ice formed.

Sarco tapped Sherman on the shoulder and motioned for him to take his place on the doll. He then turned toward his brother. "Are you ready?"

Cyrrick nodded.

Sarco looked to Uthiel and Adan. "And you?"

They nodded.

Slowly, so as to not disturb the ice shelf before he had to, Sarco knelt and plucked away the frosty sphere with the flower inside. Immediately, what was left of the ice shelf cracked.

"Get on the doll, Sarco, now," Cyrrick yelled as he lifted his arms and extended his hands toward the avalanche of snow threatening to fall. "Hurry, I can't hold this for long."

Sarco took his place opposite Sherman. He lay flat on his belly with Miss Bunny's right arm tucked tightly between his legs and gripped her shoulder. With his other hand he held high the orb of ice. "I'm in position, come now."

Adan slowly walked Uthiel backward as Uthiel held tight onto the hem of Cyrrick's shirt. Finally, just as Adan came into contact with the foot of the doll, he turned and laid himself along the length of her body, his face between her breasts.

Leeky turned and grinned at the huge barbarian. "What the picked-at green scabs on the knees of a troll trollop giving a blow job do ya think about my girl now, Adan? Ever have yourself a piece of plastic? Ya know what they say, don't ya? Once you've done plastic, nothing else is as fantastic."

Leeky cackled.

Sarco wasn't laughing. He was watching Cyrrick's arms. They'd begun to droop from the strain. "Hurry, Uthiel, grab onto Miss Bunny's leg. Cyrrick can't hold the snow much longer."

Uthiel let go of Cyrrick, turned, and leapt facedown onto the doll's leg and wrapped his arms tightly around Miss Bunny's thigh.

Cyrrick's voice sounded raspy from the strain of his efforts. "Go on, get going, all of you. I'll hold the snow back 'til you're safely away."

Sarco shook his head even though he knew Cyrrick couldn't see it. "I won't leave without you, brother. Let it go now and grab the other leg as we planned."

"I don't have the energy left to hold on, Sarco." Exhaustion weakened Cyrrick's voice. "It's all right, really it is. Allow me to do this for you, please. It's my fault you were put in this predicament in the first place."

Fear coursed through Sarco. "No, I won't allow you to sacrifice yourself. Think of Aryanna, Cyrrick, if you can't think of yourself right now."

Cyrrick's arms almost dropped. Then, with great effort, he once more raised them. "I am thinking of Aryanna."

Sarco unwound himself, tucked the frozen orb deep into a pocket, and grabbed hold of the back of Cyrrick's shirt. He forcibly dragged him down and the loud cracking of a solid mass of snow rent the air.

The last thing anyone heard before the doll slid down the mountainside was Sarco's shout. "We won't be leaving a man behind, Cyrrick. I'll hold on for the both of us 'til you can hold on for yourself."

****

When Laycee turned the key in the lock, flung the door wide open, and flipped on the light, the sight in Leeky's apartment was worse than Lark had thought possible. She turned in a circle and still couldn't take it all in.

Panties, not just a pair or two, but stacks upon stacks of them, all the way to the ceiling. There wasn't much more than a path wide enough for a person to snake through Leeky's entire apartment. The rest of the space was filled to overflowing with women's panties of every size, shape, color, pattern, and fabric.

It was Briar who dared speak first to the stunned,

open-mouthed group. "I must admit, I've often wondered what Leeky did with all the panties he's been pilfering for the last twenty years. Now, I finally know. The Academy panty thief story is a famous legend, don't you know? The stealing of panties from every female to cross the threshold of this place of learning has been a tradition and, although most suspected they knew who the panty thief was, not once has Leeky Shortz come close to being caught in the act." Lark shuddered as Briar continued, "Wow, Laycee, that rascal of a gnome must really love you. I'm pretty sure he's never shown this to anyone else."

Laycee's eyes glowed with excitement. "He is simply the sweetest, most considerate man in all of Albrath. And to think my Leeky collected all of these. What a noble endeavor for a rogue." She sniffed loudly and wiped away a tear. "I can't remember another time I've been so proud of anyone."

Shivers ran down Lark's spine at the disturbing sight. There were plain panties and polka-dotted ones, others were striped, sequined, plaid, flowered, and even bejeweled. Some were actually fashioned from precious metals. And they abounded in every style from grannies all the way to skimpy thongs.

Though she knew to hold her tongue so she wouldn't hurt Laycee's feelings, Lark was glad Aryanna didn't seem to have the same notion. Someone needed to talk sense into their governess, and Aryanna was evidently up for the challenge. "You can't be serious, Laycee. You can't really consider living here among other women's undies? That's too gross and disgusting for words."

Laycee cackled, "Live among them? Why, missy, I

plan ta do more than live among them. I plan ta put every last pair of them ta good use. Why, I bet in no time at all we could create a couch, a few chairs, a couple ottomans, curtains, even a mattress and covers for the bed out of these. I even have a picture or two in mind ta hang on the walls. Fine material and Academy history like this should not be let go ta waste. That would really be a shame. These panties should be proudly displayed."

Lark gulped.

"Now, be good girls, will ya, and sort. By color, pattern, and texture. Mind ya, I'm looking for consistency here. I don't want my furniture ta come across as low class or common. I have a sense of style ta uphold, ya know."

Ally gasped as she picked up a skimpy, bubble-gum-pink silk thong. "These are mine. Not only are they mine, but that…that panty thief stole them from my dirty clothes. Eww, now that's just nasty." She quickly tucked them into a pocket.

Laycee put her hands on her hips and glared. "If ya all insist on examining every single pair, we'll still be sorting this time next year. As far as taking them from your dirty clothes, my Leeky is the cleanest person I know. I'm sure they've been laundered. I mean, look around, do ya even see a speck of dust anywhere?

"And, Miss Allyssa Hammerstrike, ya put those panties right back where ya found them this instant. My Leeky stole those fair and square, and ya won't be shoplifting his property while I'm around. Matter of fact, ya should be thanking him for making ya part of history."

Lark didn't want to touch any of them, not even the

pretty blue velvet, bikini-cut ones that looked so familiar. But she did. How could she ask Laycee for help with what she needed if she wasn't willing to return the favor? Still, she used only the tips of two fingers to handle the garments.

Why was it, a man who had gloves for every situation imaginable, had not one single pair lying around today? She tried her best to think of something, anything, other than other women's panties as she sorted.

She sighed. Sarco had been gone less than a full day and here she was up to her elbows in women's underthings. Lark wondered how he was faring and hoped it was better than she.

Chapter Twenty-One

If ever a man should have kicked himself in the head before taking advice from a gnome, Sarco Sunwalker knew he was that man. The only thing he was now positive of was that he and five others were all going to die this day and very soon.

Ice, rocks, snow and trees—really big trees—whizzed by his head at an eye-popping, stomach-churning, scream-stuck-in-his-throat pace.

The scenery became no more than a blur as, faster and faster, the Miss Bunny sled sped down the nearly vertical mountain toward the looming, solid wall rimming the city of Alaria.

Sarco hastily glanced back over his shoulder and wished he hadn't. They were still being chased by what looked to be a ten-foot high wave of crystal-white, cold-as-the-grave snow, and the inundation appeared to be catching them. It was a toss-up as to which would go splat against the quickly approaching structure first—the group of six men crazy enough to ride an inflated plastic doll down a mountainside on their bellies, or the avalanche they'd unleashed.

Sarco gasped as something sharp scored his left hip. Pain shot straight down his leg and almost caused him to lose his grip on Miss Bunny's lifeline of a synthetic shoulder. Barely clinging with one hand as his other continued to hold onto his brother, Sarco knew what his bet on the outcome of this race would be. If he were a betting man. It wouldn't be on the survival of the doll or any of them.

The feel of powerful fingers stretching out, gripping his arm, securely drawing him in closer, and holding him in place surprised Sarco. He chanced a quick glance at the owner of the hand and yelled a quick, "Thanks," before he struggled once more with his grip.

The hulking barbarian didn't even look his way or acknowledge him. Sarco could understand why. Adan's eyes were on the sight before him. The color of his face rivaled the snow itself, and a look of complete terror was frozen on his countenance.

The massive barbarian's fright didn't do a thing to alleviate Sarco's own fears, and it took him totally by surprise when Adan yelled back, "You're welcome, Sunwalker. Didn't do it for you, though." Adan's wide-eyed gaze stayed riveted on the disaster that awaited them at the bottom of the mountain. "Still not sure how I feel about you becoming part of my family. Lar—I mean, Aryanna would never forgive me if I let you die in our own homeland. I'm doing it for her—"

At that moment, they hit a ridge and caught air. The sound of little girl screams rent the air, and somewhere in the back of his mind, Sarco realized they'd come from him. Even in the frigid cold, heat crept up his cheeks. No one else noticed, however, as, with a thud, the doll and all six of her passengers hit the frozen ground hard and kept going.

"Left, Leeky. Steer her to the left," Adan shouted. "See the entryway through the wall? Yes, that's it, now straighten her up. Faster, Leeky. The snow's catching us."

Time and space slowed, and Sarco could see every detail of each passing tree, rock, and snowbank. He could smell the tang of pine and wood smoke in the air. He could hear the howling of the wind and feel his heartbeat as it pounded in his chest.

He tried to keep his eyes trained on the finish line, the beckoning opening in the wall below, but he couldn't. The sight of Leeky playing a real-life version of Ride 'Em Cowboy down a mountain of ice while straddling a plastic doll was more disturbing than it had ever been to stumble on Leeky playing the silly game with Laycee.

Leeky "the daredevil" Shortz, with his salt-and-pepper tufts of hair flapping in the wind and a look of total exhilaration on his face, rode Miss Bunny as if she were a bucking dragon and he some bizarre tournament-of-champions star.

Leeky "the wrangler" Shortz kept one hand firmly fisted in the doll's hair while his other red-mittened hand reached back and periodically slapped Miss Bunny's boob.

Leeky "the slightly touched in the head" Shortz yelled at the top of his lungs with what sounded suspiciously like glee or perhaps insanity, "Didn't I tell ya she could do it? Giddyap, lass, faster, giddyap. Yee haw!"

The doll gave the gnome what appeared to be a conspiratorial wink and if possible, her smile grew wider. Sarco shook his head. If he hadn't completely lost his mind, and he wasn't sure he hadn't, their speed *did* increase.

He caught sight of Sherman out of the corner of his

eye and wished he could've said or done something to help the halfling. The little guy's eyes were closed. His hands gripped the doll's other shoulder so tightly his knuckles were completely white. From the way his lips constantly moved, it was obvious he was praying, and his face had taken on a green hue. Sarco sympathized, but when this ride came to a halt, he knew he wouldn't want to land anywhere near poor Sherman if he could possibly help it. There was no doubt in Sarco's mind that when they did finally come to a stop, the first thing the halfling would do, if still alive, was barf or piss himself.

Sarco had no idea his stomach could lurch harder than it already was until they flew over a small outcropping. Miss Bunny crossed legs in midair like a ballerina, and Uthiel was suddenly beside Sarco. He was still clinging to a thigh, with his body draped across the doll, and Cyrrick and Sherman were now side-by-side in the same manner.

Uthiel yelled over the roar of the rushing snow right behind them, "Should've brought Briar after all. We're going to need a healer when this is over. If we live through it."

That did make Sarco laugh.

Until they hit the ground.

The laughter and the air were knocked from his lungs. At least a couple of bones creaked if not cracked and muscles he hadn't realized he had spasmed as the doll went head-over-hindquarters on the cold, hard ice. Right through the open gates of Alaria they slid and came to a stop in the middle of the courtyard.

The deafening sound of the avalanche hitting the solid rock wall shook him to the core, but the pounding of Sarco's heart rang even louder in his ears. The wall held the onslaught of snow. They had done it. They were safe. And as he looked around, he realized they were all still alive.

"What the pink-plaid tutu on the torso of an ample-busted, black-haired ogre miss plying her trade on the street corner do ya have ta say about that, lads? Wasn't that just as much fun as I said it'd be? Who's for taking her back up ta the top and doing it again?"

No one raised a hand or even looked at the gnome as the group slowly stood up and dusted snow and debris off themselves.

After a few moments of silence, Adan asked the question everyone else was afraid to. "Well, Sunwalker, did the flower make it? I'd hate to think we just did that for naught."

Five pairs of eyes waited anxiously as Sarco stuck his hand into his pocket and drew out the frozen orb. With a sigh of relief, he held up the fist-sized, perfect sphere of ice for all to see.

Sunlight reflected off and through the globe. Inside, still frozen solid, glittered a perfect, golden-petaled Maiden's Desire bloom. Six deep breaths were let out in a rush. None louder than Sarco's.

"You wouldn't happen to have a safe, cold place to store this in your castle, would you, Adan? Just until we finish the next part of the quest? I'd sure hate to try and keep it frozen where we're heading tomorrow."

For the first time ever, Sarco heard Adan laugh, and the sound, though much deeper than hers, reminded him of Lark. For a moment, his heart contracted painfully with loneliness, and he wondered what she was doing right now.

Adan's next words, though they didn't alleviate the pain, helped a little. "This is a land of ice, Sunwalker. I'm pretty sure I can find some to spare around here someplace. The royal vault comes to mind. We can stoke it with plenty of the frozen stuff to keep that thing from melting for a millennium if need be. We'll put it in the vault first thing when we get to the castle. I can't wait to be back in my own home, if just for the night. I've a powerful need for a warm fire to thaw out our bones, hot food to fill our bellies, fine ale to sooth our souls, and a good night's sleep. I don't know about the rest of you, but every muscle in my body hurts and, if I'm not mistaken, I think half my teeth have rattled loose. I've had all the questing I can stand for one day."

For the first time all day, Sarco felt the comforting effects of a genuine smile cross his face as he followed Adan toward the castle. But the sound of the clearing of a gnome throat stopped them all in their tracks, even the hulking barbarian.

"Where the frozen dingleberries hanging off the bare, hairy arse of a high-mountain polecat peeing on a flat rock do ya think you're going, Adan Hammerstrike? Aren't ya forgetting something?"

Adan whipped around, and Sarco enjoyed the expression on the face of the other man. The barbarian prince at first looked confused, then understanding dawned. He walked up to Leeky, plucked Miss Bunny up, and cradled her in the crook of his arm. With his other hand, he hefted the gnome and placed him onto his other shoulder.

"What are the rest of you waiting for? Let's get a move on. I'm not carrying everyone. It's been a long day, and Leeky, I, and Miss Bunny here are mighty cold, tired, and hungry."

****

Good to his word, Mr. Authorn Hawthorn had the library open bright and early the next morning, a fact Lark was thankful for. Glancing around at her companions, she wondered how thankful they were. With their droopy eyes, grouchy expressions, and loud yawns, she doubted thankfulness was what they were thinking.

When she'd roused them from their beds before the sun had begun to peek over the horizon, her only thought had been to get an early start. Perhaps she should have at least allowed them to break their fast before dragging them to the library. If nothing else, she could offer them the opportunity. "Anyone need to eat first?"

Five sets of eyes looked up and brightened as heads nodded in unison toward her.

Aryanna spoke for the group. "I think we might concentrate better on the task at hand if we at least have a bite first. Don't you?"

It was on the tip of Lark's tongue to tell the group to go and eat without her as she looked longingly down row after row of history books. She didn't care about the grumbling of her stomach. When had she last eaten? She couldn't remember.

But, with a sigh, she followed the women out of the library and down the long hallway. She wouldn't be able to do Sarco, herself, or anyone else any good if she didn't take care of herself first. But knowing what was right and doing it instead of what her heart was begging her to do were two entirely different things.

Out the big, double doors of the library and across

277

the bailey the group of women retraced their steps. Lark kept her head down and her eyes trained to the front until they stepped through another door and were safely inside a hallway.

The feeling of warmth on her arms had been the only thing telling her the sun was shining. She hadn't been able to bring herself to look around outside at the debris still scattered around the grounds. The last thing Lark wanted was to be reminded of the devastating storm she had caused. She couldn't afford to dwell on it. There was work to be done, and distractions and guilt would only serve to sidetrack her from her task.

Because she hadn't been watching where she was going, she was caught off guard when the group stopped abruptly as they entered the cafeteria. Lifting her eyes, she saw her father sitting at a table all by himself, gazing at them with a questioning look on his weathered face. There was no way to avoid it. They were going to have to face him.

"Isn't it rather early for princesses to be up and out of bed? The sun has barely broken the horizon. Your mother won't rise for at least four turns of the hourglass yet." His smile suddenly faded. "I don't suppose any of you know how to spar on the practice field, do you? Longswords? Broadswords, blades, daggers, axes? Anything sharp?" He shook his head. "No, I suppose not."

Words stuck in Lark's throat as if she were three again and had been caught red-handed, filching her favorite cookie from the big blue jar that always sat on the counter in the corner of the kitchen, just out of her grasp.

Thankfully, Aryanna didn't seem to have the same

problem. "Good morning, father." She laughed. "And, no, swordplay and such was always forbidden to us females, remember? That was your rule. Princesses read, princesses do needlework, and princesses look pretty. Princesses never spar."

To anyone else's ears the sound of the tremble in Aryanna's voice would have been joyous, but Lark could hear the undertone of nervousness and the touch of anger Ary tried to hide. She sent a quick prayer skyward for Lord Draka to help them all.

Alfred Hammerstrike motioned to the empty chairs surrounding his table. "Well, if you can't join me out on the lists for swordplay, the least you can do is break bread with me. Come now, all of you, sit. It's not often I get time alone with my girls. A king's life is very busy, you know. There are always matters of state to deal with and the queen to keep happy. Then there's the warriors to see to and make sure they keep their skills honed. You never know when they may be needed to protect the realm. Your brother normally handles the warriors for me. He also usually spends at least a turn of the hourglass sparring with me each morning. I wonder how long he'll be gone."

The king sighed and the sound struck a chord deep in Lark's soul as she took her seat along with the rest of the group. For all his power and position, King Alfred Zavier Caden Hammerstrike was a lonely man.

Her father chewed off a hunk of bread and took a long draught of his Alarian apple ale. "So, then, which is it for my princesses this morning? Reading, needlework, or looking pretty?"

Lark was surprised when the corners of her mouth lifted and she giggled right along with the rest of her sisters. She suddenly realized that before this day, she'd never been in his presence without her mother. This was a side of her father she'd never seen before. He was almost…approachable.

The gleam in Aryanna's eyes told Lark she was thinking the same thing, and before Lark could stop her, Ary answered her father. "Reading. Well, to be precise, Father, we're going to be doing research in the library all day, after we finish here, that is."

King Alfred looked confused. "Research? What on Albrath would you girls have to research, the newest tapestry pattern?"

The sound of Aryanna clearing her throat settled like a rock in the pit of Lark's stomach. She stopped smiling and set her eating utensil down, her appetite now gone.

"Human rules and regulations pertaining to the order of marriage." Lark's belly grumbled as Aryanna continued, "You see, Father, I don't wish to marry Sarco Sunwalker, and I'm not going to. So, I need to find a way around the who-marries-whom-and-when rule."

King Alfred Zavier Caden Hammerstrike choked, coughed, and sputtered as ale ran down his chin. His face turned bright red, and he no longer appeared jovial in the least.

Lark cringed as her father stood, slammed down his eating knife, and roared. "Just a minute here, young lady. What do you mean, you don't wish to marry Sarco Sunwalker? I can understand you being upset about his insult to our family and all, but give the lad a chance. After all, this very moment he's off on a quest to make up for his mistake. And, human rule or no, it's not up to you, it's up to your mother and me who you'll marry. Don't you want to be a Lady of the Realm, Aryanna? Every little princess wants to be married to a powerful leader when she grows up."

Lark grasped Ary's hand and squeezed. Aryanna looked at her and smiled, but there was no humor in it, only sadness. "No, Father, I don't wish to be the wife of the next Lord of the Elves. I wish to marry his brother, Cyrrick Sunwalker. I wish to be the wife of a diplomat. It is he I love."

The fist of the king came down on the table top with a resounding thud, and Lark glanced around quickly to see if they were making a spectacle of themselves. Luckily, this early in the morning, there weren't many others in the cafeteria, only a solitary troll sitting off by himself in a corner. He didn't seem to be paying attention to anything other than the bowl of gruel before him.

"Cease this ridiculous prattle this moment before your mother gets wind of it. Do you have any idea what she would say or how she'd react or the trouble you'd cause? Of course, you'll marry Sarco Sunwalker when he returns and be happy to do it. Your mother and I have declared it. It's final."

Aryanna and King Alfred glared at each other. "I'll not marry a man—any man—I don't love. No matter what you or Mother decree."

The king's face contorted with rage. "Are you so selfish as to wish war on your people then, daughter? Because, that's precisely what will happen if the prophecy isn't fulfilled. Don't you think it's a little late to be bringing up all this love nonsense? Love is a fleeting thing, child, a dynasty is forever. And even if

281

you find some way around the human rule and our dictates, just who do you suggest marries the wizard in your place so the prophecy can be fulfilled and war avoided, one of the twins?"

"Oh no, not us father," Ally piped up. "As long as we are talking wishes, we wish to marry Sherman Bobert Limburger the Ninth. You know, the amazing halfling wizard whom Sarco chose to accompany him."

Lark was positive her father was going to explode with anger and braced herself for it. He opened and closed his mouth three times before any sound came out again. "Has this entire family lost its mind? One daughter who wants to marry a diplomat instead of becoming a lady, and two others who want to marry the same...*same* man. And not even a barbarian man, but a squat little cheese-smelling halfling. Next thing you know, you'll be saying marry Lark off to the heir of the elves and make her his lady. Wouldn't that just make your poor, dear mother have a fit she'd probably never recover from?"

Though her voice came out in no more than a squeak, her words were clear as Lark faced her father. "I do wish to marry him. I love Sarco more than life itself."

Her father sat down heavily and put his head in his hands. It was long moments before he looked up. Weariness lined his face as he held out his hands toward his daughters, palms up. "What do you want of me? I am but a man who tries to do his best for his family and his people. I have always done what is right and just and honorable. I would give you all there is in Albrath if it were in my power to do so. It isn't. What you're asking is simply impossible. Your mother's heart is set on this match just the way it stands. I can't go against her wishes. All of you know what she's like if she doesn't get her way. Who do you think I am that I can simply flaunt tradition and rules and decrees as if they do not matter?"

With resignation and soul-deep sadness, Lark stood. Though she knew it was probably a really big mistake, she couldn't force herself to remain quiet and simply walk away as she had so many times before. She was no longer the silent, obedient daughter she once was. She had changed. Sarco's love had changed her.

"What a fool I've been, Father. All my life I thought you were the king and it was you who upheld the traditions, made the rules, and spoke the decrees. I guess I was mistaken."

Without another word, Lark walked out, the girls on her heels.

Chapter Twenty-Two

If ever a man regretted even thinking the word *dragon* this morning, Sarco Sunwalker was that man. The sun was already high somewhere in the cloud-filled sky, and still the small group of questers stood anxiously waiting in the courtyard to take their leave of this place. The hope of an early start was now a long past aspiration.

With the very first whisper of the possibility of encountering dragons during the quest today, the head of the royal guard had sent a missive back through the portal to the king and queen and, until an answer arrived, they were stuck here. Not only stuck, but under heavy guard so as to not slip away.

Sarco sighed. Could he blame the rulers of the kingdom for being concerned about Crown Prince Adan's safety? Certainly not. But that didn't make it any easier, knowing that unless they got under way soon, it would be nightfall by the time they arrived at the mountains high above Castle Kuropkat. And the combination of nightfall and dragon was a volatile concoction at best.

Dragons were known throughout the land to be the source of magic. Though they were helpful to humans and quite peaceful in the light of day, at night their temperament was another story all together. Their primal instincts were heightened, and they were known to become testy and willful with the setting of the sun. Stories had been written concerning nocturnal dragon activity. It was the stuff with which elfin adults frightened their children into obedience.

Even though he'd personally met two dragons when he'd helped Uthiel fulfill the fable of Castle Kuropkat the previous year—and lived to tell about it— the long ago childhood rhyme still came back to haunt him.

*"Watch when ye wander, little children, and where.*

*Be careful. Don't disturb a dragon in its lair,*
*Be it high on a mountain or deep in the wood.*
*Walk softly, tread lightly, and always be good,*
*For dragons read hearts, be they obedient or not.*
*In the darkest of night, the naughty will be sought.*
*For though dragons by morning can be quite gay,*
*And afternoon dragons may be found in play,*
*When the sun doth set and dusk draws near,*
*If you've misbehaved, you'll have reason to fear.*
*For by darkness of night, wings will take flight*
*And seek out the naughty to devour by next light."*

A chill ran down his spine and Sarco shook it off. This wasn't the time for childish fairytales. It was a time for action. Glancing at Cyrrick, he gestured. "While we're waiting on Adan, Cyrrick, tell us about the stone we seek today."

His brother's eyes suddenly lit with an interest Sarco hadn't seen in their depths for quite some time. Cyrrick slipped his hand into his pocket and drew out his small notebook. Flipping it open, he made eye contact with Sarco, then Uthiel, Leeky, and Sherman.

A grin tugged at the corners of Sarco's mouth.

After the last couple of days of Cyrrick's moodiness, it was good to see him excited about something.

Cyrrick glanced between his notebook and the group of men. "After you've collected the Maiden's Desire bloom, you must next obtain a Spirit Alexandrite. It's said, both the Alexandrite and Opal needed to form a Spirit Alexandrite can be found in the dragon caves above Castle Kuropkat. One of the entries I discovered in my research states, 'Spirit Alexandrite, a gem forged by fire but not consumed. Can be held in the hand, a pledge from a groom.' The *Geological Text of Minerals and Precious Gems* says that Spirit Alexandrite is formed when the intense fire of dragon's breath comes in direct contact with the rare metal Alexandrite and the gemstone Opal, forever fusing them into a single stone."

Sarco nodded. "So all we need do is find a dragon cave and chisel off a hunk of rock. Sounds easy."

Cyrrick didn't look as confident as Sarco felt. "I wish it were that easy, brother. The problem comes in finding a dragon willing to cooperate with us. They don't normally breathe that intense a fire in their own caves unless seriously provoked, and provoking one can prove to be an extremely dangerous endeavor. So it'll be a challenge. After all, it's not as if we can simply walk up to a full-grown dragon and ask him politely to melt some rock for us."

Uthiel chuckled, and at first Sarco didn't realize why, then understanding dawned. Carnelian.

"Of course we can," Uthiel said. "Though it'll be a *her*, not a him. Male dragons are extremely rare."

Sarco smiled at the confused look on his brother's face, already knowing what Uthiel would say next.

"I know a dragon who'll be more than glad to help us. She's a friend of mine, and the biggest, blood-red-scaled dragon I've ever seen. Carnelian's her name. She lives above my castle in those same caves you spoke of, Cyrrick, with her dragling, Obsidian, who is one of those very rare male dragons. When we get close, I'll contact her. We have a mental bond, she and I."

Sherman hopped up and down while waving his hand, his eyes as big as the second full moon of Albrath had been last night.

Sarco sighed. "You don't have to do that, Sherman, remember? This isn't class. Just say what you have to say."

The halfling puffed out his chest. "I took a class on dragons once. That, of course, was before I saw one up close in real life. It was almost as big as our home. It tried to get our cheese. I've been told dragons really like cheese. Scared it off all by myself. Took one of the skewers we use for kabobs and poked it right in the foot, and it flew away. I sure wish Prince Adan could've seen that. He wouldn't mind his sisters spending time with me then, I bet."

Leeky Shortz harumphed, "What the slimy green belly of a Landis bullfrog jumping over the head of a lopsided troll do ya take us for, lad? Ya know for a fact ya've never seen a dragon, let alone run one off. If ya did, ya'd piss yaself right then and there, for sure. There'd be no shame in it either. Dragons can be fierce creatures. They scare much bigger men than ye. And don't ya be worrying about Adan seeing ya as a coward. If that barbarian does get ta go along with us, I'll talk ya up ta him and make sure he doesn't know how afraid ya truly are."

Sherman stretched to his full five feet and one inch and glared down at Leeky. "I have too seen a dragon, I tell you, and they do like cheese. When we find one, I'll prove it to you. And I'm not afraid of any ole dragon. I'll show you, I'll show all of you."

The ground beneath their feet rumbled as Prince Adan Hammerstrike, along with a full contingent of fifteen soldiers, marched into the courtyard. The discussion of dragons was forgotten as Sarco waited for the decision.

The barbarian prince looked almost sheepish when he finally made eye contact with Sarco. He cleared his throat, then did it again, trying to delay what he obviously had no choice but to say. "I'm not a coward. I want you to know that, Sarco Sunwalker. There has never been and will never be a dragon I'm afraid to face one on one. I'm not a child who needs protecting. I can take care of myself in any situation. I am, however, Prince of Alaria, and as such, am required by my parents, the king and queen, to bring these men along to ensure my safety. It isn't my choice, but it is my duty."

Sarco sighed with relief. Duty, he understood. "I don't care if you bring the whole city with you as long as we can get on our way."

The tenseness around Adan's mouth eased. "Well, thankfully, we don't have to take the whole city, only these fifteen. Shall we ride, then?"

Leeky twiddled his thumbs as he glanced at the barbarian. "Where the frost-bitten pecker on a short-legged billy goat do ya think ya're going? Isn't there someone ya just might be forgetting, lad?"

Adan bent low from his horse and collected the plastic doll from Leeky. He placed Miss Bunny securely in front of himself on the saddle and wrapped an arm protectively about her middle. "What the whatever on the whenever by the wherever are ya talking about, gnome? I'd never forget our favorite girl. Unlike you, though, I fill out my saddle. I was simply scooting back to make a little room so Miss Bunny would be comfortable. After all, it's the princely thing to do." He winked.

Leeky suddenly stopped. "On second thought, we better leave Miss Bunny here until we come back for the flower. Where we're going there's gonna be dragon's-breath fire flying everywhere, and as we learned last year, fire and plastic don't mix well. I don't know what the short and curlies betwixt the legs of a goat-humpin', barefoot-stompin' ogre I'll do without her, though, while we're gone."

Adan passed Miss Bunny down to one of his men. "Place the lass in my royal suite and guard her as if you were guarding me." He winked at Leeky. "Treat her like a queen."

****

"Nothing."

Despair filled Lark with a darkness to rival the night. Even the two full moons and the almost-full third one couldn't shine enough light through the large floor-to-ceiling windows of the library to lessen her feelings of helplessness. As a matter of fact, the sight of them only served to remind her that time was indeed running out.

Flecks of dust floated about her face as the musty library smell of old parchment and ink filled her nose to the point of nausea. Her head pounded, her stomach rumbled, and her rear end had long ago gone numb.

Twelve hours of non-stop reading. Twelve turns of the hourglass as sand trickled, hoping that perhaps the next volume she picked up might hold the key. Row after row of shelves had been emptied, and books lay scattered on the surface of the long table. Piled four and five high in places, the remnants of a full day's toil had still not yielded a single word to help their dire situation.

There had been pages, chapters and sometimes even entire books concerning human history, anatomy, physics, physiology, psychology, chemistry, and to some extent mating rituals, but nothing helpful concerning the order of marriage.

Volume after volume stated the same thing: In the organization of marriage in a royal family, it is the proper way of humans to marry their daughters by order of their birth. The only footnotes as to why, and what possibly might be exceptions to the rule, had been found only in the collection of the oldest reference tomes.

These digests, a set of three volumes, were rumored to have come to Albrath from the original human world galaxies away and centuries ago. Manuscripts of such importance were not to be found in a simple Academy library, so the question remained, where did they reside? There were only four copies of the set known to still exist in all of Albrath, and they were all privately owned.

*VoT! What was she going to do now?*

"That's it, then. There are no more books to look through." Lark yawned and stretched as kinks and aches in her muscles reminded her once more just how long she'd been sitting in one place. She glanced around the table at the faces of her sisters and friends. They all held the same expression of desolation she was trying to hide. One by one, they laid down the manuscripts they'd been reading and quietly closed the covers.

"So, what now?" Aryanna asked while rubbing her forehead. "Do you think there's any way to find a set of those three old volumes in time?" Tears filled Ary's eyes, and Lark wanted to cry right along with her as she continued, "This is all my fault, and I'm so sorry. It never occurred to me our human half would be that important, but it should have. We can't give up now, we simply can't. I promised Cyrrick I would find a way."

Lark took Ary's hand in hers and smiled even though she didn't feel it. "We aren't going to give up. I promise. We'll find a set. We must."

The dark-elf librarian, Authorn Hawthorn, walked over to the table. "I'm so sorry to disturb you fine princesses, but it's well past closing time and I still must put these books back in order before I can lock up. My significant other is going to be very angry with me. He's probably been holding the night's sustenance for at least two turns of the hourglass by now. Perhaps you can return tomorrow and continue your search?"

Lark shook her head. "There's no need for us to return. What we're looking for isn't here. We do appreciate all your help, Authorn, really we do. We're sorry for being such a bother and making you late for your evening meal."

The dark-blue of the librarian's skin brightened to almost a glow as a smile relaxed his face. "No bother at all. It's my job, and I take it very seriously. If there is ever any way I can help, please don't hesitate to ask. It's not often we get royalty in the library."

A thought occurred to Lark and for the first time in hours her smile felt genuine. "I know they aren't here in this library, but you wouldn't happen to know where we might find a copy of the three ancient human history texts, would you?"

Authorn appeared to be deep in thought for a moment. He tapped an indigo-blue finger against the side of his dark cheek. "*The Chronicles of Shak-spere*? I don't know their exact location, but I do believe I might have an idea of whom to ask. I remember someone once mentioning that High Mystic Purrell is a collector of extremely rare books. Perhaps he has a copy. That's who I'd check with if I were you."

A sudden gasp caught Lark's attention. Briar's face had gone completely white and looked as if she'd seen a ghost.

"What is it, Briar? What's wrong?"

Briar shuddered before she spoke, and her voice sounded shaky. "Remember when I told you about what happened to Ray? It was because of that same *High Mystic Purrell* Authorn is speaking of. And trust me, I'll never forget my one and only experience with that man. If we must go, then I suggest we stick close together, and whatever you do, under no circumstances, let him get close enough to touch you," Briar grimaced. "I won't shock you with the details, but trust me when I say it was scary."

Lark nodded, concerned with having to face the powerful mystic but at the same time, her heart raced anew with the hope of possibility. After all, how bad could it be? There would be six of them to Mystic

Purrell's one. Safety in numbers. She smiled. "It's settled then. We'll meet at the cafeteria first thing in the morning, and after we break our fast, we'll pay High Mystic Purrell a visit."

\*\*\*\*

Darkness enveloped him and Sarco's senses leapt to keen awareness. The only light available to the group was the glow of lit torches held high in the hands of Adan's soldiers. Even if it hadn't been for the clouds, the light from Albrath's three moons and the brightness from the stars would have been mostly obscured between the towering solid rock walls of Castle Kuropkat's high mountain pass.

Still, he climbed without hesitation, leading the group ever upward.

The smell of sulfur and brimstone hung heavy in the air and burned his lungs. His throat hurt to swallow, it was so parched, and his eyes stung and watered. Waves of heated air drifted toward him on all sides, and even though it should have warmed him, it had the opposite effect.

Sarco shivered.

The fine hairs on the back of his neck bristled and his skin tingled. They were breathing down upon him, watching his every move, whispering among themselves and waiting for a signal of some kind.

The ground below his feet pulsed through the soles of his boots with an energy of its own, and he could not only feel the hypnotic beckoning of the throb, but also hear the steady, rhythmic cadence of at least a hundred huge hearts beating in unison.

Occasionally, he glimpsed a flickering glow in the distance that looked suspiciously like angry, piercing eyes blinking back at him. Sweat ran in rivulets down his spine as he carefully placed one foot in front of the other and trudged ever upward.

The unexpected sound of a gravelly voice breaking the silence from somewhere behind stopped him in his tracks and he nearly jumped out of his skin.

"What the oozing, pus-filled pockets between the toes of a barefooted troll standing knee deep in a vat of melted butter marinating do ya make of that, lads? We have company. I can almost taste the venom dripping off their teeth. I'm glad I had Adan leave Miss Bunny at his castle. After what happened last year ta poor Miss Kitty, I wouldn't want a sweet little thing like her ta get melted or eaten. Even though I've never heard of the scaly beasts having a taste for plastic. Now, cheese…that's an entirely different story. I've been told they really like cheese."

The sound of a garbled gasp coming from Sherman's direction only added to the overall tension of the moment.

Sarco sighed deeply as he glanced toward the halfling following closely on his heels. "Nobody's going to get eaten tonight. That is, unless Carnelian is in the mood for a midnight snack of gnome. If so, I think I'll feed Leeky to her myself."

The gnome's cackle didn't do a thing to ease his apprehension, and for the first time since leaving Adan's castle that morning, Sarco was glad they'd arrived well after nightfall. He knew sometimes it was better not to see what you were walking into until it was too late to turn back.

A chill ran down his spine as an iciness deeper than the one he'd experienced high in the Alarian Mountains infused him from head to toe. His sweat turned as cold as winter rain.

Dragons. They were now deep in the land of the scaly beasts, and Carnelian wasn't the only dragon close by. The air literally hummed with the presence of many. Oh, yes, there were dragons here, and even though Sarco had no doubt they were being watched, he was infinitely glad he couldn't see them.

## Chapter Twenty-Three

If ever a man longed for the night to be done and yet dreaded the coming of the dawn, Sarco Sunwalker was that man. The clouds that had earlier obscured the party's vision were gone, and the group was now high enough in the mountains that the three moons of Albrath could be seen shining brightly. Two of the moons were already as full as full could be, and the third was but a sliver away from the same.

Time was running out, and there was still so much to be done.

A bone-deep weariness enveloped him, and his fear of dragons had dissipated to a nagging uneasiness during the hours of constantly trudging upwards. It had been replaced with an urgency to see this quest finished.

Soon it would be morning, and still the cave they sought was at least a quarter turn of the hourglass away. Not once had they stopped for sustenance or rest during the long trip. Not from the moment they'd left the bailey of the barbarian kingdom of Alaria and ridden through the portal to Castle Kuropkat, nor during the long trek up this mountain they now climbed. Sarco lifted his head and gazed at the stars for a moment. There would be time for rest later. He hoped.

He stopped suddenly. Directly before them gaped the opening to a cave. He glanced at Uthiel, who nodded. This was the one. They had arrived. It was time to fulfill the requirement of the second part of the quest.

A familiar warmth seeped deep into the recesses of his mind and, for an instant, Sarco's heart leapt with glee. "*Lark?*" his mind shouted.

"*Lark? I am not some creature called Lark, elf friend of my Lord and Master Uthiel. I am Carnelian.*"

Sarco's mind pounded with the coursing power of the dragon's thoughts, and he closed his eyes tightly as he rubbed his temples, trying to alleviate the pain.

"*Elf, my Lord and Master Uthiel says you have need of me. What is it? Be quick before the limitations of your mind break our bond.*"

Taking deep breaths, Sarco fought to form a response. "*I have need of a Spirit Alexandrite. Will you help me obtain one, Carnelian?*"

The dragon chuckled, and the vibration rolled like a shudder throughout Sarco's being. Chills pebbled his skin, while heat flowed in waves from the top of his head to the tips of his toes. He grasped for something, anything, to hold onto and was relieved when the strong clasp from Uthiel's hand held him upright.

"*And if I do help you,*" Carnelian sighed, "*what will you give me in exchange, elf friend of my Lord and Master Uthiel?*"

"*I am called Sarco, and I am a wizard friend of your Lord and Master Uthiel.*"

The impact of her laughter booming in his mind buckled Sarco's knees, and if it hadn't been for Uthiel's grip, he would have collapsed to the ground.

"*It is no matter what you are called, though I do think I like your bravado, Sarco the Elf. Now, what will you give me in exchange for my service?*" She sniffed from somewhere deep within the cave, and Sarco's lungs emptied of air. He struggled to reinflate them as her next words filled him with horror. "*Ahh, cheese. And not just any cheese, but a pungent, full-bodied cheese, wafting this way from the essence of the halfling traveling with you. It has been ever so long since I had a truly fine aged halfling. That would be a fair exchange. Don't you agree?"*

Sarco shook his head, the weight of it so heavy upon his neck, the effort left him panting.

"*No. Sherman is my friend. You may not have him. Ask for something else."*

When next her voice came, it was almost a whine. "*But halflings are scrumptious—a delicacy, even. I would be the envy of all to have been awarded such a prize."*

A thought occurred to Sarco, and his own chuckle caught him by surprise. "*I can't give you the halfling. I promised him he wouldn't be eaten, but might I interest you in a gnome?"*

The sudden shriek within his head blinded him momentarily.

"*A gnome? You offer me a gnome? I'd eat a troll before I would a gnome. They're bitter, nasty-tasting creatures, with way too much gristle for my taste. Perhaps I won't help you after all, Sarco the Elf."*

Sarco bowed his head toward the cave. "*Forgive me, Carnelian. I do not mean to taunt you. I was teasing. Even the gnome is a valued friend. It's not in my power to give you what you wish. The men who travel with me, all of them, are important to me. Is there something, anything, else I can give you in return for your help?"*

He heard a low-pitched whisper in his ear, as if the dragon were standing right at his side, telling him a secret. Understanding of the price of Carnelian's help flowed like water across synapses in his brain and straight into his heart. The weight upon his mind lightened.

*"That is truly all you wish?"*

Sarco felt the dragon's nod within his mind. *"Yes, if you don't mind. I know it is a lot to ask, but it's been even longer since I had that, than it has been since I last tasted halfling."*

*"Doesn't Uthiel ever do that for you?"* Sarco inquired.

Her sigh rippled throughout him. *"Oh, I could never ask such a thing of my Lord and Master Uthiel. He is the Protector of all dragons, and as such, must never appear to show favoritism."*

*"So be it, Carnelian. It would be an honor,"* he whispered to her.

The warmth slowly faded from Sarco's mind, and he opened his eyes. With wonder, he stared at the brightening horizon and the first glimpse of the rising sun. The long night was finally over, the end to this part of the quest was right before them, and a brand new day lay ahead.

\*\*\*\*

As far as doors went, Lark thought this one was quite pretty. It was a soothing, welcoming blue-green, almost an ocean blue, inspiring trust. It was serene, inviting, magnetic even. She was drawn toward it.

The words "High Mystic Purrell" were stenciled in the middle of the center panel in four-inch-high glittery silver letters that she found nearly hypnotizing. She blinked, and turned to look at her three sisters, then at Briar and Laycee.

"Well, here goes." Tentatively, Lark smiled, shrugged her shoulders, and turned the knob. Opening the door, she took a step inside. Mist surrounded her and swirled about her ankles. The distinct sound of breathing in the distance was her only guide forward as she and the girls ventured farther inside. "Hello? High Mystic Purrell? Are you here?"

The mist immediately cleared, and for a moment, Lark wished it hadn't. There, standing not more than three feet in front of her, was a man. Not just any man, but a golden-haired, bronzed-skinned, completely naked man, who had his erect phallus cradled in his hand and a grin on his face.

"Ahh, you must be the Hammerstrike Princesses and friends. My secretary informed me you wished to seek an audience this morning. How may I be of service?"

Lark opened her mouth to speak but didn't get a chance to say a single word before the Mystic turned, picked up a tiny silver bell and rang it. A panel on the wall of the office opened and in walked a young, female high-elf dressed in business attire.

From behind her, Lark heard Briar gasp, but she was so enthralled by the sight of the woman now standing before her that she didn't even wonder why.

The lovely woman's long, thick hair was the color of raven's wings. It was attractively bunched up on top of her head, and tendrils curled around the peach-blushed skin of her face and neck. Her tiny tongue flicked out and licked already moist, full, red lips. Eyes, dark brown, the shade of hot cocoa, looked out from behind wire-rimmed glasses. She appeared to be in a trance as she walked toward the Mystic, carrying a plain pad of paper and a white pen with a bright blue feather on one end.

For a moment, Mystic Purrell looked directly at Lark and her group. "This is my secretary, Ms. Bea Hayven. She was once a boring little librarian before I rescued her from that horrible fate." He turned his attention back to his secretary. "Bea, I have an urge."

A confused look came over the young woman's face for a moment, then she smiled. A voice as sweet as honey purred, "Hmm, an urge?"

High Mystic Purrell picked up what looked to be a blackboard pointer and tapped the woman lightly on the top of her head. "Yes, an urge."

In a single motion, Bea let her hair down, took off her glasses, stripped off her clothes, dropped to her knees, and took High Mystic Purrell's cock between her moist red lips. And sucked.

The Mystic closed his eyes for a moment as he chanted, "Suck, swish, swirl, swallow. Suck, swish, swirl, swallow. Good, my dear."

Lark stood in shocked silence. Her pussy ached, and her nipples hardened. Other than the few required experimental encounters when she'd been a teen, she'd never truly been attracted to another female before today. She loved Sarco with all of her heart, but her body was definitely responding—and then some—to the scene before her eyes. Tearing her attention away from the perfect lips sucking the impressive cock, Lark once more looked up at High Mystic Purrell.

By this time, he'd turned his attention back to Lark and the group of women. "Now, how may I be of help?

You must be here to learn the mysteries of the cock. It always pleases me to instruct the cockless unfortunate on the care, maintenance, and comfort of the most important appendage in Albrath."

Briar tugged on Lark's sleeve and whispered, "Remember, don't touch him or let him touch you, or you'll be right down there beside Ms. Bea Hayven, doing all manner of despicable things."

For just the fraction of a second, Lark was tempted. Then she remembered just why they were here, and she swallowed back her unexpected lust.

The mystic leaned down and picked up a small pile of paperbacks from a table close by. He reached over the top of Ms. Bea Hayven's bobbing head and handed them one by one to Lark as he rattled off their titles, "*Me, Myself, and My Magnificent Cock. The Journey of a Cock.* And, my latest best seller, *Great Cocks through the Ages.* I'm sure whatever questions you may have, the answers can be found somewhere in these pages. I'll even be happy to autograph them for you. And be sure to pick up a signed bookmark on your way out the door. Now, will there be anything else? I really am quite busy, as you can see."

Aryanna tried to speak. "We would like to—"

A hand went up to silence the princess, and High Mystic Purrell shook his head. "Now, now, no need to be thanking me. It's the least I can do." He waved in dismissal. "Now, shoo, be on your way. I have much to do."

He glanced down as he patted his secretary on the top of her head. "Very good, Ms. Bea Hayven. Yes, suck, swish, swirl, swallow. Suck, swish, swirl, swallow."

The base of Lark's neck throbbed and tension radiated upward. The whisper in her ear of, "See what I meant? Didn't I tell you he was something?" from Briar didn't help to soothe the anxiety. As a matter of fact, it intensified her sexual tension. Why today, of all days, and why this woman and this man? There was no love here, like she had for Sarco. This was lust, pure and simple.

Lark cleared her throat and forced the pounding of her heart to slow. She missed Sarco so, and it was him she truly wanted, needed. With determination, she put her own desires from her mind and tried once more to make the mystic understand their plight. "Mr. Purrell, if we could but please—"

The mystic glared. "Oh, you're still here? Off with you, now, all of you. I have no more time for groupies and autograph seekers."

Lark seethed and any hint of desire faded. How dare the arrogant man label her and her friends as…as *groupies*. As if! She was about ready to give the mystic a piece of her mind when Laycee pushed her way through the group.

The little gnome stood before Purrell and wagged her finger. "We don't have time for this nonsense. Did you not see how full the three moons were last night?" Laycee walked up to the mystic, reached around the secretary's head, and poked him in the balls with a fingertip. "My girls here have something important they need ta ask ya."

Lark gulped, then held her breath, waiting to see the strange man's reaction.

High Mystic Purrell looked down his nose at Laycee. "There is no touching of any part of the cock without invitation, tiny female-gnome-type person. I'm a very busy man, and if they," he pointed toward Lark and her sister, "have something to ask, then simply have them ask it."

Lark cleared her throat and spoke as fast as she could, hoping she'd get her question out before he interrupted her again. "We don't wish to be a bother, but do you have a copy of the *Chronicles of Shak-spere*, and if so, may we peek at them? It's extremely important."

High Mystic Purrell scoffed, "Do you, for the space of a single grain of sand, think I would let strangers, especially cockless, female strangers, walk in off the cobblestones and look at—let alone *touch*—my priceless book collection?"

Nausea threatened, and Lark felt like she'd been punched in the gut. So close, so VoT close.

"I barely allow trusted scholars to touch my priceless set, let alone…vagina-wearing princesses."

Lark wanted to hit him. Not just hit him but drive her fist so far down his throat it would pop right out his vagina-less ass. She couldn't do that though. Getting the chance to look through the *Chronicles of Shak-spere* was too important, and Sarco was too important for her to lose her temper now. If only the mystic ass would shut up for a moment.

"You do see how impossible your request is, don't you? Perhaps you could send a representative who actually has a cock, and I'll make him an appointment for some time…next summer, at the latest."

Lark clenched her fist and shook it at the mystic. "My representative, who has a cock, is only God Draka knows where on a dangerous quest, and I don't even know if he'll come back alive." Tears welled in Lark's eyes and her voice shook. "Please, Professor Purrell, just a few minutes."

Laycee patted her hand and pleaded with the mystic. "Isn't there something ya could do for the poor lass? Look at her. I can't take it anymore." She spread her arms and encompassed all the princesses. "Have ya ever seen a group of women go all PMS ninja? It's not a pretty sight, and I'm warning ya, it's about ta happen."

The gnome governess broke down in tears, and before another breath could be taken, Lark, Aryanna, Ally, Audrey, and even Briar were crying.

The mystic closed his eyes and tapped Ms. Bea Hayven once more. "Suck, swish…umm, swallow." His eyes popped open. "No, no, no, that's wrong. It's swirl before swallow."

High Mystic Purrell's secretary had stopped sucking when he'd made the mistake and now just stared up at him with a confused look on her face.

He sighed and looked at the sobbing women. "You must stop. I can't abide crying. It isn't conducive to a happy cock, and if the cock isn't happy, then no one is. If you cease this instant, I swear, I'll allow you a few moments to glance at my copy of the *Chronicles of Shak-spere*. Just the time it takes for a few grains of sand to slip through the hourglass, though. I can't be bothered with looky-loos all day."

Lark's heart soared with hope as the mystic pointed to the panel in the wall the secretary had come through minutes before. "Through there, in a golden box on the center shelf of the bookcase. But be extremely careful please. Even for copies, they're very old and delicate."

He tapped Ms. Bea Hayven on the top of her head once more. "Now, where were we, my dear? Oh, yes. Suck, swish, swirl, swallow. Suck, swish, swirl, swallow."

## Chapter Twenty-Four

If ever a man was grateful he had a friend who even knew a dragon, let alone a comrade who had a personal relationship with one, Sarco was that man. At the same time, his childhood fears of the mighty creatures caused him to hesitate one last time before entering the cave.

He turned to his companions. "I want you all to know, I do appreciate everything you've done for me. A man couldn't ask for better friends. I'm not sure how safe it'll be or how much room we'll have to maneuver, so, Adan, you and your men might want to wait here, out of harm's way. We understand the limitations your duty to your people puts upon you."

The barbarian prince sputtered, and his face reddened. "There'll be no leaving me out here cowering in the bushes while all of you rush headlong into the cave. I didn't come this far to miss witnessing you face down a dragon. There has never been a beast born who frightened me, and if you're to wed my sister, I'll be a witness to that same bravery in you. To think an elf would march into a dark cave and face the wrath of a dragon while a barbarian prince waits outside is beyond ridiculous."

Sarco smiled.

Adan turned and pointed a finger at Sherman. "If you're truly worried, then leave the halfling out here as a lookout. His knees are knocking together so loudly, I bet even the townspeople down at the castle can hear them, and he looks near ready to pass out. He'd probably even thank you."

Sarco chuckled. "You think Sherman's frightened? If you do, then you don't know the halfling at all. He might be small, but I've never seen him turn from danger. Can you say the same of *all* of your men?"

Adan glared, but Sarco simply folded his arms across his chest and stared at the big barbarian until Adan looked away.

Leeky winked at Sarco, then poked Adan in the side. "What the smelly belly button lint under the fingernails of a one-platt troll trollop dancing nakey in the moonlight are ya thinking? The purpose of Sherman's knee-knocking is ta prevent himself from running in ahead of everyone else and stealing our glory. Don't ya be worrying about the Shermanator here. Even though he knows how much dragons love the scent of halfling, let alone him smelling like a fine, aged Limburger himself, when things get hot, he'll be right there mixing it up with the best of us. I guarantee it."

An idea formed in Sarco's mind, and for the first time in hours, he relaxed. With purpose, he stepped across the threshold and into the cave.

The moment darkness surrounded him, warmth once more invaded his being. This time he knew it wasn't Lark. This time he was better prepared when the power of Carnelian's voice slid deep into his mind. Still, the intensity left him with shivers running like rivulets of water from head to toe.

*"Sarco the Elf, which of your companions is going*

*to assist you?"*

Sarco smiled into the darkness as he formed a fireball to light their way. *"If you don't mind, Carnelian, I would have the help of the halfling. It would go a long way to raising his status with the barbarian prince. May he be the one to do what you've asked as payment?"*

He felt her sigh in the very marrow of his bones.

*"I suppose, if you feel he's big and strong enough. I like it rough."*

Sarco chuckled. *"I'll make sure to explain to him exactly what it is he must do."*

*"So, Sarco the Elf, what then of your brother? Will his duty be to make sure you do not falter?"*

Surprise flowed like waves through him. *"How did you even know my brother is one of my companions, and why would I need his help? Trust me, I may be an elf, but I'm quite capable of taking care of myself. I am also a fire wizard, as you can see, and I can withstand the heat. I won't put my brother in danger, Carnelian. We can do this, the two of us. We need no other."*

The shaking of her head made him dizzy. *"Arrogant species. No wonder your lifespan is so short. And here I was beginning to like you. You know nothing of the forming of a Spirit Alexandrite, do you? Did you really think all you need do was hold up two rocks and get a dragon to melt them together for you? If that were the case, anyone could do it."*

Dread filled Sarco. He really had thought that all he'd have to do was hold the rocks.

*"The bond it takes to form a Spirit Alexandrite is special, Sarco the Elf. It is true, the heat forms it, but it's the slice of the holder's spirit that keeps the Opal*

*and Alexandrite forged together forever. You must give a piece of your very soul to the stone. Therein lies the danger. It's a risky and painful proposition, and not always survivable. And though I'm sure you're a brave and strong elf, you will need help."*

Sarco shook his head. "*No, I can do it alone.*"

*"Why, then, did you choose companions to accompany you? To chronicle your brave deeds? To sing your praises around the campfire at night? I sense your brother, Cyrrick, has as much a need to see this quest accomplished as you do."*

Her words rang true to the core of his being, and Sarco hung his head for a moment. He had been arrogant for so long, it had become a way of life. Carnelian was right, even about Cyrrick. Especially about Cyrrick. Although he wished to keep his brother safe, he also realized the outcome of this quest was as important to Cyrrick as it was to him. And not just the quest, but their relationship for the rest of their lives, hinged on what would happen in the next few minutes.

He let his mind merge once more with the dragon's. *"Tell me what to do and I'll do it."*

The response he heard was no louder than a whisper of wind in his mind. *"Come to me now, Sarco the Elf, and we shall do this thing."*

The narrow passage of the cave wound around and up and down. Every once in a while, a soft green light flickered in the distance. Sarco had seen Carnelian the year before when she and Uthiel had been forced to work together, and the thought of the huge dragon traversing the narrow hallways struck him as funny. He laughed, and immediately the warmth infused him yet again.

*"Is there something you find humorous, Sarco the Elf?"*

He chuckled. *"I was just wondering how you got in this cave, Carnelian, and if you're feeling cramped. I've seen you, remember?"*

Bright lights flickered behind his eyes until Sarco was blinded, and he stumbled headlong into the hard rock wall in front of him.

*"Pathetic creature, did you forget my kind brought magic to this world? Dragons were here long before those without scales walked this land, and magic is strong in us. Don't concern yourself with my comfort or how and where I get about, Sarco the Elf. It's your own smooth, thin hide you should worry about."*

The passageway opened into a cavernous room. The sound of gasps, gulps, and groans echoed off the walls as the source of the flickering green light was finally revealed. From the face of a huge, blood-red-scaled, talons-as-long-as-boat-oars dragon, two bright, blinking, intelligent eyes glowed eerily upon the group that had followed Sarco inside.

Carnelian's mouth opened wide and a stream of fire warmed and illuminated every crevice of the inner chamber. The walls glowed opalescent and upon the dirt floor were strewn numerous chunks of greenish metal.

Sarco almost didn't recognize Adan's voice as stuttered words tumbled from the man's lips, "Ma-ma-mother of God Draka, that's gotta be the big-biggest dragon I've ever seen."

The fifteen barbarian soldiers took up positions behind their prince.

It was on the tip of Sarco's tongue to put Adan's

fears to rest by telling him the true relationship with Carnelian, but the man's next words put a quick end to that thought. "Bet you wished now you'd left the halfling outside. Look at him. I think he just peed himself."

Instead, Sarco motioned for Sherman to come near.

With visibly shaking legs, the halfling complied. Leaning down close, Sarco whispered in Sherman's ear. "When I point, I want you to climb the side of that big rock over there and punch that dragon in the jaw as hard and fast as you can. Don't quit until she stops breathing fire, okay?"

Sarco had always realized Sherman was pasty-white, but now, with the blood draining from the halfling's face, he was beyond white. He patted the little wizard on the shoulder. "Do you trust me, Sherman?"

The halfling gulped. "With my life, my lord."

"You won't be harmed," Sarco promised.

Sherman took three deep breaths and pushed the rims of his glasses firmly up the ridge of his nose. "Well, I did take a class on rock climbing and pugilism once and have never gotten to use my knowledge, so, I'm ready. My life for you, sir."

Sarco braced himself as he allowed the warmth of his thoughts to flow toward the dragon. *"Carnelian, the halfling is ready. He's never 'petted' a dragon before, so go easy on him. Are you sure all you wish is to be petted, and that is how one goes about petting a dragon?"*

Carnelian smiled, and the full impact of it sent ripples of pleasure skittering down Sarco's spine. *"Oh, yes, it has been so very long since I felt the gentle caress of a hand. The last time was back before the war, when I was but a dragling. And it must be done hard in order to feel it through the scales. Make sure he doesn't hold back. I will know if he does. I'm quite excited."*

Sarco pointed toward Carnelian.

Sherman gulped once again, squared his shoulders, lifted his head, stood to his full five feet and one inch, and climbed.

Adan sputtered, "What are you doing, Sarco? I didn't mean to taunt you into trying to prove anything. That dragon will kill him."

Sarco shook his head. "Never underestimate the power of the little guy in a fight, he'll always surprise you."

Bending to the floor of the cave, he picked up a chunk of the greenish metal Alexandrite then faced Cyrrick. "Would you help me, brother?"

Immediately, Cyrrick stepped forward. "Whatever you wish."

Sarco drew out a blade and chiseled away a piece of opal from the wall of the cave, then held both the stone and the metal together in his raised hands. "I need you to hold up my arms, Cyrrick. No matter what happens, don't let them drop. Even if I scream or plead with you to make it stop, you must promise you won't listen to me until the last flame has died away. I'll put a Protection from Fire spell around us to shield us from the heat."

A fine sheen of sweat broke out on Cyrrick's forehead that even in the dim light of the cave Sarco couldn't miss.

"I'll do whatever you wish, brother, but perhaps

you should ask Uthiel in my stead. He's stronger than I." Cyrrick leaned in close to Sarco and whispered, "And he's friends with the dragon. Surely she would let no harm come to you if he were close."

Sarco looked his brother in the eye. "It's your support I need. No other will do."

"So be it," Cyrrick nodded.

Sarco glanced at Adan, his fifteen men, Leeky, and Uthiel. "I suggest you step back. It's about to get...*warm* in here."

He looked toward Sherman, who was now level with Carnelian's snout. The dragon leaned and swiped the halfling with her tongue from head to toe. Sherman almost toppled.

*"Are you certain I can't eat him, Sarco the Elf? He smells and tastes so yummy."*

Sarco shook his head and chuckled, *"Not if you want to be petted, you can't. And you gave me your word, remember?"*

Her sigh wafted through him. *"As you wish."*

Sarco filled his lungs to capacity and yelled to Sherman, "Now!"

He almost laughed as he watched the halfling ball up his stubby little fists, close his eyes tightly, and, with a flying flurry, punch Carnelian square in the jaw, over and over.

The last thing Sarco heard, before the deafening roar of the dragon's blaze drowned out all other sound, was Adan's expletive, "For the love of Draka. That's gotta be either the bravest or stupidest halfling I've ever—"

Sarco held himself erect. A wave of heat radiated up and through him. The very act of breathing became almost an impossibility. Tender, scorched airways burned and even the blood coursing through his veins heated so much he wanted to shriek.

He burned. Not the burn of flames licking at exposed skin, but a deep, consuming, incinerating burn from the inside out. A burn that seared all the way to his soul. Pain coursed through every fiber of Sarco's being as he fought back the desperate urge to scream.

He opened his eyes and concentrated on Cyrrick's face, but his vision was partially obscured by the heat from the wall of flames enveloping them. Time stood still. His consciousness threatened to abandon him. His knees buckled more than once under the onslaught of the slashing pain, and his heart raced, as if it were trying to escape his chest.

Still, the security of Cyrrick's arms beneath his own never once wavered, not even when every muscle, every fiber of Sarco's essence was begging for the relief only oblivion could afford. From somewhere far away he heard himself plead for the end to take him, yet with the help of his brother, he stood.

A sudden, shearing, cold-as-death gash shot through his belly, across his ribs, to finally land and explode deep within the recesses of his mind. Sarco's world finally became what he had wished for—nothing more than a floating sea of cool white.

As if from a far distance, he heard someone ask, "Is he alive? Did it work?"

Slowly, Sarco cracked open a lid and peeked up into the concerned face of Uthiel. He stirred, but the arms of his brother tightened about him. It took more energy than he had to resist, so he smiled instead and let his hand fall open.

What he held pulsed with a life of its own. A stone, no bigger than his thumbnail. Warm to the touch, almost hot. A deep metallic green with ribbons of opalescent fibers dancing within. To his eyes, it was the most beautiful stone Sarco had ever beheld. A perfect Spirit Alexandrite.

He tried once more to move and was reminded of the price he had paid as pain exploded up his chest, all the way to his neck.

Cyrrick placed a steadying hand on his shoulder. "Careful, brother. Lie still or you'll have it bleeding again, and I just got it to stop."

His mouth was dry as cotton, but still he fought to speak. "Bleeding?"

Cyrrick yanked back the front of Sarco's tunic to expose his chest. There, between the fourth and fifth intercostal spaces of his ribs, right at the point of maximum impulse of his heart, was an angry-looking, lightning-shaped scar.

Warmth infused his mind, and Sarco welcomed it. *"I am glad you still live. I warned you it would require a piece of your soul. You and the stone are now one, Sarco the Elf. And thank you for the petting from your halfling friend. Tell him for me he did well."*

The warmth faded away and even without looking up, Sarco knew Carnelian was gone.

****

Lightning streaked across the angry-looking, midday sky. Thunder clapped loudly in the distance.

Lark's gaze flew toward her sisters and the rest of the group. "It's not me, I swear."

Aryanna shrugged but didn't bother to look up. "It doesn't matter. I say let it rain, let it storm even, so hard that it washes away every book in the land. At this point, nothing much matters. I really believed we'd find a way around the stupid human rule in the Chronicles of Shak-spere. What are we going to do now?"

The tears Lark had been trying valiantly to hold back all day flowed, and she was just as powerless to stop them as she was to prevent the rain from pelting the group as they hurried across the bailey on the way back to their rooms.

All the long hours of research had been for nothing. In the end, they had failed.

The Chronicles of Shak-spere, written thousands of years ago, and most probably very specific at that time concerning the order of marriage, were now nothing more than a tattered group of paragraphs and pages with entire sections missing. In the three fragile volumes, it was difficult to make any sense of what must have once been beautiful prose.

Granted, the writings of the great historian, Sir W. Shak-spere, even now were regarded as the ultimate authority on all things human. The entire culture of Albrath had been closely fashioned after his writings when they'd first been discovered.

The castles, the monarchies, the knights, the lords of the realm, even their speech and mannerisms, were taken straight from the crisp, printed pages of the three volumes when they were still new to this world.

The books were nearly the most researched and coveted writings in the whole world, second only to the Alarian Scrolls of God Draka.

From what was left of the original writings, Lark couldn't decipher how the humans had gotten the ill-conceived idea to embrace such a rule of marriage. And if what there had been left to read was any indication, she wasn't sure the historian himself had agreed with it, but simply stated random facts.

It would have been helpful to read Sir Shak-spere's writings in their entirety when they had been consistent within the world he lived in. All that was left now wasn't consistent with anything.

The very-much-in-demand chronicles were now no more than scattered thoughts with large sections missing that made no sense. They spoke of a far away world called England-Rome, in a cold and foggy place dubbed London and a barbaric city named Verona that was now no more than some other world's ancient history.

Lark sighed. Why should what happened on a tiny, inconsequential planet light years away and more than a few millennia ago so impact her life today? It wasn't fair and it wasn't right.

The wind picked up, and thunder roared so closely the ground beneath her feet shook with it. Lark thought to deny once more she was the cause, when it occurred to her perhaps she was responsible after all.

She tried her best to quell the turmoil within herself as she quickened her pace. Stopping for a moment, she closed her eyes, lifted her face toward the heavens, and whispered, "Sarco, I pray you're having better luck than I am."

# Chapter Twenty-Five

If ever a man was more confused about how to make separate parts of a quest come together, Sarco would definitely like to see that man.

He stood in the middle of the icy cold vault in the Barbarian city of Alaria with the Maiden's Desire bloom frozen solid in one hand and the warm, pulsating Spirit Alexandrite stone in the other, and no clue how to proceed.

Cyrrick had recited the quest to him again less than a turn of the hourglass ago. The words still ran through Sarco's mind.

*"It's ice and fire that forms a maiden's desire.*

*It's searing heat where metal and gemstone first meet.*

*It's with love in mind that a treasure becomes divine.*

*It's a champion you must defeat for a heart you wish to seek.*

*It's your choice to make for the wife you will take."*

With a to-the-bone weariness, Sarco carefully placed the frozen flower and the stone on a nearby table, then he slumped to the floor and leaned his back against the cold wall. He put his hands in his lap and closed his eyes. All day and late into the evening, they had marched down the mountainside and then ridden through the gates of Castle Kuropkat. Just as the three moons of Albrath were highest in the heavens above, the group had passed through the portal and returned to the barbarian capital.

Time was running out. Not much longer could even a sliver of darkness keep the third moon from being completely full. Tomorrow he must return to the Academy and complete what he had started.

So this was it. Right now. The time to finish the third element of the quest and be done with it, and still, Sarco had no idea what to do.

*It's with love in mind that a treasure becomes divine.* What did that mean, and what did it have to do with the flower and the stone?

He knew what love meant. His mind drifted back to the Academy and to the very definition of love. Lark. What was she doing right now? Was she sleeping? Was she well? Did she miss him as much as he missed her? Had she, by chance, found a way for them to get around the human rule? And what if she hadn't? What would they do? He knew deep in his heart he could marry no other and still have a life worth living.

The thought of an existence without Lark had his breath catching in his chest and an ache settling in the pit of his stomach. Could he manage to get through a lifetime without the sight of her smile or the twinkle of mischief in her molten silver eyes? Did he even care to try?

Would his soul shrivel and die if he never again ran his fingers through her chestnut mane or touched her body in reverence? Would life lose purpose if he couldn't hear the tinkling of her laughter or feel her soft sigh as she slept curled against him?

His cock hardened at the thought of her, and

though he sat in a chamber surrounded by ice, he burned. How long had it been since Lark had sheathed him? When was the last time she'd taken him in her mouth and sucked him until he'd exploded? Too long.

The tightness of his breeks became uncomfortable, and Sarco undid the laces. His pulsating cock sprung free.

He closed his eyes, envisioned Lark's luscious mouth sliding up and down his shaft, and stroked himself. At first slowly, allowing his hand to tease, squeeze, fondle, and caress his shaft, savoring the fantasy of Lark. Then, faster, harder, more demanding, with purpose.

His breathing quickened, his heart pounded, and the blood coursing through his veins heated to boiling. Pressure built at the base of his balls, rising up the length of his cock like hot magma from a volcano. When the explosion happened, Sarco shuddered from the force of the spasms. Hot cum coated his fingertips, and loneliness enveloped him.

Not that his orgasm hadn't been pleasurable, for it had, but it hadn't been what he craved. He wanted Lark, needed her. He missed her more now than ever. What was he going to do?

Sarco threw up his hands in frustration and accidentally bumped the table. He grabbed for and caught the rolling stone and frozen flower before they had the chance to topple to the floor. Staring at them, he gauged their meaning.

Lark…He couldn't get her out of his mind.

His fingers itched with the need to touch her instead of stone and ice, or at least that's why he thought they were tingling until he glanced down. With awe he gaped as a soft glow pulsed and darted back and forth between the flower and the stone.

Before his eyes, what had once been two, became one.

Sarco blinked three times. There, in the palm of his hand, lay a ring. Not just any ring, but a shiny, deep-green, faceted treasure of a ring with a tiny, opalescent flowering bud. The small blossom rose from the middle of the ring to form a setting that could only be described as divine.

He turned it over in his hands as a grin broke out on his face. This was no petite band meant to grace the delicate finger of Princess Aryanna. It was a sign. It had to be.

He knew there was but one woman in all of Albrath whose finger this ring would fit. It had been forged from the love in his heart, and the seed representing the future generation they would forge together. It was meant for Lark, only for Lark.

The heaviness that had settled over him earlier now lifted. With newfound energy, Sarco rose, refastened his breeks, and stepped with purpose into the night air.

He looked up at the three moons and winked as he slipped the band into the pocket of his tunic, close to his heart. With a smile on his face and a new determination in his heart, Sarco headed off to find his bed. Tomorrow was going to be a big day.

\*\*\*\*

Lark hesitated before the large, wooden doors of the royal suite and tried unsuccessfully to draw a deep enough breath to quiet the uneasiness settling in the pit of her belly. As if the sleepless night of a few turns of the hourglass ago hadn't been bad enough, and the even longer unending gloominess of the day still hadn't come to an end, now she was being summoned, and not by just anyone, but by Mother.

Her hands trembled and tiny rivulets of moisture formed and made their way down the middle of her spine. Lark hated this about herself. She was a woman full grown. Why did she still fall prey to the all-encompassing fear of the unloved little girl she'd been every time she was in her mother's presence?

She turned to flee instead of facing the woman when, with a loud bang, the door flew open and out rushed an angry-looking Laycee Titwilder with Tug's head bobbing up and down under her arm.

The gnome wasted no time making sure the whole Academy and probably the majority of Albrath heard every word of her displeasure. "Oh, I'll be glad ta move my things out of the princesses' quarters, don't ya be worrying about that. After almost twenty-six years of looking after and loving those girls, ya have the nerve ta tell me I'm mettlesome, disloyal, and my services are no longer needed? Well, ya can't make me stop loving them, but ya can take ya governess position and stick it straight up yare hinny hole with a toothpick. As tight as yare arse is, I'm sure that's all ya could fit up there. That's probably what's wrong with ya. If ya could loosen up and take a good shit, ya might be a tad less full of yaself."

Lark wanted to laugh. She wanted to follow Laycee and get as far away from this room as possible.

She didn't do either. Her mother, the queen, stared straight at her. There was no escape.

"You're late, as usual. I summoned you a quarter of a turn of the hourglass ago. Get in here and close the door. There is much to discuss."

Lark's knees almost buckled as she slipped into the room and took her place beside her sisters. Chancing a glance toward Aryanna, anger replaced her fear when she couldn't help but notice the dark smudges under her sister's eyes and the tear tracks down her face. The twins didn't seem to be faring much better. They were gripping each other's hands and both had complexions as white as death.

Lark lifted her head, thinking she was now ready to face whatever her mother had to dish out. She soon found out how wrong she was.

Queen Allanna Zanlynn Calista Hammerstrike stood and made a production of smoothing wrinkles that weren't there from the skirt of her white-as-snow gown. She patted her golden curls and straightened her glittering, jeweled crown.

Then she looked down upon her daughters and sighed. "I can't tell you how disappointed and distressed I am. I've been hearing rumors that simply can't be true, except of Lark, of course. I would believe such treachery from her. But the rest of you? My sources must be false. My own dear, devoted daughters wouldn't really try to thwart my plans, would they?"

Lark held her breath.

The queen made a production of fluffing her gown before taking a seat upon a golden throne. She patted her husband's hand, and for the first time since walking into the room, Lark realized her father, though silent, was also present. At his wife's touch, he flinched but didn't look directly at any of them.

Lark's throat tightened, and the air in the room thinned. Her breathing became labored.

The queen, however, wasn't having any problem speaking. "What is this I've been hearing, Aryanna? You don't wish to marry the elf?" She laughed. "Of course, you don't wish to marry the elf. Who would? Look at the sacrifice I've made for this family by marrying your barbarian of a father. One does what one must, not what one wishes."

Stars floated before Lark's eyes, and she forced herself to breathe in and breathe out. She tried to form even one coherent thought, but her mind was the blank canvas her mother's words were being imprinted upon.

"Marriage isn't about all that love nonsense. It's about power and prestige. You, my daughter, will be a great lady as is your birthright, and your children will have prestige. To have you become the next Lady of the Elves will add to my power and popularity. It's a boon to have a firstborn daughter so highly placed. I've worked hard to see this match come to fruition. You'll not disobey me in this."

Aryanna stiffened her spine and glared at her mother. Lark had always been proud of her sister, but never more than this moment. "It isn't the fact Sarco is an elf that I object to Mother, it's the fact he isn't *the* elf I'm in love with. I'm in love with his brother, Cyrrick, and that is whom I wish to marry. I want to be the wife of a diplomat. I'm not you. I don't care about power or prestige, and I don't want to be a lord's lady. I refuse to marry Sarco Sunwalker, and nothing you say or do will change my mind."

The queen smiled at her daughters, and the sight of it made Lark cringe. History had proven that nothing pleasant ever followed one of those smiles.

"Well, then you're in luck. After all, what do you

think Sarco Sunwalker's chances are in the arena against your brother? Adan is the barbarian champion and has never lost a challenge. So you see, my darling girl, we'll both get what we want. You will have Cyrrick the diplomat. Though it's beyond me why anyone would actually want an elf. And, with Sarco out of the way, you'll still become a lady."

Lark's gasp radiated throughout the room, but she didn't care. She glanced at Aryanna and awaited her response. It wasn't long in coming. "You would have our brother take the life of a good, decent man? Is getting your way in this really so very important? Why can you not understand I simply don't wish to be a lady, anyone's lady?"

Lark swallowed back the sob stuck in her throat and closed her eyes. This was useless. There was no reasoning with the queen. But Aryanna continued to try.

"It's Lark you should be embracing. She and Sarco love each other, and she'd make a fine lady, really she would. And…and you'd still get to reap the benefits you so desire. I know you've always had an irrational displeasure with Lark, but she's a wonderful person, Mother, and can make you proud if you'd but give her half a chance."

Lark opened her mouth to speak, but before she could get a word out, Aryanna clenched her fist and shook it toward their mother. "If you dare cause or allow a single hair on Sarco Sunwalker's head to be injured, I swear, I'll leave this place and you'll never see or hear from me again. Then it'll be on your head when the prophecy is not fulfilled and a war to end all wars rips your precious kingdom apart. What will happen to your power and prestige then, Mother?

You'll lose everything you hold dear."

Lark waited for the explosion. But the fact that the queen didn't erupt scared her more than if the woman's screams had shaken the walls down about their heads. Instead, her mother's quiet smile and words of "Oh, really?" as she glanced toward the twins had ripples of nervous chills scampering up and down Lark's backbone.

The queen clasped her hands together and addressed the two identical sisters. "Ally, my sweet, I have news for you. I've been in negotiations for the past few days and the Prince of Karza has agreed to take you on as a second wife. Isn't that simply grand? You are to become a member of the harem he's building. I realize it isn't as grand as the wonderful opportunity Aryanna is trying to throw away, but then, neither are you. And best of all, his entourage is here, at the Academy, this very moment and can whisk you away to his kingdom with no more than a single word from me. I'm ever so happy for you, dear."

Lark's heart stopped for a moment and then raced. *Trolls.*

Ally gasped, but it was Audrey who rushed forward.

"You can't be serious, Mother. The Prince of Karza is still more a child than he is a man, I mean, troll. I don't think he's even attained his thirteenth year yet. And even if he wasn't a…a…a…troll, which is totally disgusting, Karza is halfway around the world. We'd never see Ally again."

Lark's breath caught and her chest hurt from the exertion it took to simply breathe. Her mother would actually marry off one of her daughters to a troll? They were huge, green, horrid beasts with tusks, who didn't bathe often and were known for their propensity to pick the remnants of their meals from between their teeth with the bones of their victims.

Lark was used to hatefulness being directed toward her from her mother, but to see and hear the vindictive poison unleashed upon her sisters was a new experience.

The queen chuckled, "Don't worry about seeing Ally again if your older sister doesn't do as I wish, my sweet. You'll be much too busy. I've found a match for you also. Since I've been told you have a preference for men of a shorter stature, the dwarf duke himself has offered for your hand. You, my special girl, are to become a duchess."

Lark heard Audrey's quick intake of air and watched in helpless horror as her sister's face turned an alarming shade of purple.

"You'd marry me off to a man older than Father? Not only older but smelly and wrinkly and who has already buried three wives? And a man who lives on the opposite side of the world from where Ally will be? We can't be separated. We wouldn't survive it. Please, Mother, I beg of you, don't do this."

The queen laughed and it was the scariest sound Lark had ever heard. "Then I suggest you talk some sense into your sister. There will be a wedding to celebrate tomorrow, and she will become the future Lady of Landis or else. Yours and your sister's fates depend on how selfish Aryanna wishes to be."

Lark couldn't stand the anticipation or the anger bubbling from deep inside any longer. Even though the thought filled her with fear, she had to know what her mother had planned for her, for she had no doubt the queen had something equally, if not even more horrible, in mind.

"And what of me, Mother? Who have you arranged to marry me off to, an ogre?"

The queen really did laugh then, and Lark wished she hadn't asked after all.

"You, married? Don't be absurd. I care more about our family than to try and pawn you off on some poor unsuspecting soul. I wouldn't do that to even our worst enemies. Oh, no, Lark, for you I have a special surprise. All of your scheming and trying to steal your sister's place hasn't gone unnoticed."

Lark forced herself to breathe normal and remain calm. Not willing to allow her mother to see her fear.

"I had a nice long chat with the head of the Rector yesterday, Lark, and he's agreed to take you off our hands. He'll put you where you can get help for your particular, umm, ailment. He even believes with enough time and prayer, the evilness within you can finally be expunged. And this opportunity doesn't depend on what choice your sister makes."

Lark swallowed, and the lump that had been sitting in her throat hit the bottom of her stomach like a brick. So there it was. Mother had finally found a final solution for her spiritmaster-daughter problem.

"Whether Aryanna marries either of the Sunwalkers or not, Lark, the day after tomorrow you leave here for a life in service to our Lord God Draka for the rest of your days. I've been told this particular abbey is situated in the middle of the desert close to VoT itself. As dry and hot as it must be there, I'm sure they'll welcome a few cloudy days and a little rain. You may now thank me."

She couldn't help herself. Lark's knees buckled. VoT. Her mother was sending her to The Valley of Torment. Before she hit the ground, her father spoke for the first time since they'd entered the chamber.

"Now, Allanna, my sweet queen, perhaps we're being just a little hasty. Maybe we should take some time and discuss this further."

The only thing scarier than watching her mother systematically attack all four of her daughters was watching her turn on her husband. With a screech that sent shock waves through Lark's body, the room came alive with her anger.

"Alfred, how many times must I tell you, if you don't have something useful and supportive to say, then keep your mouth shut? There's nothing left to discuss. I'll have my way in this and that's final."

Lark developed a tiny spark of respect for her father as he bristled. "Allanna Hammerstrike, I promised my dear mother on her deathbed I'd treat my wife like the queen she was meant to be, but I must admit there are days you sorely try my patience. I am king, remember? *I* have the final say."

The queen laughed yet again. "If you wish to pretend you have some authority then so be it, but we both know who rules, don't we, Alfred?"

Queen Allanna Zanlynn Calista Hammerstrike clapped her hands. Immediately the doors opened and in strode a contingent of barbarian soldiers.

"My royal guard. I'm pleased to inform you, just this very evening I have been in contact with your prince. Adan tells me he'll be returning to the Academy shortly after sunrise with Aryanna's betrothed. The quest is almost complete and we must prepare for the wedding that will take place as the sun sets tomorrow evening.

"Please be so kind as to escort my…daughters to the princess quarters and guard them closely. No one is to be allowed access to them, and they are not to leave their chambers or speak to anyone until Aryanna is escorted down for her wedding. If they attempt to disobey my orders, inform me immediately. There will be dire consequences."

Lark hung her head. There would be no happily ever after for anyone. Nothing mattered anymore, so why even try to play nice. She lifted her eyes and glared at her mother as she once more rose to her feet, straightened her spine, and lifted her chin. "Do what you wish with me, I don't care, but leave my sisters alone, you fucking witch."

The queen paused and then smiled as she continued speaking to her guards as if Lark wasn't even there. "This is much too delicate a diplomatic situation to allow anything to go wrong at this juncture. After all, there is the possibility of a war if we don't hold up our end of the bargain."

With a flourish, the queen made a motion, and then Lark and her three sisters had no choice but to follow the guards through the doors.

In the distance, thunder roared and lightning struck.

\*\*\*\*

Even though the sun was shining brightly over the Barbarian city of Alaria, it might as well have been freezing cold and pouring rain for the mood the day had taken on.

Sarco sat upon his steed in the center of the

courtyard, shaking his head. He didn't understand. The men should be jovial. They were on their way home. The quest was almost done. And yet, to a man, there was an oppressive, uncomfortable aura surrounding them. Something was wrong, very wrong. All he wanted in all of Albrath was to get back to the Academy and to Lark.

He'd first noticed the changes in moods last night when he'd returned to the castle with the ring and shown them all the divine treasure. What should've been a celebration had been received with silence. Well, almost silence. There had been Leeky's comment. *'What the blue balls beneath the short stinky pecker of a homely red-headed dwarf too broke ta afford a hand job do ya make of that, lads? Looks a might big for Princess Aryanna's hand, don't ya think. Ya sure ya did it right?'*

Adan's face had lost all color, and without a word, the barbarian prince had turned and left the room. Sarco hadn't seen him again until a few minutes ago when he'd ridden into the bailey and joined the others.

Leaning, Sarco whispered to Uthiel. "What's with everyone this morning, especially Adan? He won't even look at me."

Uthiel sighed. "Think about it, Sarco. What's the next part of the quest? *'It's a champion you must defeat for the heart you wish to seek.'* Who do you think the barbarian champion is? I have no doubt he's feeling sick about the fact he's going to kill you in a few hours, or at the very least, give it his best shot. Just so you know, Adan Hammerstrike has never known defeat. Ever."

Suddenly, the mood of the day made perfect sense.

## Chapter Twenty-Six

If ever a man was more relieved to see the castle, with its spires rising in the distance, that housed the Academy of Magical Arts, Sarco couldn't imagine such a man. It didn't matter that gray clouds rolled across the sky or cold, fat drops of rain steadily pelted down or that lightning flashed across an angry sky and thunder shook the ground.

Soon now, he'd be with Lark.

It wasn't even important that this very day he'd be forced to face Adan in the arena, finish a quest, and fulfill a prophecy. All that mattered was getting close enough to Lark to reestablish their bond.

Sarco sighed. He hadn't realized when he and Lark had spoken the spell to block their mental bond what the cost would be. Never in his life had he been so utterly alone as these past few days. Having her joined with him in his mind had become essential to his well-being. No less important than the blood coursing through his veins or the air going in and out of his lungs.

Without her presence in his mind, *alone* had taken on a whole new meaning. No longer did it just mean being by himself. Instead, his aloneness had morphed into a bottomless well of despair and an endless aching need to the very depths of his soul. He would never again be whole without her.

As the group of six men rode through the gates of the Academy and into the bailey, Sarco didn't slow. He simply threw his leg over the side of his saddle, slid to the ground, tossed his reins to a nearby page, and took off in a run.

Taking the stairs of the tower two at a time, he didn't pause until directly in front of Lark's door. His hand was on the knob when, suddenly, from the other side, it was pushed wide open. For a moment, he wasn't sure which of them was more surprised, him or the female gnome standing before him.

He glanced past her, anxious to see Lark's face.

"She's not here. Lark, that is. None of them are." The sadness in Laycee's voice drew his eyes back to the gnome. "The queen has them under lock and key. Nobody can get in or out of their chamber. I was just tidying up in case Lark gets ta come back and at least get her things before she's sent away forever."

Tears streaked Laycee's cheeks.

Sarco knelt to her level and took her gently but firmly by the shoulders. "What has happened?"

In between hiccups and sniffles, Laycee explained. "She fired me. The queen, that is. But I didn't leave, like she thought I did. I stayed and listened at the door. It's horrible what she's gonna do. Poor Ally's being forced ta marry a troll and Audrey, an old dwarf. Aryanna has ta marry ya, if Adan doesn't kill ya first, and Lark's getting sent away ta some abbey in the middle of VoT no matter who marries whom."

Chills flooded Sarco from the inside out, and shivers skittered from head to toe. VoT? Not even the queen could be that cruel, could she?

Laycee plucked a red hanky from her pocket and

blew her nose. "There's no hope, ya know. She has them all locked up tight in Aryanna's rooms. There are even guards on the door. My girls will be gone by this time tomorrow, scattered ta the wind. I'll never see them again."

Laycee pushed past Sarco. "If ya're back, that means Leeky is, too. Get outta my way, wizard. He'll know what ta do."

Sarco easily passed her on his way back down the stairs. He knew where to find Leeky, Uthiel, Cyrrick, Sherman, and even Adan. They'd be right where he'd left them, still in the bailey dealing with their horses.

He needed to get to them before a babbling Laycee did. With the girls locked away and being guarded, Sarco was going to need all the help he could get from his friends.

****

Lark paced.

There were no windows in this room, and the stuffiness—combined with the unceasing drone of her sisters as they took turns sniffling, sobbing, and ranting—only added to the dull ache in her head and the throbbing muscles on the back of her neck.

The wailing in the room reached a fevered pitch, and Lark placed her hands over her ears and closed her eyes, trying to block out the misery. She couldn't take any more.

If it hadn't been for the sudden reverberations created by someone or something landing hard against the door and the added sound of a familiar voice outside, none of them would have realized anything was happening.

"How dare you tell me I'm not permitted. My

sisters are in there, and you will grant me access. I am your Prince."

The girls rushed to the door as it shook with the force of someone or something hitting against it yet again.

"Please forgive me, Prince Adan, but we can't allow even you to enter. The queen gave very specific orders. No one gets in or out until we escort Princess Aryanna down for her wedding this evening."

Lark's heart raced. If Adan was here, and he obviously was, then Sarco must be also. She almost yelled out before remembering the silence spell the queen had ordered to be put on the room. Even if they all joined voices and shouted and screamed, not one squeak would be heard through the door. Glancing toward her sisters, she could tell they were thinking the same thing. So instead, Lark settled for straining to hear Sarco's voice. It was no use. No one had ever been able to outshout Adan.

"I don't care what my mother has dictated. You'll open this door, and that's an order."

The voice of the guard sounded anything but confident, but his message was clear. "I wish I could, sir. I'd give anything to do as you wish. I simply can't. The queen would have my liver for her dinner. I'm more afraid of her than I am of you."

A familiar female voice joined the mix and even through her veil of tears, Lark couldn't help but smile.

"Didn't I tell you they're being held prisoners, Uthiel? Draw your sword this minute and run these guards through. You know what I'm talking about, do that paladin stuff you do. Or better yet, give me the sword and I'll do it."

Lark couldn't prevent the smile that graced her lips as Uthiel answered his wife. "Now, Briar, don't be getting excited. You know bad things happen when you do. Just calm down and let us men handle this, please."

"Like you handled me? Why, do you plan to drug them? Oh, wait, I forgot, that's not how a big, strong paladin handles men. That's what he resorts to when dealing with his wife."

Uthiel groaned, "Not now, Briar, please. Later you may make me pay for my actions to your heart's content."

Lark glanced at her sisters and they, too, were smiling for the first time in days. They all knew Briar would have no problem making Uthiel pay in spades for his lapse in judgment when this was all over.

Another voice came from somewhere beyond the locked door. "I once took a class on escaping if that would be of any help. Of course, I was on the other side of the locks, and there weren't guards blocking my way."

Sherman's voice faded, and Ally and Audrey sighed. Lark just shook her head.

"What the black spandex leggings rubbing betwixt the chubby thighs of a toe-tapping, tango-dancing trollop out on the town are ya thinking, lad? We don't need ta pick the lock. All we need ta do is find the one with the key and take it away from him. I've got a dagger that says I'll get ta search at least four of them before they know what hit them."

Adan words were like steel. "There won't be anyone attacking anyone. These guards are of my realm and as such under my protection. And we have ladies present, remember? I won't put Briar or Laycee in danger."

Lark's heart sank. There would be no rescue for them. Though she knew her brother loved all his sisters, first and foremost, he was the prince. And his next words confirmed her fears "This tactic isn't getting us anywhere, and it's wasting valuable time. I will go speak with my parents and get to the bottom of this. At the moment, the girls are safe."

The sound of feet shuffling off into the distance told Lark more than she wanted to know. She looked at Aryanna and could tell she was thinking along the same line. Neither had heard the voices they'd longed to hear. Not once had Sarco or Cyrrick Sunwalker said a single word.

Were they here? Did they survive the quest? And what about the quest itself? Had it been a success? Or perhaps the brothers had simply decided the Hammerstrike sisters were more trouble than they were worth, and who could blame them?

Adan made one last comment before his voice completely faded. "Hear me well. No harm is to come to my sisters in any form, or God Draka have mercy on all of your souls."

Then silence. Cold as death, lonely as the grave, dark as the longest night…silence.

\*\*\*\*

Sarco waited with Cyrrick, Uthiel, Leeky, and Sherman in the challenger's corner of the arena, his hand wrapped around the hilt of an ancient, rusty barbarian broadsword. Slowly, he turned, glancing about.

The spectator seats were quickly filling, and excitement hummed in the air. It had been just past midmorning when they'd first stepped back onto the grounds of the Academy and more than three turns of the hourglass had passed since they'd attempted to rescue the girls. It felt more like days.

What was he going to do? Had he been wise in agreeing to remain silent and allow Adan a chance to work things out his way? Every instinct he possessed had screamed for him to form fireball after fireball and if necessary burn the walls of the Academy down in order to free Lark. His fingers still itched with the need to do just that. But agree he had, and so had Cyrrick, and now time was running out.

The sun was well past its zenith, the three full moons of Albrath would rise soon, and Lark and her sisters were still locked away. The contest between him and Adan was quickly approaching without a single word of resolution being spoken.

Horns suddenly trumpeted from somewhere above and bright lights illuminated the stadium. He stared, dumbfounded, at a procession, the likes of which he had never seen.

The Council of Elders entered, with Great-Uncle Arizon in his midnight-blue robes in the lead, followed by Lark's grandmother Ava, and the remaining members. The council members seated themselves in the section cordoned off especially for them and looked expectantly toward the floor of the arena.

Next, Headmistress Seychelle sauntered in with her pet human, Ray, in tow. The human looked directly at Sarco, jumped up and down, and yelled, "Ray loves cock."

*Quite the greeting.* Sarco almost wanted to hug the pathetic excuse for a human as the first real smile he'd felt all day crossed his lips.

The headmistress didn't even acknowledge Ray's outburst. She simply smiled and chatted with onlookers as she made her way across the arena. At the last possible moment, just before she took her seat of honor, Seychelle turned and gave Sarco a quick, sorrowful glance. One that could only be described as a too-bad-you're-going-to-die look. Sarco didn't respond. He didn't know how.

The tinkling of a thousand bells joined the booming of horns as the King and Queen of Alaria and the Lord and his Lady of Landis made their presence known in royal splendor. First, his own parents, Lord Tylindius and Lady Jillian Sunwalker, with plastic-looking smiles plastered on their faces, waved in his direction as they walked by.

Sarco wished he had the magic to somehow wipe away the worry lines etching his mother's face. Even her practiced Lady of the Keep smile couldn't hide her concern.

Then came King Alfred and Queen Allanna, with their noses high in the air and their eyes forward. They marched arm in arm to the royal section of the arena and took their seats upon thrones next to Sarco's parents.

With a roar, the barbarians, occupying the majority of the bleachers, rose and cheered. The sound filled the arena until it echoed off the walls and the ground below Sarco's feet shook with it.

The reason for the roaring became evident as Prince Adan Zeth Conner Hammerstrike entered the arena. He was a sight to behold. Attired in a traditional, barbarian kilt of emerald green and royal blue, along with his shining broadsword swinging from his side, he certainly looked the part of a formidable opponent.

Sarco gulped. Adan's muscles bulged as his mighty fist gripped the hilt of his broadsword and hefted the thing high into the air as if it weighed no more than a toothpick.

The crowd cheered.

A fine sheen of moisture peppered Sarco's forehead and upper lip. *Yep, he was going to die*.

As if on cue, every barbarian within shouting distance stomped their feet and chanted the Prince's name.

"Adan. Adan. Adan."

A sudden prod at knee level got Sarco's attention.

"Do ya remember what I told ya, lad? Stick and jab, stick and jab. Then, when ya've got him reeling, go in for the shot that'll put him on his knees. A well-placed kick ta the willy-whackers ought ta do the trick. Then, strafe ta the left, that's his weak side, and melee him if ya can with that there piss-poor excuse for a sword they gave ya. Don't be killing him if ya can help it. I've developed a fondness for the lad. Though the offer's still open if ya wanna use my special daggers."

Sarco patted the gnome on the top of his almost-bald head. "I appreciate the offer, Leeky. Really I do, but I must use the weapon the barbarian queen ordered given to me for this task. It's one of the rules of the battle, right along with no use of magic, and no outside help. Only the king himself can override her decision."

Sarco glanced at his brother and each of his friends in turn. "Promise me, all of you, you won't interfere, no matter what."

Cyrrick shook his head. "If it looks like you're in

danger of being killed, I can't give you that promise, and you know it."

Uthiel coughed and cleared his throat. "It'd be very unpaladin-like of me to stand by and watch my best friend cut down and not interfere, don't you think? There isn't much I wouldn't promise you, Sarco, but I can't and won't promise you that."

Sherman lifted his hand.

Sarco sighed. "What is it, Sherman?"

The halfling pushed his glasses up the ridge of his nose and ran his fingers through the stubble of his hair. "I once took a class on swordplay, and I could give you pointers, if you like. That wouldn't be taking unfair advantage, would it? Oh, and I'm with the rest of them on the promise, I'm afraid. I've ridden a plastic doll down the side of a mountain of ice, and I've punched a dragon in the face. I'm not going to stand by and watch you slain now that the quest is all but finished."

Sarco chuckled. "That's what I thought. I appreciate your loyalty, all of you, really I do. You have no idea what it means to me."

He lifted a hand and immediately eighteen high-elf soldiers in full war armor surrounded Cyrrick, Uthiel, Leeky, and Sherman, forming an impenetrable wall between them and Sarco.

Ignoring the protests of his friends and feeling more alone than he'd ever been in his life, Sarco walked slowly but purposefully to the middle of the arena.

He turned first toward the Council of Elders and bowed low, then did the same in the direction of the headmistress. Finally, Sarco faced the king, the queen, his parents, and then finally Adan.

He opened his hand revealing a greenish opalescent object. Holding the ring high above his head for all to see, he addressed the room. "With the help of the men I chose, I plucked the flower from where ice and fire formed a Maiden's Desire. I withstood the heat where metal and gemstone first meet. And it was with love in mind that this treasure did become divine. When this champion I must face is defeated, I will place this ring upon the finger of the woman I love and make her my wife. This day I will fulfill the prophecy."

Cheers rang out and Sarco waited patiently for them to die down. "But first, there is this challenge to complete, and I gladly face it."

Sarco pointed to Adan. "It is an honor to battle your barbarian champion to complete the quest and win the right to choose my bride."

Queen Allanna laughed. "You have high aspirations for an elf, Sarco Sunwalker. My son has never been defeated, and defeat him you must to complete the quest. There has never been, and will never be, an elf born who can best Prince Adan. Perhaps after your unfortunate death, your brother Cyrrick will be able to use the ring for his bride. From what I've been told, Aryanna prefers him over you."

Sarco ignored Queen Allanna as he made his way back to his brother and friends. He reached through the wall of soldiers and held out the ring to Cyrrick. "Would you hold this for me and keep it safe?"

Cyrrick nodded.

Sarco returned to the battle circle and whispered to Adan, "I know I've asked much of you these past days, but there is one more thing I request. We both know I'm not much of a swordsman and most probably will die this day, for I am known for my magic, not my brawn. But Lark is innocent in all of this and she is being held prisoner. There is nothing I wouldn't do to see her set free. Even try my best to kill you, my friend."

He locked gazes with Adan. "Let us make a pact, shall we? You have a duty to your people as do I to mine. Duty we both understand. Promise me, Adan. Promise me no matter what happens in this arena today, you'll personally protect Lark. You'll get her somewhere safe. Don't let your mother send her to VoT, I beg of you."

A hush fell over the crowd as lights dimmed and a single spotlight illuminated the two men.

Adan nodded to Sarco then turned in a circle, encompassing the crowd with an angry look upon his face. "Do my fellow countrymen consider me a weakling?"

A mighty roar of, "No, never!" went up.

The barbarian prince held out his arm and pointed. "Then, do you consider Sarco Sunwalker, the elfin heir to Landis, to be a superior swordsman to me?"

Again the crowd yelled their nays.

For a moment, Sarco didn't understand why Adan was doing what he was doing, then understanding dawned, and he grinned.

After a few moments, silence fell and Adan shook his head as he looked first toward his parents, then back to the crowd. "Then I don't get it. If I am the champion and I am expected to win, why would any noble barbarian give this man a rusty weapon with which to fight? Is this how you wish your champion, your prince, to win? I can only conclude it must have been a horrible mistake, for barbarians are men of honor, are we not?"

The crowd roared.

Adan hung his head and Sarco chuckled at his theatrics.

"Now, is there not a single warrior in this arena willing to let this...*elf* use a real blade for a few moments?"

The sound of a thousand swords being unsheathed at the same time was deafening, and the glare of the shine off their blades so blinding, Sarco didn't even see the man walking toward him until the barbarian king stood mere inches away.

King Alfred Hammerstrike bowed before Sarco and handed him his own gleaming broadsword hilt, then turned and made his way back to his throne. The crowd became as silent as death itself and stood at attention until the king once more took his throne.

Adan raised his hand and silence fell. "Now that we're equally armed, we shall see who is victorious this day. Prepare to defend yourself, Elf."

Again, the crowd rose to their feet and roared as the two men faced off. Sarco took a deep breath and braced himself for a quick and sudden death.

Adan hefted his broadsword high above his head, and Sarco almost forgot to fend off the first blow as the barbarian prince looked him straight in the eye, winked, smiled, then brought his sword swiftly down. With a loud clang and a teeth-rattling blow, metal struck metal.

The crowd gasped.

Over and over, the two men sparred, trading blows and maneuvering for position. The crowd continued to cheer as sweat trickled down Sarco's chest as fast as the grains of sand were dropping through the hourglass.

Before long, his arms burned beneath the weight of the sword and his muscles quivered. All he could hear was the ringing of metal upon metal in his ears. Still, he sensed Adan was holding back, not using all the power he had at his disposal, but Sarco wasn't sure why.

Just when Sarco's energy to fend off one more blow failed him, Adan's huge barbarian arm wrapped around his neck. With a loud smack, their foreheads collided. Pain shot through Sarco's head and with the ringing in his ears, he almost missed Adan's words.

"We must make this look real. The crowd expects it. We both know our honor and duty, my friend, but we also understand loyalty. When I tell you to, I want you to trip me and place your sword at my throat. Until then, keep defending against my blows."

Sarco shook his head to clear it. "You would…let me win?"

Adan Hammerstrike smiled. "Before this quest I would've gladly killed you, but over the past days, I've found you to be a brave and honorable man, Sarco Sunwalker."

Adan raised his sword and swung. The bones of Sarco's arm ached as he once more blocked the blow.

The barbarian price smiled. "I'll be proud to call you my brother at the end of this day, no matter which of my sisters you wed. A man doesn't raise his sword against his brother in anger, but only in defense thereof. From this day forward, you have my loyalty and my sword if ever you need."

"And my magic is yours, brother, now and forever." Sarco smiled.

Adan nodded. "Time for the big finish. We wouldn't want to disappoint our spectators."

In the next heartbeat, Sarco found himself flat on his back with the wind knocked from his lungs, gasping as a sword came ever closer to his chest. From the vibrations reverberating through his bones, he could tell the crowd was on their feet stomping along with their yelling.

Adan mouthed the word *roll* a split second before the sword would have split him in half. And roll out of its way was precisely what Sarco did. With a flourish, he leapt to his feet and once more faced Adan.

Again the barbarian prince mouthed a word, but this time it was *now*.

Sarco swept his foot in a circular motion from left to right and, even though they'd planned it, he was still surprised when Adan fell backward. With lightning-quick swiftness, Sarco brought his sword down until the very tip of the blade rested against the pulse of Adan's neck.

The arena became silent. The falling of a single grain of sand through the hourglass could've been heard. When Adan spoke, there wasn't an ear in the building that didn't hear. "I forfeit. You win your challenge, Sarco Sunwalker."

There was one more moment of absolute, perfect silence before an earsplitting shriek shattered the air.

## Chapter Twenty-Seven

If ever a man had no idea whether to jump for joy or cry with despair, Sarco knew himself to be that man. He stood in the middle of the arena, enormously relieved the quest was now complete, but at the same time, he dreaded facing the next task—that of trying to convince a reluctant king and a totally irate queen they'd made an error in judgment choosing Aryanna as his bride.

And there was still the human rule of order of marriage that needed to be dealt with since, according to Briar and Laycee, no way around it had been found.

It was difficult to form a coherent thought, however, with Queen Allanna Hammerstrike giving her son the dressing down of a lifetime at the top of her lungs.

"You forfeit? What do you mean, you forfeit? How dare you forfeit, and to an...an...an elf of all things. I'll never live down the shame of this day. You've disgraced not only me and your entire family, but also the crown and every barbarian who breathes. I can't believe such a coward as you actually came from my body. You must be your father's son. You certainly aren't mine. No son of mine would've ever—"

"Cease!" The sudden shout of the single word from an unexpected source silenced the queen and shocked Sarco all the way to his toes. He stared at the throne.

Queen Allanna glanced in the direction of her husband, lifted an eyebrow, glared, then continued. "As I was saying before I was so rudely interrupted, no son of mine would've ever forfeited. No. My son would've died before dishonoring himself and his people in such a fashion."

Adan Hammerstrike stood tall, straight, and silent before his parents and the full arena with an impassive look on his face. The only thing that belied his calm was the twitch Sarco observed every now and again in his jaw, and the tiny shake of his head toward Cyrrick, Uthiel, Sherman, and Leeky when it looked as if they were going to speak in his defense.

The queen opened her mouth once more, but King Alfred surprised them all. "Not another word. Do you hear me, Allanna? You will cease this instant. I am king, and it's high time you knew it. I will be obeyed in this. You will now sit down and be silent, or I'll be forced to have you bound to your chair and gagged until these proceedings are finished."

Queen Allanna didn't bother to look at her husband as she flipped her hand in his direction and laughed, "You wouldn't dare."

King Alfred snapped his fingers and immediately guards from every corner of the arena formed before him. "This is your last chance, Allanna. Sit down."

The queen made a production of turning her back to her husband and addressing the guards. "Return to your posts this instant. I command you."

Not one guard moved.

She stomped her foot. "I said go."

The guard closest to the throne shuffled his feet and looked sheepishly at the king. "What kind of rope will you be wanting, Sire? I have a few lengths of sturdy hemp with me and an extra handkerchief if that'll do the job. "

For a moment, Sarco thought the queen was going to strike the man down as she raised her hand and screamed. She never got the opportunity.

As gently as if dealing with a small child, the barbarian king lifted his human wife, set her upon her throne and placed the offered hanky between her teeth before she could say another word. Then, he tied it swiftly and securely behind her head.

She squirmed and kicked, fought and twisted, but to no avail as King Alfred used five lengths of rope to tie his wife to her chair. One on each of her arms and legs and one about her middle. When he was finished, he turned toward the people gathered in the arena.

"Now, my sweet queen and I are prepared to watch and enjoy the wedding of our daughter and the fulfillment of the prophecy. We sincerely hope you will all stay as our guests and enjoy the festivities of the coming evening. There will be a formal reception afterward."

King Alfred Zavier Caden Hammerstrike took his seat and patted his wife upon the hand as he addressed Sarco. "Are you now prepared to do your duty by joining our two families together, Sarco, heir of Landis?"

Having glanced in the direction of Adan to see if the man had any last-minute advice as to how to proceed, Sarco was a little surprised when Adan leaned toward him and whispered, "You're on your own in this one. If you have something to say, now would be the time."

Sarco took two deep breaths before kneeling before the barbarian throne. He closed his eyes a moment to still the racing of his heart. After one more long cleansing breath, he spoke. "Your Majesty, my greatest hope is to join together our two families for all time and finally fulfill the prophecy spoken almost nine hundred years ago. And as God Draka is my witness, I do not mean to offend in anyway, but I simply cannot marry Aryanna. I love Lark. It must be she or none."

The crowd went wild with boos and hisses. Even the Council of the Elders pointed and frowned. Except for Grandmother Ava, who Sarco could swear was smiling at him.

The king raised his hand for silence then rubbed his chin thoughtfully. Sarco looked toward Queen Allanna to see her reaction and, for a moment, was afraid the woman was having seizures from the way she was twisting and flopping around.

King Alfred simply leaned over and patted his wife's hand once more. Finally, he looked up. "And what precisely would you have me do about the human rule of marriage? Lark is the youngest and as such must marry last. What should I do about the other three? Perhaps marry them off to the highest bidder just so you may have the wife you wish? Life is at times hard, young man. We don't always get what we wish for."

Sarco stood straight and faced the king. "It's true we don't always get what we want, but it's also true you should never be willing to settle for something you don't want, either. Aryanna is a beautiful, wonderful woman, but she isn't for me. However, I know for a fact, my brother, Cyrrick, loves Aryanna with everything he is, and she loves him the same way. They belong together, and I implore you to allow them to be the first to wed this day."

The king looked around the crowd. "And is your brother, Cyrrick, here and ready to speak for himself?"

Cyrrick stepped forward, stood beside Sarco, and bowed before the king. "What my brother says is true, Your Majesty. Aryanna and I do love each other very much and have for some time. She is a strong, intelligent, young woman and will not only make a wonderful diplomat's wife, but a powerful diplomat in her own right. Without her, I am but half, longing to be whole again. I ask you for her hand, and if you grant my fondest wish, I promise I'll cherish Aryanna the remainder of my days and treat her as your mother would've wanted, like a queen."

Cyrrick bowed and stepped back into the shadows.

Queen Allanna shook her head violently, and for a moment, Sarco thought he saw foam forming in the corners her mouth around the gag.

The king paced before his throne before turning once again toward Sarco. "And the twins, what would you have me do with them? Do you have suitors waiting to marry them also? There is that troll prince and the dwarf duke, but…"

The king didn't get the chance to say another word as Sherman jumped up and down waving his arms. "Point of order. Point of order."

King Alfred sighed. "What is it, halfling?"

Sherman gulped twice as he made his way forward, until he was standing directly in front of the king. "You can't marry Ally and Audrey off to a troll or a dwarf. You simply can't."

The king looked down his nose at Sherman. "And

why can't I?"

Sherman shuffled his feet, straightened his spine, then looked King Alfred in the eye. Sarco had never been as proud of the little halfling as he was this moment.

"Be…be…because I'm in love with them."

The king shook his head. "You're in love with which one of them?"

Sherman cleared his throat, but his voice still came out in a squeak. "Both."

The king laughed, "No man gets to have two women, halfling, especially two barbarian princesses. Not that you'll get either, but just out of curiosity, if you had the choice, which of my daughters would you choose?"

Sarco slipped an arm about Sherman's shoulder for support. Though the halfling's voice quivered as he answered, the squeak was gone and the tone rang true.

"How can you ask a man to choose between his next breath or his next heartbeat? For that is what you're asking of me. Ally is like the air I need to sustain my life—fresh, crisp, and full of promise. And Audrey, she pulses with an energy and exuberance that feeds my soul. You mustn't separate them. That would be beyond cruel. Together they make the most amazing *One* there has ever been. Apart, they would wither and die. If you can't find it in your heart to give them both to me, I'll understand, but please don't ever force them to be separated. They wouldn't survive it."

Not even the taking of a breath could be heard from the crowd. Even the queen herself sat in stunned silence.

King Alfred sat heavily upon his throne and looked

toward his son, and Sarco held his breath. "Above all men, it's your council I respect the most, Adan. Someday it will fall upon your shoulders to take my place and rule our people. Do you have an opinion as to how I am to proceed?"

Adan Hammerstrike faced his father. His voice rang to the very rafters of the arena. "I have quested with these men, Father. Together we've eaten, slept, and faced many dangers. We have overcome much. From each and every one of them, I've learned another aspect of honor, duty, bravery, and true kinsmanship. They are my friends, and I would trust any of them with my life and lay down my own for them. I am proud to call them my brothers, and I would count my sisters, *all* of my sisters, lucky to call any one of them husband."

The queen fainted.

King Alfred slowly nodded. "I need time to think. Let us adjourn to the Hall of Ceremonies."

He glared at Sarco, and Sarco felt the seriousness of his stare all the way to his toes. "No matter what decision I make in the next little while, this day you *will* wed one of my daughters."

He turned to leave, then as an afterthought, twisted back around and pointed toward four guards and then to the unconscious form of his wife. "Bring her along. The queen does so love an event, and I wouldn't want her to miss a moment of this evening."

\*\*\*\*

Lark squeezed her sisters tighter as they huddled together in the darkness. She strained to hear even the slightest sound from the outside world. There was none, only cold silence.

Ally was the first to break it. "It's been an awfully

long time since Adan was here. What do you think is going on? I don't want to marry a troll, really, I don't," she cried.

Lark patted Ally's back and stroked her hair.

"I won't let that happen, I promise." Aryanna heaved a deep breath. "I'll do whatever I have to do to appease Mother."

"Even marry Sarco?" Audrey asked the question Lark was too afraid to ask herself.

Though she couldn't see her sister's response, Lark could feel it as Aryanna nodded her head before she spoke in a voice no louder than a whisper, "Yes, even that."

The door to the room burst open and in marched a full contingent of guards. One held up a parchment.

"Princess Aryanna Zahanna Clemencia Hammerstrike, you've been summoned to the Hall of Ceremonies."

The sisters held onto each other as Aryanna asked, "Will they be allowed to accompany me?"

The guard shook his head. "I'm sorry, Princess. The decree is just for you. We cannot allow anyone else to leave the room. The others must wait here until called for."

A moment later the door slammed shut with Aryanna on the other side, and silence invaded the chamber once more. Lark closed tight her eyes, trying to hide her tears from Ally and Audrey. It did no good. They seeped out and ran down her cheeks anyway.

If Aryanna was being summoned to the Hall of Ceremonies it could mean only one thing. Somewhere in the recesses of that hall, a groom was waiting.

Conflicting emotions and thoughts fluttered

through her mind. Did he still live? Had Sarco somehow managed to beat Adan in the arena? Doubt and fears filled her. Lark knew her brother and his skill level.

So, was Sarco dead then? Pain so intense it took her breath away shot straight through her heart. She had to know. This not knowing was driving her mad.

Lark concentrated her energy and sent fingers of it out in all directions, seeking a mind, any mind, to probe for information. Just as quickly as they had gone out, the slivers of mental energy rebounded back and left her reeling. Someone, probably Grandmother Ava, had placed a Prevention of Probing spell upon the Academy.

Lark shook her head. How could she have forgotten such a spell would be in place? After all, it was common practice when important diplomatic decisions were being made. Without it, undue influence could be applied from those who were well-versed in mind control.

She crumpled to the floor, no longer capable of holding back the sorrow.

Her two remaining sisters rushed to her side. Ally held her hand and cooed softly, "It's not as bad as all that, you'll see. You just watch. Everything is going to be fine."

Lark shook her head. "No, it won't."

Audrey patted her back. "Mother won't really send you to Vo...Vo...VoT, Lark. Even she can't be that horrid. You know how she is, mostly hot air. She didn't really mean it. She couldn't have."

Lark wiped her eyes and hiccupped, "It doesn't matter where she sends me anymore. Don't you understand? If Sarco still lives, then this very moment he's marrying Aryanna, and if he isn't marrying her, then he's…he's…he's dead. Either way, I've lost everything."

They sat in the middle of the floor holding each other, and that's where they were when, minutes later, the door swung open once more.

They all jumped at once, but they weren't fast enough to avoid being surrounded. The same guard who spoke before again held a parchment high. "Princesses Allyssa Zoe Carmen and Audrey Zana Constance Hammerstrike, you've been summoned to the Hall of Ceremonies."

The two women screeched and clung to each other while Lark stood protectively in front of them with her arms stretched wide."I won't let you take them!"

The guard made a motion, and before Lark could even think to act, four guards surrounded her and separated her from her sisters. The last thing she heard before the door slammed shut was Ally's cry of, "Lord Draka help us. I don't want to marry a troll!"

Lark pounded on the door until her knuckles bled and she could no longer feel her fists, then turned and staggered to the center of the room. They were gone. All of them. Ary, Ally, Audrey, and especially Sarco. Gone, and she would never see any of them again.

Soon the door would open again and this time it would be the guards coming to escort her. It would then be her turn to go to the Hall of Ceremonies where her mother would hand her over to the Rector. He'd then take her to the Abbey in VoT where she would spend the rest of her life.

Her eyes burned with the need to cry, but there

were no tears left to shed. In their place, right there in the middle of the room, clouds formed, the wind roared, and cold rain splattered down upon every surface.

Lark lifted her face and embraced the droplets of water, hoping and praying lightning would form, strike her, and send her to an oblivion where the Rector, Mother, and her memories of the love she'd lost would never find her again.

Her knees buckled, and if it hurt when Lark hit the floor, she didn't feel it. There was too much competition coming from the torment in her heart.

Anger built and filled her to overflowing. What right did her mother have to manipulate not only Lark's life but the lives of her sisters as well? What right did the queen have sending Sarco on a quest that had probably meant his death? What right did Allanna Hammerstrike have to lock her away, when the only crime she'd ever committed was loving the one man not meant for her? Why was she still even sitting here, crying like a baby, when her sisters were facing their fates alone?

Perhaps it was too late for a future with Sarco. Perhaps she couldn't prevent Aryanna's marriage to him if he were still alive. But, as God Draka was her witness, she didn't have to sit here and allow her piss-poor excuse of a mother to marry off the twins to such hideous creatures as a troll and a dwarf.

She didn't have the slightest hint of what was about to happen, and it certainly wasn't a conscious thought on her part when it did. She wasn't even sure what prompted her to look up at the exact moment lightning flashed across the room and the door splintered into a million pieces.

If the situation hadn't been so dire, the looks on the faces of the guards would have been humorous. They stood in the doorway with their eyes big as saucers and their mouths gaping. For a moment, Lark thought perhaps she should explain, then realized she simply didn't wish to.

Instead, she faced them, her anger spilling forth. "Haven't you seen it rain before?"

The same guard who had read the summons for Ary, Ally, and Audrey held up a parchment and opened his mouth, but no sound came forth. He cleared his throat and tried again. Still, not an audible word crossed his lips.

After a third attempt, he managed to squeak. "Princess Larksong, you've been…"

Lark couldn't take it. With her hair dripping in her face and her hands on her hips, she glared at him. "Don't bother. I've decided to summon myself to the Hall of Ceremonies."

The guard nodded and moved aside.

Lark glared at the other guards one at a time, and man after man stepped back into the hallway and out of her way. She walked past the entire group with her head held high. "Come along. There's no one left here to keep watch over."

The faster she walked, the madder she got. Memories of everything from her lost love, to her lost sisters, to her sad childhood, flooded her mind as rain poured upon the floor in sheets and the wind whipped ferociously. She could hear the guards slipping and sliding behind her, but Lark didn't care. She didn't even care that her tunic was plastered to her body or that water dripped continuously from the tip of her nose.

She didn't give a thought to the fact her hair was a soggy, wind-blown mass of tangles, and she looked a fright. All that mattered was opening the door, which now stood directly before her.

This time she did it on purpose. This time it was no fluke. Lark concentrated every speck of magic she'd learned from Sarco, and combined it with her own natural gift of controlling the weather, to form a ball of pure lightning and aim it straight at the door.

Right before it hit, she heard the guards behind her scrambling for cover. In the space of a grain of sand dropping, a huge hole gaped where a solid wooden door had once been.

When the debris settled, Lark saw three things.

Her mother tied and gagged, sitting upon her throne, which she didn't understand.

Both twins bending and kissing Sherman at the same time, which she also didn't understand.

And Aryanna smiling within the circle of Cyrrick's arms, which Lark understood perfectly.

So that was it then. If Aryanna was with Cyrrick, then Sarco was truly dead. She didn't realize she was falling. All Lark knew was the warmth of oblivion surrounding her.

She welcomed it.

****

*"Wonderful, wake up."*

She didn't want to. Awake meant a world without Sarco. Here in her mind, she could still be with him. *"Not yet, my love, please. Let's stay here awhile, shall we? I've missed you so much."*

*"Lark, I need you to wake."*

The voice was more persistent now, and Lark

stirred. *"No…no…no, I don't want to lose you again. Please, don't make me."*

He chuckled in her mind and shivers raced down her spine.

*"I love you, Larksong Hammerstrike, and you must wake and become my wife. You've kept me waiting long enough."*

Tears seeped from the corners of her closed eyes, and her breath caught. *"I so wanted to be your wife. I love you."*

She felt a shake on her shoulder and strong arms lifting her. Though she fought it for all she was worth, Lark's consciousness returned. Slowly, she opened her eyes, then blinked as comprehension of what she was seeing finally settled in. "Sarco?"

He nodded.

"You're alive?"

He nodded again.

She laughed. "You're alive!"

"Yes, I am," he chuckled. "Now, will you marry me?"

Lark sat up and looked toward her mother.

Sarco answered her unspoken question. "She was misbehaving, so your father subdued her."

Lark grinned. "And the twins?" She turned in their direction.

"Both newly wed to Sherman, again courtesy of your father."

She shook her head. Could miracles really happen? "And…and Ary and Cyrrick?"

Sarco looked gruff, but there was no anger in his voice, only anticipation. "Lark, you're killing me. They are now married also. We have the rest of our lives to chitchat. Right now, we are all waiting for you to say you'll marry me so we may get this wedding going. Will you?"

She looked down at herself and cringed. "Perhaps I should go change first. I look horrid."

Sarco shook his head. "Oh, no, my lady. There's no way I'm letting you out of my sight until we've said our vows. And you are wrong, Wonderful. I've never, ever, seen a more beautiful bride."

Lark smiled and hugged him close.

Within moments, bells rang and horns trumpeted in the distance as the three moons of Albrath, all as full as full could be, rose high in the evening sky. A rainbow arched across the length of the hall as Lark's voice rang loud and true for all to hear.

"I, Lark, take thee Sarco…"

## Epilogue

If ever a man looked more handsome, more sexy, more exuberant, more…well, simply *more* than Sarco Sunwalker did this very moment, Lark couldn't imagine such a man.

Her husband was resplendent in his royal purple wizard's robe, and he was hers, now and forever. She watched him from the corner of her eye as he thanked their guests.

He gave her a look of total exasperation and she couldn't hold back a smile. For the last quarter of a turn of the hourglass, they had been trying diligently to make their exit from the Academy's Hall of Ceremonies. Apparently, it wasn't to be quite yet, as more and more well-wishers lined up to say their congratulations.

It really had been a wonderful party. Especially once she had returned to her room after the vows, combed her hair, and dressed herself in something more befitting the occasion than her soggy tunic. She had chosen the same white gown she'd worn the very first night she'd met him at Carnalval. It was appropriate, and the tiny flowerbud on her beautiful wedding band matched it perfectly.

When Lark returned, the hall had been transformed and the rubble from the mess she'd created had been cleared away. Even the puddles of water on the floor had been mopped.

Everywhere she looked, tables overflowed with food, goblets overflowed with wine, and friends overflowed the boundaries of the room. And dancing. Oh my, there had been dancing until her feet ached.

The thought of dancing reminded her of her father, and Lark almost laughed out loud at the memory of that dance. While she had been splendidly twirled about the room on the arm of her father, poor Sarco had been left to dance with her mother, who'd remained tied to her chair. The sight of the guards carrying the still very angry woman upon her ornate throne as they followed Sarco in what more resembled confusion than dance steps was something Lark would cherish forever.

A tug on the fabric of her dress got her attention, and Lark glanced down. Laycee grinned at her with tears brimming in her eyes.

"Ya are a beautiful bride, my girl. Ya all were. And don't ya be worrying your head a minute about that door either. I'll have my Leeky fix it up all right and proper. He's quite handy with tools, ya know. And he's the sweetest man. He's gonna take me out on a date later this very evening. Says he's taking me ta the best show in all of Albrath. Why, we're even gonna leave Bunny and Tug at home. Says he wants it just ta be the two of us. Isn't that the sweetest thing ya've ever heard?"

Lark hugged her governess and planted a kiss on the top of her head. "Thank you, Laycee, for always being there for me."

Laycee sniffed loudly and blew her nose into her hanky as her welled-up tears spilled over and ran down her pudgy cheeks. She tried to speak once more but was too overcome by emotion.

Leeky, however, didn't seem to have that problem. "What the paisley-plaid panties on the over-sized, zit-covered behind of a bald-headed dwarf doing the cha-cha on a barrel of pickles are ya thinking, lass? If I live ta be two thousand, and I have no doubt I will, I'll never understand sentimental females."

He grinned up at Lark. "Don't ya think it was bad enough when we said goodnight ta Aryanna, the twins, and their fellows? Took me nigh on half a turn of the hourglass ta calm her down, and here she is blubbering again. What's a gnome ta do? Come along, Laycee. We wanna get good seats before the first act starts, don't we?"

****

Finally alone.

Lark smiled up at her husband as Sarco carried her, not only through the portal, along the path, and up the stairs, but across the threshold of his room. He gently sat her on the edge of the huge bed in his castle suite, high atop the city of Landis. Quickly, he retraced his steps and locked the door. The light from the glow of a hundred candles gave the room a magical feel, and rose petals strewn across the quilt added to the fragrance of romance permeating the walls.

Sarco chuckled. "Uthiel and Briar must've guessed I'd bring you here. Appears they came before us and prepared the room. They used it just last year for their wedding night."

He sounded nervous and Lark held out her arms. "Come love me, Sarco. It's been much too long."

Instead, he paced for a moment before facing her. "I want to make love with you more than I want to breathe. It's just…" He ran his fingers through his hair. "You're my wife. My *wife*, for God Draka's sake, can you believe it? I want this night to be perfect. I'm afraid if I touch you this moment, I may not be able to hold off long enough to see you satisfied. I feel like an untried teenager about to embarrass himself."

Lark hopped off the bed and strode purposefully toward her husband. "I wouldn't worry too awfully much over it, my love. We have the whole night, and every night for the rest of our lives to perfect your technique. I'm pretty sure you'll see me satisfied more than a few times over the next, let's say, hundred years or so. Right now, though, what would satisfy me the most is to have your sweet, hot cock deep inside my pussy…pounding me…all night long."

She grabbed the lapel of his robe and tugged. He found her lips and she his, as, for the space of a breath, time stood still and all that existed in all of Albrath was this man, this woman, and this moment.

A heartbeat later Lark found herself on her back with her legs dangling over the edge of the bed. Sarco grinned as he made a production of slowly slipping his robe up and over his head, revealing his gloriously naked body to her one inch at a time. His cock, already hard, beckoned to her.

"What my lady wants, my lady gets," he whispered.

Sarco lifted her dress above her waist, teasing as he went with the touch of his fingertips on the inside of her thighs. In a single motion, he ripped away her panties, parted her legs wide, placed his hands beneath her ass, and plunged deeply into her pussy.

Tremors of excitement shot straight through her

spine, landing quick and hard on her already swollen clit. It hummed and throbbed in response. Lark held on to the side of the mattress. Her thighs quivered and her heart raced. Their eyes locked and their breath quickened as, over and over, he slid his cock into and out of her tight opening. Her muscles contracted about him.

Suddenly he flipped her onto her stomach, and entered her from behind, and pumped furiously. "God, what you do to my soul, Lark. One lifetime won't be anywhere near long enough to make you understand how much I love you. How much I need you. How much I can't even breathe without you near me."

"Shhh," she whispered. "Remember what you always say to your students? Now is the perfect time. Show, don't tell, my love. Show, don't tell."

Sarco chuckled. "Your wish is my command, Wonderful." His hands clutched tightly to her hips. The intensity of his strokes doubled.

Lark closed her eyes and let the sensations consume her. Blood coursed through the veins of his cock as it pulsed deeply within her and matched the beat of her own heart. She could hear his sharp intake of breath, and then the explosive exhalation as he thrust wildly.

He flipped her again until she faced him once more. "I want to fuck you in every position possible before this night is through. I want to look in your eyes as you orgasm over and over again. I want to see your pleasure, Wonderful. Share it, taste it, be responsible for it." He leaned forward and took her mouth in a hot, wet embrace that scoarched her soul and thrilled her heart.

The aftermath of his kiss upon her lips tasted of lust, and the essence of the man wafted through her nostrils, exciting her further. He smelled of magic and sunlight, dreams and desire.

In a single motion, he lifted her completely off the bed and turned them around. Flat on his back now, he lay with Lark impaled upon him. With fingers quick as lightning, he divested her of what was left of her gown, and Lark gasped with pleasure as warmth flowed like waves everywhere his eyes touched. He stared at her nakedness with a lecherous grin.

She laughed. "My…my, Professor Sunwalker, how talented you've become."

He shook his head slowly, his eyes smoky and languid. "It's not talent, Wonderful. It's greed. I want to watch as you ride me." He playfully tweaked one nipple then the other. "I want to touch every inch of you, taste every crevice, and hear you scream my name so loudly every citizen of Landis will hear you before this night is over."

Ever so slowly, she rose until just the tip of the head of his cock remained still sheathed within her, then quickly plunged back down. His breath whooshing out made her grin. "Let's just see who screams first, shall we?" she challenged.

The bed became a blur of arms and legs and body parts as Sarco and Lark both took turns on top and bottom, front and back, without their bodies ever completely coming apart. Soft sighs met sudden gasps, and pleas met promises fulfilled, as, together, they rode the waves of passion. Muscles clenched and throbbed, and everywhere, pressure built, and the world around them exploded in unison. They shouted together, then fell exhausted, still wrapped in each other's arms.

Slowly, the world righted itself, and in a cocoon of warmth, they slumbered.

It had been no more than the dropping a few grains of sand later when Lark heard a sound she couldn't quite make out. Sarco must have heard it also, because he stiffened behind her. She listened intently, and there it was again. Kind of a...crunch, coming from the shadows in the corner. She started to rise and investigate, but Sarco held her firmly in place.

They both held their breath, listened, and heard the first hint of a familiar voice whispering.

"What the fart-covered backside of a constipated troll trollop in too-tight granny panties did ya think of that, lass? Pretty sure they're sleeping. If we keep our voices low, we can discuss it for the time it takes a few grains of sand ta trickle through the hourglass. Gotta be quiet though. Won't be long before they're at it again, mark my word."

A crunching noise came once again, more muffled this time. Then Leeky giggled, "Didn't I tell ya this would be the best show in Albrath tonight? A better performance than either his brother or that halfling, if ya ask me. Though Sherman was handicapped having ta do two. Ya gotta give him that."

Another whisper, female this time, had no problem at all reaching Sarco's and Lark's horrified ears. "Ya're right there, the show was amazing. It's the best one I've seen tonight. Why, I'd even give that wizard a solid nine for effort, flexibility, and ingenuity. And, ya gotta admit, my Lark wasn't half bad herself."

The gravelly whisper came once more. "Yea, she held her own. But what the pustulated scab on the pox-infected who-ha of a female dwarf are ya talking about? A nine? When it comes ta Sarco's performance he did better than a nine. Why, I'd bet my left ball sac that was closer ta a nine point five. His dismount alone was worth a nine."

The tugging of something paper rattled through the room. "Now, quit hoggin' the popcorn and pass it this way before they wake. If I know my wizard and his little apprentice as well as I think I do, this is just a short intermission and they'll be back at it any moment."

Only one more word was spoken before both gnomes were unceremoniously tossed from the room.

*"Leeky!"*

## About the Author

Maxine Mansfield writes fantasy, erotic romances for The Wild Rose Press. From the comfort of her home in the far northern state of Alaska, where the summer days are long and the winter nights even longer.

She has one very special man, his three equally special children, and their six delightful grandchildren to keep her busy when not typing away on her next book. Not to mention her very bossy African Grey parrot named Gabriel.

Oh, and Gnomes! Many, many gnomes

Visit Maxine at
Web site: WWW.maxinemansfield.com
Blog: http://www.maxinemansfield.com/blog.html
Email: Maxine-mansfield@hotmail.com
Twitter: https://twitter.com/LeekyShortz

To chat with Maxine Mansfield and other Wild Rose Press authors of erotic romance, join us at www.groups.yahoo.com/group/thewilderroses.

Also Available

# Touched By The Magic

by

## Maxine Mansfield

New to The Academy of Magical Arts, Briarlarn Tumbleweed wants to learn the art of a True Healer, but her nerves get the best of her when she's paired in the sexually dynamic healing class with Uthiel Stoutheart, Paladin of the Realm. Between burning off his eyebrows and overturning a candle on certain exposed male parts, she isn't making a very good impression. But how can she focus when Uthiel is strong, brave, and touches Briar in a way that leaves her weak in the knees, quivering with pleasure, and begging for more?

Falling in love with the accident-prone but talented Briar was not what Uthiel had planned, but life with the sexy healer is adventurous, hilarious, mind-blowingly stimulating, and clearly his destiny. His soul awakens while taking her to new heights of ecstasy, yet he can't allow his own pleasure. There's no getting around it—he must leave The Academy and pursue his quest to right the wrongs done to his people if he can ever hope to find happiness with Briar.

But is their love strong enough to mend the magic so desperately needed to preserve their world, and that touches both their souls with a searing heat?

*"When a man whose heart is stout and true*
*joins with a woman whose love flows*
*through and through,*
*And together they embrace a soul who forgiveness is*
*due, in order to save a life barely started and new,*
*Then and only then will the shadows of ancient wrongs*
*become light and the mist of misunderstanding be lifted*
*and the world become bright.*
*The time of waiting will come to an end*
*as a leader steps forward of both dragon and men.*
*Tried by fire and forged of true love,*
*ruled by a heart as pure as a dove.*
*United again Castle Kuropkat will be and a time of*
*peace like no other all of Albrath will see."*

## Chapter One

Briar pressed her face farther between the large, purple leaves of the pandronium plant in order to get a better view. She knew she was breaking the rules but simply couldn't help herself. After listening all week to the stories floating around The Academy of Magical Arts concerning the castle's most talented healer, to literally stumble upon her in this manner was amazing. Not only amazing but so incredibly lucky, it had to be fate.

Who would have thought a simple wrong turn on the way to Healing the Soul class would've conveyed her, Briarlarn Tumbleweed, to this particular small, out-of-the-way conservatory and the sight now before her eyes? Could any remotely rational person really expect her to avert her gaze, walk away, and pass up this opportunity? Certainly not!

To observe the magnificent Ursula at work was a dream come true. If she had the chance to witness an actual healing, Briar had no intention of missing it.

The beautiful healer mounted a bronzed, godlike man, whose muscles bulged and rippled beneath her touch as she rode him to a rhythm only she could hear.

It was incredible. It was hypnotic. It was primal. It was healing at its most basic and yet, at the same time, exquisite.

Over and over, ever so slowly, Ursula rose, and the thick, hard, swollen cock beneath her threatened to spring free. At the very last possible moment, she plunged downward, and the golden-brown man moaned—yes, actually moaned—with the pleasure of it.

Briar slipped the leaves back in place, once more hiding the couple from view, and blew out the breath she'd been holding.

Heat radiated from her insides and spread outward. She fanned her fevered face with both hands as she took in great gulps of air, trying to slow the pounding in her chest. A throbbing Briar didn't quite understand pulsed in her core to the rhythm of her erratic heartbeat.

So, this was the sex act used for healing—the millennium-old, sacred treatment to heal the soul she'd been trying to envision all week. Not that the concept of sex for treatment or even simply for pleasure was entirely foreign to her. After all, she wasn't a child; she was a woman fully grown, twenty-one as of the second moon's last phase. It was just that her previous experiences with coupling had all come from watching animals mate for the sake of procreation.

Well, a couple of things were for certain. She was no longer in her beloved Dak Forest, and people definitely performed the sex act much differently than animals.

Briar sighed. Would she ever be so powerful a healer as to make a man like the one Ursula rode moan? Her body tingled with the possibility as she parted the leaves again, leaned in much closer to get a better look, and peeked once more.

Ursula wasn't riding him anymore. The healer now straddled his chest, and had the very tip of the man's cock between her lips. Her hand barely reached around his shaft, it was so thick.

He suddenly lunged upward as his body spasmed and shook. A trail of white fluid trickled down the side of Ursula's perfect, pink mouth, and her tiny tongue slipped out to capture it.

The throbbing became more demanding as it pulsed from the pit of Briar's belly all the way to the junction between her thighs. She clamped her legs tightly closed in an attempt to impede the persistent sensations.

It didn't work.

They grew stronger, and faster, and more exacting as Briar struggled to take in enough air to remain conscious. The hairs on the back of her neck and arms rose as her nipples pebbled and ached for something, though she wasn't sure what. A quiver she had no control over scampered along her spine, marking its path down to the tips of her toes.

As the leaves fell back in place, Briar wondered if she would ever be attractive enough to entice a man like this one to give her a second glance, let alone actually do with her the things this blond Adonis was doing with Ursula.

If she could, then she wouldn't have to worry about her secret. But how did one go about letting the opposite sex know you were interested in such things?

A twinge of regret at the fact she'd been raised in small, out-of-the-way Dak Forest stung Briar, and not for the first time since she arrived at The Academy a short week ago.

Though she loved her home and her father with all her heart, a mother's advice, a proper sex education, and a city upbringing would have come in handy.

It's not as if she considered herself unattractive, for she didn't. If her own eyes hadn't seen her reflection many times, her father certainly didn't have a problem telling her how much she looked like her elegant, high-elf mother. Nor was she a classic beauty like Ursula, although Briar knew her features complemented each other. Still, not a single one of them stood out in her mind as unique or truly memorable.

Like her hair, for instance. More the color of dull rust than shiny copper, it was at least healthy, if not manageable. Even though it hung well past the halfway point of her back, and the weight of it alone should have kept it straight as an arrow, it tended to curl on the ends and go every which way. And her eyes—though they were the exact shade of the deep-green moss on the forest floor—had none of the exotic tilt so prevalent in most elves. They were definitely rounded, due to her father's human heritage.

Her ears had only the slightest tendency to come to a point—nothing like the crispness she'd seen in pictures of her mother. Her waist was neither petite nor wide, her legs neither short nor long, and her feet, thanks to the Good Lord Draka, each had simply five toes. For the most part, she was average.

Ursula, on the other hand, was flawless. From her pointed, high-elfin ears and porcelain skin, to her below-the-waist blonde tendrils, her rose-tipped breasts, and legs long enough to easily wrap around even the largest of barbarians, Ursula was perfection personified.

Briar sighed once more. She would never come anywhere close to achieving that degree of beauty.

She grimaced at the self-deprecating way she'd let her thoughts run. Perhaps she wasn't as pretty as Ursula, perhaps she never would be, but Briarlarn Tumbleweed knew her worth, and she had dreams.

With a start, she realized she was now late for one of those dreams. Healing the Soul class.

Standing and turning to leave, she ran straight into a solid wall. No, not a wall. A chest. A wide, warm, living-and-breathing wall of a chest.

She forced herself to look up, and up, until she could finally see the face it belonged to.

Eyes the blue-green of a stormy sky rimmed with thick, dark lashes stared back and held her captive with their intensity.

An apology was ready on her lips until he smiled. The air dissipated from her body. She couldn't speak, she couldn't think, she couldn't budge an inch.

He was gorgeous.

Actually, not just gorgeous, but eye-popping, heart-racing, weak-in-the-knees gorgeous. Her own knees buckled and she placed a palm against his chest to steady herself.

Time slowed as two very solid arms wrapped and sheltered her in a haven of warmth. The fingers of his hands pressed into her back, leaving tingling imprints in their wake.

Realization rocked her. This is what she'd been craving moments before while watching Ursula and the man with a body to die for.

To be touched. Not the touch of just any man, however. What she craved was the caress of a hot-blooded man like this one.

His life force exuded energy beneath her fingertips and it pulsed with a vivacity matching the pounding of her heart. Oh yes, this man was definitely sizzling hot and then some.

"Damsel in distress?" he asked.

Briar gulped. She couldn't take her eyes off his mouth, and she couldn't force herself to look away as his lips—so full and ever so slightly upturned at the corners—widened into a broad smile.

"I do so hope you're a damsel in distress, my lady, for damsels in distress are my particular specialty," he chuckled.

Briar flushed as the sensual, deep tremor of his laugh infused her with even more heat. She spoke, but what came out at first was more a squeak than a word.

"No."

She swallowed the lump in her throat. "No, sir, I'm

fine. You simply gave me a fright. I thought for a moment I'd been discovered by an Academy official. You aren't one, are you? I know I'm not supposed to be here, and I know it's forbidden to watch a healing unless it's part of a class demonstration. I swear I simply couldn't help myself. It was so…breathtaking."

He leaned forward until their foreheads touched and his lips were no more than a whisper from hers. "See, you are a damsel in distress. I knew it. And, nope, not an Academy official. I'm a graduate student, my lady, and your secret is safe with me."

She wasn't sure why she believed him but she did. He looked trustworthy. Older than she, but not by much, he appeared to be perhaps twenty-five.

Leaning in even closer, he brushed her lips with his so lightly, Briar wasn't sure it had even happened. Her heart knew it, however. It pounded so hard, she feared it might explode.

His shoulder-length hair—the color of rich, dark chocolate—tickled her cheek and sent tiny spurts of excitement scurrying every which way. His strong, princely nose flared at the nostrils as his breath further warmed her overheated skin. But it was his intense stare, so full of both sincerity and mischief, that held her mesmerized.

He'd said her secret was safe with him. What if…? What if she did dare to share her most important secret with this man who now held her so close? Would it be safe—would *she* be safe? Could she take a chance and tell the one fact about herself that, if it got out, could spell the end of her dreams?

"Just what, may I ask, are you two doing here? This area is off limits to students at this time of the day."

She jumped, but the man holding her didn't let go. He simply turned them as a single unit toward the sound of the speaker.

Briar wished for the words and skill needed to cast

a disappearing spell. The stern voice belonged to none other than Mr. Ohmni, the assistant administrator, and he was scowling.

Instead of demanding an immediate answer, Mr. Ohmni glanced through the partially opened leaves of the pandronium plant. "Ah, I see. You've been watching a healing in progress, haven't you? That's forbidden, and you well know it. As soon as the day's classes have been completed, report to Headmistress Seychelle's office." The frown lines in his already too thin face deepened as he scowled at Briar and the man whose very heartbeat thumped strong and steady through the thinness of her tunic.

Briar wanted to tell Mr. Ohmni that the man who was still holding her so close hadn't been watching anything at all and was completely innocent, but she never got the chance. Her safe-shelter-against-a-cold-world guy placed a finger against her lips and spoke for them both.

"We'll be there." Taking her hand in his, he tugged, and Briar automatically followed.

By the time she'd slowed the pace of her racing heart and formed her next coherent thought, they'd arrived in front of the door to her Healing the Soul class.

"Why'd you do that? You weren't watching the healing, and you didn't break any rules. There's really no need for you to take any part of the blame for something I did entirely on my own."

The man bowed slightly before Briar. "Allow me to introduce myself, my lady? I am Uthiel Stoutheart, protector of the realm, paladin by trade, and rescuer of fair damsels in distress when the opportunity arises.

"And you, my dear damsel, appeared to be in great distress. Being the stouthearted rescuer that I am, I couldn't very well allow a lady as lovely as yourself to take punishment alone. It would've been highly unchivalrous of me and not paladin-like in the least.

Now, might I inquire as to who you may be?"

Her breath caught in her chest. A paladin? An honest-to-goodness paladin. She'd heard rumors of their existence, even stories of their exploits, but had never seen one up close, let alone been held by one.

Briar once more grew warm, her nearness to the gorgeous paladin playing havoc on her nerves. Her voice sounded breathy even to her own ears. "I'm Briarlarn Tumbleweed, though my friends call me Briar. I'm here at The Academy to become a True Healer. It's nice to meet you, kind sir. I mean, Uthiel Stoutheart. And thank you."

He bowed before her, and Briar couldn't resist the question almost burning her tongue, demanding to be asked, so she blurted it out. "Have you seen a real live dragon? I mean, I've been told paladins take an oath to protect them. That's what warriors of the light do, isn't it? Protect the dragons, and therefore the magic that is Albrath?"

Uthiel suddenly looked uncomfortable, and the teasing glint in his eyes dimmed. Guilt engulfed Briar for asking something that obviously he didn't wish to talk about. Something was wrong, very wrong, and she shouldn't have pried.

As quickly as the tense moment happened, it disappeared. Uthiel graced her with such a smile, her panties dampened from its effect.

"I've seen a dragon or two in my time. We can discuss them later if you like. But for now, I suggest we get inside."

She started to open the classroom door, then hesitated. "You're in my Healing the Soul 101 class? I haven't seen you here before."

"I have not been. This is indeed the first day of the semester for me. I was unavoidably detained…elsewhere, but I'm normally a quick study. I hope to catch up without too much trouble. Perhaps you could help me…study."

Briar glanced over her shoulder at Uthiel. "Why would a paladin in the graduate program take a Healing the Soul 101 class? No offense meant, of course, but don't paladins normally *cause* damage, not heal it? I mean, I could see the value of, perhaps, a Healing the Body class. That would come in handy in your chosen field. You know, for those times when you fall off your horse or scrape your knee with your sword or such?"

Uthiel's face had changed. Gone was the easy smile. His eyes were lifeless, and his stance stiff.

Briar clamped her mouth shut, suddenly realizing she'd said the wrong thing again.

"Trust me, my lady, by outward appearances alone there is no way of telling who may or may not have need of a Healing of the Soul class. I don't require this course to finish my degree. My father, however, believes this class will…benefit me, so I agreed to take it.

"Headmistress Seychelle is a friend of the family. When my father asked her to get me admitted to Healing the Soul 101, she did it. That's it."

Uthiel looked as if he wanted to say more. Briar held her breath, waiting. She didn't know why it was so important he trust her, but only that it was.

An expression that could have been relief softened the planes of his face, and his pupils dilated ever so slightly as he sighed and relaxed his stance.

"Though my father and I aren't on the finest of terms at the moment, I know he has my best interest at heart. And I am nothing if not a dutiful son, at least in most things."

Briar smiled, hoping to encourage him to continue with the explanation she somehow doubted he shared with very many.

"But, if you ask me, you're right," he shrugged. "It probably will be a waste of time. I have no doubt I'd be better off out in the lists, learning advanced techniques with my sword in order to better protect the realm. But then, who ever really knows why things turn out the way they do. Perhaps it's destiny, my lady, and by being in the same class with you, there may be no end to the important secrets of healing I might learn."

Briar nodded. If Uthiel was willing to trust her enough to honestly answer her questions, could he possibly be the one person in all of Albrath her own secret would be safe with? If her trust in him turned out to be a mistake, it could mean her immediate suspension from The Academy.

Divulging her secret wasn't a chance Briar was willing to take lightly. Becoming a True Healer was more important than the omission of the tiny but extremely important fact that she was still a virgin.

But what was she going to do about her secret? How was she ever going to remedy the situation without confiding in and receiving help from someone? These were the questions that plagued her thoughts almost every waking moment and had been the themes of her recent nightmares since arriving at The Academy.

How had she managed to overlook something so very basic for so long?

More importantly, would anyone really consider the smudge she'd placed between the yes and no answers to question number five on her entrance application…a lie?

Thank you for purchasing
this Wild Rose Press, Inc. publication.
For other wonderful stories of erotic romance,
please visit our on-line bookstore at
www.thewilderroses.com.

For questions or more information
contact us at
info@thewildrosepress.com.

The Wild Rose Press, Inc.
www.thewilderroses.com